Isabella Fyvie Mayo

**The Occupations of a Retired Life**

Isabella Fyvie Mayo

**The Occupations of a Retired Life**

ISBN/EAN: 9783337424398

Printed in Europe, USA, Canada, Australia, Japan

Cover: Foto ©Andreas Hilbeck / pixelio.de

More available books at **www.hansebooks.com**

# THE OCCUPATIONS OF

# A RETIRED LIFE

# By EDWARD GARRETT

AUTHOR OF "THE CRUST AND THE CAKE"

*Anchora Spei*

# STRAHAN & CO., PUBLISHERS

## 56 LUDGATE HILL, LONDON

1869

# CONTENTS.

# INTRODUCTION.

HERE are few things which it is altogether pleasant to do for "the last time." I daresay many brides feel a little heartache when they give their parents the evening kiss the night before the wedding. I think most clergymen would falter a little over a farewell sermon, though next Sunday they were to preach in an ancient cathedral instead of a little country church. And so my heart is not altogether merry as I draw my chair to mine ancient hearth for "the last time."

It is only a lonely hearth in the second floor of a great house of business. The room is rather low, but quite large enough for me ; and it has one advantage which I have always appreciated : its windows overlook a narrow strip of graveyard belonging to a vanished London church. There is a great elm which touches my panes, and makes a ghostly pattering when the wind is high. I

A

wish the church were still there. One Sunday, its pastor preached in it for " the last time," only he did not know it ; and in the week the red flames came, and withered it up before the eyes of the congregation. I have seen a picture of it, and it was a pretty Gothic church. If it were here to-day it would not have a score of worshippers. I should be one ; or sometimes I might remain at home and listen to the anthem and the preacher's voice through my open windows.

I am an old man—I must be, for I have been in this very house, one way or another, for fifty years. I entered as junior clerk—a *very* junior clerk, just fourteen years old, penniless and fatherless, and without home or friends in the great city. But a home was kept for me on the banks of the river Mallowe,—thanks to the courage and industry of my only sister Ruth. She was some years older than me ; and when our father died she took his place, and ruled everything for our poor, crushed, feeble mother, with that quiet tenderness which belongs to strong characters. Ruth settled all about my situation, and then she prepared my little outfit, and at last accompanied me to meet the stage-coach. Mother did not come further than our own gate. It was a very hot, bright summer day, and the green lanes and fair meadows looked more tempting than I had ever seen them before. When we reached the corner of the common the coach had not come, and we stood beside the sign-post and talked. Ruth did not exhort me ; she only told me in what parts of my trunk she had stowed away certain treasures ; and at last, when a white cloud of dust in the distance announced the coming coach, she put her hand on my shoulder, and said—

" Now, Ned, never think you are free to go wrong because you fancy it won't hurt anybody but yourself. IT WILL. It will break up our home at Mallowe as much as if it depended on your support and you failed to send money. I shall not have heart to bustle about in the shop and among strange people unless I have cause to be proud of you, Ned."

And then she bent and kissed me, and stood there, smiling, while I climbed the coach. She did not move as long as we were in sight ; and very often during my first nights in London I dreamed of my sister standing alone by the sign-post on the broad common.

Yes, Ruth was a wonderful woman. When my father died, people advised that the shop should be given up and a school opened in its stead. That would be proper woman's work, they said, which the business was not. It would have been all very well had it been only the village library and stationery goods ; but it was something beside. In or near our village were two solicitors, with large connexions among the farmers and landed proprietors about, and my father kept in his shop all the requirements of their offices, and, what was more, he undertook their copying. He had taught Ruth to help him, and she had been his only assistant,—a fact over which there had been much shaking of heads among the old ladies. Of course she must give up that now, they remarked. Ruth said nothing at first, but when they pressed her very vigorously, recommending particular houses as suited for her visionary school, and even giving hints as to what furniture she should keep, and what she should sell, then she opened her mouth and spake.

" We know the worst of old things, but we can't guess the worst of new ones," she said. " So long as I can I shall keep what I have."

And so she did. The labours which she and her father had shared, she managed to do alone. God knows (I say it solemnly) how she did it. We had been orphans for a year before I left home, and her example during that time was a great boon to me. She was a living picture of self-denial, patience, and cheerful industry, all the more edifying because she did not see it herself, but was only a little proud of her success as a woman of business. I fear our mother never quite appreciated her. But Ruth will not let me say so. She always remarks, " Ah, Ned, there was nothing to appreciate ; I am very glad that our mother kept me in mind of my faults." But then why was mother so blind to *mine ?*—and I might have had many more, and worse ones, and I know she would have continued as blind. Dear mother ! she is gone where she is doubtless grown strong enough to understand the daughter who puzzled her so sorely on earth.

London seemed very dismal to me when I alighted from the old " Highflyer." It set me down at the " Saracen's Head," and as I wandered out of the quaint inn-yard, I felt a strange sinking of heart. The great world around was so strong, and stern, and remorseless, and I so weak and lonely ! It is not at first we can realise that the vast tide of humanity is composed of little individual waves, one not much stronger or swifter than another, and all, and each (such comfort in that *each!*) carried along by the pitiful hand of God, who remembers every face in the vast throng, whether fair or faded, and knows every heart, and understands all about each life! But at first we only feel the terror of our own littleness. Coming from sweet country villages, where we recognised every one we met, we shrink from the unheeding crowd, with their blank, regardless eyes.

I was duly installed in my humble duties in the counting-house of this establishment. I don't think I was very bright; but every one was kind, and ready enough to give a helping hand to the poor dazed lad from the country. To me they seemed very clever those handsome, well-dressed, gaily-speaking young men, my superiors. I did not believe I should ever be competent to fill places like theirs. As I have said, they were very kind; but I knew they laughed at me, and would not care to converse about such things as I took interest in. For the first few days this great house was as lonely to me as the streets. But one fair, cool morning, I was told that "the master" had returned from his summer holiday, and wished to see me—little Ned Garrett, from Mallowe. This was the head of the firm,—the other partners had been wisely chosen from among his best and longest-tried clerks. I had never seen Mr Lambert; but I knew his history—how he was the son of a far-descended fallen country family; how he put aside the prejudice of his rank and entered business life as humbly as myself; how by God's blessing on his diligence, he succeeded, until at last he bought back the old family mansion, but still remained in business, because he could not bear to give up the influence which he used for good in London.    I felt a little awe as I approached his room—this very chamber.    It was Mr Lambert's then ; it has been Ned Garrett's since.    To-morrow it will belong to somebody else.

He said very little to me.    He was a tall, slender man, with a beautiful old face and long silver hair,—no less a gentleman because he was a merchant.    He sat in a great brown leather settle, behind a huge writing table, and he bade me be seated on a little cane chair opposite. He asked if I had heard from home since my arrival, and how were my mother and sister—"your sister Ruth," he called her, and the sound of the old household name was like a breath of the breezes that blow over the sunny Mallowe.    Then he said he had heard good reports of me, and he should always like to hear the same, and stretched forth his hand—a white, warm, wrinkled, aged hand—and shook mine kindly, and I knew I might go.

But after that I never felt alone.    I generally saw him once or twice a day, only for a minute, and quite in the way of business ; but that always sent me back to work comforted and content.    The great millionaire—the man who had declined royal honours—could not hold conversation with such a unit as me, as he might have done had he himself been an old clerk with two hundred a year, and a wife and children in a six-roomed house at Clapham.    The tide of life breaks into streams, the boundaries of which it is not wise nor pleasant often to overflow. But the very character of the man was a friend to me. From it I could imagine the counsel he would give, and that it would be but an echo of the brave womanly words I had heard under the sign-post on Mallowe Common. I put the image of the quiet old gentleman into my heart beside that of my dark-eyed, accurate sister. They were the *lares* of my soul. I did not know all this when I was fourteen, but I know it now.

Well, I prospered, and rose one step after another, and when I was twenty-one I was in receipt of a fair salary for that age. Early every autumn I took a run down to Mallowe, but not at Christmas, because in those times we had no holiday then but the one day. I never wanted a better change than to go home. Early autumn was a slack time in the shop, so Ruth was free to roam the country with me, and many pleasant rambles we had sometimes together and sometimes with young people from the village, whom I had known all my life. Ah, not even in London, had I forgotten one—little Lucy Weston. I shall not speak about Lucy's looks ; I don't suppose she was a beauty to any one but me, and I don't suppose she was clever. She was only a good little girl —a daisy among women ; and we always love the daisies most, because we knew them best when we were young ! Her father kept the Meadow Farm, a dear old-fashioned gabled house, overgrown with creepers, which wreathed round its quaint white-curtained lattices, and made the whole place like a huge nest. Lucy was the only daughter ; but she had five brothers, great curly-haired,

grinning, tramping, good-natured lads, who came crush-
ing round me to hear about London, until, not having
grown much since I first left Mallowe, I always felt quite
overwhelmed and breathless.   Yet Lucy was a very
quiet thing in manner, and voice, and look.   Just to see
her was as soothing as to hear an old psalm tune sung
softly by little children.

I have not got a vivid memory, but any minute that I
like I can fancy myself in the great parlour at Meadow
Farm—a long low wainscoted room, with some curious
wood-carving about the ceiling and fireplace, and wide
windows along one side, beyond which lay a splendid
prospect of lane, and field, and hedgerow, mingling
summer charms with autumn wealth.   The floor was
bare except for two narrow strips of plain green carpet-
ing, which set off the cleanness of the boards.   There
were heavy old chairs with cushions of some kind of
chintz, and a long well-polished oak table uncovered,
except when clad in white drapery for meals.   The
room boasted no ornaments beyond a fox's head and
brush, and a few firearms over the mantelpiece, and
three great beau-pots of flowers, one set in each window.
And what a noise the farmer and his sons made, as they
came tramping in, with loud honest laughter, and good
old jokes that could stand an airing almost every day,
and among them little Lucy with the breezes in her hair,
and her cheeks a wee bit redder from the family kisses.
And last of all, " the mistress," with her cambric cap and
kerchief, and her broad sunshiny face, that looked as if
it remembered all the good harvests and forgot every

bad one. And then after them came tea and cake and fresh fruit, borne in by a stout serving-maiden full of old-school deference to her superiors, but always able to throw back a saucy word to the boys, if necessary. And then we all gathered round the long table, Lucy and I, somehow, side by side, and after a moment's hush, there burst forth the Westons' customary tea-time grace—Lucy's silver voice rising among the others, like a minstrel's harp amid the clang of martial music,—

"Praise God from whom all blessings flow,
Praise Him, all creatures here below,
Praise Him above, ye heavenly host:
Praise Father, Son, and Holy Ghost."

After such a meal as that, on the last night of my visit in the year of my coming of age, Lucy and I wandered out upon the greeny downs behind the house. I was a little disposed to envy the easy course of life in that nest-like home, and I manifested this tendency by setting forth, somewhat vauntingly, the advantages of city life. Perhaps I did it to hide my discontent, perhaps to argue myself into satisfaction with my lot. But Lucy went straight to the root of the matter. " There's a 'best side' to everything, Ned," she said, " and there's much to be gained by living in London, but because we grant that, don't let us cry down country life. I'm rather sorry your favourite Mr Lambert thinks there is so much more to be done among the houses than under the trees. I wish he would come down here and try."

" But life in the country is so narrow," said I.

She looked at me and smiled. " No one can do

more than he can, Ned," she answered; "and the narrowest life is wider than most of our hearts. When people have a great many ways of doing good, they sometimes get so confused that they do nothing."

I knew she was right.

"So you have made up your mind never to return to the fields 'for good,'" she remarked after a short silence.

"I don't say that," I answered. (We were standing on a slight eminence, facing the sunset.) "I daresay you would refuse to live in the city."

"I don't think I should," she replied, shading her eyes; "it would all depend upon circumstances."

"I shall not be able to afford to live in the country till I am quite old," I said—"perhaps not then."

"Well, everywhere is God's world," she answered, turning towards me; then added playfully, "but when you do come, don't make up your mind there's nothing to do but water flowers and go to sleep. There's plenty of work wherever there are sin and sorrow; and sin and sorrow are everywhere. 'The harvest truly is plenteous, but the labourers are few:'" and her voice was solemn then.

Ah, pretty Lucy! at the harvest supper some will meet us whom their Father called into the shelter of His own house before the burden and heat of the day!

"Dear me, but I'm grown quite a cockney," I said, after a long pause. "If I am to live in the country again, I shall want some one to show me how."

"You can easily find some one," she retorted.

"Will you?" I asked.

But at that auspicious moment we heard Farmer Weston's lusty voice shouting our names, and Lucy sprang up with damask cheeks, and ran fleetly to the house. I did not see her alone again all the evening. But next morning as I passed the farm, on my way to meet the coach, I saw her toying with her beau-pots in the parlour. So I unfastened the wicket, and crossed the garden, meaning to ask for an answer to my question. But the moment I reached the window, Mrs Weston advanced from the recesses of the room, and overwhelmed me with good wishes for my journey, and an enormous cake and some ripe pears wherewith to beguile its tedium. So perforce I returned to my city abode with an unsatisfied heart.

After a fortnight (scarcely a fortnight—I think it was only ten days) came the accustomed budget from Ruth. It opened with a bulletin of my mother's failing health, and good news of the business, but the third page went on thus :—

"It has been a sorrowful week at Mallowe. Our dear Lucy Weston was taken suddenly ill on Tuesday afternoon. She was unconscious from that time, so no one was sent for, not even her grandmother, and on Wednesday night she died. I know you will be so sorry."

That was all. My sister passed to other topics.

Of course I went as usual to business, but I felt myself worse than useless. The long rows of figures meant nothing to me, and I was blundering on, with flushed, throbbing face, when Mr Lambert came in.

"You are not well to-day, Garrett," he said, in his soft, modulated tones.

"Not quite, sir," I replied.

He looked kindly at me for a moment. " Have you heard from home ?" he asked. " All well there, I hope ?"

" All quite well, thank you, sir," I answered.

He sat down opposite me, and wrote a letter. I could feel his eyes upon me now and then. When he had finished, he spoke again :—

" Leave off work to-day, my boy, and take a drive out of town. You're worrying about something—I shan't ask you what. I don't believe it's your fault, so it will be sure to come right again, Garrett." And once more he shook hands with me—the second time since I had been in his house.

I did as he bade me. And I returned, not comforted, but calmed, and strong enough to bear my sorrow. Comfort came by and by, but not completely—not till I had been through a simoom of misery which was destined to teach me that I and my first love had been parted by the best and kindest separation which God can ordain.

Ah, Lucy, and it cannot be many more years before I shall hear you singing again ; this time a better Doxology than the one in which I can always hear your voice to this very day. I have never forgotten you ! Looking upon my life, people might say I did forget, and not too slowly ; but where you are, perhaps you know better.

I sent an ordinary condoling message to the bereaved family, and then I settled into my old life, and in due course the time came round for my accustomed visit to Mallowe. I half thought I would not go, but I forced myself not to flinch. I found everything exactly the same. I thought Ruth gave me one or two searching glances, but that was all. I believe it was only my fancy.

"You will go to Meadow Farm this evening, Ned," she said, after tea; "you always gave them the first visit, and they might feel hurt if you didn't now, poor things."

"I shall certainly go," I answered, looking from the window. "Shall you come too, Ruth?"

"I think not," she said. "I am rather busy, so I will stay at home, and then I shall be ready to take a walk with you to-morrow."

The Meadow Farm looked as nest-like as ever, and the beau-pots were still in the windows. But the flowers missed the dainty fingers which had arranged them so well, and they looked faint and drooping. I entered the open door; the house was very silent, but presently one of the brothers, crossing the back-garden, caught sight of me, and came forward to bid me welcome. He was as yellow-haired and ruddy as ever, but his step seemed quieter—perhaps it had grown hushed while *she* lay in her coffin. He led me to his parents. The father was laughing and chatting as usual, but his voice and laugh were those of an old man. The mother's face was as sunshiny, but not so broad. They were seated in their great orderly kitchen. Mrs Weston explained "that they felt the parlour chilly of an evening; they liked to be where the fire was." The five brothers came in and sat down in a half-circle. Presently the mother spoke about "her Lucy," and her husband joined in. They both shed a tear or two. The eldest brother shaded his face, as from the firelight; another got up and looked into the garden; a third asked if the horse were put up for the night, and then went to the stable to satisfy himself. It was very touching. They were evidently trying to pursue their life as cheerfully as possible, but they could not make it what it had been. I stayed to supper. The elder brother stood up, and offered "thanks." There was no singing. " We could not do it at first," said the poor father; " it was nothing but breaking down, and so we got out of the habit."

That visit did me good: the sight of their cheerful resignation braced my own soul, and I returned to London, stronger and happier than I had been since my last country visit.

After that, several years went quietly past. I advanced in the office, until I was fairly a well-to-do man, and though still but a salaried clerk, not without private dreams of ultimate partnership. At last, when I was nearly thirty years old, I found myself constantly a guest in the home of a fellow-clerk—a young man, who lived with his widowed mother and a sister. Their small neat house at Hackney was very different to great rambling liberal Meadow Farm, and the occupants were as dissimilar. Yet I believe competent judges would have considered Maria Willoughby much more handsome and talented than the little daisy of Mallowe. Of course, Maria was a town-lady, quiet, polite, and self-contained—a conservatory exotic; while the other was

just a little flower, dropped from God's hand, and un-
touched by horticulturists. But I grew to love Maria—
not with such love as I had borne for *her*, but with
grave, reverent affection, which would have placed her
"in my home and near my heart," and kept her there
safe and honoured even to the end. In due time I
opened my suit; it was courteously received, and I believed myself happy in a sensible, middle-aged kind of
way.

Well, I don't want to say much about what followed.
Let this suffice. Here am I, Ned Garrett, a settled old
bachelor, and there is Maria, the wife of a wealthy City
man, the son of a long line of prosperous merchants. If
she had come to me and said, " I love this man—I
loved him before I knew you ; " or, " I see him for the
first time, but I know that I can love him as I can never
love you," I could have forgiven her and forgotten my
own loss and humiliation. But no ! Only her mother
wrote to me, saying Maria had received a proposal from
a gentleman who could offer her a comfortable establishment and handsome settlements ; and as I could do
neither, she had advised her daughter to act in a way
most conducive to the well-being of all parties, and
Maria had been prudent enough to consent. Do you
suppose I was satisfied with this ? Not I. I insisted on
seeing the girl and making sure there were no under-
hand dealings or false representations. But she only
confirmed Mrs Willoughby's letter ; and I don't know
what I said, nor how I looked, but both women quailed
before me, and I have never spoken to either since.

I think that would have cost me my faith in woman-hood, had Maria been my first love. It was then I learned to thank God for Lucy's grave—for the gentle Hand that had not shattered my idol, but only removed it to a place of eternal safety. And from that time my heart has never yearned for a new allegiance. The bitterness slowly wore away, together with the remembrance of her who caused it. I know that Maria was pretty, graceful, and refined; but her face never comes to me in sleeping or waking dreams—while as for Lucy's, I could draw her portrait directly, if my fingers had as good a memory as my heart!

Not long after that I got my partnership. It was but a sober triumph for me. I wrote a letter to my mother and sister, and then I walked out in the darkness alone. There was no one else to tell. I knew Maria Willoughby would hear the news from her brother, and I blushed at the coarse pleasure I felt at her possible mortification, for I was now in the way to become a much richer man than her intended spouse. Oh, if she had only stood the ordeal! Yet even then I did not wish my success had come earlier and spared her the trial. One would rather go without jewels than pass through life decked out with pinchbeck, in the fond belief that the glass and gilt were diamonds and gold. We may regret the baseness, but not the detection. Let all false things go!

Not very long after that my dear gentle mother died. She had been so long ailing that she slipped out of life almost unconsciously; and I am glad to remember that

her last word was Ruth's name.   After the funeral I remained at home many days, assisting my sister in her
final arrangements.   Had everything been realised, there
would have been a slender competency for her, and I
wished her to share my London home, and rest herself
for the first time in her life.   But she resolutely refused.
She would live in the old house and carry on the business,
aided now by the orphan daughter of our village doctor.
"When I'm an old woman and you're an old man, Ned,"
she said, " then we will live together if we choose, but not
before.   You might wish me away if I came.   Now, don't
exclaim.   I should be glad if something happened that
would make you wish me away.   Shall you never marry,
Ned ?"

I laughed, and told her, as she was the elder, I was
waiting her example.

"Don't talk nonsense," she said, giving an energetic snip
to some stuff she was cutting out.   And there the matter
ended.

But now, after many years, the time is come when
Ruth is content to rest assured I shall never need a
fresher face than hers for my *vis-a-vis*.   For I find the
long rows of figures dazzle me, and the new-fashioned
ways of business confound my old-fashioned mind.   And
I also long for green fields, such as that where I talked
to Lucy more than forty years ago; and to fortify this
failing and yearning, I have argued with myself that it is
almost a sin for an out-of-date old fellow like me to keep
on grinding and moiling for more gold, which I shall
never need for wife or bairns, thus filling a post which

B

might be better occupied by some clever young man with both. So we two mean to live and die together in a quiet country corner; and this very day I have said good-bye to all my clerks, and left some remembrance in the hand of each, just as Mr Lambert did thirty years ago, when he came among us for the last time only the week before he died ; and I patted the head of a curly-haired lad from Glasgow, the very image of Ned Garrett fifty years ago, and I have told him if he ever want a friend not to forget his old master, buried in a certain snug cottage, where I know even now Ruth is passing about the rooms to see that all is in apple-pie order for my arrival to-morrow.

Yes, I, the old merchant, mean to rest for the remainder of my days. Yet, at the same time, I remember *her* charge, that in the quietest life "there's more to do than water flowers and go to sleep." Ruth will help out my slow comprehension with her keen eyes and clear voice. I only wish there had been a touch of romance about her. It would have made her as perfect as mortals can be. But romance is always sorrow. Therefore I thank God for my sister's escape.

Now for one more star-lit gaze from my narrow window ! To-night I see the dim moonbeams over the graveyard of the vanished church, and so far as silence goes, I might be on Snowdon, instead of in the heart of London city ; but I know that almost within a stone's throw of my window nestle courts and closes where infamy need never hide its head, even in such polluted daylight as can enter there. I know, too, that in some of the giant houses round me toil men whom the world respects and honours, but whom God ranks with those other felons who snatch watches to buy bread they are too cowardly to earn. And I own that Lucy's words are true ; this vineyard has been too large for me. My heart has not been strong enough for its burden. I have done a little, or rather I have helped others to do it, but it is such a little that I have no temptation to stand where the Pharisee stood, and boast of my good deeds.

To-morrow night I expect to look out on a far different scene—on quiet meadows with great hills rising behind them. Perhaps I shall hear the nightingale below my windows, and the lights will all be out in the few cottages within ken, just as if each were an abode of domestic peace and love. But I must not forget my Lucy's words,—"There's plenty of work where there are sin and sorrow, and sin and sorrow are everywhere."

Yes ; God has brought me thus far on my way, and I can trust Him to guide me to the end. He never gave me one sorrow or one pang more than I needed. I find now that the days which were hardest to live through are not darkest to remember. I only wish I had known this at the time, for I was often haunted by a dreary picture of lonely old age brooding over memory of sorrow as painful to endure as sorrow itself. It was my own fault. I should have trusted God's promises. It is rather late to begin to have faith, when one is on the brink of the cold river, and can almost see the gleaming gates beyond. But God is very reluctant to say, "Too late."

# CHAPTER I.

LEFT London at dawn, and arrived here before noon. My new home is not at Mallowe, but a little higher up the country, within an easy drive of that dear old place. This afternoon I have taken a fresh survey of my premises, and I am as well satisfied as on the day I bought them, for I am not one to like a thing less after it has become my own.

The house stands on a hill, gradually rising from the river side. Between the trees, by the use of a field-glass, I can catch a glimpse of the Mallowe, like a silver thread wandering on a greeny robe. Valleys are very beautiful, with their wealth of vegetation, and their well-like coolness; but I prefer the hill-tops. I think a valley is like youth, a lovely place to saunter for a while, but where we do not wish to stay, and where we could not stay even if we would. I don't say we never wish our-

selves back again, for many hill-sides are very bare and
dreary. But age is like a bower near the summit,
whence we can see the path by which we came, and
from which many things which seemed ugly when we
passed them, look beautiful in the distance. And from
that resting-place we can survey the little bit of journey
which still lies before us, and we see that it is very easy
and very short. I know age is generally called "the
descent of the hill." What! go down to rest amidst the
dampness and chills, and mists, that always haunt
valleys? No, no!

A narrow scarcely-used road, running between hedges,
passes our front door. It leads direct from our nearest
village, or rather attempt at a village, for I saw scarcely
a dozen houses as I drove through it. But there are a
few great farms standing back from this road, and enlivening it with their sweet sights and sounds. One in
particular seemed to come as near as possible to my
typical homestead. The dwelling-house stood in a
bend of the road, and a long, fair, dazzling flower-
garden stretched before the white curtained windows of
the best rooms. At the back lay the farm buildings,
loading the air with scents of hay and new milk, and
stretching about, as such buildings do in pleasant
places where ground-rents are unknown. A great curly
dog stood at the stable door and looked at me reflectively, as if he knew I was a new neighbour whose
acquaintance he must soon make. All around stretched
broad meadows, rejoicing under the warmth of God's
hand. I could not resist alighting from my chaise, and

leaning over the hedge. Suddenly I heard a horse's step in the path behind it, and a middle-aged man rode up mounted on a stout cob. He wore light garments and a. brown straw hat, and he looked full at me as he passed. I almost think he muttered. I am afraid he grudged my enjoyment of his possessions, for as he left the field, he shut the gate with a sharp bang, and rode on to the house. The sight of his face spoiled my plea-sure. He reminded me of an old spelling-book picture of " the dog in the manger." I began to pity the women who lived in that beautiful house, with no glimpse of the outer world except what he brought home to them. I looked compassionately at an old labourer who was carting some soil, an ancient man, with that patient, pathetic look which comes upon the aged when at work. I feared he never got a single penny more than what he could legally claim for his poor failing toil. But, any-how, he at least knew of another Master, for as I passed I heard him singing in a queer cracked voice—

> " The Lord's my Shepherd, I 'll not want.
>   He makes me down to lie
> In pastures green : he leadeth me
>   The quiet waters by."

There he paused to raise another shovelfull, and then went on to the last verse, as if it and the first dwelt specially in his mind—

> " Goodness and mercy all my life
>   Shall surely follow me :
> And in God's house for evermore
>   My dwelling-place shall be."

I was struck by the Scotch version and accent in an English lane.   A few yards off, a young man was mending a gate, and from the likeness I concluded he was son, or more likely grandson, to the cheerful patriarch. But he was not singing either psalm or ballad.   His face was quite gloomy—a handsome face, with noble features, such as one rarely sees except in the highest or lowest ranks.   He could not be more than nineteen. Ah, you see I am right.   The old man was near the hill-top, and in the brightness, but the lad was under the shadows of the valley.

Another twist in the road brought me to my own gate. So that surly farmer is our nearest neighbour.   Well, I hope I got a wrong impression of him.   Perhaps, before this day week, I shall be sorry for my judgment.   I hope so !   I hope so !

Ruth was waiting at the wicket, and I wish a painter had been with me to immortalise the scene—the little red-brick house standing against the warm greens of very early autumn, the bright geraniums in the foreground, the solid pillars of the entrance, relieved by their snowy stone globes, and my sister in her black satin gown, with a lace cap on her head, and a cambric kerchief fastened about her throat by the one heir-loom of our family, a little diamond brooch presented to our great-grandmother by the famous Duke of Marlborough when he was *fêted* in some town where her husband chanced to be mayor.   Two prim serving-maidens stood in the background waiting to do me honour, and I could hear the deep bay of a house-dog in the rear.   Their

decorous faces broke into smiles when I entered, as if
something in my countenance promised to relax the reins
of domestic discipline. Oh, Edward Garrett, why are
you not dignified! You and your sister have both been
business-people till now; you have made a fortune, and
she but an independency, yet she looks quite a *grand
dame*, and you! do you look like a gentleman of fortune? Go and see yourself in the glass, and be humble: your house, and your sister, and all that is yours,
are far too fine for you, old fellow. Go and hide your
diminished head!

Then we had our dinner, and we ate it in the sunshine, at the open window. Perhaps it was this, and
Ruth's company, which made it so much nicer than my
chop or steak yonder in the city. We were attended
by a neat-handed Phillis. That is not a quotation.
The girl is really a Phillis—Phillis Watts, a ploughman's
daughter, who has doubtless derived her fanciful cogno-
men from some relative on whom it had been bestowed
by a sentimental fine-lady godmother. The other servant came in to help her to remove the dishes, and
not thinking it right that I, her future master, should
sit by in perfect silence, I inquired her name, and was
answered in a quiet, refined voice—

" Alice M'Callum, sir."

The tone made me observe her more closely. She
is a slight girl, with brown, waving hair, pushed very
clearly off her brow. Her face looked pale and worn
beside the ruddy Phillis. There was nothing striking
in the features, but much in their expression, more par-

THE FIRST DAY IN THE HOUSE ON THE HILL. 25

ticularly when seen in a country-servant. Presently she
removed the cloth and withdrew

"That is a Scottish lass," said Ruth, "and a very
superior girl."

"Has she a brother and a grandfather?" I asked,
"for I saw two Scotchmen on my road here."

"She has some male relatives who work at the farm
below," answered Ruth, taking up her knitting.

"Have you learned much about our new sphere,
Ruth?" I ventured to inquire after a little pause, for she
had already resided here nearly a month.

"Really, I have not troubled myself about any sphere
outside these rooms, Edward," she replied; "they have
kept my hands full until now."

"You have certainly arranged them admirably," I
said, looking round. It was no compliment. I never
saw better appointed chambers.

By and by I brought out this, my note-book, and
began to write. Ruth's knitting needles clicked awfully
fast. I know she thought me trifling.

"Is that your correspondence, Edward?" she inquired,
in that cool voice of hers, which always makes me feel
so deferential.

"No; I'm only writing about—about "——

"Your sphere, eh, Edward?" and the voice was
cooler still.

"Well, yes," I answered, growing desperate, "and
yours too, Ruth."

"You needn't trouble yourself about mine," she
said. "'Whatsoever thy hand findeth to do, do it

with thy might.' That's all the sphere I care about, Ned."

"That is just what I wish to illustrate," I explained.

"The words are plain enough as they stand," said she.

"Yet, Ruth, many seem to read them, 'Whatsoever thy hand findeth *not* to do, fancy thyself doing it with all thy might.'"

"They are fools," she answered, decidedly.

"So are all of us," I remarked, "in one way or another;" and then followed a long silence.

"Nevertheless, Ned," my sister began, in her softer manner, "I own even the wisest take long in learning that there is no better work for them than the bit God puts into their hands. I know I have often neglected some duties, because it was out of my power to perform others."

I could hardly restrain a smile to hear her use her own shortcomings as proof of the weakness of "the wisest." But I knew it meant no harm. It was only a habit she had acquired through being the sole responsible person in the old home at Mallowe.

"And, Ruth," I answered, "there are also people who perform the far-off duties before those near at hand."

"Ah, yes," said she, "like the young woman who could play the piano, but had not learned the use of a thimble."

"And there are still others," I went on, "who yearn after blessings they cannot get, and undervalue those they have."

" Ah, feelings are different from deeds," she said. " To them we can scarcely say ' I will,' or ' I will not.' "

" I think God will help us through our yearnings for what He withholds," I remarked ; " but He will surely punish our undervaluing what He gives, perhaps by making us realise that old school-book line—

' How blessings brighten as they take their flight.'

And speaking of school-books, reminds me that many people will not learn what they may, because they cannot learn what they would, not knowing that the path of possibility often guides safely through the maze of improbability; and they seldom find out their error till too late."

"Yes, truly," assented Ruth, clenching my meanderings with a proverb :—

" He who will not when he may,
When he will, he shall have nay."

And then she rose and went off about some household arrangement, leaving me to puzzle out a few more thoughts on the wisdom of doing first the thing which lieth nearest.

But it would not do. The silent beauty of the prospect stretching far before my windows wooed me from my papers, and after a few ineffectual attempts at perseverance, I put them aside, got my hat (oh, joy ! not a dingy beaver, but a cool, light straw,) and sauntered out. Now, it's just like me to want to know more about what I know already. So, instead of turning to the left and taking the road I had never seen, I turned to the right and pursued the path along which I had travelled at noon.   It was cooler now.   The sun was getting low, and the shadows were broader and darker.   Very soon I came in sight of the Great Farm, with its outlying houses. The young workman was still lingering by the gate, which was now mended, and beside him stood a slight figure in white cap and apron.   As I drew near I recognised the pale face of my servant, Alice M'Callum.   She turned and acknowledged my presence.

"A fine afternoon, Alice," I said.   "Do you know, when I saw you at dinner, I fancied I had met relations of yours in the morning, and I suppose I am right."

"This is my brother Ewen, sir," she answered.

"And you have a grandfather too?" I went on.   "I heard him singing the Scotch psalms as I passed."

"Ah, he's always cheerful, sir," she said, and I thought her lips quivered a little.

"Has he gone to his tea?" I inquired, looking round, for he was not in sight.

"No," said the young man.   "He's just inside yonder tool-house."

The words were civil enough, though rather abrupt, but the voice startled me.   Like his sister's, it was a refined voice, yet there was in it a harsh tone of defiance, as if he were ready to direct me anywhere, so as it took me away from him.   I looked at the girl.   Her eyes were fixed on her brother's face, with an expression of mingled pity and terror.   There was something in her countenance which made my heart ache.

"I will go and speak to your grandfather, Alice," I said.

As I drew near the tool-house, the old man came out. Seeing me approach him, and recognising the traveller of the morning, he gave me a sort of half-military salutation, and stood still.

"I find your grand-daughter Alice is one of my household," I said. "She does not seem a very strong girl; but our service will not be hard."

"Alice is quite content, sir," answered the old man cheerfully.

"Were your grandchildren born in England?" I inquired.

"The boy was; Alice wasn't," replied the patriarch. "Alice was born in the Highlands of Scotland. She says she can just remember the place; but I doubt, sir, that's more from my talk than from her memory. Ah, I see it as if I'd only left it yesterday—aweel! I don't say it was bonnier than this, nor so bonnie maybe," and he looked round, "but for a' that, sir, to auld folk there's nae place like the auld place."

"What made you leave it?" I asked.

"Ye may well believe, no o' my ain will," said he, "but the Earl, to whose forefathers mine had paid honest rent for a hundred years, took it into his head to make a great sheep farm. So we had notice to quit. Not us only, sir. More than thirty homes were broken up on the same day. One or two hearts were broken, too, I'm feared. Yet the Earl was a kind man, sir, and had never been hard after a bad season. I suppose he didn't know people could care for old walls that had no 'scutcheons on them.  I don't doubt he did it never thinking.  But that didn't save our sorrow."

"Was there any resistance?"

"No, sir; there were a few fierce words at first, but we understood well enoo' that the Earl could do as he willed wi' his own.  And if his agents were kind-hearted folk, why should we make their work painfu' tae them?  And if they were cruel, why should we resist what we couldna' withstand, and gie them the pleasure o' conquerin', as they were sure to do?  We don't like being conquered, sir; if we can't keep a field, we leave it."

"And what became of the evicted people?" I asked.

"They mostly went to Canada.  All those I've heard of, have prospered.  If the Earl ever frets about the few old people who were sent to their graves a little before their time, he may comfort himself wi' the thocht it was a good change for the many in the long-run.  That's the way the Lord brings good out of evil, sir."

"Your family didn't go abroad?" I queried.

"No, sir," he said.  "I had only one son, and his wife was a poor ailing creature, who would have died on shipboard.  Yet she had a wonderfu' spirit: there was no one said harder things of the Earl than she did.  At the same time, sir, if she could have shown him a kindness, I 'm sure she'd hae done it.  So, instead of going abroad, we came down here, and my son got a place as manager on a farm, and we all did very well, only the wife died when little Ewen was born.  My son lived till both his children were 'most grown up.  We have had hard lines, sir, since then, but I'm glad he died when he did?"

'Why, how is that?" I inquired.

"Ah, sir, it's a terrible story, and might be better untold. But you seem kind, sir, and however you may judge about the boy, what I can tell will help you to understand Alice."

"Your grand-daughter certainly looks unhappy, Mr M'Callum," said I.

"She's just witherin' up," said the old man, with the strange pathos of solemn calmness.

During our conversation we had strolled down the lane past the farmhouse, and as M'Callum spoke thus, he paused beside a rude fence which enclosed a low-lying woody meadow, through which ran a narrow stream.

"It happened there!" he said.

But Alice came running behind us, quite white and breathless. "Grandfather," she cried, "Ewen is waiting for you to go to tea. You know he must make haste back to finish his work,' and as she spoke she gave an appealing look, as if she only wished she knew what was told and what remained unsaid.

"I'll come—I'm comin'," answered the old man, with a humility like that of a child detected in some indiscretion. "Mind, sir," he whispered, "it has nothing to do with *her*, except that it's hurrying her away to be an angel in heaven."

We retraced our steps very slowly, for the old man was unmistakeably feeble. Alice walked by his side in silence. We found Ewen waiting for us where we had left him. Their home lay down a narrow lane, leading from the road. I caught a glimpse of it—a rude wooden cottage, with bulging windows.

"I have made your tea ready, grandfather," said Alice.

"Thank ye, my girl; and I'm sure, sir, we're kindly obliged to Mistress Garrett for giving her leave to run out whiles, and do us a turn at housekeeping. Good evening, sir."

"Good evening, Mr M'Callum," I answered; "good evening," I added, turning to the young man, but he walked away as if he had not heard.

Alice stepped before me and opened the garden gate. She held it while I passed in. Then she said timidly, "Don't think hardly of my brother, sir. His manner is strange, but he has been through seas of trouble."

"Is he quite ashore now, Alice?" I inquired.

She did not answer for a minute, but her lip and brow quivered. "I'm afraid, sir, it's as right as it ever will be," she said, and burst into tears.

"My dear girl," I began, "I don't want to hear anything you do not wish to tell, but"——

"You'll hear it all soon enough, sir," she said, with a desperate effort to stop her tears; "but I wanted you to know us a little before you heard."

"Yet, would it not be best for you to tell me your own story? Why should I be left to hear what other people say?"

"Then I've got no story to tell, sir," she answered with

sudden calmness. "The only story is what the people say, and they say a lie!"

There was a clear emphasis in her voice which made me look down at her. Her tears were dried, and her eyes were bright and fixed, like those of a person fronting a railing mob.

"Then I should not heed them, Alice."

"Yes, sir, you would," she replied. Her flat contradiction was quite respectful. She saw life from a position in which I had never stood. She was the wisest in this matter.

By this time we had reached the hall. I held out my hand to her, as Mr Lambert had given me his on the day I heard of Lucy's death.

"Well, at least, Alice," I said, "remember, I am ready to hear whenever you wish to tell. Do not be too sure that a friend's aid is useless."

She let her hand stay in mine for about a minute. It was very cold. Then she raised her eyes and opened her mouth, so that I saw rather than heard her thanks.

I went into the parlour. My papers still lay about the table, and Ruth had not returned. I wondered if she knew anything of the tragedy of which I had caught a glimpse. I resolved not to ask her about it yet, for I believed she had a practical person's strong dislike to mystery. And what was this mystery? It seemed connected with that handsome, abrupt young workman, scarcely more than a youth. His sister denied its truth, whatever it might be, but I knew that loving women

c

have a happy gift of disbelieving what they choose. Her grandfather had certainly spoken less decidedly; and I could not forget his words as we stood beside that low, deserted meadow, with its sluggish stream. "It happened there." What happened?

It pained me greatly to see the suffering written on my servant's face. When she brought in our tea she was as composed as possible; but I had been behind the scenes, and I knew there was a reason for her worn cheeks, and for the strange note that sounded occasionally in her voice. Yet what could I do to help her? It occurred to me, I might find an opportunity of speaking to the young man alone. I know some people suffer from a strange reserve, which makes them more willing to open their hearts to strangers than to their dearest friends. This arises from a morbid sensitiveness which cannot bear constantly to meet eyes that understand all about us. Now this disposition ought not to be punished or preached at. It is a spiritual disease, and must be pitied and cured. At the same time, I doubt if it ever wholly disappears. To this day, I am glad Ruth never guessed about Lucy Weston.

After tea, my sister resumed her knitting, and as I fumbled with my papers, I caught her dark eyes watching me with an arch expression. Presently she said—

"How did you like your afternoon walk, Edward? Had you any adventures?"

"Hem—no," I answered, guiltily; "at least, I met Alice in the lane, talking to her brother and grandfather. The old man seems a shrewd, pleasant Scotchman, and he sent his thanks to you for permitting Alice to look after his household arrangements."

"Ah, poor man ! I should think myself a hard woman if I denied him any comfort in my power to give," said Ruth.

"Any special reason for saying so ?" I inquired.

"I believe the young man is as bad as he can be," returned my sister. "There's one very dark story whispered about him in the neighbourhood. He was tried for a fearful deed and acquitted. So, of course, human eyes must henceforth regard him as innocent. I shall not repeat the story, for I don't know any particulars."

"I gathered something of this from their talk in the afternoon," I said. "At any rate, his sister believes him guiltless."

"She's one of those women who are made to be heart-broken," remarked Ruth ; "she'd not love him less if she knew him guilty."

"Thank God for such love," I said. "It helps us to understand His own."

"Yes, that's all very fine," returned my sister, "but it seems hard one should be a martyr that others may learn a lesson."

"Yet it is often God's will," said I.

"Well, Edward," she answered, "I don't suppose He wishes it, but as He permits it, of course we must be satisfied. He will make it up to the sufferers in His own good time."

"He makes it up now," I said. "Love is ever its own reward. It purifies the heart which holds it."

"So does fire purify silver," retorted Ruth, "but I doubt if the silver likes the process while it is going on."

"Yet I am sure Alice would not give up her sisterly love even if she could," I pleaded.

"Ah, she can't give it up, so that settles the question," returned Ruth. "There is no laying down the crosses that grow out of our own hearts, and they are always heaviest ? "

"The heaviest cross makes the brightest crown," I said.

"I suppose so," she answered. "But when one is over-tired with carrying a burden on a long journey, one has not always strength to look forward to the very end. The little bit of road under each footstep is often quite enough ! "

"Just so," I said, "and so doing, we shall suddenly find ourselves on the threshold of Home ! "

Then followed a long silence. At last I asked, " From what service did you take Alice M'Callum ? "

"From Mallowe Hall," answered - Ruth. "I knew her by her coming to my old shop, and I always had a liking for her. She was lady's-maid there, and she left because all the servants took sides against her brother, and that she could not bear. Besides, she wished to be nearer her relations in their 'trouble,' as she called it. So I offered to take her, and she was quite thankful to come, though our service is much inferior to what she left at the Hall. I told her plainly she was a simpleton. But she only answered, 'Never mind.'"

"Well, Ruth," I said, "I am truly thankful you acted

as you did. Few women would have courage to engage a servant who expressly wished to be near a relation with ' a very dark story.' "

" I am not in the habit of judging individuals by their connexions," she answered, " and I liked the girl's faithfulness. Besides, for the matter of fear, I may as well tell you I keep pistols."

" Bless me, Ruth !" I ejaculated.

" Well," said she coolly, turning her needles, and beginning another row, " better do that, than not do what you wish because you 're frightened."

" When did you begin that custom ?" I inquired.

" Twenty years ago," she answered ; " at the time when I hired a youth to be messenger and odd man about the house and garden at Mallowe.

" Then you took two or three means of protection at the same time," I said.

" I didn't know whether the lad would be a protection," she replied drily. " He had been a convict, and he hung about the village, saying he could not do anything, because no one would give him a chance. I resolved he should not have that excuse any longer. So I rode to Hopleigh and bought two pistols, and took some lessons in their use. Then I hired him, and he slept in the room over mine. He never knew about the firearms. He thought I trusted him entirely. I think it was a harmless deception. Had he shown himself unworthy of trust he would have found out his mistake."

" Then you were not disappointed in him ?"

"No," she said, "he is now highly respectable, and is head man on one of the best farms near the village."

"Ruth," said I, gazing earnestly at her, as she sat opposite me as upright as a dart, "you never told me this before."

"Why should I?" she replied, returning my gaze with a sharp glance from her keen hazel eyes. "You would have urged me not to do it, or not to do such things again, as the case might be. And yet I'll engage you 've been doing the like in London. We 're all willing to be a little brave or kind ourselves, but we 're prone to wish our friends to shut themselves into safe, selfish cupboards, just to save our own feelings and fears."

"Well, Ruth," I said, (thinking this was a good opportunity,) "I 've come to the conclusion I 'll have a little conversation with young Ewen M'Callum myself."

"Very well," she replied, "only you need not speak to him beside pools in lonely fields."

"But supposing the best opportunity occurs in such a locality?" I said smiling.

"I cannot get into you to direct your conscience," she answered. "But don't follow my example in everything *except* the pistols!"

At that moment Phillis brought in our supper, and our conversation fell into very ordinary channels, until we finally said good night, and retired to our respective chambers.

I wonder if Ruth has really had no romance in her life. I am not so sure of it as I was last night. She is certainly like some apples I have seen, which have green, tart rinds, yet are very sweet at the core. But if God has ever sent my sister one of those special sorrows with which "a stranger intermeddleth not," she must have suffered very much, as such strong natures do. They always shut their sorrows in their own hearts, which is very like covering a crown of thorns with an iron helmet. God bless her! I almost wish she had been born to rank and wealth—she seems just the woman to save a country, like Joan of Arc, or Elizabeth, or Maria Theresa.

Yet, after all, but few are needed to do these out-of-the-way tasks which startle the world, and one may be most useful just doing commonplace duties and leaving the issue with God. And when it is all over, and our feet will run no more, and our hands are helpless, and we have scarcely strength to murmur a last prayer, then we shall see that instead of needing a larger field, we have left untilled many corners of our single acre, and that none of it is fit for our Master's eye, were it not for the softening shadow of the Cross.

# CHAPTER II

## THE MYSTERY OF THE LOW MEADOW.

HE two following days were very rainy, and I spent them in-doors arranging my books and papers according to my own fashion. But on Saturday the weather was glorious.

I did not go out till afternoon, and then I made my way down the lane wherein stood the M'Callums' wooden cottage. I found it empty. I could see the glimmer of a fire on the hearth, and a fine gray cat was seated on the window-sill, but the other inmates were evidently out. So I sauntered on.

I had not gone very far before I came to a gate. It led into a field where two cows and a donkey were feeding. It was a clear open meadow, lying full on the slope of the hill, and commanding a fine view of the valley and of my dear old Mallowe. I went in, and rambled about. I attempted a friendship with the cattle, fully believing myself quite alone in the open eye of heaven, when suddenly I caught sight of a man seated on a fallen tree, resting elbows on knees and hiding his face in his hands. It was Ewen M'Callum.

I stood still. I feel an awe in the presence of speechless suffering, for, with all its agony, I know it very often sits close outside the golden gates of God's Paradise. In this case I could scarcely hope so. Yet anyhow there is royalty about anguish. I stood still; and it seemed as if a solemn silence dropped over the meadows.

He sat as if he would never stir, and I scarcely wished him to look up and find me watching him. So I went towards him with a brisk step, and when he raised his head I bade him a cheerful " good afternoon."

He responded and got up, gathering together a little cane and two books which lay near him on the grass. He intended to go away, and I was forced to devise an excuse to detain him.

" This is a fine prospect," I said. " Where does this field lead ? "

" Into the road that goes to Mallowe," he answered.

" I suppose you leave work early on Saturday," I went on. " I hope your grandfather has not suffered from the wet weather."

" I believe he is very well," he replied.

I felt that our conversation was torture to him, and that he was merely enduring it by great effort of will. It was like holding a wild animal, which only waits till our grasp relaxes, and then bounds away to its hiding-place, henceforth to be shyer than ever. I saw I should never

get at him through the ordinary avenues of neighbourhood and friendliness.   To such entrance his heart was
closed.   My only chance lay in a sudden attack on
some unexpected corner.

"I should like to ask you a question," I said, and was
almost frightened to hear my own words.

His face changed colour and his lips moved a little;
yet there seemed a thaw in his manner as he answered,
"Very well, sir."

"I hear something is said against you in the village.
I have not heard what it is.   Will you tell me?"

There was a long silence.   We stood just beside the
fallen tree.   I could see some little boats on the silver
breast of the distant Mallowe, and thin smoke wreaths
rising from the house on its shore.   I heard a church clock
strike four.   My companion stood motionless beside me,
the outlines of his face clearly chiselled against the pale
blue sky—a handsome face, full of passionate sensibility,
from which the old look of fierce endurance had fallen
like a mask.   At last he spoke: "They say I am a
murderer!"

I did not shudder at the dreadful word, and somehow
there was no query in my voice as I turned to him and
said, "But it is not true."

"No, it isn't," he answered; "but it might be better
for—for the others—if it were!"

"No, no," I said, "the more the sin the greater the
sorrow."

"Well, I don't know,' he went on in a choking voice.
"If it had been found true, and I had suffered for it,

every one would have pitied them ; but as it is, they are only blamed and scoffed at for taking my part."

"But you don't suppose they mind that?" I inquired.

"If they don't, I do," he said.

"Sit down again and tell me all about it," I said ; "surely there must be some way out of this misery ; tell it from the beginning, and take your own time over it," for I saw he was greatly excited.

We both sat down side by side on the fallen tree.

"It is a pity I was born," he said.

"Don't say that," I interrupted ; "that might have saved your past, but it would also cost your future."

"My future!" he ejaculated bitterly.

"Yes," I answered. "What do you call the future? If you measure it by the few fleeting years of mortality, you may as well style this field the world."

"I 'm a living text for all the sermons in the neighbourhood," he broke out after a short silence. "There is not an idle reprobate in the place who does not set forth my ruin in excuse for not caring about his children's education. I 'm quoted as an instance of the folly of parents trying to elevate their families above the station in which it pleased God to place them. Every one is sure I should have been a better man if I had not known how to write or read. They can't argue the subject, but they can point to me in illustration."

At this moment it struck me that the young man's whole manner was not that of a country labourer. I had not noticed it before, because my ordinary style of

conversation is so homely that I need seldom lower it
for the simplest comprehension.

"Then your father brought you up carefully?" I
remarked.

" Yes, indeed he did," answered the youth ; "and he
would have been angry if any one had called us poor
people, and I was sent to the best school he could find.
But from the first there was something wrong in me.
The schoolmaster did not like me, and I had not a friend
among the boys.  They knew who I was, and they did
not care to receive me as an equal.  When I discovered
that, I turned it over in my mind, till I made out that
according to their reckoning I was their superior; for
however poor we were, I came of a nation the English
could never subdue.  They drove me to say so, and
then they hated me, and I used to go to and fro with
black bitter anger in my heart.  Oh, what folly it all
was !  What folly !—if I had known then what real
trouble means—— Nevertheless," he went on, " I liked
school for the sake of learning, and I believe I got on
pretty well.  But when I was fourteen my father died,
and somebody got me a place in the builder's counting-
house at Mallowe.  The builder's son had been my
schoolfellow, and the same week that I entered his
father's shop he went to college.  I suppose I envied
him.  I don't know how it came about, but I grew a
very bad lad.  There was something in me which would
not be satisfied with my work and my home.  Then
Alice got a situation as lady's-maid, and grandfather
went into lodgings, and there was nowhere for me to go

of an evening. And yet it was not that either, for whenever grandfather called to see me I made some excuse to get rid of him, and when Alice wrote to me I seldom answered her letters. One of the young men in my master's shop was a Londoner, and he seemed to have so much more life in him than the others that I made friends with him at once. I got so fond of him that he could persuade me to anything. I used to go with him to all the cricket-matches and regattas within reach. Those things are harmless enough if one goes to them in good company. But poor George was not good company. And so I went on from bad to worse."

"Until"—— I remarked, to lead him on, for he paused.

"Oh, the story is just like a common report out of a dirty newspaper," he said, writhing.

"Never mind that," I said; "and we should not call such things common if we only realised what anguish they each bring to somebody."

"Well, I got in debt to George. He gambled, and often had plenty of money. Then we grew quarrelsome. One Saturday afternoon last summer twelvemonth we went together to a boat-race. He drank a good deal, and betted and lost. I tried to get him away, but he only became very angry, and used violent words about the money I owed him. At last we left the place together. He had lodgings up here, and I meant to see him home. But he got so aggravating that my temper was roused, and I left him, and returned towards the river. Just as I was passing the church I saw Alice riding in her mistress's carriage, and she looked from the window and recognised me. After taking a walk, I went back to my master's house and slept there ; and on Sunday morning we heard that George was found drowned in the water in the Low Meadow."

He spoke these last words in a low, horrified tone. It was the first time he had told the story. I did not break silence, but waited till he resumed the narrative.

"I was arrested that evening," he went on, "and I own everything was against me. I was last seen with the dead man, and we were heard to be on bad terms. One or two people swore to seeing us together on the road a good way from the river. One man, an ostler, knew the exact time when we passed his tavern. It was half-past four. From that house it would take about three-quarters of an hour to reach the Low Meadow. I did not re-enter my master's house until half-past six, which allowed me full time to go the whole distance and return."

"But your sister had seen you in the interval," I remarked.

"Yes ; and as she was driving past the church, she had happened to notice the time, and it was then about ten minutes to five. Her mistress remembered this, and also that Alice had nodded to some one on foot. That was all the evidence I could bring forward in my favour."

"Slender as it seems, it was sufficient," said I.

"It might have been if Alice were not my sister," he

replied.  " But every one is quite willing to believe that she swore falsely to save me."

" But her mistress partly corroborated her," I re-marked.

" Not in the main point," he said.  " The lady knew that my sister nodded to some one as they passed the church at ten minutes to five ; but she did not see *who* it was.  So the coroner gave a verdict of ' found drowned,' and I was discharged, because ' there was not evidence whereon a jury could convict.' "

" But didn't they take into consideration the poor man's intoxication ? " I inquired.

" Yes ; they consulted on the possibility of his slipping into the pool ; but many swore that he was sober enough to take care of himself.  I believe that was true."

" Then, what is your theory of his death ? " I asked.

" That he was murdered, or, at least, that a struggle took place on the bank, which ended in his falling into the water.  There were footprints of two people up to a certain point where the ground was much trampled, and after that, there was only trace of one."

" It is very dreadful," I said; " and no one else has been arrested since your discharge ? "

"No," he answered, hopelessly.  "Suspicion did not point at anybody but me, and so I must go through life as the murderer of the man who was my companion and destroyer.  There is no appeal from suspicion !"

" Then you left your old service at Mallowe ? " I asked.

"I was dismissed," he said, "and there was no chance of getting a similar situation. But I had been with my father a great deal when I was a boy, and so I am handy at any out-door work. But even that was not easy to get, till Mr Herbert at the Great Farm took me on as a kind of general hand."

"There, at least, is a blessing," I said; "that saves you from being a burden to your grandfather and Alice, and "——

"I wouldn't have lived upon them while there was a rope in the house or water in the river!" he interrupted, in the old desperate tone.

"What! sooner than bear the weight of gratitude, you would plunge those who love you in despair?" I said. "I am sorry you are so selfish!"

He groaned aloud—"O sir, have mercy on me. If you could only know how I feel "——

"Ah, that is it," I said, laying my hand on his arm. "If I only could! But, my boy, God knows all about it, and He does not willingly afflict His poor children."

"But this false accusation—this wicked scandal—cannot come from God!" he exclaimed.

"He permits them—He does not wish them," I replied, recalling Ruth's remark. "No more did He wish a youth, the son of godly parents, to go with evil company, and fall into wicked ways. You must learn to pardon your neighbours' mistake. Your conduct has led them into this breach of charity. You have been to them an occasion of falling."

" And must the world always go on thus ?" he cried.

"Remember, God overrules all these troubles," I went on. " He saw you were proud and wilful, and He has been pleased to humble you, and to put your steps into straight and painful paths. He changes your neighbours' mistake into a merciful rod to correct you. You must not cry out at the rod, you must be thankful for it, and repent of the sins which brought it upon you."

"But the innocent suffer with the guilty," he said, raising his eyes. " *They* feel the rod as well as I do."

" That is part of your punishment," I answered. " But do not understand me that affliction follows sin as a judgment. God sends sorrow to draw us back to Him, or nearer to Him, as the case may be. The judgment of sin lies in our remorse for it, and our grief at consequences which we cannot undo. It is right you should smart to see the troubles of your dear ones ; but yet those troubles may be a blessing to them."

He had buried his face in his hands, and I saw a tear trickle between his fingers.

" Your grandfather bears it very bravely," I said, presently. " I daresay he thinks little of any sacrifice which serves to steady you."

" That's just what he says ; but it's killing Alice," he answered, without looking up.

" *You* are killing Alice," I said, firmly. " She cannot bear it because she sees you do not bear it cheerfully. Now, will you not candidly own that you often speak sharply to her ?"

" Who told you so?" he asked, in astonishment.

" My own knowledge of human nature," I answered : " when she comes near you, the sight of her recalls all the misery and bitterness, and doubtless you see she is whiter and thinner than she was two years ago. Then your heart rebels, and you ask yourself grievous questions which you are not able to answer, and meanwhile you forget the smile and the pleasant word which would send her away rejoicing. Next time she comes back whiter and thinner than ever, and the same weary work is done over again."

" But what am I to do?" he said, looking at me with eyes of such despair that I could hardly confront them.

" Humble yourself, and leave the past alone," I replied. " Remember that you have sinned, and forget that you have been sinned against. Draw your thoughts from your injuries to your errors."

He sat in silence for some minutes, then the church clock chimed five, and he arose suddenly.

" Then you believe I am an innocent man, sir?" he said.

" I do, sincerely," said I.

" I'll try to do as you say, sir," he remarked presently.

" You must excuse my plain speaking," I said; " I don't often take folks by storm as I have taken you."

" I wasn't worth the trouble," said he.

" Don't forget you are worth a good deal to two or three people in the world," I answered, "and you 'll set a value on yourself some day soon."

He smiled sadly and shook his head, and so we parted, and I retraced my way alone.

I had plenty to think about, in this grim commonplace tragedy which had met me on the threshold of my retired life. I felt a warm interest in Ewen M'Callum. He had passed through a dreadful trial, but I could see it was just the trial he needed. Think of his schoolboy pride in belonging to a nation which had never been subdued! Ah, now he knows his own weakness, and one has to know that before one can be really strong.

Then I pondered over the mystery of the Low Meadow. Even Ewen concluded that his unhappy comrade had not met his death by mere misadventure. If this were true, the young man's character might yet be cleared by the discovery of the real criminal. But Ewen himself owned that suspicion had pointed to nobody but him, and surely the police would have tracked every possible clue they could find. It made me shudder to think that the murderer might yet be haunting the neighbourhood, not even aroused to confession by the danger and misery of an innocent person. Now, what would touch such a heart as that? I should say nothing, only I know that God can do anything.

As I drew near home, there came through the open window a pleasant clatter of spoons and china. It was tea-time. In the hall I met Alice carrying the toast rack.

"I think you will find things get much better soon, Alice," I said, cheerfully.

She looked up at me with sudden brightness and asked: "Have you been speaking to Ewen, sir?"

" Yes ; and I believe I have got into his heart," I replied.

" Did he mind—I mean, how does he seem now, sir?"

" Well, Alice," I answered, smiling, " I think he is quite as well as can be expected after the operation ! "

Then we went into the parlour, and Alice deposited the rack on the table, and Ruth looked at her and then at me, and quite understood that I now knew all about it. She is a wonderful quick woman, one of the sort that know things before they are told. I can never make out how she did not guess about Lucy Weston.

" So you 've had your conversation with the young man," she said, as soon as the girls had left us.

" Yes," I answered ; " and I have come to the conclusion that he is as innocent as I am."

" Why, surely you didn't talk to him of—what they say, Edward ?" she exclaimed.

" Yes, I did," I replied. " I asked him to tell me all he could about it."

" Well, that 's delightful simplicity !" said Ruth, laughing ; " nevertheless, I believe simple people often do the wisest things. Let me put another lump of sugar in your tea, Ned."

" Thanks for your compliment," I said, holding up my cup for the proffered sweetness. " Don't you know, Ruth, that my pet theory is the mission of Thoroughfares ?"

" I want a report of that mission," said she. " I don't quite understand its operations."

"Well," I answered, "when I was in the City, I used to notice that streets through which no one could pass were always miserable. The houses got bad tenants, and the bad tenants grew worse every day. I remember one instance in particular. It was a long narrow street, opening from a road and ended by a dead wall. The houses near the road were well enough. But as you passed down the street, you saw that each dwelling was shabbier and dirtier than the last, until close to the dead wall you found broken windows screened by torn shawls or dirty blankets, through whose tatters you could see family operations not usually carried on in the eye of the public. It was a hopeless street—a property so bad that the landlord vainly advertised it for sale. But in the course of some improvements the dead wall was pulled down, and the lower end of the street thrown open to a rising thoroughfare. And before a year was out, either the old tenants had departed, or they had mended their ways, for there was no untidy window or slatternly woman to be seen. Now I believe it is just the same with our hearts. Sin or sorrow sometimes closes them so that no friendly voice can echo through. And gradually all foul things congregate therein. Then some hand must break down the barriers with kindly violence, so that God's comfort may blow through like the healthy north wind which leaves a blessing behind it. And that makes suspicion and despair get ashamed of themselves and sneak out of sight, while love to God and man passes up and down the new thoroughfare."

"That's all true enough," said Ruth. "But don't

you think that in due time most hearts re-open without any interference?"

"Perhaps they may," I answered, "but they may remain closed too long for their own happiness or the good of the world."

"Yes, that's quite possible," said she, and she looked very grave. "But still, Edward, don't you think some sorrows are best endured and conquered in silence?"

"I do think so," I replied; "but then sorrow is not meant to close the heart, but to open it, and if we feel our heart closing, we may be sure we are neither enduring nor conquering, but succumbing."

There followed a long pause.

"A false accusation is a terrible thing," said Ruth at last, "for it is very dreadful merely to be misunderstood."

"I don't believe you would mind even that," I remarked; "you are brave enough to say, 'If God and my conscience approve, let others think what they may.'"

"You are a wise man, Edward," said Ruth, drily. Now what she meant by that, I cannot tell. I am sure she did not mean exactly what she said.

"It is to be hoped that you practise what you preach," she added presently. "If you have made a thoroughfare in this young man's heart, make a thoroughfare in his life as well."

"Please explain yourself, Ruth," I said.

"Why, don't you see he is cooped in a corner," she answered, taking up her knitting-needles, "with a lie behind him, and the whole village in front, hunting him back upon it? I suppose the world has more places in it than Mallowe and Upper Mallowe."

"Well, now I think of it, I wonder he did not go abroad," I said.

"Yes, of course, brother," answered Ruth; "because you know people can travel about so easily who have neither money, nor friends, nor character, particularly if they have aged or feeble relatives with whom it is their duty to stay. I must repeat, Edward, that you are a very wise man!"

"But if he went to London," I said, "then he wouldn't be too far from his grandfather and sister—certainly he might go to London."

"Certainly he will," said Ruth, "if you send him."

"But still, out-door work there would be worse than here," I remarked, "and, under the circumstances, other employment would be hard to get."

"Then never talk to me again about your City influence," said Ruth, knitting furiously.

"But, my dear," I pleaded, "we have only our own impressions to go by, and "——

"Edward," said she, laying down her needles, and looking at me awfully, as she used in the days of my youth when I faltered in repeating "my duty to my neighbour,"—" Edward, do you believe this young man innocent, or do you believe him guilty?"

"I have no doubt of his innocence," I answered.

"Then do your duty according to your lights," said she; "that's all the best of us can do."

" But I could not recommend him to any one without telling him the whole story," I remarked.

" Certainly not, but I repeat, if you cannot get anybody to share your convictions, or at least to trust them, I would not give much for your City influence."

" But would he be better off anywhere, when once his story was known?" I queried.

" I should think so. I presume a respectable merchant could hear such a narrative without telling it over to all his clerks and errand-boys. Were no confidences ever placed in you, Edward?"

" Well, my dear," I answered, " let us call Alice, and if we can ascertain from her that the scheme is likely to prove agreeable to her brother, I will write to my old partners, and the youth's mind need not be disturbed about the matter till we have a definite offer to make him."

" There! that will do," said Ruth; and she got up and rang the bell, and in half a minute Alice's patient face appeared at the doorway.

" Alice," I said, " come in; I have some questions to ask about Ewen. We all believe him innocent—my sister, you, and I—but we fear it is very hard to defy a general bad opinion. Do you think Ewen likes remaining in the neighbourhood?"

" Oh, sir!" exclaimed the maiden, wringing her thin fingers, " do not set him thinking about going abroad!"

" Don't be a simpleton, Alice," said Ruth; " now you are feeling for yourself instead of your brother."

" Hush, Ruth," I interrupted. " Alice is only nervous because she is weak and weary with sorrow. I am not speaking of abroad. I think it is a great blessing that he could get honest work close at hand, for Mr Herbert had as much reason as other people to mistrust him. By the way, I wonder that did not help to re-establish Ewen's character, Alice."

" It could not, sir," she answered. " Every one knows that Mr Herbert would not care if he were guilty, so as he could get him cheap."

" Now I fear that is rather uncharitable, Alice," said I.

" It may not be so, Edward," remarked Ruth. " 'Charity thinketh no evil,' that is to say, she does not suspect, but she cannot shut her eyes to facts."

" I am not ungrateful to Mr Herbert, sir," said Alice. " His work has been a blessing to us, for the other gentlemen round here would not hire Ewen at any price."

" Well, what I wish to ask is, do you think your brother would be better off in London ? Take time to consider. There are many questions to answer. Has he had sufficient warning to steady him ? Can you and his grandfather bear to part from him ? "

" Oh, sir," said Alice, with streaming eyes, " if he could get work more fit for him than field-labour, and be out of sight of all the people that shun and scorn him, grandfather and I wouldn't think about ourselves."

" Now I believe you love your brother," remarked Ruth quietly. But the girl dropped her head and wept bitterly.

" I suppose he would have no objection to any plan of this sort ? " I said presently.

" He would bless you and thank God for it, sir," sobbed my servant.

" Then don't repeat our conversation at present, and I will see what can be done. Trust me, he shall not be left in his present misery if I can help it."

" Though he must not forget it is principally his own fault," said Ruth, parenthetically.

" And now you may go, Alice ; and you may tell Phillis to get supper ready."

" No, I 'll tell her myself," interrupted Ruth ; " and if Alice likes, she can go straight off to bed, else Phillis will think she has had a very bad scolding."

" I don't care what any one thinks, ma'am," said Alice, joyfully, though the tears were still streaming down her cheeks.

" Now isn't that extraordinary ? " remarked Ruth, when she was gone.

" What in particular ? " I inquired.

" That girl's love for a brother who has never made her happy. People who are wicked, or useless, or unlucky, seem always the most thought of."

" I suppose it is a provision of God," I said. " He longs to save them from themselves. If we stood on shore and beheld a shipwreck, we should throw out most ropes to those who could not swim."

" But still it seems hard," said Ruth.

" Well, so it did to the prodigal's brother," I answered, " but, depend upon it, when they both sat down at the family feast he was the happier of the two; or, at any rate, he would have been, had he loved his brother as he ought. You see, he might have watched at the gate beside his father, and then he would have been better employed than weighing and measuring affection, and disturbing himself with reproachful thoughts."

"Ah, yes, so he would," said Ruth; "of course I know God in His wisdom manages these things best; and that just shows us how foolish we must be; for if we had the reins we should do almost everything differently."

"And yet, Ruth, I believe no fiction ever points so clear a moral as one life lived fairly through," I observed, "and that is how God sees every life from its beginning. We only read one or two chapters out of each history, or if we happen to see nearly all, we do not possess the key, which would show us a hidden meaning."

"I suppose it is so," said she, folding up her knitting; then, with a change of tone, she continued, "but if I were you, Edward, I would write that City letter directly, so that it may go off by the next post."

I wrote it, and when it was signed, sealed, and stamped, my vigilant sister was satisfied, and we had our supper and went to bed in peace.

I did not go to sleep directly, for my room was glorious with moonlight. I lay still and pondered over the events of the day; and most of all, I mused over the depths of sin and suffering that might lie hidden behind the calm smiling front of such a tiny village as Upper Mallowe. When I passed Mr M'Callum and Ewen in front of Mr

Herbert's farm on the day of my arrival, how little I dreamed of the tragedies in which they were both called to bear part! And so it often is. We read of saints and heroes, of martyrs and sorely-tried folks, and then we go out into the world, and marvel why we meet nothing of the sort. All our own fault! We cannot see the romance because our eyes are too weak to pierce its commonplace vulgar wrappings.

"Just like a common report in a dirty newspaper," said poor Ewen of his sad story. And yet, if we move the scene from an obscure village to a great capital, and change the persons from unknown working people to princes and generals, this is the stuff of which much history is made. We are all so taken with glitter and grandeur, that many who would shudder to come in personal contact with "common" crime like this, are ready to spend years in writing the defence of some royal "suspect," long dead and gone beyond the reach of calumny or justice. But I suppose my mind is not strong enough to love great heights and long distances. I would rather confine my interest to the little world lying close round me. I always find that it contains far more than I can manage, and I should often be quite disheartened if I did not remember that our Saviour approved her who just "did what she could."

Then I fell asleep. And when I awoke the room was bright with sunshine, and I heard a low sweet voice softly singing—

"Praise God, from whom all blessings flow;
Praise Him, all creatures here below;

Praise Him above, ye heavenly host ;
Praise Father, Son, and Holy Ghost."

For a moment I forgot forty years ; but when I remembered all about it I felt no pain, for I know Lucy is still singing in our Father's upper chamber ; and next to the sweetness of a dear voice, is the sweetness of a voice which we have made joyful.

Alice was the singer.

# CHAPTER III.

"WHAT are your household arrangements for Sunday, Ruth?" I inquired of my sister when I joined her at the breakfast-table.

"Why, of course, you and I go to church, Edward, and so does one of the girls, and in the evening I shall stay at home, and they can both go out."

"Shall you send them to church?"

Ruth shook her head. "I haven't hired their souls as well as their bodies," she said. "I never speak about such things to my servants until I am their friend. Because a girl is in domestic service, why should we conclude that she is naturally disinclined to her duty, and must be preached and driven into it?"

"But as a mistress you have a right"—— I began.

"To set a good example, as far as I can, to give them time and means for self-improvement, and to encourage them to do right by not suspecting them of doing wrong," interrupted my sister. "And, by the way, Edward, what 'rights' did you exercise 'as a master' over your clerks? Not many, I expect, and I'd rather follow your practice than your precepts."

The parish church of St Cross was not very far from our house. As we approached it, its appearance did not gladden my heart. It stood in the angle of a small green, flanked by a few straggling houses of the meaner sort. In the midst of the green was a wide pool of sluggish water, inhabited by a colony of ducks. The church itself was a long low edifice of no particular order of architecture, with an insignificant spire, and a single dismal bell, more like a signal for an execution than the summons to God's house. Around lay a little graveyard, wherein most of the graves were covered down with huge flat stones, which, not to be blasphemous, always suggest the idea that the survivors had resolved to do their utmost to prevent a resurrection. Up to the porch, between these gloomy tombs, ran a narrow path of rough sharp stones. Certainly that path would never tempt any shoeless wanderer. The porch itself was narrow, and the inner doors were closed, and guarded by an injured-looking female in a widow's cap. I paused in the porch and looked round,—and I pitied the little children who would remember that church as the place where they first went up to worship God.

Passing through the folding doors, which opened with a dismal creak, we found ourselves in a passage-like interior, lit by narrow windows filled with opaque glass.

Now, I dislike opaque glass even in city churches, for I think a ragged back wall is better than a blank, and I don't see why a cat, peaceably creeping along a coping, need disturb the sanctity of any congregation. But opaque glass to shut out green trees and open sky! With a shudder, I turned to the pew which the disconsolate widow opened for us. It was not far from the pulpit, and was snugly cushioned and carpeted. I did not discover the narrowness of the seat until I had risen from my knees, and was, I trust, in a more contented and devout frame of mind.

Then I looked towards the communion-table, hoping to find some comfort there, but I only saw bare white walls, relieved by two tablets whereon was written the ten precepts of the law. The table itself was small and high, and grudgingly covered with shabby crimson velvet, edged with tarnished gilt fringe. On it stood two straight candlesticks. But above all rose the single adornment of the building—a painted window representing the Descent from the Cross. The colours were laid on so thickly and darkly that the picture was only illuminated round the central figure— the dead body of our Saviour, gaunt and wrenched, half-wrapped in blood-smeared cloths. The painting suggested no idea but that of fearful physical pain and exhaustion. I think angels veiled their faces before the reality of that scene. Why should we hold it up for our children to gaze upon while they weary of the sermon, and long for the Sunday pudding? It was frightful!

Slowly the congregation gathered in. I saw Alice

and her grandfather, but not Ewen ; I saw other faces which I had seen pass my gate, but with which I could not yet connect any idea. But just as the bell gave its last lugubrious stroke the bereaved attendant bustled up the aisle with increased alacrity, followed by the brisk step of a middle-aged gentleman. I recognised his bronzed face and beetling brows : it was my nearest neighbour, Mr Herbert of the Great Farm.

Close at his side walked a young lady, dressed very quietly in gray mantle and bonnet trimmed with purple and black. They both entered the great square pew immediately in front of ours, evidently *the* pew of the church, with seats on all sides, and an oaken desk in the middle. When I caught sight of the young lady's face, in the midst of that dreary building, it came to my mind like a line of poetry quoted in a dry theological tract.

Yet it was not a beautiful face. I do not suppose an artist would have been satisfied with one feature. I think its charm must have been that the veil of flesh was so delicate and frail that the soul shone clearly through —a sensitive, shivering soul, which would need a very warm mantle of love to pass safely through this chilly, blustering world. There was nothing about the face which will stand description, except perhaps the dark hazel eyes, very intense and bright, yet with a look that somehow suggested they had often glistened through tears.

She gave just one glance towards us, and then stood up and opened her book to join in the service. For by this time the clergyman had entered.

E

He was a young man, with plain features, and resolute, sensible bearing. I knew his name was the Reverend
Lewis Marten. And the clear, distinct tone of his voice
was the first thing in the whole church which gave me
unmingled satisfaction. But when we kneeled down for
the Confession of Sins, imagine my horror to find that
we were expected to go through it in an undefined chant,
rendered absolutely ludicrous by an attempt to join, on
the part of some old people on the free seats. And I
found the same thing went on whenever the congregation should respond. I never say a word against cathe-
dral-services—they have trained choirs, and audiences,
as a whole, highly educated. But can the same arguments be used for little churches, dependent on a sing-
ing-class or charity schools, and where the main object
should be to render the whole service intelligible and
profitable to such as cannot read, or have no book ? I
don't suppose God's Word has any exact precept for or
against such performances, but does not St Paul say, " All
things are lawful, but all things are not expedient ?"
And he uses some other arguments which wonderfully
suit these customs when viewed from another aspect. I
should like to hear what the Reverend Lewis Marten
thinks of the 14th chapter of Romans.

We got through the prayers, and through an anthem
which was not in our hymn-books. It was performed
only by the schools and a few giggling boys in a pew
behind the reading-desk. While this went on, Ruth
kept her seat, with that awful expression of countenance which I know means a great deal of anger, with a

strong spice of contempt. I stood up, for I don't think
such a matter is worth a breach of the peace. I only
think it a great pity—a very great pity!

My hopes revived when the young clergyman mounted
the pulpit in his black gown. His face was so rational
and open, so free from the covert humility of priestcraft,
that I felt sure his ideas were not so mediæval as his
customs. I was right. But still I was disappointed.
Everything he said was true, but it was only half the
truth. He spoke of the sin of our hearts, the utter empti-
ness of the world, and he garnished his discourse with
pithy aphorisms, and flashy poetry. But scriptural words
of healing and comfort were not set therein, like "apples
of gold in pictures of silver." He showed us the suffering without the salvation,—Golgotha without the Saviour
who died thereon. And the old men and women fell
asleep, the charity boys "swopped" their marbles, the
singers giggled and whispered, and the dark eyes of Mr
Herbert's companion turned ever and again to the fearful picture above the altar. And I could not help being
glad when it was over, and so I am sure was the
preacher.

When I turned to leave, I found the church had been
but thinly attended, and that the majority of those present belonged to the classes which have but a loose hold
on the stirring interests of life,—young boys and girls,
aged people, and those miserable-looking objects who
haunt the regions of clerical almsgiving. Now that is
a view of religion which I can never understand. To
me, it seems that it should have the strongest claim on

those who are in the front rank of the battle, that they should find God's house verily a house of refuge, wherein to rest and recruit their strength for each new campaign. And I am sure there is something wrong in the religion which fails in this.   By my own heart, I could trace how the declension might proceed.   Next Sunday morning, if it were wet, or if I were weary, it might seem to me more profitable to remain at home with my Bible and good books, than to attend a service which chilled and dis- heartened me.    And thus, a church-going habit once broken, I might get so accustomed to my good books, that I might long for a change, and take to essays and history, and so on, till at last I might fall to the depth of newspapers and gossip.   And thus it may have been with the honest yeomen and buxom matrons who left their empty seats before God in the church of St Cross.

In the pebbly graveyard we overtook our Alice, with her grandfather leaning on her arm.   I thought I should like a little talk with the old man, for his face had been the best lesson of the morning,—a sermon beaming with the comfortable truth that one may be very old, and very poor, and very tired, and yet very happy.

" What, Mr M'Callum," I said, stepping to his side, " are you a deserter from the kirk ? "

" Na, na, sir," he answered, with his blithe smile, " I 'm just a sheep that 's been carried frae its ain field, and must e'en pasture where it can ; and, praised be God, there 's grass growin' everywhere."

" Is there no Scotch church within an easy distance ?" I asked.

"Na, sir," he said ; "the nearest is full fifteen mile frae this. Aince on a time, I made shift to get there every Communion Sunday—which was four times a year. But noo-a-days I go but aince, so that I 'm broucht back to the privileges o' my young days. For ye see, sir, we lived in a country parish, and only gathered for the Lord's Supper just after the harvest was in."

"I daresay you wish there was a Scotch church close at hand ? " I said.

"Aweel, sir, of course, there 's nae kirk like the auld kirk, to my mind ; but still there 's a poo'er o' grace an' glory i' the Church o' England,—the twa are sisters like, sir ; only the ane is a sonsie gudewife in her braw white mutch, and the ither is a grand princess in her jewels. They fa' oot a bit sometimes, as sisters will, but there 's the same heart i' them baith, sir, and they 've but ae Father."

"I am sorry to see St Cross has not a larger congregation," I remarked.

"The people hereaway don't go much to church, sir," he said : "I 've aften spoken tae them about it. Ye see, I 'm an auld man, and I 've come frae sic a far-awa' place, that maybe they 're mair patient wi' me than if I was a poor body that had ne'er been ayont the parish. I tell them about the shootin' grunds, and the moors, and the deer-stalkin', and they 're glad to listen, and then after a bit, I can bring the talk roond—ye understand, sir ?"

"And what do they say about neglecting church ? " I inquired.

"Some say it 's a dour place, and gies them the

miserables; and some say parson doesna tell them ony-thing new, only that the world's a wicked hole, which they ken well enough already; and some canna stand the chantin'."

"And no wonder!" ejaculated Ruth.

"Aweel, mem," he went on, turning to my sister, "I think it some queer mysel', mair especially as I canna hear what they say, and I'm ow're blind noo to read the biggest print. Hoo the honest Church o' England should want to mak' herself look a bit like the Lady of Babylon, is what I canna understand. But still, I aye say to mysel', if ane gies up the kirk, he gies up Sunday, and then the days rin on without sense or meaning, like print wi' the stops no put in. Anything's better than that."

"Has Mr Marten been clergyman here long?" asked Ruth.

The old man shook his head. "It seems but the other day he came, mem, but time passes quickly. How long is it, Alice?"

"Just two years, grandfather," she answered.

"Aye, aye, just two years," repeated he. "I remember, I remember, Alice. I think he's a good young man; he was verra kind to us when—aye, you know now, sir! Only he thinks a college education maks mair difference than it does, sir. He's feared it keeps folk frae understanding him. And he looks at things in a gloomy way; but that's aften the case wi' young folk. Life comes unco hard tae them at first, puir things," and the old man glanced at his granddaughter.

"Ah, by the way, Alice," I said, "I 've a letter in my pocket that you may as well drop into the post now, for I should like it to go off the first thing to-morrow morning," and I handed her the epistle bearing the London address. It caught her eye, and she smiled brightly as she hastened down the turning leading to the post-office, whilst we and her grandfather waited at the corner.

"Your granddaughter seems a blessing to you, Mr M'Callum," I said.

"Aye, she is that; and so is the boy, poor fellow— he 'll be a brichter blessin' some day. Thank you kindly for your goodness to him yesterday, sir."

"What! did he tell you of the talk we had?" I asked.

"Yes; he seemed main thouchtfu' all the evenin', and yet he wasna sad or sullen. An' at supper-time, he said, 'There 's some one else thinks I 'm innocent, grandfather,' and then he told me all about it."

"Does he never come to church?" inquired Ruth.

"He hasna come regular for a long time—and never since *then*, mem," answered the old man. "Ye see, the folk would hardly have sat in the same aisle wi' him ! But he seemed inclined to come this mornin', and I hope he 'll mak' up his mind to be there the nicht; he 'll tak' courage i' the dusk, maybe."

"If Alice would like to pass the day with you, we will spare her," said my sister, as the girl rejoined us. "Phillis can manage to-day, and Alice must do as much for her in a Sunday or two."

Alice looked up into my sister's shrewd, brown face, and she let that look be all her answer, leaving the audible thanks to her grandfather. And so we parted.

"That was very kind of you, Ruth," I said, as we went on alone.

"May it not be their last Sunday together?" she answered. "Don't you think I know how a woman feels before a parting?—the more fool she, for a man never cares!"

That is Ruth's way of speaking, whenever she is caught doing a kindness. And it is astonishing how she always brings in something complimentary to the male sex. And the worst of it is, sometimes I can't say these compliments are unmerited. So I generally let her take the field, whilst I retire into the nearest ditch.

"I'm afraid you don't like St Cross?" I said, presently.

"Like it?" she said, with bitterness. "Edward, I've endured it four Sundays, and I wouldn't allow myself to say a word to you about it, because I wanted you to see it with unprejudiced eyes. But it drives me mad! If I could get at these boy-singers in their white gowns, wouldn't I find out whether they know their catechism! And I'll engage they don't! What can a clergyman think about to put a parcel of lads into a seat together, instead of each of them sitting beside his own father and mother, and learning to behave in a reverent, godly manner?"

"It seems a mistake," I said; "but no doubt Mr Marten does it in hopes of rendering the service attractive."

"Attractive!" she answered; "if any one wants such attractions, why do they put up with shams? Why don't they go where they can get the reality—to the Church of Rome?"

"But the sin of the Church of Rome is not so much her ritual as her doctrine," I pleaded, rather wildly.

"Don't the two go together?" said she. "I wonder the Israelites didn't plead that it was only 'harmless ritual' when they danced round the golden calf! Perhaps Aaron meant it so."

"But, my dear Ruth, the innovations at St Cross are very few and faint," I expostulated.

"They're as much as they can be," she answered, grimly. "There's a choir in white, and they and Mr Marten all turn to the east two or three times in the prayers, and every response is chanted, and there are candlesticks on the communion-table. Anything more would cost money, and the church doesn't look as if it had any to spare."

"These things seem to me so pitifully trivial as to be beneath mention," I said.

"Is it wisdom to overlook the egg until the serpent is hatched?" she asked.

"Mr Marten has a pleasant, sensible face," I remarked, "and there is something I regret much more than these petty ceremonials, and that is, the cold, repellant tone of his sermon. I should like a little talk with him.   He is a young man, and a glimpse of an old man's experience can do him no harm."

"It would be less trouble to build a new church at once," said Ruth, cynically.

But that is just like her.   I hope for the best, and she prepares for the worst.

As we entered our house, it struck me painfully, that instead of returning with God's peace on our hearts and tongues, we had come back in a criticising, flaw-detecting spirit.

And what seemed worse, I could not conclude it was altogether our own fault.   I resolved, however, that Ruth's hopelessness should not dishearten me.   I must try to do good in my own way, and I am always inclined to mend rather than remake.   So in the course of the afternoon I startled my sister by announcing that I should write to our young rector, and invite him to spend an evening with us in the course of the following week.

"It is his place to call upon us," said she.

"Certainly, Ruth, and doubtless he will do so; but you see I do not care about a call, I want a long, friendly visit."

"Then I wish I could go to tea somewhere, and leave you to fight out your battle by yourselves," she remarked.

"There will be no battle, Ruth," I responded.   "I only want to ask him the general position of affairs in the parish, and how I can best make myself useful."

"Then he will say they want a new altar-cloth—not

to say a new organ—and also more funds, that the choir may be enlarged," said she.

"Well, I'll tell you what the church does want, Ruth," I answered, "and that is, new windows. It is a sin that thick glass should come between us and the blue sky."

"What, let in more light to the candles on the communion-table?" queried Ruth, sarcastically.

"The candles are not lit," I said.

"But I suppose they will be some day," she returned. "They are not there for nothing, surely."

"Perhaps the sunshine will put them out, Ruth," I said.

"I hope it may!" she retorted, grimly.

I did not answer, but opened my desk, and began to indite my letter to the clergyman.

"Won't you help me, Ruth?" I asked, after putting down the date.

"It is quite your business," she replied. But the dear woman is far too active-minded not to interfere in anything when asked. So presently she said, "You may send my compliments, I suppose. And what do you mean to say, Edward?"

"Will this do?" I asked her, and read :—

"Mr and Miss Garrett present their compliments to the Rev. Louis Marten, and hope he will do them the honour of spending an evening with them in the course of the week. Mr Garrett is anxious to get acquainted with the neighbourhood, and trusts that Mr Marten will be willing to advise how he may become useful therein."

" I suppose that will do," commented Ruth ; " and yet, brother, the fact is you want to advise *him !* "

" I don't deny that, but it is quite true I wish information which he can give."

Ruth looked at me for a moment, and then her grave face broke into a smile.

" Any one would say I managed you, Edward, but I doubt if I do," said she. " I think you know how to get your own way without making a struggle. But, by the way, I don't like letter-writing on Sunday."

" Why, this is only an act of neighbourly kindness ! " I said, surprised. " We are always free to do good on that day."

" Certainly, Edward ! and yet I think we should keep up every possible distinction between the Sabbath and other days."

" You don't think the day of rest should be a day of idleness, Ruth ? " I asked.

" No," she answered ; " but I think with Mr M'Callum that Sundays should be the ' stops ' in our life. I know some people laugh at Scotch notions of Sabbath-keeping, but that is because they never tried the refreshment afforded by the day, when life stands still before the throne of God, and care and weariness are swallowed up in His glory."

" But, Ruth, may it not be that while we try to keep the letter of the positive law, we are in danger of neglecting some moral duty ? " I inquired.

She shook her head. " I don't think so. The very day of rest helps to discipline the mind to distinguish between what it wants to do, and what it should do. If a letter would prevent a mistake, or save an hour's unhappiness, or give comfort, I should say, write it—aye, and carry it yourself, though the task occupied your whole Sunday. I was glad to see you give that letter to Alice this morning. But what will do quite as well on Monday, leave till Monday, and certainly this note can wait till to-morrow."

I felt that Ruth was right. And I put away my desk.

# CHAPTER IV.

HERE was rain on Sunday night, and when we looked from our windows on Monday morning, we found but a dreary prospect. Many leaves had fallen, and lay sodden and decaying in the garden path, and the few remaining flowers looked as if they only lingered to bid us a last good-bye. A light mist hung over the scene, and shut out the distant meadows. Ruth ordered fires to be lighted, and advised Alice to put on a warm shawl when she went to carry my letter to the rector. Winter never finds my sister unprepared, and perhaps there is no instance in which forethought saves more health, comfort, and good temper.

Alice returned in due time, saying she met the rector at his gate, and he detained her while he read my missive and penned his reply, which proved a very courteous one, stating he would have great pleasure in waiting upon us that very evening.

Five o'clock found Ruth and me seated opposite each other, with the lamp on the table between us—I lingering over the pages of a monthly periodical, and she busy with a huge bagful of gay scraps, by which I understood that patchwork was on hand.

"Phillis is a terrible blunderer with her needle," said she; "she shall not live in the house with me, and not learn better. Patchwork is good practice, and as the quilts get made, I can give them away to the old people round."

"I fear they need blankets more than quilts," I ventured to say.

"Very likely. That is your concern," she answered coolly. "Money buys blankets, and you are a rich man. But if you were bedridden, Edward, you would know the comfort of a bright quilt to cover the fuzzy blanket. And patchwork is quite a fortune in a house with a sick child. Do you remember ours at home?—the silk quilt which mother used to show us on holidays." And when I glanced at my sister, some minutes after, her face was still soft and tender with the recollection of the faded finery.

Every day, sitting opposite Ruth, I am struck with the exceeding beauty of good old age. In youth, my sister was plain; her features harsh, and her figure and movements too decided for grace. But Time has dealt with her like a patient artist with his picture; so that she is a noble old lady with a grand brown face, crowned with white hair, and lit up by eyes which have not forgotten to flash and sparkle.

Presently the gate clanged, and in a moment Phillis ushered in the clergyman, who brought with him the peculiar damp chill atmosphere of an autumn evening. I think he was glad of the welcome offered by our cheerful fire, and he seated himself on a chair indicated by Ruth, and rubbed his hands in the genial warmth. They had no fires yet where he lodged, he said. He had not noticed the deficiency until he saw ours, but he remembered he had been very cold while studying. He must speak about it to-morrow.

And so we kept up a good-humoured chatter till tea was brought in, and when we were fairly established round the table, with cheering cups before us and a pleasant prospect of tea and toast, Ruth inquired if St Cross were a comfortable church in winter.

"I regret to say it is never comfortable," replied Mr Marten; "in summer it is close and dark, and in winter cold and damp."

"Yet it is well situate," I said. "The darkness is only due to the narrowness of the windows and their thick glass."

"You are right, sir," he answered. "And why a church should be so built I cannot understand."

"Nor I," I said. "To shut God's light from God's house seems to me worse than foolish. Why do you not remedy it?"

The young man looked at me, and smiled grimly. "Neither my predecessor nor I have been able to muster more funds than barely suffice for whitewashing and cleaning," he replied. "The parish is not rich, and the people do not seem liberal. At the present moment, the church is absolutely falling out of repair. We have had one or two collections in its behalf, but the money comes so slowly that I fear the building will be in ruins before the requisite sum is made up."

"Why don't you repair first, and collect afterwards?" I asked.

"Sir!" exclaimed the young man in astonishment.

"Yes," I said; "why don't you get some kind friend's promise to make good the deficit—if any?"

The rector shook his head. "I wish we had such a friend in Upper Mallowe," he said.

"Are you sure you have not? Have you asked every one?" I inquired.

"There is no one to ask," he answered, adding suddenly—"unless it be you!"

Ruth laughed outright.

"I should not wonder if it were me," I said.

"My dear sir, I did not expect this," said the young clergyman, very radiantly indeed.

"You need not thank me, Mr Marten, until you see whether I have any balance to pay," I observed.

"Ah, I know you will," he replied, shaking his head. "I know my parishioners. You are a stranger among us, sir."

"We shall see who judges them best," said I.

"My brother is always hopeful," remarked Ruth; "but I must say he is generally right."

"We must not attempt any serious repairs until spring," I said, "but in the meantime cannot we make some little temporary improvements? I observe that the old people sit about in cold parts of the church, where, if they be at all deaf, they cannot hear a word. Why don't you give them those comfortable seats round the reading-desk?"

"They are kept for the choir, sir," answered Mr Marten, reflectively.

"Excuse me," I said, gently, "but in many churches, and certainly in St Cross, I think a formal choir is a mistake."

"So do I," returned the young man, frankly, and Ruth gave an unmistakable look of pleasure. "It was established by my predecessor, who thought otherwise. I found it when I came, and I have not abolished it because I dread meddling with existing arrangements, and because I fear to deprive our services of what is generally considered an attraction, lest our small congregation should become still smaller. Many people believe they derive benefit from the full carrying out of the ritual of the Anglican Church."

Here Ruth broke in. "They like fine singing and pretty altars. If the ritual be performed shabbily, they don't care for it. Since I have lived in this parish I have learned that many of your young people walk to Hopleigh, five miles off, because the church has a splendid choir and enticing decorations. Unless you can afford the same, your ritual will never secure them, though it may drive away people better worth keeping."

"I do not belong to the High Church party," said the young rector, quite humbly, "and I am always sorry that St Cross.wears the badges of the same. But what can I substitute for the choir? We have no charity-school on which to depend."

"Of whom does the choir consist?" I asked.

"Of the sons of farmers and tradesmen in the parish," he replied. "They meet for practice twice every week—after the Wednesday evening service, and on Saturday night."

"You don't have them in a Bible class, then?" queried Ruth.

"I have nowhere to receive them," answered Mr Marten, dismally. "If they came to my lodgings, the landlady would complain of their wearing out her carpets, and our parish school-room—I dare say you saw our little school in the aisle—the parish school-room is such a rookery that their parents would think it an insult if they were invited there."

"A good opportunity to hint they should build a better one," put in Ruth.

Mr Marten smiled, and shook his head in resigned despair concerning the efficacy of such hints.

"Can't you have them in the vestry?" asked my sister.

"Why, so I can!" he exclaimed. "It's rather small, but it will do. I wonder I never thought of that!"

"Where there's a will there's a way," said Ruth. The young clergyman blushed slightly.

"Mr Marten must pardon us," I said, "we are getting old," ("We are old," said Ruth.) "and we forget some-times that we have no parental rights over young people.

We are only anxious to do a little good before we go away."

"And old people can seldom do better than set the young ones to work," observed Ruth. "I only made the suggestion because I thought the class would keep them together, and they might go on with their practising: and I think they would sing better standing decently at their mother's side than now, when they are always ready to burst into a giggle."

"Ah, I'm afraid they behave very badly sometimes," sighed the rector. "But as the stoves will be lighted next Sunday, I will take the opportunity to direct that the old people shall sit round the desk and enjoy the warmth, and I must manage about the boys as well as I can."

"Mr Marten," said Ruth, "you cannot tell how glad I am that it is only a matter of 'management.' I feared we should have to fight out a battle about apostolic succession, and an infallible Church, not to say the Real Presence, and other dogmas."

"Ah, Ruth," I observed, "if Mr Marten were the staunchest advocate of these doctrines, I should not attack them; I should only say—'Think of the old people, and do not keep them in the cold—remember the people who can't read, and don't sing to them,'" (and I glanced at our guest, in hopes he would take a hint from my words.) "Differences of opinion will never be reconciled by argument, but any sect will shrink from confessing that its theories will not let it work under Christ's great banner of 'Love to the brethren.'"

"I do not adhere to one High Church doctrine," said the young rector; "but yet I cannot help thinking some of their innovations are improvements."

"Certainly," I responded. "For instance, I like the idea of free churches: the rich and the poor equal before God."

"I don't," said Ruth. "The rich and poor are equal before God; and no arrangement of seats can make any difference. You look at it from the wealthy point of view, and you like to flatter your spiritual pride by a semblance of self-abasement. Some people seem to think the poor are only made to practise their virtues upon, particularly humility, like the cardinals at Rome when they wash the beggars' feet. But just view it from the other side. Would not you rather sit among your own people—the pensioner and the farm-labourer and the servant-girl together—than flourish your rough hands, and poor, coarse clothes among the silks and velvets of the gentry? There are two sides to every question; but I always think it is best to let people stay in their own places, just because I believe that in God's sight one place in the world is quite as good as another, and that the labourer's horny hand is as honourable as the prime minister's worn brow. But their outward conditions can never be the same till they're both in heaven. And if they be wise men, and recognise their true equality, they will not wish it otherwise."

"Very likely you are right," responded the rector. "Viewed in that light, probably the poor, as a rule, are happiest among the poor. But dropping the subject of free seats, I am sure you would not wish to check honourable ambition.    One is often struck with a great disparity between the mind and the position."

"Certainly," said Ruth, with a humorous twinkle in her eyes.    "I knew a man who blamed statesmen, and censured clergy, and had splendid ideas of what he could do in their place, whilst his own home was in disorder, and one or two of his children might have given him valuable information about prisons and workhouses.    There was a great disparity between his mind and his circumstances, only it was the wrong way!"

"Oh, Miss Garrett, you refuse to understand me!" cried Mr Marten, smiling.    "I mean that a great mind is sometimes found in a lowly place, and surely you would not wish such to remain in the position wherein he was born."

"He'll often wish himself there before he dies," answered Ruth.    "He'll find God gives hard work in the upper classes of His school.    But he's sure to be promoted, not because he was too great to do the easy tasks, but because he was great enough to do them well. God wastes nothing, Mr Marten.    If He make a genius, He has got something for him to do besides breaking stones; but most likely He will keep him doing that, till by virtue of the power that is in him, he does it better than any one else.    Don't you remember it is said when Shakespeare got his living by holding horses, he did it so well and was in such demand, that other men hired themselves under him, that they might call themselves 'Will Shakespeare's lads?'"

"But still many geniuses are sad failures in the ordinary walks of life," remarked Mr Marten.

"Ah, those are poor, unhealthy geniuses, who slip from God's grasp into the devil's," answered Ruth. "They let go their Father's hand; but I think He generally catches them against their will; only they get so torn to pieces in the struggle that the best work they can do for Him is the warning of their example."

"Still, there remain a few sad cases which cannot be classed under any rule," said the clergyman, thoughtfully; "Chatterton, for instance."

"Yes, poor Chatterton!" replied my sister, in a tone so different from her own that I looked up. "Almost every writer has said something fine about Chatterton: heaps of sentimental pity, with a spice of blame for his wrong-headedness, or recklessness, or want of faith, which they seem to think brought down his miseries in punishment. Not one thoroughly realises that he was only a boy—a child—and that none of his faults and blunders need be wondered at. It was his time for being checked, and chidden and comforted afterwards. But he was dropped upon the world with no one to screen his follies until they were corrected. If he had only known a little love "——

"I always understood his mother and sisters "—— began Mr Marten.

"His mother and sisters must have been weak, shallow women," interrupted Ruth. "They believed all his poor, fine stories! Love gives the greatest fool more wisdom than that. All you men blame Horace Walpole.

So do I; but I blame those women more. That boy
had lived with them sixteen years, and they did not
understand him. It was a noble wish to keep all his
struggles to himself, but it was cowardly in them to
allow it. I can't believe they thought everything right;
God help them if they did, for the revelation came too
late."

"They were very poor, and doubtless ignorant of the
world," pleaded Mr Marten; "but the whole story is sad
and mysterious, like a psalm of humanity with the love
of God left out."

There was a pause.

"But the misery is," added Ruth, suddenly stirring the
fire, "that the same thing may be going on somewhere at
this moment, and we don't know."

"God can do without our help," I said, softly, "if He
does not show us where to give it."

And then followed a long silence, which I broke at
last by asking the rector if he knew much of the
M'Callums.

"I saw a good deal of them about eighteen months
ago, when they were in some difficulty," he replied;
"but I have not called upon them lately. The old man
is very kindly, and the grand-daughter—your servant,
Miss Garrett—struck me as a good girl. But the young
man is as ill-conditioned and morose a fellow as I ever
knew. Their trouble was about him, and I fear there
is little doubt he was guilty of the crime imputed to
him. He avoided me as much as possible, but I ventured to speak to him once, saying I hoped he would

be warned of the wickedness and danger of neglecting his religious duties and consorting with evil company, and he turned and answered me in a terrible way—a terrible way, Mr Garrett."

"What did he say?" asked Ruth.

"His manner so astonished me that I can scarcely recall his words," returned the rector; "but it was to the effect that it was not his fault if some bad people were more attractive than some good ones, and that he guessed, in my day, I had done as much as he to deserve suspicion."

"Dreadful, dreadful!" said Ruth; but she smiled as she said it.

Mr Marten looked aggrieved, and turned towards me. "I had only spoken the truth with the authority of a clergyman," he observed.

"Why didn't you try speaking the truth 'in love'?" I asked; "that is St Paul's counsel."

"I certainly did not speak it in malice," he replied.

"Should you have said the same thing to your brother, had you such a relation in Ewen's place?" inquired my sister.

"Well, not exactly," confessed the rector—"circumstances make things so different."

"Mr Marten," I said, "will you take a hint from an old man, who has lived in the world more than twice as long as you?"

"Not one hint, but twenty," responded the young man, cordially.

"It is this: Never address the vilest outcast as you

would not speak to your dearest friend. Even were
this young man the criminal you think him, you and
he have the mutual ground of a common humanity.
The gentleman-parson should not have lectured the
peasant, but the man in you should have spoken to
the man in him."

"You are right, sir," said the rector, heartily, "I
accept your reproof;" and he took my hand and shook
it, adding, "and I only wish the young man had shown
himself wiser than me, by taking my blunder in a more
kindly spirit, for it is not pleasant to recall his answer."

"Yet there was truth in it," I observed, "and he
did not mean it for the insult it seemed. He declares
himself innocent of the murder, and conscious of this,
he felt the sting of your implied suspicion, and retorted
with the conjecture that, in your days at school and
college, you had perhaps fallen into many misdemeanours,
such as those he confesses, and which your wiser guar-
dians regarded as the foibles of youth, but which in his
case exaggerating gossips blacken into confirmed bad
character."

"I can understand that," said Mr Marten, reflectively.

"Ewen was wrong to speak so," I went on; "but
I fear he was almost in despair. The gentlest animal
will turn upon its pursuers when it sees no way of
escape. He cannot justify himself further than he has
done, and his tormented soul was ready to take shelter
behind the mask of ruffianism. And if that mask be
worn too long, Mr Marten, it is rather hard to throw
aside."

"You speak as if you believed his innocence, sir?" observed the rector.

"So I do," I answered. "I noticed something strange in his manner, and I heard dark whispers concerning him. So I asked him to tell me all about it. And he did not omit one shadow from the gloomy picture. I believe he is as innocent as you or I."

"Then I feel as if I could go and beg his pardon directly," said the rector.

"That's right," said Ruth; "we shan't make mistakes in the next world, so this is our time to practise penitence."

"He was with his sister at last evening's service," remarked Mr Marten. "I daresay he came because his heart was touched by your kindness. He sat in a lonely corner in the shadow. And when I noticed him, I thought, 'That reprobate has come to God's house because it is too damp to wander in the fields.'"

"And if it had been so, what did it matter?" observed Ruth. "If God drives a man into church by wet weather or a snowstorm, all you've got to do is to say something which will make him come again."

"Oh, dear, I am so sorry!" bewailed the young man; "I feel as if I should never be uncharitable again."

"Oh yes, you will," answered Ruth, "and be sorry afterwards, I hope. That's about the best we can do, from the cradle to the grave."

"It is always safe to hope for the best, Mr Marten," said I.

"So long as you prepare for the worst," put in Ruth.

"I daresay I have often done harm where I have tried to do good," said the rector, ruefully. "I am so lonely in this dull country-parish, that my mind gets sour and jaundiced. I am inclined to envy my brethren whose lots are cast in London. They have earnest work to keep their souls healthy. If they wear out, that is better than rusting out."

"Whoever can't work here, couldn't work in London," answered Ruth, decisively. "If a man is not strong enough to walk to his own gate, he needn't wish to climb mountains."

"Now, for my part," I said, "I think a country clergyman is a very happily placed man. His work is ready for him, and it is not more than he can do, if he go about it honestly and heartily. He is surrounded by means of healthy relaxation, in the proper use of which he can set a good example. He is known and honoured everywhere, and he knows and cares for everybody. His education and knowledge of mankind enable him to widen the narrow village life, and connect it with the busy world beyond. Sometimes he can help his city brother, for the restless tide of labour often throws a few wanderers on his quiet shore, and he has it in his power to link some holy memory with their recollections of his fields and farms. That is my portrait of your life, Mr Marten."

"It is so flattering that I do not recognise it," said he, with a smile—rather a melancholy one.

There was a pause, for Ruth sat lost in thought. Suddenly she roused herself, and asked, "Have you a refuge in the village, sir?"

"No, ma'am," answered the rector. "If belated travellers cannot pay for a bed, we inhospitably refer them to the workhouse at Hopleigh. If they die on the road—they have done so once or twice—there is an inquest, and the Union buries them. That is our English version of the Good Samaritan. It is useless to disguise the truth."

"Then let us try to make it truth no longer," I said. "I know you will have an earnest helper in Ruth, for refuges are her favourite form of charity."

"Because, if they are well managed, they do so much good at so little cost, and in such a kindly way," she remarked. "If we give hungry men a tract on the goodness of God, need we wonder if they throw it away with a curse? A meal and a bed would preach a far better sermon."

"Certainly, if their hearts were sufficiently open to receive it," said Mr Marten, dubiously.

"There must be something to put them in mind," replied my sister, "but I don't believe many people are so hardened as you think. Anything roughly knocked about gets battered and black outside, but the tough rind may keep something very soft within."

"I shall be only too happy if you will help me to try the experiment," said the rector; "my heart has often ached to see the poor creatures starting on their long journey to the tender mercies of the Casual Ward."

"Ay, you may well say 'tender mercies'!" responded

Ruth; "I am quite astonished to find, that as a rule, workhouse chaplains think they have no duty to discharge towards these strays. They don't want preaching. But surely they might go in and commend the great family to Him who remembers every one of them. That would comfort some, and a good word can't harm the worst. And in the morning I think the chaplain might go again, and see if any one wanted advice. A little counsel is sometimes worth more than a fortune. If the chaplains can't do it, I wish some one else could get permission."

"It will take us some time to get a refuge organised," remarked Mr Marten, presently.

"We only want a six-roomed cottage, no matter how rough or old-fashioned—the more so the better; it will be more like home," replied my sister; "and then we must get a nice, comfortable couple to live in it, and act host and hostess. And of course you must persuade all the village to help us, Mr Marten."

"O dear, dear!" said the rector, despairingly.

"Never venture, never have," I observed. "I will help you. I believe I am a good beggar."

"You have let them lose the habit of giving," said Ruth. "Like everything else, it grows easier by practice, sir."

"Well, Miss Garrett," he said, rising, "I must thank you for originating so excellent a plan. I shall mark to-day with a red letter, in commemoration of this visit, and in a few days, I daresay, I shall bring you word of suitable premises."

He would not stay to supper : so, after a little more talk about the best ways and means to further our plan, Ruth and I escorted him to the door. The ground was still damp, but there was a pleasant drying breeze, which made me long for a little ramble under the starry sky. So I proposed to walk home with our guest. Ruth expostulated, but I put on my great-coat, and had my own way.

The clergyman lived down the road, past the Great Farm, and as we walked we chattered cheerfully about divers things, and it gratified me to believe that the young man was in better spirits for his visit to us old people. I know some of Ruth's words were very sharp, but so are mountain breezes, and yet they do us good. They make us turn about and look at things under different aspects, and that is a healthier proceeding than standing still, peering through our own little glasses, which perhaps are yellow !

We turned the corner occupied by the Great Farm, and presently the sound of hurried footsteps warned us of a wayfarer advancing towards us. In a moment he came up.

There were no lamps on the road, and I could only distinguish a tall figure, muffled in a cloak, and a face which looked very pale in the moonlight. He was walking rapidly, but the rector turned and watched his form as it swiftly receded into total darkness.

" Surely that is young Herbert," said Mr Marten, half aloud ; " and what can he be doing here ? "

I remembered the name of the family at the Farm,

and concluding this individual to be one of them, nothing seemed more natural than his presence close to his
own home.   And so I silently wondered at my companion's wonder.

We parted at the rector's gate, and he detained me a
moment to congratulate me on having such a sister as
Ruth.

"Her society is like a draught of quinine," he said.

"Ah," I replied, "her words have bristles on their
backs, but we all want brushing up sometimes!"

"I hope she won't spare me," he said; and I think he
was sincere.

"Never fear," I answered.   "Good-night."

But as I walked back, I wondered what made my
sister so terribly earnest about Chatterton.

# CHAPTER V.

N Thursday, there came to me a letter bearing the London postmark. I saw Alice look at it as she took it from the postman, and she brought it into the parlour and laid it on the breakfast-table with its superscription upwards. I recognised the writing of the kindest man in my old firm, and I had little fear about its contents, so I bade my servant wait a moment.

The epistle was short enough. The "house" regretted that my first recommendation was not a case which they could take up with more zeal. But they would stretch a point to oblige me. So, if the young man liked, he could take a subordinate place in their counting-house at a salary of eighteen shillings a week.

Now, I did not read the letter to Alice. I knew it was very kind, but to her it would seem cruel. I only told her the result of my application. She took it very

G

quietly, with a few grave thanks, spoken slowly and laboriously, like words in a half-known tongue, ending with the request that she might go and tell Ewen.

I reflected for a moment, and then said, "No, I should like to speak with Mr Herbert first; he has been kind to your brother, and I should not wish to entice him from his service without his knowledge. I will make everything right, and your brother shall have the offer before the afternoon."

And Alice thanked me again, and went away to the kitchen.

I wanted Ruth to accompany me to the Great Farm, but she refused, saying I suited strangers better than she did, and she hated morning calls. I learned afterwards that she and Alice passed the time in consulting over the outfit necessary for the lad's decent appearance in his new situation.

I saw neither Ewen nor his grandfather on the way to the farm. I proceeded to the dwelling-house, and found the garden-gate open. The bad weather had made sad havoc among the shapely flower-beds, but a few chrysanthemums smiled from the withered leaves, like country faces in a London crowd. So I reached the broad old-fashioned porch, and pulled a bell whose handle I found among the ivy leaves.

The door was opened by a middle-aged woman, tall and gaunt, clad in a dark clinging gown, and thick white cap and apron. She might have been portress at a nunnery.

"Is Mr Herbert within?" I inquired.

"Mr Herbert has just gone out among his fields," she answered, in a sour tone, eyeing me like one who has reason to suspect a stranger.

"Can you tell me where I may overtake him?" I asked.

"H'm—ye see he's moving about; and as you went in at one gate, he might go out at the other. I don't know whether he'll be long. If ye'll step inside I'll just inquire."

She admitted me into a square wainscoted hall, pushed forward a heavy oaken chair, and retreated with noisy steps through an arched doorway.

The place reminded me of dear old Meadow Farm, only on a grander scale. There was the same wide fireplace, surmounted by hunting trophies and blunderbusses, the same bare walls and floor, only these were of oak instead of deal. But it was very silent, and there was no cheerful family litter on the hall table—no whips, or dog-collars, or battered gardening-hats. I had scarcely time to notice all this, when the tall servant returned.

"Will ye just step into the parlour to Miss Herbert?" she said, and turned about and led the way. She had never asked my name. It seemed that unexpected visits were so rare in that house, that she had forgotten the customary etiquette of such occasions.

The "parlour" was reached by a short passage leading from the arched doorway. This passage was very dark, and as my guide opened the door at the end, I was almost dazzled by the sunlight in the white-ceiled and delicately-papered room beyond.  The servant made way for my entrance, but did not retire.

Miss Herbert advanced to meet me.  As I expected, she was the lady whom I had seen on the previous Sun-day, but in her in-door apparel she looked much younger. She met me close to the door, and her face seemed anxious and fearful.  There was a dog at her feet, a curly honest-eyed fellow, but not such a one as usually frequents feminine boudoirs.

"I apologise for disturbing you," I said; "but I wish a little conversation with Mr Herbert.  I must introduce myself as Mr Edward Garrett, your new neigh-bour."

"Oh, indeed!" she responded, in a relieved tone; "will you please take a chair?  I expect Mr Herbert will return in half an hour.  If you can wait, he will be very happy to see you."

Then she resumed her seat, and the attendant, who had remained till now, closed the door and left us to-gether.  Like all English people, we entered into a con-versation about the weather, from which we passed to the scenery in the neighbourhood, and similar topics. On Sunday, my companion's face had awakened my in-terest, and as we talked this interest deepened.  Her manner was refined and kindly, and her smile was that beautiful smile which suggests a burst of sunshine on a rainy day.  Yet there was a preoccupation about her, as if her thoughts perpetually slipped away elsewhere, and had to be forcibly recalled and kept at their duty. As we talked, there came upon her face the anxious, laborious expression sometimes seen in deaf people, and then she spoke with a fitful, forced vivacity, as if she feared she was failing in her part, and threw out all her energy to succeed. Altogether she was exactly the reverse of the calm healthy woman one expects to meet in a farm-house parlour.

"I hope your papa is not so busy this morning that I shall be troublesome," I remarked, after one of our very natural pauses.

"Oh, no," she answered, rousing herself with a start; "but Mr Herbert is not my father; he is my uncle."

"I beg pardon for the mistake," I said. "Then are you one of the household here, or are you on a visit?"

"I have lived here since my father's death three years ago," she replied. "Up till that time I was with him in London."

"Ah, so we shall be able to talk about the great city," I said. "But I daresay you do not know much of the part most familiar to me—eastward of Temple Bar."

"Oh yes, I do," she answered. "My father was a literary man, and we went about a good deal."

"A literary man." I knew that means such different careers—a refined retirement graced by many of the comforts and privileges of rank and wealth, without their restraints and responsibilities, or a hurrying life in rest-less homes, shiftless labour, improvident speculation. Perhaps this was the key to the overwrought face before me.

"Which do you prefer, town or country?" I asked.

She shook her head. "I cannot say—one may be happy in both, or miserable in either."

"Then, at least you do not dislike rural solitude?" I remarked.

"I was always accustomed to solitude," she answered. "Mamma died years ago, and I was an only child, and my father was generally much engaged."

"Ah, then you may be less lonely in a family house among the fields, than in rooms overlooking London streets," I observed.

She smiled faintly, and did not reply. Presently she rose and said we had best find our way to the dining-room, as her uncle sometimes came in by a side-door, and sat there looking over his papers, long before any one knew he had returned from his rambles.

"I am sorry to give so much trouble," I apologised as I followed her guidance; "my business is only a little matter about one of the farm people. If I could see young Mr Herbert"——.

We were crossing the hall when I said this. She stopped short, looked up at me, and repeated my last words. Surely it must have been the effect of some stained glass above the door, but her face looked scared and white.

"Have I made another mistake?" I queried. "Is there no young Mr Herbert? I fancied so, because I was out with a friend a few evenings back, and I thought he called a gentleman by that name. Such are the difficulties of introducing one's-self, Miss Herbert."

God forgive us for the pain we unintentionally give!

She moved forward again, and led the way down another short passage.  As she paused to open a door,
she turned and said in a very soft, low voice—" We are
a small family at the Great Farm—only my uncle and I."

The room into which she ushered me was a long, low,
wainscoted chamber, with a window at either end, one
opening into the garden, and the other into the conservatory.  The furniture consisted of high-backed, red-
cushioned chairs, two or three carved chests, and a table
spread with a white cloth, and sundry preparations for
lunch.  The walls were enlivened by a few heavily-
framed portraits in oils.  Now, I always take interest in
family pictures, but, as I glanced over these, I saw something which gave me a sudden chill.

It was nothing dreadful.  Household skeletons are
generally shut in very commonplace cupboards.  There
is no unpleasantness in the back of a canvas when we
scan it in hopes of finding some clue to its pedigree.
But it brings an awful revelation of domestic agony when,
in a pleasant family room, we come upon a picture
TURNED TO THE WALL.

Miss Herbert made no effort to renew our conversation.  She drew a chair towards the fireplace, in mute
invitation for me to be seated, and then went to the conservatory and began gathering dead leaves into a little
basket.  It occurred to me that she had brought me to
that room expressly that I might understand there was
delicate ground in her uncle's dwelling, and so be warned
to tread warily.

In a few minutes the master of the house came in, and

greeted me very cordially. Now he knew me as a respectable neighbour—not as an unknown lounger peering over his hedges. But it's an ill compliment to be suspected till one's credentials are shown.

"Come, Agnes," he called to his niece, "come and take your place at the table, and do the honours. Rather a young housekeeper, you see, Mr Garrett, but as discreet as if she were fifty," he added, as the young lady obeyed, with a pale ghost of a smile flitting over her face.

I would have excused myself from his bluff hospitality, pleading "that I would not detain him five minutes, I only wished to speak about a little business "——

"And what business on earth is not better for being discussed over ale and ham?" he answered.

So I had no alternative but to accept a chair and a plate.

"You have in your service a young man named Ewen M'Callum," I began very primly.

"Ay, that I have," said the farmer. "And there isn't a better workman in the place—can turn his hand to anything. Good job for me that he's rather under a cloud, else he would not be hired for my price."

"Then, Mr Herbert," I responded, "I fear you will not thank me for asking you to give him up?"

"What! do you want him yourself?" he asked. "Upon my word, you city gentlemen are keen in detecting the value of a good article."

"No, I don't want him myself," I answered; "but I dare say you know the youth has capabilities rather above farm-work."

"Certainly I do," said he, "and that's just the reason why he's so good at it. Everything's the better when done with brains. I only wish they would get so cheap as to be included in engagements."

"I have succeeded in getting him a place in the city, something of the kind he had before he—before he passed under the cloud, as you say," I explained.

Mr Herbert's face clouded, and he asked very shortly, "Does the young fellow know this?"

"Not yet," I replied. "I would not name the subject to him, until I had conferred with you."

"That's right," he said, clearing up. "'Pastors and masters,' and all that, you know. We must stand up for it, sir. The young ones are always ready to throw us over. Well, let 'em if they can. If they won't have our rule, they can't want our help."

Now, I felt that Mr Herbert spoke truth, and yet I could not assent. It pains me to hear truth spoken dogmatically, or maliciously, or selfishly, and though the farmer's seemed only a coarse, good-humoured, give-and-take selfishness, nevertheless it profaned what it touched. But he did not notice my silence.

"I'll not stand in the lad's light," he went on. "We'll go out together, and we shall find him somewhere about, and then you can tell him, and he shall have his wages, and a bit over, may be. He's been worth double the money he's cost; but, of course, I shan't say so. He's a civil lad, too, though he's short-spoken, and doesn't say two words, if one will do."

"He will be all the better when he is out of the way of suspicion," I said.

"I don't see why he need care for suspicion," responded Mr Herbert, with a contemptuous emphasis on the word, "except that it lost him a good place. But anything else might have done that. Suspicion can't hang a man, and so far as I can see, it doesn't hinder his enjoying any comforts he can get."

"But a man does not live only to eat and to escape the gallows," I remarked. "That's a dog's life, Mr Herbert."

"Let who can live for better things," he said, recklessly. "Let 'em have fine hopes and visions, they'll find 'em less substantial than this," and he slapped the ham with his carving-knife.

"Certainly, sir," I answered, "just as the perishing body is, to our gross senses, more substantial than the immortal soul."

Mr Herbert made no reply, but helped himself to some ale, and told his niece she ate no more than a chicken, and there was a silence, until I inquired if Miss Herbert's London training permitted her to be a good walker.

"Oh yes," she answered, with that same aroused manner. "I think nothing of what many women call long distances."

"But you hardly ever go out now, Aggie," said the farmer, in a softened, kindly tone.

"I wonder at that," I remarked, "for I know there are beautiful walks about here, and I am sure you must have plenty of leisure."

" Yes, plenty of leisure," she repeated absently.

" Can you sketch ?" I inquired.

" I used to do so," she answered.

" Now, how interesting that would be," I said, " for you might bring all the beauties of the neighbourhood into your uncle's house to brighten a rainy day."

She laughed a little, and then answered, " There was nobody to see them. Uncle would not care," and I thought she glanced towards that picture with its face turned away.

" But anyhow it would occupy your time very pleasantly," I went on. " Don't the days seem long to you, alone in this house among the fields ?"

" Oh, the days pass somehow," she replied with such a short, sad laugh.

" I wish she would not shut herself up," said Mr Herbert, uneasily. " She's always willing to go out if I ask her, but she never proposes it of her own accord."

" Then, sir," I said, " I wish you would now ask her to accompany me to see my sister. Ruth will be very glad to have a young thing about her as often as the young thing likes." But even as I uttered the words I felt that my sister, with her white hair, was far less weary and worn than this twenty-year-old girl. Agnes Herbert's sweet, tired face positively pained me.

" Then Agnes must be at her service," said the farmer promptly. " So, my girl, go and put on your wraps, and you can come with us through the fields. The walk will do you good, this fine sunshiny day."

She rose to obey, smiling and silent. It was the

silence about her which was so pitiful.   For silence is
the leaden shield with which we meet the inevitable.
Hopelessness is silent.   So is Death.

She was ready in a few minutes, and we three started
from the back-door—"the field way," as Mr Herbert
called it.   He was quite eager to show me every object
of interest, and I don't for one moment suppose that he
identified me as the Cockney traveller whom he had
half anathematised for peering at his crops.   Agnes
stood beside us, while we discussed sundry items of
agriculture, and she answered when addressed, but when
left alone, I don't think she listened.   However, when
the conversation passed to haymakers, and similar "odd
hands," and I remarked that we hoped to establish a
little village refuge, which might be useful to such, or to
others in distress, she suddenly looked up into my face,
and said,—

"That will be very good."

"Ay, so it will," observed her uncle; "they can put
up there on days when we farmers don't want them, and
then they'll be at hand when we do."

"I shall ask you to subscribe, Mr Herbert," I said.

"Well, I'll give something—it will save me bribing
'em to hang about idle,—picking and stealing."

"And you too, Miss Agnes?" I queried.

"I have so little money," she answered.

"Then Ruth must find out how else you can help us,"
I remarked.

"I'll thank her if she does," said Mr Herbert.
"Aggie sat and looked at the fire all last winter, and

all this summer she has looked at the grass. Anything will be better than that—whether it does good to others or no."

So we walked on through meadow after meadow, yet we did not find Ewen, but only his grandfather, who told us the young man was "away in the cart." I announced my proposal to the patriarch, who received it with very eager gratitude. "It will be the making of the lad, not that he ever said a word against his work, but it's no the richt sort for him—ye'll grant that, sir?"—to Mr Herbert.

"I'll not grant anything of the kind," returned the farmer, with his bluff laugh; "but every man must stand up for himself, and I don't blame your boy for following his fortune."

"Ye'll no think him ungratefu'," said Mr M'Callum. "He'll ne'er forget that wantin' your kindness he couldna ha'e bided here till the bricht turn came. He'll aye remember that, sir."

"There's nothing to remember," said Mr Herbert; "I had a chance of a good workman cheap, and I took it. Tell him he can go away whenever he likes, M'Callum; he need not wait to give me proper notice. And you can hand him that from me," and he slipped something into the old man's hand, "just a kind of farewell blessing, you understand."

"Ewen will be prood, prood, if he can e'er serve you or yours, sir," returned Mr M'Callum, but the farmer waved off his thanks and strode on, calling on us to follow.

"I'm called a 'near' man, Mr Garrett," he said presently. "So I am. I wouldn't give a man high wages for the world. Bad principle. Keep 'em in their place. Make it up in presents. High wages make 'em independent in their service. Presents bind 'em to it. High wages set all the labourers round plaguing their masters for the same. Presents only make 'em anxious to get to the master who gives them."

"But, Mr Herbert, is it *just* to give a man less than he is worth, and then bestow his own upon him as a boon?" I asked.

"Justice is an excellent lady, sir," he answered jocularly; "only she's blind, and there's no knowing where she'll lead one. She has taken some people so far that they think it's sinful for one to be rich and another poor. They may go on till they find out that some have no right to be tall while others are short."

"That is mistaken, indeed," I said; "but the rich have no right to grind the poor because they are poor; and in a crowd a tall man looks none the shorter for letting a little one stand in front."

"Ah, right enough," assented my companion. "'Live and let live' is a good motto. But when you stand aside to let another pass, I like him to notice that you needn't do so if you don't choose."

"Then you are very fond of power, Mr Herbert," I remarked.

"Indeed I am," he answered candidly. "And if any one under my control is sensible enough to understand me, he can get pretty much his own way; but if he flies in my face and rebels—well—as I said before, I don't govern him, and I don't help him, that's all."

"But then you throw away the much stronger influence which patient forbearance would win," I observed.

He looked a little blank, but he only gave a whistle and stopped short, saying that he must turn back, and would send for Agnes in the course of the evening. So he shook hands with me, and sent his respects to my sister, and Miss Herbert and I proceeded to our house.

My sister received the young lady very kindly. I saw she noticed how girlish and transparent the fair face looked when the lace bonnet was removed. But she only rattled on in her sweet, old-fashioned hospitality, calling Miss Herbert's attention to sundry quaint knick-knacks scattered about our parlour, and giving their little histories. Our visitor merely answered "yes" and "no;" but she listened in the grave, pondering way of those who strive to bring every new idea to bear upon some old problem. After dinner Ruth let the conversation flag, and Miss Herbert did not take it up, but leaned back in the easy-chair, and seemed quite satisfied with the silence. As her uncle had said, she sat and looked at the fire, and I will confess that I sat opposite and looked at her. Gradually twilight stole over us, and as I watched her with half-dozing eyes, I became conscious of one of those strange revelations which come to us at such times, when out of the familiar face grows another face, different and yet the same, sometimes showing how the old man looked when he was young, sometimes prophesying how the boy will look when he is old. And lo! the hopeless face before me grew calm and firm, but no longer girlish, and the peace thereon seemed not of the simplicity which looks up at life's struggle, but rather of the wisdom which looks down upon the same. But the spell of my dreamy gaze was suddenly broken by Phillis bringing in the lamp, and Ruth rousing herself from the sofa behind me, and saying she guessed Miss Herbert would think us a fine set of sleepy-heads.

So the fire was stirred and tea ordered. Alice brought it in, and when she left the room Miss Herbert made her first spontaneous remark—

"That is Alice M'Callum, is it not?" she said. "She looks happier than she has looked for a long while."

"I daresay you know she has been in great trouble," observed Ruth; "but, thank God, there is no sorrow so dark that it cannot be lightened in God's good time."

"If it be God's will," Miss Herbert whispered softly.

"And I think it is always God's will," answered my sister in a clear, cheerful voice. "Sometimes He chooses not to take away our cross, but it is our fault if He do not help us to carry it, and when once He does that, the worst is over."

And I saw Miss Herbert paused, and let those words print themselves on her mind.

"Let us hope that in every sense the worst is over for Alice," I observed.

"Alice has never lacked blessings," returned Ruth. "Her troubles have not wasted her life, but rather ennobled it. Her calamities have compelled her to work harder than before, and more for other people than her-self. All sorrow should lead to that, only it's a great blessing when we're put between two hedges, and so can't mistake the meaning of the signpost."

"Yet it seems to me that those who have done most for the world have been happy people," remarked Miss Herbert.

"Certainly," said my sister, "just because those who do good cannot be miserable. If we make smiling faces round us, we learn the habit of smiles."

Just then there came a gentle tap at the door, and Alice's face appeared very bright indeed as she said, "Ewen has come up, if you please, sir, because he would like to thank you."

"Show him in," answered my sister.

The young man entered, and his sister retired. He was not in his farm clothes, but in such dress as he must have worn in the office at Mallowe—a suit probably never used since that time. He was a tall, well-made fellow, and I was glad he would certainly make a good first impression on my city friends, and I noticed that Miss Herbert looked at him with surprised interest. Naturally enough, he spoke shyly and stiffly. He was evidently very glad of the impending change, yet in the gladness was a reservation which he seemed unwilling to express. It came out at last. "Grandfather will be so lonely."

"Ah, we must see about that. For the first few days Alice can stay with him, and come to her work here while he is out," answered my sister. "And after that, some new plan may suggest itself. Does Mr M'Callum speak of it ?"

"Oh no, ma'am," replied Ewen ; "for that matter, I 've been such bad company that he won't miss me much."

"Have you seen Mr Herbert ?" I asked.

"Yes, sir; I happened to meet him in the road. He was very kind," with a glance at our guest.

"Well, Ewen, you are the first person I have recommended to my old firm," I said, "so you must get me a good name for insight and discretion, just for the sake of those who may come after. Do you know any one in London ?"

"Not a soul ! " he answered, with the gaiety of one who is not sorry for oblivion.

"Then take care what friends you make," I responded. " There are one or two Scotchmen in the office, to whom your nationality will serve as introduction. And for the matter of evening recreation—I know you are well educated—have you any favourite pursuit—chemistry, or anything ?"

Ewen smiled and blushed a little, and then answered, "I always had a taste for drawing, sir."

"Oh yes, I know," exclaimed Agnes Herbert, and checked herself.

"Then go to a drawing-class as soon as you can afford it ; and even before that, there are many free evening lectures and exhibitions by which you can improve yourself. An inclination for any study is the cheapest and best pleasure a man can have. Pursuing it, he gains in-

sight into other things, and is thrown in the way of con-
genial company. But don't let your taste run away with
you ; don't let it intrude on business, or sleep, or exercise. Don't allow yourself to be an indifferent clerk,
for the sake of being an indifferent artist. Be thorough
in your duties, and you will elevate the standard of your
taste."

"And don't forget to be regular in your letters home,"
said Ruth, practically. "Let them be expected on certain
days, so that Alice need not waste her time waiting for
the postman."

"And write to me whenever you like," I added, as the
young man rose to depart. "But I suppose we shall see
you again before you go."

"I don't think so, sir," he answered. "Alice and I
have talked it over, and she says I can be ready to go by
the train to-morrow morning, and she'll send the rest of
my things after me."

"You are indeed glad to get away, my boy," I said,
as we shook hands.

"I'll not deny it, sir," he replied, "but please God,
I'll win to such a life that those who believe that black
chapter will be willing to forget it."

"And is there no one else to whom you should say
good-bye ?" I asked. "A journey is none the worse for
a few ' God speeds.'"

"Well, there is one," he said, reflectively ; "but I was
once so rude to him that I don't like to go. I mean our
minister, sir."

"Go by all means," said Ruth, smiling. "You own

you were rude to him ; so if you get a rebuff, it will only serve you right."

" Ewen," I interrupted, " if you go, take my word for it, you won't get a rebuff."

" I 'll go," he said. " I 'll go before I return home."

And so he shook hands with Ruth and me, and was going away with a bow to Miss Herbert ; but that young lady sprang up briskly and shook hands too.

" One of Nature's gentlemen," I remarked, when he was gone.

" A brave, honest man," said Ruth.

" You think him innocent ? " queried our visitor.

" That we do," answered Ruth.

" Supposing he were guilty ? " said  Miss Herbert again.

" Then, as he asserts his innocence, he would be very base indeed," returned my sister.

" I think him innocent," observed the young lady after a pause.  " I always thought so."

" Did you express that opinion whenever you could ? " asked Ruth.

" I said so to my uncle ; but he did not care  whether or no ; and I don't speak to any one else."

" Then you should," answered Ruth, decidedly ; " we should all keep a seat for ourselves in the parliament of public opinion.  A single vote may turn the scale sometimes."

" But I am so fond of solitude," pleaded the girl ; " yet still," she added, eagerly, " I would make myself like society if I could do good in it.  But if I had gone to all the village tea-parties, and lifted up my voice for Ewen's innocence, I could not have helped him as you and your brother have, Miss Garrett."

"Certainly not," returned Ruth; "your time for that has not come. Youth is the season for gaining a place and a voice in the world. Influence is like everything worth having: we must work a long while to gain it."

"Well, Ruth," I said, "Miss Herbert has her uncle's permission to help you about your refuge. That will be a beginning for her. I think she is like you—in favour of refuges."

"Is that so, my dear?" asked Ruth.

"Yes," answered the girl, very softly indeed; "because they give one more chance to the lost ones."

"There are none 'lost' between earth and heaven," said my sister; "wherever they go they can't get away from God. And He gives them chance after chance to the very end."

"But He is angry with the wicked," whispered Agnes Herbert, with dilating eyes.

"Just as a loving father is angry with his naughty children," returned my sister. "He loves them none the less for His anger. He is angry because He loves them Like a father, too, He waits to forgive."

"But some fathers are not ready to forgive," said Agnes.

"Then they need to ask their children's pardon for their hard-heartedness," replied Ruth; "and God help them to see the necessity before it be too late!"

There followed a short silence, which Miss Herbert broke by the abrupt inquiry,—

" Do you think many people go to heaven, Miss Garrett ?"

" Surely many more than go elsewhere," answered Ruth, " for God's love is stronger than Satan's malice. And heaven is broader than our charity. There will be some there whom we scarcely expect. Ah, it would be a woeful world if we could not always hope that ! "

At this the strange, reserved girl suddenly sprang up, and kissed my sister with the bursting enthusiasm of one who has just heard unexpected tidings of joy. She would have subsided as suddenly, but my sister held her for a moment, and kissed that sensitive forehead—once, twice, thrice. Agnes's impulsive embrace was like the electric shock which flashes across the sea the glad news that two nations have but one heart.

Here Phillis entered with the announcement that Miss Herbert was fetched, and that the rector's servant had brought a letter, which she handed to my sister, who presently passed it to me ; and while Agnes put on her bonnet, I read aloud :—" The Rev. Lewis Marten sends his best regards to Miss Garrett, and he has found a house which he thinks exactly suits her ideas of a refuge. If convenient, he will wait upon her to-morrow morning, and take her to see it. He must add that he has named the subject to some of his parishioners, and has secured one or two donations ; which is very promis· ing."

" Would you like to join us ? " inquired Ruth of Miss Herbert. " Come over here early, and take the walk with us. Remember, I shall quite expect you."

"Tell your uncle, and then he will take care to send you," I said, smiling. And so the matter was settled.

"A very sweet girl," remarked Ruth, when our visitor had departed. "At first I thought her listless. I don't think so now. And she has an energetic face."

"She seems like one defeated," I said, "who has no heart to re-commence the battle."

"Then we must get her into it unawares," returned Ruth.

And I told her all I had seen and heard at the Great Farm about the girl's loneliness and her uncle's evident solicitude, and about the strange shadow of household tragedy that haunted the family dining-room.

"Doubtless she will tell us about it in due time," said Ruth, meditatively. "In the little intercourse I have had with people round, I have heard nothing about the Herberts. Very likely Alice could explain it. But she is not the girl to tell, and we are not the people to ask her. Whatever it be, they had better have taken the picture down and put it out of sight. Turned to the wall, indeed! What folly?"

## CHAPTER VI.

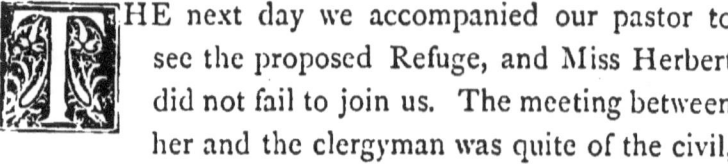

THE next day we accompanied our pastor to see the proposed Refuge, and Miss Herbert did not fail to join us. The meeting between her and the clergyman was quite of the civil, distant order—so much so, that I wondered if the young man's exercise of his ministerial functions had ever extended to a visit at the Great Farm. I expected that he and Ruth would lead the way, and leave the young lady in my charge, but as Miss Herbert attached herself to my sister, Mr Marten and I had no alternative but to follow.

Our destination was a large old cottage at the quieter end of the row, which Upper Mallowe honoured as its " High Street." There was a narrow strip of garden in front, cut in twain by a flagged path, leading to the door. At each side of this door was a wide, latticed window, and there were three casements on the upper story. The rector had armed himself with the key—a very primitive instrument—and in a moment we were all rambling over the place, opening doors, and discovering cupboards and shelves, and such like appliances of domestic comfort.

"I think it will do," said Ruth.

"You must not say so yet, Miss Garrett," returned Mr Marten; "for you have not seen its chief beauty." And he ushered us into a long low room at the back, evidently an addition to the original building; for it had no chambers above it.    "There!" said he, "I think that will make such a capital—what shall we call it, ma'am?—feeding-room—*salle à manger*?"

"So it will," responded Ruth: "the other two rooms can be male and female dormitories, and the floor above will do nicely for the housekeepers' home."

"But there are three upper rooms," said Mr Marten, mounting the stairs, and rapidly opening their doors. "See! two will suffice for the housekeepers, and we shall have one superfluous."

"A great comfort for an ailing woman or a sick child," I said.

"Certainly," answered Ruth; "and now, Mr Marten, can you tell us the rent?"

"The landlord has always asked sixteen pounds a year," replied he; "but the cottage has this disadvantage: it is too large and expensive for the poorer class of tenants, and too rough for any others, and so he says he will part with it entirely for one hundred and twenty pounds.    What do you think of that offer, Mr Garrett?"

"I will accept it," I answered; "and then the remaining expenses will be a small salary for the housekeepers, who will have their rooms rent free, and who need not be wholly without other work, and a little fund for meals, and general assistance for the poor wanderers."

"And furniture?" suggested Miss Herbert, timidly.

"Oh, every bit of that must be begged," said my sister.

The Reverend Lewis Marten put on a very wry face.

"Come, come," said I, "you have made a good beginning already, and you know I am pledged to help you."

"You two look after the money," advised Ruth. "Do you suppose the village mothers will promise *you* old pans, and kettles, and pillows? Leave those things to us."

"I have read of a very good plan," said that sweet voice, which only spoke too seldom. "When some good German wished to furnish an orphan house, he made a little blank book, and wrote on each leaf such headings as 'bedding,' 'earthenware,' and so on. Then he sent the book about, and every one wrote in it what they would give, and thus each might be quite sure they were not giving what was already had."

"Thank you very much, Miss Herbert," returned my sister: "that is a good idea. Whenever anything like that strikes you, mind you tell us."

"Of course, I shall," said Miss Herbert.

"No 'of course' about it," replied Ruth; "you hesi-

tated before you said that. And you'll have other wise
thoughts come ; but you'll be so afraid they're foolish,
that you'll let us old folks go blundering on without
their help. Now promise me you won't ?"

" I'll try," said the dear girl.

And Ruth looked at her, and gave her head a queer
little shake which I could not understand.

" Well, I think we are getting on very well," remarked
the clergyman. " I'll just get my memorandum-book,
and take a note of our position. But, dear me, I have
not a pencil ! "

" Oh, I have one," answered Miss Herbert, producing
a dainty " lady's companion." Its fastening was a little
intricate, and she drew off her gloves to undo it. In
the course of this action, I saw something I had not
noticed before. On the " engaged " finger she wore a
broad, richly-chased gold ring—one of the kind known
as " guards."

" Thank you," said Mr Marten, accepting the proffered
pencil. " Now, ' Edward Garret, Esq., £120 '—that
looks handsome ! Then, ' Miss Ruth Garret '—what did
I understand ?' " and he glanced archly at my sister.

" You did not understand anything," Ruth retorted.
" I've got very little, and I mean to keep it to fill up
odd corners where Edward's grand subscription won't
go."

" Well, I've written your name," returned Mr Marten,
" and I shall let it stay. Then there's the two old ladies
to whom I named the Refuge—Mrs Withers, one pound
one ; and Miss Tabitha Vix, five shillings—that's all for

the present. Total, one hundred and twenty-one pounds, six shillings, and an unknown blank, you see, Miss Garret."

"Uncle says he will give five pounds," whispered Agnes Herbert.

"Oh, come! this is famous!" said the rector, resuming his notes; "and may I put down anything from you?"

"Half-a-crown, if it's worth while," she said, softly; "and one shilling from Sarah—that's our servant, Sarah Irons, you know. Perhaps we may get something better out of the lumber-room. Uncle lets us give away anything we find there; but I haven't looked over it for a long time."

"The first thing we have to do," said Ruth, as we left the house, "is to get a good housekeeper, and then we can say, 'Gifts thankfully received at the Refuge.'"

"And who is to hire this housekeeper?" asked Mr Marten.

"I will, please," responded Ruth. "If you like, you may set that down as my subscription. It may prove worth more than Edward's."

Both the clergyman and Miss Herbert resisted our pressing invitation to lunch. So we returned home alone, and Alice admitted us—red-eyed, but smiling, after the parting from her brother.

In the course of the day Ruth paid another visit to the Refuge. She and Alice went there in the twilight, and stayed some time. I half guessed the mischief they were plotting, and I was not mistaken. Alice and her grandfather were appointed hostess and host at the Refuge.

" It will be so nice to tell in my first letter to Ewen ! " said Alice.

Now you may be sure the opening of this Refuge made quite a commotion in our sleepy village of Upper Mallowe,—more sensation even than the sudden curtailment of chanting in St Cross. The two events happened simultaneously. Before gossip could circulate any particulars about the new " charity," it was announced that the Reverend Lewis Marten was to preach a sermon thereon. Out of curiosity, some of the people who usually walked to the Ritualistic church at Hopleigh, turned their steps to St Cross. Also, out of curiosity, some of the old farmers laid down the local paper, and went to hear the local discourse. They found the creaking doors set wide open to receive them, and the bereaved pew-opener's temper was all the sweeter for being spared the trial of the singing-boys in the vestry. The lads, themselves, conspicuous by their absence in an official capacity, occupied seats about the church, either under the surveillance of their parents, or steadied by the charge of junior relatives.

The service began. Neither Mr Marten nor I had exchanged a word on the subject beyond what I have related. He read the sentences and exhortation in his usual clear ringing tone, and there followed a brief expectant silence. Then he lifted up his voice without the intonation with which he was wont to accompany the chanting. The scattered choir-boys, previously instructed, were the first to join, but by the third or fourth petition of our glorious old confession the whole congregation responded. The farmers looked approvingly at each other, and I think the Ritualistic strangers were too surprised to be displeased. The same reform went on throughout the service, and the old people, too blind to read, had the full benefit of those beautiful reassuring psalms, which so marvellously suit every circumstance and experience.

It was the Twenty-second Sunday after Trinity, and the rector took his text from the Gospel for the day. " Shouldst not thou have had compassion on thy fellow-servant, even as I had pity on thee?" His heart was warm with the subject : and his words were eloquent in proportion. As usual, he dwelt strongly on the spiritual wickedness of the world, but only to show the depth of misery from which Christ had saved it. And his closing remarks struck me so much, that I can recall them almost word for word :—

" Christ has forgiven us the ten thousand talents, that dreadful debt which Adam contracted, and which descends to us with accumulating interest. The greatest saint and the greatest sinner are both included in the bond which His mercy remits.

" Yet people rarely realise this brotherhood in evil and misery, this participation in proffered forgiveness. God draws no distinction between sin and crime. The world does. It must. But do not let us say this is because crime injures society, while sin may be left to God, as a matter wholly between Him and the sinner.

Crime grows from sin, as the tree springs from its root. Law only punishes crime, simply because sin is too subtle for it.   Why, brethren, the sins that really injure society, and from which issue the crimes which fill our prisons and reformatories, are sins to which none of us could truly plead 'Not guilty.'   First and foremost is the little seed of self, sprouting into wilfulness, and sloth, and apathy.   Who has never preferred his own weal to another's, never driven his own will over another's com-fort, never held back his hand when he should have stretched it out, or kept silence when he ought to have spoken ?   If these questions were pressed upon us, who would not be convicted by his own conscience ?

"Justice can punish the murderer or the thief, but human justice cannot reach the influences which may have raised his hand against his fellows.   Do not suppose these influences excuse his crime.   No one need be a victim to circumstance.   Circumstance is only given us to conquer.   But neither does circumstance excuse the man from whom proceeded the evil influence.   Ah, my brethren, when the shadow of a great crime darkens the length and breath of the land, who of us can safely say, 'I have had no share in this !'   A mere want of punctuality or promptitude, by souring tempers, and em-bittering hearts, may be the first step on the dark road which ends with a gallows !   The devil takes care that sin shall be a maze, wherein nobody knows where each path may lead.

"But you will answer, 'Christ came to deliver us from sin.'   Truly He came to redeem us from its bondage.

He came to show us what we were in Eden, and what we may be again in Paradise. He came to throw the mantle of His own spotless righteousness over the ragged holiness which clothes the purest earthly saint. He came to hold up before us that perfect humanity which fell in fragments round the tree of the knowledge of good and evil. Yes, my brethren, He came to do all this, and what is the result? Those whom He draws closest to Himself—those whose purblind souls are so anointed with the balm of His forgiveness, that henceforth they can see clearly—those are the very ones who cry with St Paul, 'The good that I would, I do not: but the evil which I would not, that I do.' Such walk in humility and gentleness, ever watchful lest some unwary stumble of theirs crush a soul 'for whom Christ died,' ever praying, 'Lord, pardon us for the sins which we mistake for virtues!'

"Yes, Christ himself tells us that 'it must needs be that offences come.' The world is God's work, but Satan's tangle is in it. Every one of us—you and I—have done our little share to perpetuate that tangle. And so long as we carry about our mortality, the devil will sometimes catch our fingers, and set them at the old mischievous work. But in the meantime we must put our hands to labour on God's side. There is always a task ready for us. Wherever we see pain, or sorrow, or poverty. or death, let us remember we confront suffering born of sin, *our* sin.

"My brethren, I am about to suggest a solemn thought. · It has been said of some holy men, that they never knew how much good they did. It may be truly said of all of us, that we know not what evil we have caused. You, the regular worshipper and communicant —some permanent inconsistency in your life may have given a forgotten acquaintance a lasting prejudice against religion. You, parents, bewailing rebellious children— perhaps you 'provoked' them to wrath and sin. You, neglected wives,—by your own peevishness and self-con- sideration may have alienated the love which you should have held next to God's. I, myself, lamenting over the empty seats I too often see in this temple, may have driven my flock away by my own coldness and apathy! And alas! alas! my brethren, the evil our own hands have done, our own hands cannot always undo. Those whom we injure, die or go beyond our influence. There are words and deeds which we cannot recollect without remorse, yet which can never be cancelled. Then, as we pray that other hands may efface our wrong-doing, let us remember that some may be so praying on behalf of one whom we can succour, either in mind or body. How happy we should be to hear that God had per- mitted a good man to destroy our evil work! So, let us be up and doing, that in our turn, with God's blessing, we may confer that happiness on others. Let it no more be said that the homeless, the erring, or the miser- able, pass among us unsheltered, uncounselled, and un- cheered. Christmas again draws near—to some of us it will be brighter than ever before; to others its earthly brightness may be departed. But the gayest, as well as the poorest and the saddest, and the utterly bereaved,

1

will be none the worse for winning 'the blessing of those that were ready to perish.'"

Mr Marten spoke so earnestly and pointedly, that the interest of the most sluggish was aroused, and the church was solemn with the breathless silence of rapt attention. There was but one interruption. When the rector's warning touched on family miseries, Mr Herbert suddenly rose, left his seat, and walked down the aisle. At the front, however, he paused, passed his hand reflectively over his whiskers, and returned to his pew. But immediately after the final benediction, and before any one had risen from prayer, he and his niece both left the building.

There was a collection made at the door, and when we passed out, the "plates" seemed in a tolerably prosperous condition. The rough church-path was not so clear as on my first visit to St Cross, for neighbours were lingering to greet other neighbours whom they had not seen there for a long time. As we went through the crowd I heard many remarks such as these :—

"Parson gave us a moighty fine sermon. He seems quite awaukened up."

"Ay, you may say that ! He spoke as if he meant it."

"A'most as if he wor preachin' to some 'un there, and knew ezactly what they wanted."

"Perhaps he wor'."

Next day when Mr Marten came to confess his mistake, and to own that the people of Upper Mallowe had proved liberal beyond his hopes, I told him this. He smiled at the rough criticism, but his reply was—

" They were right.  I was preaching at some one,—
at myself.  All the time I bore in mind my miserable
blunder with that poor fellow Ewen."

" Ah, you had a visit from him before he left for London," said Ruth.

" So I had," he answered.

" And what did you say ?" inquired my sister.

" We each begged the other's pardon," returned the
rector, " and I think he 'll count me among the friends
ne has left at Upper Mallowe,—or at least not among
the enemies.  He is not at all an ordinary chip of
humanity.  You did a great work in saving him, Mr
Garrett."

" Edward just did a common Christian duty," said
Ruth ; " if God bless it, to Him be all the glory !"

" And you think the people felt my sermon last Sunday ?" queried Mr Marten presently.

" Yes, just because your heart was in every word," I
answered.

" I feared I was, as usual, too gloomy and severe," he
remarked.

" No, no," said I ; " you own you were preaching at
yourself,—therefore you loved the sinner, understood his
errors, and felt a human pity for his remorse.  Now, you
must ask God to enlarge your sympathies till you can do
the same in every case, and then your severity will be
only truthful love."

" And if your preaching suits your own heart, it will
certainly suit somebody else," added Ruth.

# CHAPTER VII.

ND thus Christmas drew near. By that time the Refuge was fairly established, Miss Herbert's " Contribution Book " having secured sundry very useful gifts, which went far to spare our little cash account, and Mr M'Callum and Alice were settled in their new abode—both made exceedingly happy by punctual and comfortable letters from Ewen. And so Ruth and I jogged on in our quiet way.

But we saw very little of Agnes. She helped my sister in all the Refuge arrangements, yet we could not allure her to our house for a leisurely visit, nor even detain her for such when she made a call. She was always quite anxious to return home, as if it were some post of imperative duty, from which absence was absolutely desertion.

" How shall we keep Christmas, Ruth ? " I asked one evening in December.

"Just like a Thanksgiving Sunday, I suppose," said she. "There are no children coming home for the holidays."

Now, of course I knew that. But Ruth will say things.

"Christmas is a birthday feast," I remarked, "and so it should be kept."

"Ah, but birthdays are drear times," she answered, "when there's no one to stoop over us and give us a kiss and a keepsake."

"I suppose that is why old people leave off keeping them," I said. "I think they are wrong; let them rather give kisses and keepsakes on the dear date when they used to receive them. So with Christmas. Ah, Ruth, you were mistaken when you said we had no child to gladden us at this season. Is there not a Babe in a manger at Bethlehem which is ours for ever?"

Ruth did not reply. She never replies to such remarks. I believe she thinks the more for her silence, for by and by she said—

"Then what should you like to do on Christmas day?"

"I want to give as many little bits of pleasure as I can," I replied; "such little bits of pleasure as made me happy when I was a boy, Ruth."

"Ah, you were easy to please, Edward," said she; "and a very good thing, too!"

"Any one who can be pleased at all is as pleased with little as with much," I replied. "A Christmas card gives as much delight as a Christmas-box. A child is as charmed with the discovery of a blackberry bush, as is a miner with his nugget. And perhaps the one 'find' is as valuable as the other."

"To the child, may be; but not to the man," retorted Ruth. "Recollect, grown-up people have no leisure to go blackberry hunting unless they've first got a nugget of their own, or are degraded enough to live on other people. Don't you pretend to under-value money, Edward. It's God's gift as much as any-thing else. It depends on us whether it be a blessing or a curse."

"That is how you always pull me up when I grow poetical," I said, smiling.

"Talking rubbish is not poetical," she answered. "Sham sentiment is too often mistaken for poetry, and when people find common-life tears off such rags as she goes along, they foolishly fancy they are too fine for every-day wear, and so put aside the tinsel for best occa-sions. Now real poetry is just naked truth."           .

"You are far too clever to argue with, Ruth," said I.

"Ah, you see I kept a circulating library, and the best books were always at home," she remarked drily.

Presently, being really willing to fall in with my humble plans, she observed,—

"But a little consideration makes money go very far in giving pleasure. It prevents you sending coals to a widow at Newcastle, or presenting a farmer with a turkey, or a schoolboy with Euclid, or a blind man with a tract."

"That is to the point, Ruth," I said; "now I just want to give a little bit of genuine delight to every one I know. I wish you had second sight, and could reveal the secret desire of each friend and neighbour."

"Then you would find out you could satisfy none," she returned. "Do you think folks are so shallow as to long for aught you could send as a Christmas gift?"

"No," I answered; "but every one has some dear little wish, whose gratification makes the great want easier to bear."

"You are right there," responded my sister. "If you cannot give a man dinner, you may give him a biscuit for lunch."

"We must send some pretty surprise to every house which has young folks," I said.

"And we must not let them find out where it comes from," added Ruth. "Nobody will set greater value on anything because sent by you or me, Edward. If they cannot guess the giver, it will make them feel kindly towards all their friends."

"But yet we cannot tell what will please each child," I remarked.

"A book or a picture with a little innocent mystery about it will satisfy all the young people," answered Ruth. "It will be harder to hit the fancy of the elder ones."

"The elder ones will be pleased in the young ones' pleasure," I said; "and as I find there will be cheap railway excursions to and from London at Christmas-time, I shall buy a return-ticket and send it to Ewen, and his arrival on Christmas morning shall be my gift to that family."

" Bravo, Edward," exclaimed my sister ; " that is just the right thing.    You are cleverer than I am, in your own way."

" Only you think it a small sort of way," I said, laughing.

" As you know my thoughts, I 'll not contradict you," said she.    " And what shall we do for Mr Marten ? "

" Ask him to dinner ? " I queried.

Ruth shook her head.    " Very likely he would have somewhere better to go," she said, " though he might come, thinking to please us ; while, for my own part, I 'd rather have only ghosts at the Christmas-table."

" And yet you have never known the bitter changes which some know," I remarked ; " you can only miss our father and our mother, and they were spared till their time was fully ripe."

" I know the changes in myself," Ruth answered. " It 's my own ghost that comes to see me on feast-days."

" But you would not object to any guest who had nowhere else to go ? " I asked.

" Certainly not," she said ; " such a presence would lay the ghost.    Not that I wish it laid.    I like to see what a fool I was once.    I only wish I could be such a fool now ! "

" Age is higher and happier than youth," I remarked, harping on my pet theory.

" I know it," she answered ; " but yet some folks like climbing mountains better than sitting at rest. You must not judge every one by yourself, Edward."

" I wish I could guess what would please Agnes Herbert," I said, presently.

" If we only knew what ailed the girl!" observed Ruth.

We little dreamed who was then walking across our garden. We heard the back door slammed, and in a moment Phillis appeared in the parlour, announcing that a gentleman had brought a little ragged boy to our gate, and had bidden him ask for Mr Garrett.

" Is the gentleman in the kitchen ? Who is he ?" asked Ruth, rising, in astonishment.

" Please, ma'am, I could not see him out in the dark," answered the sapient Phillis, " and he wouldn't wait ; but says he to the boy, when I opened the gate, 'You're all right now,' says he. And, please, sir, the boy seems stupified-like."

" It's only some stranger who has heard of us in connexion with the Refuge," said I. " Is the lad in the kitchen, Phillis ? "

" I've kept him out in the passage," replied Phillis ; " for it's a bad night, and he's awful muddy, and would muck the kitchen-floor, if you please, sir."

" No, I'm not pleased, Phillis," I answered. " If cleanliness is to follow godliness, then kindliness must keep between."

" Ask the boy to the fire directly," said practical Ruth ; " at the same time let him rub his feet well upon the mat."

"This is a queer adventure," I commented, as the girl obediently departed, and we prepared to follow.

"I daresay it will put your Christmas cards and keepsakes right out of your head," said Ruth.

"A very good suggestion,' I retorted. "Your doubt will help me to remember them, my sister."

We found the boy seated by the kitchen-hearth, with his dirty feet tucked up on the rung of the Windsor chair, perhaps by Phillis' directions. He seemed a coarse, vulgar, neglected lad, and he gave an introductory snivel when he saw us. Of course he was a scrap of God's writing, but the divine characters were sadly blurred.

"Do you want to speak with me—Mr Garrett?" I asked, taking a seat opposite him.

"The gen'leman said so," he answered.

"What have you to say?" I inquired.

"I dunno," he replied, hopelessly, whirling his thick, dirty hands; "only the gen'leman said, 'There, you're all right now.'"

We had heard as much from Phillis.

"Who was the gentleman?" I questioned.

"I dunno," replied the boy.

"What were you doing when he spoke to you?" asked Ruth. Her clear, quick tones penetrated his thick skull deeper than mine. I fancy they had a magisterial echo, for he instantly thrust his red fore-finger into his bleared eye, and jerked out, whiningly, "I warn't a-doing of no harm. I only arst him for a penny."

"You're a stranger here," remarked Ruth, in the same

sharp voice, which seemed to keep his mind awake;
"where do you come from ?"

" I comed from Lunnon—I tramped it," he answered ;
" mother only died this day was a week."

He did not look so vulgar and coarse when one heard
that history. God help the boy !

" What brought you here ?" asked Ruth.

" Mother said father was summat here ; he 'd run
away from her, years ago. She niver wanted to be arter
him herself, but she bid me look to him, when she wor
gone."

" What is his name ?" I inquired.

" George Wilmot," said the lad, " and that 's mine
too."

"I don't believe there 's such a name in the place, sir,"
said Phillis, aside.

" You say you asked the gentleman for a penny," pursued Ruth ; " then what did he answer ?"

" Please, he catched me by the shoulder, an' turned me
round, an' stared at me for a minute or two, and didn't say
nothin'."

" Not at first, perhaps," continued Ruth, "but what did
he say when he spoke ?"

" He said 'God help us !' just like mother used ; and
then he asked my name," said the boy.

" And then ?" queried Ruth.

" Then he said, ' I haven't anything to give you.'
But he kep' hold o' my shoulder, an' I walked along with
him, till he says, ' Where are you going to-night?'
And I telled him I must sleep under an 'edge or summat.

And he says, 'God help us!' again; and fell a-thinking like."

"What made him bring you here?" asked my sister.

"Well, he says, 'By the by, there's a Refuge somewhere near,' and asked if I knew what a Refuge meant, and I said, 'Didn't I!' An' then he stood still, and looked about, and says, 'I've never seen it, and don't know where it is, but I'll take you to the good people who opened it!' and then he went on muttering about devils giving kind folk a deal to undo, which I couldn't make out.    He telled me this was the house as we came to the gate, but says he, 'We'll go round the other way, for I'm fittest for backdoors now,' and he laughed out, 'Ha! ha! ha!'"

The bright fire was evidently thawing the lad's frozen wits, for he gave his last words in another tone, in imitation of his strange guide.

"Should you know your father if you saw him?" inquired Ruth.

The boy shook his head: "He's not been nigh us sin' I wor a babby," he said.

"What was this gentleman like?" queried my suspicious sister.

"Tall," answered the boy, "and he had on a cloak."

"Was he young or old?" asked Ruth.

"I dunno, ma'am," staring as if the answer was quite beyond his powers.    It was the first time he gave my sister a respectful title.    I believe he thought her question showed a high opinion of his faculties, and so honoured her accordingly.

"Was he as old as your mother, do you think?" pursued Ruth, after a moment's reflection.

"Oh, no," said the boy, grinning at the idea, "*she* was quite an old woman—she allays said so!"

"What was her age?" inquired Ruth, trying to get at the truth by a side-path.

"Thirty-three," replied the lad succinctly.

Ruth glanced at me with elevated eyebrows; this was her first experience of the statistics of a London street-boy.

"When did you have anything to eat?" I asked.

"A baker gave me a clump o' bread this morning; it was not a right dinner, to say," he answered, "but coming along past the public, the hostler had a half-empty pot, and he telled me I might drink it up. That was good," he added, smacking his lips at the recollection.

O thou Father of kings and beggars, which thanksgiving makes the sweetest incense before Thy throne, —the formal calling upon Thy name of one who is discontented with his venison, or the gladness of another who picketh up the coarsest crumbs of Dives' table, and thanketh Thee ignorantly, as do the beasts and birds?

Phillis instantly brought forth a loaf and some cold meat. I am thankful to say, she understood her master sufficiently to do this without asking direct permission.

I resolved to take the lad to the Refuge myself. The M'Callums were old inhabitants, of intelligence far superior to Phillis, and they might know some clue whereby to discover the boy's runagate father. I had

a faint idea of my own in this matter, a most unreasonable one, inasmuch as it was attached, not to the cog-
nomen "Wilmot," but to the simple name "George,"
which my common sense told me might belong to a
dozen men in Upper Mallowe.

The lad made a considerable supper, without taking
long in the process, and then we started off together.
Ruth's questions had given him the notion that we
took some interest in the stranger who had brought
him to us. So as we trudged along he suggested,
"Mayhap the gentleman will be about yet."

"Whereabouts did you meet him?" I asked.

"Just here," he answered.

Now at that instant we passed the Great Farm.

We were not long in reaching the Refuge, and Alice
promptly admitted us, and led us to her little sitting
room on the upper floor. From Ruth's accounts, I
knew that she used this chamber as her sleeping apartment, the other being occupied by her grandfather,
while the third, by Alice's own wish, was kept for such
extra uses as might arise from the necessities of the
Refuge.

"Grandfather is down-stairs," she explained; "there
are two poor men here for the night, and he's in the
upper room, talking with them. Shall I fetch him, sir?"

"If you please, Alice," I said; "but you may promise that I shall not keep him long."

The old man soon presented himself, with that cheery
face, which must have beamed on the poor refugees like
a sudden sunrise after a dreary night. I hastened to in-

quire if he knew any one in the village called George Wilmot.

Mr M'Callum shook his head.

Alice said, " No."

" Do you remember such a name at any time ?" I inquired.

Neither of them could. So I called the boy forward, and made him repeat his story.

" Hech, sirs ! but it 's a waefu' tale," said the good old Scotchman. " I 'm thinking the laddie had best bide here the nicht, and look aboot you the morn. He 'll maybe hae to bide here a wee, sae ye 'd best mak' his bed i' the little room, Alie. And if he gaes doon stairs, he 'll find some warm parritch ; and the twa puir callants below are nae sic bad company."

" He 's had some supper already," I observed, as the boy seemed disposed to obey with extraordinary alacrity.

" Ou ay, sir," replied Mr M'Callum ; " but a little het parritch canna do him ony harm. Let the laddie gae. Ye see, sir," he continued, when we heard the supper-room door close behind the boy, " I wadna hint a dis-parceging thing afore the bairn's face. Let him think o' his father as weel 's he can ; but, verra-like, if he were George Wilmot when he married, he wasna George Wilmot after he ran awa'. The man that does ae base thing is fit for anither."

" But was it not strange about the gentleman in the lane ?" observed Alice, who was engaged at the cup-board, searching for blankets.

" At first, I wondered whether he were the father," I

said.  " His strange kindness might be the working of remorse."

Mr M‘Callum shook his head.

" Differin' natures hae differin' remorses," he remarked.  " A cauld-bluided scoondrel, wha didna ken gif his bairn had starved or no, would be verra unlikely to fash where the lad passed ae nicht.  Maist like, sic a one would say to himself—' Gif the laddie 's used to it, the wayside 's as guid to him as my bedroom to me.' That 's the way the deevil comforts his ain while they 're his.  He doesna trouble them much, till God gets a grip o' them.  An' if God had got a grip o' him—bein', as he waur, the father—I dinna think he 'd hae left his lang-lost bairn to strangers, e'en to their tender mercies. Maist like, the gentleman is just some puir misguided callant, wha has gotten the wrang bit in his mouth— else why fittest for back-doors, sir?—but hasna travelled the deevil's road lang eneuch to like to see ithers gangin' the same gait.  Sic a one feels anguishes of remorse—and that 's just God's grip, sir."

" But Judas himself felt remorse," I observed, getting into the argument.

" And went and hangit himsel'," said he; " and sae do mony mair.  Gif they would but bide a wee !  Why, sir, ye 'll nae say Christ's death hadna poo'r to save the puir traitor ?  Only the misguided creature went and hangit himsel'."

And so we sat and conversed till George Wilmot came up from his " parritch," and Alice returned from making his bed.

" Now, my boy," I began, " what did your mother say

about your father—what did she bid you say when you should see him?"

"She said she was afeared he'd taken her in mighty," replied the lad, "but there was no telling; and if I got to see him, I was to give him this." And he produced a folded paper, dirty and worn, which he handed to me. "Mother took a long whiles a-writin' it," he remarked, "and she used to say perhaps father a-tired of her, because he was a famous scholard. I can't read what she writ; but may be you will, sir," he added.

I took the letter reverently; for it seemed like a secret between the dead and the living. I paused before I unfolded it; but the boy repeated his request, and, indeed, to peruse it seemed the best way towards fulfilling the deserted woman's wish. This was the contents. I will not translate the strange spelling and bad grammar. They have a pathos with which I dare not meddle.

"MY DERE GEORGE,

"Why did you leve me without a wurd, this is writ to saye that i furgive yu, and hope whe shall meet in Heven, i was not good enuf for yu, but yu dident say so, when yu cam cortin me ovar master's gate, and all the gals grudgin my fortin for yu was a fine gentelman. When yu git this, I am ded and shall not trobble yu never no more. but yu aught luke to your pore boy, wich as bin a good boy to his mother, and fur his sake, i'm niver sorry I maared yu, so don't yu think it. This comes, hopeing yu are well from your luving wife

"MARY WILMOT."

K

I took a little time to decipher this letter; indeed, my sight failed over it. But when I had done, the boy said simply, " Won't ye read it out, sir ? She read it to me, she did, and it 'll be like hearin' her speak oncet more."

So I read it. And the great rough boy sobbed out loud. God's writing was clear enough upon his heart. I shook hands with him when I came away, but I did not say one word to " deepen the effect" of that letter. As soon would I have interrupted the dead mother had she stood among us in the spirit and spoken to her boy.

Alice conducted me to the door. The moon was shining brightly, and cast its blueness over her face. As she stood on the threshold, she said in a whisper—" Isn't it strange that none of us can recollect a Wilmot in these parts ? "

" Not so strange, if your grandfather guesses rightly," I answered.

" *His* name—you know whose, sir ?—was George," she murmured.

I started at this suggestion of my own thought; but, reflected in another's mind, I could see its absurdity. So I said, merrily—

" And so is Mr Smith's the chemist, and Mr Tozer's the baker. No, no, Alice, it 's a bad habit to make out coincidences. It does no good, for we can't trust them, unless they're based on facts, and if we 've got the facts, then we don't want the coincidences. But, by the way, your remark reminds me that I never heard the surname of that unhappy man ? "

"It was Roper—George Roper, sir," she answered.

"Thank you—for, considering the interest I feel in Ewen, it was awkward not to know it. But what are these sounds?"—for from the back of the house came a voice singing a spirited song, accompanied by divers notes as from some uncertain and feeble instrument.

Alice laughed—a pleasant, soft laugh. "It's only the two 'refugees' (so we call our pensioners), one is singing and the other is piping with a bit of paper on a comb. They often do it when they're not over-tired with tramping, sir."

I wonder if any rigid philanthropist would think such doings a breach of the "order and discipline of a charitable institution." I only stood and listened. I have no ear for music, but as I caught the stirring words—

> "Hearts of oak are our ships,
> Jolly tars are our men ;
> We always are ready,
> Steady, boys! steady !
> We'll fight and we'll conquer again and again,"—

I was quite satisfied with the performance. Why should we think our kindness best repaid by long faces and dead silence? Is it not unreasonable to forbid a song because we have given a supper? I remembered a great "human naturalist" said it was a happy omen for a country when the beggar was as content with his dish as the lord with his land. Better to keep our charity than to sell it at the price of enjoyment.

"There! that's grandfather gone to them," said Alice.

"He won't stop the song?" I queried.

"Oh, no, sir," she answered; "most likely he'll join in the chorus. He's fond of singing a song himself. But he thinks it's right to go in and out of the room in a friendly way. And when he's told them stories and anecdotes, and talked pleasantly, there's few so hard as to take it unkindly when he gets out the Bible, before going to bed."

I went home with a heart full of pleasant feelings. I had not forgotten my "cards and keepsakes," as Ruth warned me I should. So every time I passed a village boy, I thought, "Ah, my fine fellow, there's a 'tip' coming for you!" and then the Upper Mallowe boys appeared in my eyes uncommonly nice boys. And it was solemnly sweet to think of true-hearted Mary Wilmot in her London pauper grave—no, not there, but in heaven; for are not our trespasses forgiven, as we forgive those who trespass against us? And it was odd that her boy should come among us like a guest at Christmas time. Have not some "entertained angels unawares?" and in that case, they cannot look as we fancy angels, or they would carry their welcome with them. I don't suppose the lad is any less like an angel, because he knows the price of boy-labour in the docks, and how little one can live upon down Stepney way, and what it is to be hungry and tired—nay, there is One, higher than the angels, who knows all about that, and was a good son to His parents in a carpenter's shop at Nazareth.

But as I entered our house a hearty voice recalled me

to the world of snug suppers and warm beds, for Ruth exclaimed, "Here you are at last, Edward. Come to your supper, and don't. run all over the world, fancying you are as young as ever!"

# CHAPTER VIII.

EORGE WILMOT was still in the Refuge when Christmas-day came. There was quite a bustle in our house on the Eve. With Mr Marten's help I got off my presents, a most miscellaneous heap—tea, tobacco, knick-knacks, pictures, cards, and books ; the last three items all so pretty that if I had not wished to give them I should have liked to keep them ! The Rector was in high spirits, having an invitation to dine next day at a mansion a few miles off, inhabited by an old naval officer and his only daughter, —a fact from which I drew my own inferences. As Ruth could not let this hospitable season pass without a little delicate meddling in culinary matters, a spicy perfume pervaded the parlour, and contributed to the general feeling of festivity and good will.

Perhaps that was the gayest bit of our Christmas keeping. The day was a quiet one in our house. Even

Phillis was away, for Ruth gave her permission to rejoin her own family; and only our new servant, who was a stranger in the village, remained to wait upon us. We did not venture to invite any guests. It is cruel to allure family-people from their homes at such a season; and so far as we could ascertain, all the single folk of Upper Mallowe were already happily appropriated.

But as we took our places at the breakfast-table, a sound of sweet singing startled the clear morning air. Looking from the window, we saw the choir-boys of St Cross standing round our garden-gate. It was no unfamiliar chorale which they sang, but just the dear Christmas hymn, "Hark the herald angels sing." There are some old tunes which have such an echo in the universal heart that I sometimes fancy we shall use them in our heavenly praises.

When they ceased I went out and thanked the lads, and wished them a merry Christmas. I singled out the leader, and wanted to give him five shillings to divide among the rest. I hope the moralists will not say I was making them mercenary. Whenever I receive a pleasure I long to do something in return. But the boy said, quite sedately, that Mr Marten told them to do it, because I was doing so much for the village. Now here was a poser! I must accept their gratuitous service because it was grateful. Yet I could not put away the five shillings. A bright thought came.

"Come, my boys," I said, "I thank you very heartily for your remembrance of an old man; and as you have given me such pleasure, I should like others to have as

much.  Go to the Great Farm, and sing your hymn
again, and take these five shillings in consideration of so
employing your valuable time."   And as I did not wish
to argue through any further remonstrance from that
sedate elder boy, I ran back to the house, and the young
choristers set up a cheer.

Ruth and I went to church, and found it quite gay
with holly and laurel; and the whole service, to the very
tones of the rector's voice, was of a jubilant character.
So Christmas services should be : especially for the sake
of those who may have little rejoicing elsewhere.   The
sermon was very short and very bright, being from that
seasonable text in the eighth chapter of Nehemiah, "Go
your way, eat the fat, and drink the sweet, and send portions unto them for whom nothing is prepared ; for this
day is holy unto our Lord ; neither be ye sorry, for the
joy of the Lord is your strength."

Somehow (I say this in parenthesis), I fancied that Mr
Marten's Christmas visit was an unexpected happiness to
the young man.   But he had been less desponding in his
views for some time.   And God occasionally rewards our
efforts by sending a blessing which makes them easier.

Mr Herbert and his niece were in their pew.   Agnes
looked as if she had been crying.   I think the very gladness of the hymns and sermon tried her.   The old people
liked it ; the acute agonies had died out of their lives, and
then joy is as sunshine on an old, well-remembered grave,
which one hopes soon to share.   But to sorrowful youth'
it comes like spring sunlight on the face of yesterday's
dead.   God help the young !

They hurried out of church before us, though they paused to exchange seasonable wishes over the pew-door. But all the M'Callums waited for us in the grave-yard— the grandfather and Alice perfectly radiant with delight at Ewen's unexpected arrival. The young man himself seemed much more happy and open-hearted for his residence among people who did not suspect and shun him, and was quite eager to deliver the many kind messages he brought me from the good folks in my old house of business. Now, I knew these worthy people would not have sent these messages by him, if they had not liked him. So I augured well for Ewen.

Ruth and I dined cheerfully together, and afterwards I amused myself by droning over my holiday books, by which I mean sundry smart volumes of the poets, that I received as school-prizes in those remote ages when I was a boy. Their glories are rather faded now—like mine! Ruth occupied herself with idleness till tea-time —it must have been hard work for her. Afterwards, being incapable of further exertion in that way, I found her seated opposite me, with linen sleeves drawn over her silk ones, and a grand red and blue china bowl before her, busily cutting up candied peels for the New-Year's cake.

"Is not that the maid's duty?" I asked, heedlessly.

" Household affairs are every woman's study," she replied, cutting energetically.

Now, I like to watch an educated woman at domestic work. She makes it beautiful. So I said, "Women are never more pleasing than when so engaged."

" They are never more dignified," returned Ruth.

"Certainly it is their hereditary empire, where they reign undisputed," I remarked.

" If they leave that throne, they may wish for another !" responded my sister.

" Oh, I think in other spheres, they may at least dispute male pre-eminence," I observed.

"Let them if they like," said Ruth; "the more simpletons in the world, the better for wise people. Let who likes take pride in working out fantastic problems like any common school-boy, there will still remain some sensible women to get dinner and keep house."

" But should women have no mental discipline ?" I queried.

" Mental discipline !" she echoed; " the wise woman of the Proverbs got hers through her needlework and housewifery.    All the ' ologies ' in the world will never make greater women than we have had without them."

" But some women are called out of the shelter of home," I remarked.

" Don't say ' called out,'" answered my sister quickly; " the very duty they owe to home  sometimes *sends* them out.    A woman may do out-of-the-way tasks for very womanly reasons " (a touch of pathos in her voice,— then, with a spark of satire,) " and it 's only foolish men who can't understand that ! "

" Certainly, I am sorry that the phrase ' strong-minded,' in itself a compliment, is now perverted to describe women who bring contempt on their sex," I observed.

"I'm afraid a strong mind won't support a woman very far," returned Ruth; "but if she have a strong heart, I'll trust her wherever duty calls her."

"I really do not think brave women cry out for their rights," I said.

"I should think not," answered my sister, indignantly. "Courage does not exaggerate wrongs: cowardice does. Only weak women wish to be placed in rivalry with men; and when men accordingly treat them as they would other rivals, they cry, 'Shame! shame!' and wonder what has become of the ancient chivalry."

"Well, I must say I think them greatly mistaken when they aspire to rule rather than to serve," I remarked.

Ruth smiled peculiarly: "Christ set the fashion of ruling by service," she answered; "'ICH DIEN,' is a royal motto."

And that set me thinking. Certainly in this present, I defer to my sister, and would do anything to gratify her wishes. I am master of the house and the cash-box, yet I like best to hold my dominion as her viceroy. And why? Because I remember how she has toiled for me; how in the old past she may have sacrificed for my sake far more than I can ever know till all secrets be revealed in heaven. And, oh, when we remember that there all the secrets of holy lives will be made known, we can well understand the perfect love that shall reign among glorified spirits.  But that bright picture has also a terrible reverse.

As I looked at Ruth, cutting her candied peel, it struck me that a self-sacrificing life seems an elixir of true youth.  I wish more women would try it.  I am sure they would find it answer far better than their balms and kalydors.

"I think you would have made an uncommonly good wife, Ruth," I said presently.

"A new discovery, eh, Edward ?"—this very drily.

"Well,—you know,—I used to think that as you were such a clever woman of business, perhaps—"

"So long as men think idiots make the best wives, I hope they'll get them," she retorted.  "It's a pity you didn't try the experiment yourself."

And there was silence till Ruth finished her peels, put aside the red and blue bowl, and folded her hands on her lap.

"Well, my sister, we have had a happy Christmas-day," I said softly.

"Yes," she answered, with a nod ; "we've done with merry ones."

"We've got their memory still," I suggested.

"And don't we remember them well !" she said, eagerly.  "I can forget fifty years in a minute, and fancy that we're again at the little parties in the Clockhouse.  Half the year we expected those parties, and the other half we talked them over.  Boys and girls don't get so much good out of their pleasure now-a-days."

"How few who shared those festivities remain within

our reach!" I sighed. "Did you go to those parties long after I left home, Ruth?"

"Never," she answered.

"Why, how was that?" I asked.

"I had grown an old woman," she said, gazing into the fire.

"What! at eighteen?" I queried.

"Yes, at eighteen," she replied, turning to me with a strange smile.

Would I ask any more questions? No. I would as soon startle a sanctuary by noisy importunities. If my sister chose, I could wait for more perfect knowledge of her till our angels stood side by side in a safer home.

"Do you remember the Carewes?" she inquired presently.

"What, the girl with golden locks, and the boy with a red shock head, who used to play the piano?" I said.

"I suppose you mean the right pair," she answered; "but Richard Carewe's hair was auburn, not red, and his sister's curls were more like tinsel than gold."

"I remember her. Like all the village boys, I thought her very pretty; but, as I recall her beauty now, I think it was meretricious, like half-spoiled false jewellery. She was no favourite of yours, I recollect. What has put her in your head?"

"Simply because I see by her gravestone at St Cross that she was our Mr Herbert's mother," replied Ruth.

"And did you never hear of her marriage?" I asked, "when Upper and Lower Mallowe lie so close together?"

"Laura Carewe's friends were not mine," said Ruth.

" How such a shallow and selfish girl was her brother's sister, I could never understand."

" And what became of Richard ? " I inquired.

" Richard died," said Ruth, quietly; " he died in London on the very day you entered it."

" Dear me ! " I said, somehow awed by my sister's tone.   " He was a sort of genius, was he not ? "

" He was a genius," returned Ruth.   " I have no ear for music—no more than you have, Edward, and you know what that means—but he could make me cry the moment he touched the keys."

" I suppose he went to London to try his fortune," I observed.

" Yes," said Ruth ; " and of course he was unfortunate at first, like everybody else.   And it is not in the purest or pleasantest places that musicians often begin their career.   And there was wild blood in those Carewes.   And Richard got into trouble, and was put into the debtors' prison.   Laura was older than he : they were orphans, and their father had willed that all the little family property should go to purchase an annuity for her.   But she never went near her brother in his cell, only made sentimental suffering for herself out of his misery.   And at last, his creditor was kinder than his sister, and Richard got his liberty ; but only to die on a doorstep, Edward—only to die on a doorstep, in the broad light of the sun ! "

" But his misfortunes came out of his faults, Ruth," I said very gently, for I quite understood the solemn monotony of her voice.

" I know they did," she answered ; " but if God sent
all our faults the misfortunes which they merit, where
should we be ?  And so little might have saved him ! "
And then she added pleasantly : " There seemed a something familiar in Agnes' face the moment I saw her.  " I
can understand it now.  She is Laura Carewe's grand-
daughter, but she has Richard Carewe's eyes."

" Did Laura have other children besides our Mr Herbert and Agnes' father ? " I asked.

" I have only heard of those ; but she may have had
others for aught I know," said Ruth.

And there followed a long, long silence.  This, then,
was my sister's romance.  She would never say so—
never do more than tell the common-place story in
simple words and solemn tones,—perhaps she had never
done so much before.  And yet what a new light it shed
on all her character !  I glanced at her, and it seemed
that I must have been blind not to have seen some such
history written in her face.

" Was Richard buried in London ? " I asked at last.

" Yes," she answered, " and God only knows where !
I humbled myself to inquire of Laura, but she could not
tell—only she said it was some pauper burial-ground, and
she went into hysterics at the idea ! "

My proud, patient sister !  It was a bitter memory of
first love—the fiery, wasted genius in a beggar's grave,
How sadly different from mine—that innocent, holy
girl, laid with reverent affection in the tomb of her
fathers !  And so I am happy in the knowledge that
those who sleep with Jesus reign with Him in glory,

while Ruth takes heart, remembering WHO said to the dying thief, "This day thou shalt be with Me in paradise." Verily God plants some comfort in every soil.

"This has been quite a Christmas talk," exclaimed Ruth, rousing herself, with a dim smile.

"My poor dear sister!" I said, laying my hand upon hers.

She shook it off as if it pained her. "What's the matter with you?" she asked, starting from her seat, her old, erect self. "I daresay you want your supper. I'll go and see after it."

And when she returned, the history had vanished from her face, and the whole conversation seemed like a dream!

# CHAPTER IX.

THEN, clad in snow, the New Year came to Upper Mallowe.

But, however severe the weather, I always fancy when New Year comes, winter goes. I said so to Ruth as we started for a walk one clear, cold morning, towards the end of January.

"Though the fields be white with frost," I remarked, "there is a spring light hanging over them. I used to notice the same thing in the city."

"You had not much light of any sort there," said she.

"Oh, yes, I had," I answered, "whenever the sun shone, one narrow ray slanted across my desk. That had to serve me in place of hills, and meadows, and hedgerows ; and it did its duty very well, for it kept them in my mind."

"Ah, what we miss and long for is not lost in the blankest sense of lost," said Ruth.

L

"No," I answered; "and I will say I have never seen more lovely country than what I saw in visions in that dusty counting-house. And there is a specially solemn grandeur in sunset over the city, if one manage to get a sky-view wider than a few inches."

"Ah, that's all good for the soul," answered my sister; "but nevertheless the body wants the genuine breezes."

"I don't think the poet had true poetry in him when he said—

'God made the country, but man made the town,'"

I observed.

"One might as well say, 'Woman cuts the wood, but the fire boils the kettle,'" she answered.

"I will always stand up for London," I said, gallantly.

"That's honest," remarked Ruth; "you owe your fortune to it."

"It is the epitome of the whole world," I went on enthusiastically. "Some people will not own the analogies to be found in it, because they fear ridicule. For instance, folks laugh if one says that the bridge between the great warehouses in Carter Lane is a good suggestion of Venice."

"Well, you ought to conclude they are laughing at their own folly in not seeing it before," said Ruth.

Our destination was the Refuge. It was quite wonderful what a cheery place it looked. The inhabitants of the High Street should have been vastly obliged to

Alice for the change wrought by her industry and taste. All the tiny diamond window panes sparkled in the pale morning sun, and the ledges beneath, painfully white, were adorned with flourishing firs and laurels in bright red pots. We found Mr M'Callum busy with these plants, and accordingly we lingered to admire their prosperous beauty.

" They 're a' gifts," said he, " a' save ane, whilk root I picket up i' the road ; the ithers are puir things frae the cottages near hand, whaur they were deein' for no being understood. ' Gie them to me,' said I, ' gie them to me, and i' the richt season I 'll gie ye back a bonnie slip, and the plant itsel', gif it live, I 'll sell for the benefit of the Refuge.' An' there wasna ane that said me nay. Sae in the summer, sir, they 'll fetch us a bit siller, and their owners shall hae the slip, and naebody will be a penny the waur, and the Refuge will be sae muckle the richer."

" Do the village people like the Refuge ?" I inquired, for Mr M'Callum had been its agent and collector among many of them.

" The maist o' them do," he answered ; " if they haena kenned the grip of want themselves they ken somebody that has. But there were ane or twa said it was taxin' the industrious to feed the idle. And sae we talkit it over."

"There 's a bit of reason in that doubt," said Ruth, thoughtfully, " and I never could be satisfied with the argument that, anyhow, almsgiving is a blessing to the giver. If we give alms for our own pleasure rather than to do good, it seems to me just a selfish indulgence."

"Na, na, I didna preachify; I sat me down and talkit it over. An' first I asked, 'Did ye never need help yoursel'?' And they fired up, and said they'd never been evened wi' charity; if they wanted a little money, their master wad gie it in advance, or they had a brither in business i' the next toon, and sae forth. 'Saftly, saftly,' I said; 'suppose ye hadna a master, but just trampit the country, doing the hardest bits o' wark, which aye bring the least siller, wadna ye be glad o' a kindly hand that stood ye in stead of the master and the freends ye hadna got? Na, na,' said I, 'dinna set yerselves aboon a' the honest strivin' folk wha stand sae close to poortith's brink that the least joggle sets them over. When ye ask the master for an advance, ye wadna like if he said, "I dinna need to gang a borrowing; why suld you?" Ye'd make answer, "Master, ye're rich, ye dinna need ae pund, ye can get a hunder frae the bank."' And sae I say, 'Freends, ye're well to do; ye dinna ken the want o' a saxpence, because ye ken whaur to find a pund.'"

"And what did they say next?" I queried.

"Some paid down their shilling on that; but ane or twa--and ane I mind weel, for it was Miss Sanders, the dressmaker—stood out a bit langer. Said she, 'I'd gie anything to help a lass that would work, and couldna; ay, Mr M'Callum, and I'd gie what I could to ony puir hizzie who wanted to leave her sin and live honestly, for God only kens what drives 'em to it,—the mair credit to

such as win safely through a'; but,' said she, 'I wouldna
gie a brass farthing to those idle sluts who might work,
but will not. Don't tell me that anyhow they're miserable. Misery that could have been saved is nae recommendation—misery is nae a honest trade. It seems to
me the world's owrerun wi' miserable people, and we that
work are just the slaves to feed and keep them.' And
there was a power of truth in the words as Miss Sanders
spoke them, for, as a' the village knows it, I may tell you
she has a sister wha has just been a quiet curse to the
hail family: a woman wi' no sense of 'sponsibility, wha
seems to think her sister has a right to work for her,
and she to gie nae 'tendance nor comfort in return.
Miss Sanders canna keep baith her and a servant, and
the idle hizzie taks the servant's keep wi'out the wark,
and a' the while gangs aboot the village sae disre-
spectable and shiftless, that there's some fules found to
pity her."

"Whoever pities her should keep her," said Ruth.

"My heart was sair to see Miss Sanders's face," continued the old man, "it had sic a pitifu' overwarked
luik ; but I said, 'Aweel, mem, gif we're to stop every
wark frae which idle loons pick guid they dinna deserve,
we'd gie up everything. Na, na, we maun just do richt
—better bear a cross than be a cross. But dinna ye
say the idle have the best o' this warld, leave alone that
which is to come. What do they get? Naething you'd
want. They may share the siller o' honest folk, but they
havena the respeck. Wha seeks their word? wha cares
for their praise? Will they hae nothing to answer for

before His throne, who was constant at His Father's business? Ah, Miss Sanders,' I said, 'I dinna think there's a many such amang our puir refugees. We've mair of their victims—folk who've been so disheartened strugglin' wi' sic-like that they've thrawn aside everything to get awa'!' And then the tears streamed down her face, and she said, 'I'm thinking a' the evil i' the warld dates frae the idle people?' but she put half-a-crown into my hand."

"Are the two sisters alone?" I asked.

"They are the noo," he answered. "They're folk frae London. They're distant kith o' that unhappy callant, George Roper. I think I've heard that he was brocht up in their father's house. The puir leddy still believes her cousin met his death at Ewen's han', but she aye says she doesna judge folk by their kin; and weel I ken the schule whaur she learned that lesson."

"Miss Sanders shall have my dressmaking," remarked Ruth, in an undertone.

"And so George Wilmot is still with you, Mr M'Callum," I said, as we adjourned from the garden to the house, where Alice eagerly welcomed my sister.

"Ay, sir, and like to stay," returned the old man. "He's a decent laddie, too; and frae sweepin' up the snaw, and sich like, he gaes regular to wark at ane o' the farms. But he canna pay baith his board and lodging too, and sae he still has the empty room, waiting your pleasure, sir."

"He is quite welcome to it," I answered. "Indeed, when the Refuge funds increase, it will be no bad plan

to build two or three small chambers over the great
supper-room, so as to enable us to offer such orphans
a safe home until they become entirely independent.
It strikes me that too little has been done in that way.
What is to become of children like him, who are willing to earn what they can, but cannot possibly earn
enough? Why should they find no guardian but the
jailer?"

"Well, it is wrong," said Ruth; "nobody denies that.
But setting the wrong right is your business as much as
anybody's."

"It would make extra work for Alice," I remarked,
glancing at my late servant.

"It would be all in the day's labour," answered the
girl, smiling; "and perhaps there would be a female
orphan who could help me."

"Alice likes it," put in her grandfather: "she's been
twice as bricht since Geordie came."

"I like to have somebody to look after, you see,
ma'am," said Alice to my sister; "and I like to have
him coming in and out to his meals as Ewen used to
do."

"An' we set him crackin' aboot London," remarked
Mr M'Callum; "but it's little eno' he can tell, puir
laddie; but here he comes to speak for himsel'."

When George Wilmot saw my sister and I, he took
off his cap and gave his head a peculiar wag, intended
as a bow. His appearance was considerably improved,
for though he wore the same clothes in which he arrived at the Refuge, they were now well mended and

clean, and his face, though coarse in feature, was not ill-favoured, and his big, simple blue eyes appealed to one like a baby's.

"Well, George," I said, "how are you? I am glad to hear you are doing so well."

Whereupon he hung his head, and appeared thoroughly ashamed of himself.

"Do you like the country?" I asked—"do you like it better than London?"

He made a reflective pause, and then looked up, and said piteously, "I dunno yet."

"Where did you live in London?" asked Ruth.

"Down by Ratcliff Highway," he replied, "sometimes in one court, and sometimes in another."

"And can't you be sure whether you like this pretty village better than Ratcliff Highway?" I queried.

"I was used to it," he said simply.

"And he had his mother there, sir," said Alice softly, laying her hand on the boy's shoulder, while he moved a little closer to her.

"And you never went to school?" I inquired.

"No, sir, mother teached me to read of nights."

"Did you go to church?" I asked.

"Sometimes, in the evenings," he answered.

"Did you ever see St Paul's?"

"D'ye mean the big church in the square?" he queried.

"Yes—the cathedral."

"I only seed it once to notice—that was in the half-dark, when the stars were out. I'd been kept late at a

ware'us in Shoe Lane, and mother comed and waited for
me in the square, and then she telled me to look at the
church, 'cause it wor St somethin' or 'nother, where the
fine people went o' Sundays."

"Well, at any rate, you know the Thames?" I observed.

"I guess I do," he answered grinning; "that's fine
bathing!"

"I suppose you had plenty of friends to keep you
company in such amusements," said Ruth.

"There were lots o' boys, but I didn't know 'em, 'cept
jest to speak to on the minute," he replied. "Only little
Jem Norris—poor little chap."

"What happened to him?" I asked.

"He went a-bathing and got too far out, and a barge
knocked him on the head," he answered.

"Dear, dear!" said Alice; "weren't you afraid of the
same thing?"

"I took my chance—it's like everything else," he replied philosophically.

"Ay, ay," said Mr M'Callum; "it's little we'd do, if
we did nought by which anither had met his death. To
dee is na evil at a'—but to live fearing death is a sair
thing."

George Wilmot raised his blue eyes to the old man's
face. I wondered how much he really understood of
the patriarch's saintly cheerfulness, or if it only made a
pleasant echo in his soul, like a sweet song in an unknown
tongue.

"Alice," said Ruth, presently, "will you put on your

bonnet, and come with us, to show me Miss Sanders's house ? "

For my sister no sooner sees a way to do good than she does it. She is quick in everything, just as I am slow. But it is never too late to learn. So I took the hint of her example, and made a note in my pocket-book respecting the new orphan-rooms for the Refuge.

George Wilmot ran before us and opened the gate, blushing at his own politeness. As we passed out, I took the opportunity of slipping into his hand a little silver something which left him a very happy boy in- deed. He has no grandfather to give him a tip, and I have no grandson to receive one, so we exactly suit each other.

" Poor lad, his mind sadly wants opening," I remarked, as we walked away with Alice in attendance.

"I don't know, sir," said Alice, in her thoughtful un- obtrusive way. " He 's ignorant of some things, but he knows others better than many wiser people."

"I daresay he could pick up a living where you 'd starve, Edward," suggested Ruth ; " and because that is not an accomplishment taught in schools, who shall say it is inferior thereto ?"

"And he knows how to be patient in cold and hunger," added Alice : "he has gone through dreadful times, and don't think anything of them ! "

" I fear he has just endured like a poor animal, with- out any sense of submission to God's will," I remarked.

" Better endure like an innocent dog, than rebel like

a wicked man," said Ruth. "If we know right without doing it, we're so much the worse,—if we do right without knowing it, perhaps we're so much the better!"

"I am glad you like the boy, Alice," I said, "for it is not everybody who could see anything loveable in him."

"At first I only pitied him for being so left to himself, sir," she rejoined; "and I pitied him the more because he did not know he was pitiful."

"Did he soon make himself at home?" I inquired.

She shook her head. "At first he was very shy," she said, "just like a wild thing who fancies you mean mischief when you offer to feed it; but after a day or two he grew ill, and no wonder, for how he lived on his way from London I can't tell!"

"The God who watches the sparrows can," said Ruth.

"And during that illness, he took to me," Alice went on; "at least, then I took to him, for I was touched by his patience, which made it quite hard to find out what ailed him. I was afraid he was to have a bad fever, but it turned out only cold and weakness, and he was about again when Ewen came home on Christmas-day. And from the very first minute, he wasn't a bit shy with Ewen; wasn't that strange?"

"I daresay you've liked him all the better for that," observed Ruth.

"Your brother must carry a charm against shyness," I remarked, "for you remember I took great liberties with him in our first interview."

Alice laughed gaily.  "I asked George about it after-wards," she said, "and he told me it was because Ewen did not 'scorn' him.  Now I am sure neither grandfather nor I ever did so," she added.

"Nor do we," said Ruth; "but I know some people have a happy gift of setting every one, whether superior or inferior, on a comfortable human equality, and that without any forfeiture of respect or self-respect."

"I believe it is the temperament of genius," I re-marked.

"I think Ewen is a genius, sir," said Alice, proudly, "but he would only be angry if he heard me say so."

"In what way has he shown it?" I inquired.  "I re-member he told me he had a taste for drawing."

"He has sketched half the country-side," she answered, in the trembling voice of suppressed eagerness; "I've got the pictures at home—they're not well finished, but somehow they make me see more in the fields and sky than I ever saw before, sir."

"The true end of art," said Ruth.

"And he brought a little beauty from London," Alice went on; "he'd drawn it in coloured chalks,—an old broken boat lying on a wharf in the moonlight.  And Georgie was so struck with it—for it was like a bit of home to him—that Ewen let him put it up in his bed-room."

"Dear me," I said; "I should not have thought George had eyes for a picture."

Alice laughed again, and Ruth said, "I daresay George

is like many other people—never so stupid as when he tries to put on his best manners."

"Some day, Alice, when you have time, you must bring Ewen's pictures to show us," I observed.

"Thank you, sir," she answered.

In a minute or two she pointed out Miss Sanders's house. It was a small lodge-like place, with a tiny window at either side of the door, which bore a plate announcing the owner's occupation. Then Ruth thanked her, and dismissed her to her duties at the Refuge.

We did not call upon Miss Sanders then, not intending so to do until Ruth took her some work wherewith to make a pleasant introduction. We went home to our early dinner, which we beguiled by chatting over all we had heard and seen during the morning.

"Ruth," I said, "the new orphan rooms shall be added to the Refuge as soon as the weather is mild enough for such operations. When I ask the builder for an estimate of the repairs needed at St Cross, I will also mention this matter to him."

"That is right," she answered. Presently she added, in a clear, brave voice, "Edward, we are old people. Death *may* come suddenly to the young, but it *must* come soon to us. Let us not delay to make some future provision for the good works we are trying to do, and let us seriously reflect what will be the wisest conditions whereby to retain such provision for the objects we intend."

There was a solemn silence. Then I said, "I shall

certainly provide that these orphan-rooms be maintained expressly for orphans who are too old to enter any school, yet not old enough to stand quite alone in the world.    There is not a more forlorn class, as I said this morning "——

"And you need not say it again," she interrupted; "but just write it down on paper, and get a lawyer to witness it."

# CHAPTER X.

## A MODERN MARTYR.

ITHIN a fortnight after our visit to the Refuge, Ruth found some dressmaking to take to Miss Sanders. I wished her to go on this feminine expedition alone, but she persisted in requiring my company. We meant to go in the morning, but something prevented our departure till the afternoon.

We soon found the place which Alice had pointed out to us, and we went up to the door and knocked. Ruth always gives a good hearty knock, and in this case it seemed to shake the whole building. It was a poor shallow little sham of a house,—alas, if it were a type of the home !

Our rap was not quickly answered. I fancied I heard sounds of shouting and scuffling within. But presently the door was opened by a neat, pretty-looking faded woman, with a painfully flushed face, who indicated the way to the parlour, rather than invited us to enter. No sooner were we seated, than we heard sounds of unchecked sobs and groans proceeding from the inner apartment. Our hostess suddenly turned from us and leaned on the mantelpiece, but as suddenly recovered herself, and with a dim smile inquired our business.

"But, surely, some one is ill," I remarked; "do not let us keep you from them; we can wait."

"Nobody is ill, sir," she answered, with a firmness almost severe. "There is no need that I should detain you."

I noticed that during these remarks the sounds ceased, though they were redoubled while Ruth unfolded her materials, and issued instructions. Miss Sanders went through her part bravely, only in her face there was a little deepening of pain-lines already deep enough.

"Is that unfortunate person a lunatic?" Ruth inquired at last, in that kind of whisper which is awfully audible.

Miss Sanders threw up her hands with a disclaiming gesture, and then spread out her fashion-book.

"Yes, I'm mad,—I'm driven mad!" screamed a voice from the other room; "but there's One above knows,—He knows all the sufferings of those who never complain!"

"What is it, my dear lady?" I inquired of the trembling woman before us. "You must have heard of us in the village. Will you put no trust in us?"

Her lips quivered a little, and she wrung her thin fingers. "You know I have not said a word, sir," she exclaimed. "I wished to keep it all to ourselves. God save me from my sister!" and she burst into tears.

The door between the rooms opened, and a woman entered. I recognised her as a worshipper at St Cross's, and I concluded we saw Anne Sanders. She was a dark, sallow woman, with a bony face,—one of those countenances which seem to betray a heart too hard to be easily worn out. Though it was nearly five o'clock, she wore a dirty ragged morning gown. She rushed to her sister, and seized her arm. "What have I done? what have I done?" she shrieked frantically. "Ah, Bessie, it drives me mad to find you thus set against me. It so cuts into my heart that I am sure my last dying word will be your name!"

"The dying often remember those whom they have cruelly injured," said Ruth, quietly.

Anne Sanders dropped in a heap upon the floor, emitting incoherent ejaculations. Bessie stood aside, silent and agitated. She suffered under the degradation in which the other evidently gloried. Presently, finding herself unnoticed, Anne again sprang up and attacked her sister. "What have I done? what have I done?— tell me—tell them!" she screamed.

"If God and your own conscience do not answer, how can I?" said Bessie. "And if you don't respect yourself, or me, at least respect the presence of strangers."

"No, no," she cried. "I will not be silent,—I want justice,— I appeal for justice to God,—the Father of the helpless orphan!"

"Orphanhood is not very touching at forty," said Ruth,

M

drily. "By your own account, Miss Anne Sanders, you are an ill-used woman. Then why don't you leave your sister ?—the world is all before you."

"Oh, I wish she would," moaned Bessie.

"Where am I to go? What am I to do?" said Anne. "Nobody wants me. I'm not fit for anything."

"Then as you are useless, why should your sister be taxed with you, since there is no love between you?" questioned Ruth.

"Why should there be no love between us?" groaned Anne. "Whatever I've done—I don't know what it is —but whatever I've done, oughtn't she to forgive "——

"Oh, Anne, Anne," sighed Bessie ; "haven't I forgiven? But you won't change, and you won't go away, and you stay in the house, and make me wicked—and it is so hard to forgive that !"

"You've got nothing to forgive," screamed Anne, changing her tactics. "I work as hard as you, for all I don't earn anything. Don't I drudge about at the hard, nasty housework, while you sit in the parlour and make your dresses and get money?"

"Depend upon it, Miss Bessie will be very glad if you will do the same," remarked Ruth.

"But every one can't do the same thing," insisted Anne ; "there's different work for different people, and there's some doomed to be drudges all their days. Oh—oh—oh !"

"No work is drudgery except to an unwilling worker," said Ruth, promptly ; "and, therefore, I would not keep a drudge about me for any consideration; and it is very hard that your sister should be compelled so to do."

"What began the—ahem—the difference this afternoon?" I asked.

"I was angry—very angry—with Anne, because, although it was late, she was too dirty to answer the door if any one came," explained Bessie.

"And she called me an idle slut," sobbed Anne.

"So I did," said Bessie, wearily. "God forgive me! but at times I am so tried, I scarcely know what I say, and that's why I wish she would go away."

"No epithet stings like a true one!" observed Ruth.

"She can say nothing against me except these little trifles," said Anne, passionately. "Yesterday there was a fuss because her candles weren't ready to a minute."

"She knew I was so busy," sighed Bessie; "and I didn't ask for them till I couldn't see to thread my needles. And it's always the same."

"She might have put them up herself," shouted Anne. "It would have wasted no more time than scolding me."

"But you remember—there is different work for different people," repeated Ruth; "and the world would run into fine confusion if each left his own line of duty to take up another's."

"Every one takes part against me," said Anne, again dropping on the floor. "I've never had a friend all my life."

"Not a nice confession," remarked Ruth.

" But I hope I shall soon be taken away," she moaned, "and then I shan't be a nuisance to any one, or a burden to myself. I can find comfort in that. There's hope for me in my religion. I've kept hold of my religion through all. I've never given up my church, though no one will go with me, and I've found peace there, and so "——

"Silence, Anne," said Bessie, springing up and speaking with terrible fervour. " Your profession of religion has made religion a scoff and a byword to those who knew your useless, selfish life. Who said that if pious people were like you, he would rather try the bad ones? Who was first weaned from going to church, because he was shamed and angered by your slovenly clothes and repellent manners? Is that the religion which enjoins whatever is lovely and of good report? The blood of George Roper, body and soul, rests upon your head ! "

There was an awful solemnity in her sister's sudden outburst, which cowed the miserable woman sitting on the floor. But presently she spoke again, in a whining tone :

" I'm blamed for being idle and useless, I'm treated like a blank, and yet I'm accused of having power to do evil. How can I do harm if I'm a blank? "

" Now that puts me out of all patience ! " said Ruth, quite warmly ; " how can one argue with a person who asks such a question? Does not one dumb note spoil a tune, and one dead flower poison a nosegay? Is not every child taught that idle hands are Satan's instruments to work out his wicked will? "

" Every one is against me," wailed Anne Sanders again, finding no answer to parry these home-thrusts. " Nobody takes my part. I am forlorn and forsaken here ; but at least I can remember WHO said, ' Blessed are they which are persecuted ; for theirs is the kingdom of heaven.' "

" Don't pervert Scripture," said my sister—" ' Blessed are they which are persecuted *for righteousness' sake,*'— not blessed are they who are called to account and chidden for their own wrong-doing."

And then Anne Sanders sprang up, saying incoherently that she should go to her own room, and pour out her heart where she had never failed to find comfort. And so she rushed away, leaving Ruth and me, and Bessie Sanders, blankly gazing at each other.

" I am so sorry," said the latter gently. " You should never have known this, if I could have helped it. It has happened that you should learn more in an hour than other neighbours among whom we have lived for years."

" Depend upon it, all has happened for the best," remarked Ruth.

" I am so afraid that I am in the wrong," continued Miss Sanders, as if she feared she might gain more sympathy than she deserved. " I had such a dear good sister once, that perhaps I expect too much from Anne. And I am very sharp tempered."

" So are all overworked people," rejoined Ruth ; " of course they shouldn't be, but they can't help it, that's all."

" But the worst is that I can't love Anne," said Miss Bessie, sadly ; "and when I remember that we should love our enemies, and forgive them as we look to be forgiven, then a great cloud of despair comes over me."

" Nonsense," exclaimed Ruth ; " what do you call forgiveness ?   Fine talk and selfish actions ?   If it be not forgiveness to give another house-room and maintenance, while she neglects and torments you, what is forgiveness, I wonder ! "

Miss Bessie smiled dimly, as though she gathered a little comfort from this healthy and unsentimental view of the matter.   " From her earliest childhood, Anne always thought herself an injured being," she said.

" Then her best blessing would have been real misery," returned Ruth ; " it would have taught her to know the genuine article."

" Oh, ma'am, she may be more really unhappy than you think," said Bessie, earnestly.   " You cannot judge from this afternoon.   I fear I am too fidgety."

" I saw her dirty, ragged gown," remarked Ruth, grimly ; " a disgrace to a common lodging-house servant. Besides, she is confident she is a martyr, and you abase yourself as a sinner.   That throws a great light on the matter ! "

" So you had another sister once, Miss Sanders ?" I questioned, anxious to soften that poor pained face with sweeter recollections.

" Yes, a dear little sister, years younger than Anne,". said Miss Bessie, going to the mantelpiece and taking therefrom a little miniature in an ebony case.   " That is all I have of Katie. The picture is pretty, but not half like her, she was so sweet! And she was something like her poor cousin George—the portrait reminds me of both. If things had gone right, I think those two would have married. How different it would have been !"

" But George went wrong?" I queried.

" Yes, George went wrong," answered Miss Bessie ; " and that is the misery of it ! When he was a lad of seventeen or eighteen, we all lived together in London, and mother and I carried on the business, and the house-keeping was left to Anne. George found everything un-pleasing and unpunctual, and when he grew cross, Anne talked piously to him," (Ruth groaned,) " and of course that made matters much worse. Then he did not like going to church with her, because she never would get her winter clothes ready till after Christmas, nor her summer ones till the dog-days, and when his fellow-clerks met him with her it vexed him, and she was stiff and snappy to them besides. So he dropped going to church, and went about instead, and made friends that didn't go either, and bad habits grew where the good ones had fallen off, and mother, who was a rigid woman in her way—rigid people never punish the right ones—forbade him our house, and then he went to the bad altogether. And Katie was never herself after, and she died when she was one-and-twenty."

" But have I not heard that Mr Roper was one of your household at the time he met his death?" I asked.

" Yes," she answered. " When mother died, some

time after Katie, George heard of her death, and came
to the funeral.  He seemed very miserable ; so, when I
sold our London business and bought a smaller one here,
I got him to come with us, just for Katie's sake.  I had
more time then than before, and I managed to keep Anne
out of his way.  He got a situation in Mallowe, but he
never settled in this house, only came here now and then,
though I think he called it his home.  He kept his lively,
kindly manners to the last, and that was all, for he made
many parents rue the day when we came to the village.
He was coming to see me that summer afternoon when
—you know, sir ? "

"When his mysterious death brought a blight on young
Ewen M'Callum," I said.

Miss Sanders would make no further remark upon
that subject.  So I took up the little ebony-framed portrait, and tried to fancy what this cousin George had
been.  The pictured face was soft and girlish—a boy re-
sembling it must have had a touching look of frank innocence.  And yet it had ended in a debasing life, spread-
ing pollution round it, and closed by a shameful death,
only to be named in whispers.  Oh, what wonderful
strength and wisdom and love must dwell in Him who
has patience with a world where such things happen !

"And is this struggle between you and your sister to
go on for ever ? " queried Ruth presently.

"I suppose so," answered Miss Sanders, hopelessly.

"I could not endure it," said Ruth with animation.

"I must," replied the other.  And as the shadows of

twilight settled in the little room, the faded, lined countenance shone out of their gloom, a heroic, enduring face,
strong enough for aught which life might make its duty.
No demonstrative woman was this; she might have come
and gone about her work for years, and yet have made
no sign. She had evidently only spoken so freely to Mr
M'Callum, because she deemed her secret safer than it
really was, and did not think her words could be understood as the involuntary cry of her own pain. Surely
all her life would not be lived out in the chilling shadow
of this unreasonable and worthless relative ! But should
relief come—ay, to-morrow—it could not undo the
past; there were scars on her soul which could never
be healed on earth. Perhaps such scars shine as
honours in heaven !

We said no more about her shivered·household happiness, and after a little ordinary conversation, we left her.
She came with us to the garden-gate, and stood there till
we were nearly out of sight. Then she went back into
the house, and we heard the door close behind her. Are
there no torment chambers not underground ? There
was a fearful torture common in old times, when a putrid
body was fastened to a living man. What would it be
to drag through life with such a burden ? But is it better
to be linked with a diseased soul ?

"Now, Ruth," I said, as we walked along, "suppose
a man married a woman like Anne Sanders, what is he
to do with her ?"

"He need not marry such a one," she answered, "unless he feels that he cannot get any one better !"

" But suppose he married her under a mistake," I pleaded.

" When one makes a bargain which turns out badly, one has to abide by it," she said.

" But what comfort in life could he have ?" I asked.

" Nobody's fault but his own," said my sister.

" But don't you think this stolid irresponsibility in the woman may explain some of our wretched wife-beating cases ?" I queried.

" Probably it may," said Ruth. "When a man marries a brainless animal, he is likely to degenerate into a wild beast. Men are generally good or bad according to the women with whom they associate."

Oh my terrible sister !

" But is it not strange," I began presently, taking another subject, " that there are people in the world so ignorant as not to understand that a religious profession, unsupported by practice, is worse than nothing ? Anne Sanders consoles herself by the very principles and precepts in which she should see her own condemnation. I wonder how she reads the last chapter of Proverbs ! "

"She has her own version of it," said Ruth. "Do you suppose the Bible sounds the same to every one ?"

" Certainly not," I answered ; " but the variety ought to be, that it should seem to each full of special warnings against his own besetting sin."

" That is how it should be," replied my sister ; " but this is how it is : the lessons we most need stand as blanks in our Bibles, till God opens our eyes to see them

—just a little. The greatest saint does not know God's word as he will know it hereafter."

"I suppose Anne Sanders heard Mr Marten's sermon when the Refuge was opened," I remarked.

"Of course she did," said Ruth, "and depend upon it she sat and glorified herself that she was not as other people."

"Do you really think she would not apply a single word to herself?" I queried.

"Certainly she wouldn't," answered my sister; "she would apply it to Bessie instead."

"But if such truths were repeated to her individually, don't you think she would see their application to her own case?" I inquired.

"She would then see that *you* meant to apply them to her," replied Ruth, "and she would take it as a proof of your malice and envy."

"Then what means can be taken to convince such people of their error and danger?" I exclaimed.

"I don't know," said Ruth, "but I believe the grace of God is much nearer to the double-dyed murderer on the scaffold than to the respectable self-deceived hypocrite."

"But we must not be uncharitable in our thoughts of any, Ruth," I suggested.

"I daresay some worthy souls in Jerusalem thought Christ himself uncharitable when He called the Pharisees vipers, serpents, and whited sepulchres," answered Ruth. "Remember, He had counsel for the fallen woman, and pardon for the dying thief, yet nothing but anger for those whose lives He summed up in the awful words,—'Ye shut up the kingdom of heaven against men : for ye neither go in yourselves, neither suffer ye them that are entering to go in.'"

"Yet these people form part of the world for which He died," I said.

"So they do," she responded, heartily, "and therefore we must leave them in His hands.  Otherwise I should sometimes be inclined to think the bees set us a good example when they kill off their drones once a year."

"But all Pharisees and hypocrites are not drones," I ventured to hint.

"Not with their tongues," said Ruth, significantly. "'Whatsoever they bid you observe and do, that observe and do: but do ye not after their works; for they say, and do not.'  Such people are like a copy of the Scriptures, on whose margin an infidel has drawn unclean and blasphemous pictures, which pervert the holy words and pollute the reader's mind."

So we both returned home, and found our fire brightly stirred and reflected in our shining teapot, while Phillis stood in cheerful active attendance.  But all the evening, as I basked in the blessings God gave me, I wondered what would have become of me had my sister, Ruth Garrett, been such a one as Anne Sanders ; and as I contrasted myself with Miss Bessie toiling in her neglected home, I hoped that God does somehow make up for those strange differences in lot which no human wisdom can understand or prevent.

# CHAPTER XI.

RUTH kept up our acquaintance with Miss Bessie Sanders. I noticed that my sister required a great deal of work done in our own house, which took the quiet dressmaker out of her miserable, haunted abode. And in the course of a few weeks the silent woman appeared to take heart. Her reserved nature had never sought sympathy, but when it came, she found it good. Ruth's sympathy was of that sensible sort which proud people like. Anne was never named. Only Bessie was constantly treated with tenderness and respect by every member of our household.

And so spring brightened round our home, and with the crocuses and snowdrops, certain strange gentlemen came to Upper Mallowe, and hovered about St Cross, and roused the curiosity of the village by their note-books and measuring rods. Rumours began to fly about that the church would soon be closed for repairs : and in due time Mr Marten announced from the communion rails that donations for that purpose would be thankfully received by himself or by Mr Edward Garrett.

In the course of the following week we were startled by a visit from Mr Herbert and Agnes.  It was the farmer's first appearance in our house, and he had never been formally introduced to Ruth, though he and she had exchanged greetings when the two households met on the way to worship.  He was not at all a visiting man.  He was quite at ease among the bluff, feudal hospitalities of his great farm, with its honest oak floors and substantial furniture, which did not tremble beneath his huge weight and unceremonious movements, but he had a respectful deference for his neighbour's carpets and chairs, which caused him to sit painfully and to tread gingerly in any house but his own.  Agnes excused the long time between her visits, by the plea of severe colds and general ill-health, and I noticed that, though the weather was unusually bright and warm for the season, she still wore a long fur-trimmed mantle and a woollen veil, and held her wraps about her like one who feels chilly.  She looked very fragile and shadowy—reminding me of some early flowers in our garden, which blossomed on a prematurely sunny day, and then shivered and shrank in the pitiless rains which followed.  Yet she talked more than before, the aim of her words being to lead the conversation to such subjects as her uncle would like to take up.  Her whole manner towards him was particularly attentive and dutiful—something like the over-anxious service of a truly loyal subject, who yet has involuntary doubts about the perfect wisdom of some of his sovereign's ways. Yet this very deference seemed to perplex and trouble Mr Herbert.

"The object of my visit," the worthy farmer presently explained, (he could not understand a visit without one,) "is to pay in my subscription for the church repairs. I can't do more at present, but I may before it's all over." So saying he put a folded note upon the table. I expected it would be for five pounds, or perhaps ten; but even my sanguine nature was agreeably startled to find it was for fifty.

" But really, Mr Herbert," I said, " when you intended such liberality as this, you should have taken it to the rector himself."

Our guest laughed and shook his head. " I honour the rector, sir," he answered; " though it do come rather hard when one's 'pastors and masters' are twenty years younger than one's-self. I like the rector in the pulpit, and, as he is the rector, I would rather not differ from him out of it, and so I don't go near him, sir."

" But why should you like Mr Marten in the pulpit, and yet differ from him out of it, sir?" asked Ruth.

Mr Herbert laughed his hearty, rollicking laugh, and again shook his head with the knowing air of a man who can explain more than he chooses. " Mr Marten is pastor at St Cross," he said, " and I am master at the Great Farm, and we've each a right to do as we please with our own, and we are best not to interfere with each other. I don't reckon he has done justice to St Cross—·

till lately; and he don't reckon I act fairly with my concerns. Neither of us has ever given our opinion straight out, but I guess we each know what the other thinks. And so I keep out of his way."

"I believe Mr Marten is a truly excellent man, and always anxious to do his duty as his conscience tells him," I remarked.

"According to my mind, that's dangerous doctrine, sir," replied Mr Herbert. "Is not our conscience too likely to bid us do just what we wish?"

"I don't think so," I answered; "I think we can generally distinguish between our conscience and our will."

"I think it's best to put all that on one side," said the farmer, "and just take a sound standard of duty, and resolutely stretch ourselves up to it, even if we crack our hearts in the process."

"But by your rule, how are we to select a sound standard?" I queried. "May not our wills engage in the choice, and the harsh man indulge himself in the belief he aims at justice, and the mild man forget justice in the imaginary pursuit of mercy?"

"Oh, my ideas don't take such high flights as that," rejoined Mr Herbert; "I just follow up two or three good old precepts, that keep the world in the right place, and have no twistings and turnings."

"But everything must turn out of its way sometimes, or else crush something beneath it," said Ruth.

"Yes, indeed!" exclaimed Agnes.

Her uncle turned and glanced at her. The niece rose

from her chair, and picked up his gloves, which had fallen to the floor. It seemed as if the animated ejaculation must have come from somebody else, she appeared so utterly submissive. When an over-hasty driver hears a child's cry from beneath his chariot-wheels, how does he look? Like Mr Herbert looked then, I fancy.

After a little desultory conversation, our visitors rose to go, and then, availing ourselves of her uncle's presence, we claimed Agnes's company for the day. Mr Herbert immediately granted the petition, and the girl yielded as if she had no voice in the matter. Yet there was no scornful apathy about Agnes Herbert. One felt no repulsion—only pity. I have heard that some, who have passed through terrible physical ordeals, have henceforth found the world somewhat like a padded and darkened room, wherein all sounds were muffled and all sights misty. Would you be angry if you had to speak twice before such a one heeded you? I don't think so.

When her uncle was gone, and her bonnet and mantle put aside, Agnes returned to the parlour, and professed interest in some plain woollen knitting with which Ruth was busy. "Such nice work, for it can be done quite mechanically," she said.

"Nice work for an old woman whose eyes are not as good as they were," rejoined my sister, "but rather dull work for a young lady, who should have pretty patterns and plans of her own."

"Ah, yes; but I lose myself in a pattern," said Agnes, smiling.

"But practice makes perfect, my dear," observed Ruth.

N

"I have had plenty of practice," replied Miss Herbert. "See! I did that in London,"—and she displayed a tiny pocket-handkerchief with an elaborate embroidered device in one corner.

My sister admired it exceedingly, and inquired if she had worked any more.

"Oh yes," she answered, "I did a great many, but I have only that one."

"Have you worn them out?" asked Ruth, surprised. "Surely you don't use such things for everyday wear?"

"No," replied Miss Herbert, "but I only kept this one, and I seldom use it."

"Why don't you embroider some more?" inquired my sister.

She shook her head. "I could not do it now," she answered, a little sadly. "I should only spoil the muslin."

"Did you leave all your talents in London, Miss Herbert?" I asked.

She laughed. "Perhaps I did, sir," she said.

"Do you remember your mother, my dear?" queried Ruth presently.

"No," she answered; "and there is no portrait of her. And yet I fancy I know what she was like,"—this very softly.

"As your name is the same as your uncle's, I presume you are his niece by your father's side?" remarked my sister.

"Yes," replied Agnes; adding presently, "but my father was not at all like my uncle. Not like him in any way. I have heard he resembled my grandmother's brother, Richard Carewe."

"Family likenesses often descend in that cross fashion," I observed.

" And family characters too," said Agnes, with a shoot of that animation which occasionally illuminated her languor.

"We knew something of the Carewes, when we were young," said Ruth, " and I hope your father did not resemble your great-uncle in his fate?"

" Not exactly. But he was never what the world calls respectable or good," answered Agnes, with a hard, satiric touch in her voice.

"What does his daughter say?" asked Ruth, gently.

" That he was an angel in a strange disguise," she said fervently; adding sorrowfully, " but that is only my opinion, and, of course, I loved him."

" Depend upon it, my dear," said Ruth, " the opinion of those who love, is most like God's verdict."

Agnes looked up with great pathetic eyes. " My poor father often laughed about religious people," she said, " but he would have liked you."

" Would he?" queried my sister, with just a little quaver in her cheerful voice.

" Yes," said Agnes, quietly, " he fancied religious people were selfish, and narrow, and even cruel; those whom he had known were so, you see."

" Then it was not religion he laughed at, but only its counterfeit," rejoined Ruth ; " still, that was wrong, for it should have given him pain rather than amusement."

"It gave him pain enough," answered Agnes, "bitter pain! But it was always his way to laugh when he suffered. Oh, now, surely he knows all about it, and suffers no more!"

"God loves him far better than you can, little one," said my sister. "God knows everything, and takes all circumstances into consideration. Circumstances don't make a man good or bad, but they try him, and God knows exactly the severity of the trial, and that those who seem much better than he, might have been far worse had they lived the same life."

There followed a silence, which, at last, I broke by asking where Miss Herbert had lived when in London.

"Oh, in many places," she replied, with a little hesitation; "we lived in any neighbourhood which suited my father for the time being—in Bloomsbury while he went to the British Museum Reading Room, once on Tower Hill, often in Soho."

"And you were the housekeeper?" queried Ruth.

"Yes, but there is not much housekeeping needed for two people in lodgings," Agnes answered, laughing.

"How did you amuse yourself?" I asked.

"Oh, I had plenty to do," she replied, bending over Ruth's knitting—"my embroidery and a little drawing, and so forth. Sometimes I could help papa with his manuscripts."

"For what did your father write?" I asked.

Agnes coloured, and explained rapidly. "My poor father was unfortunate from the beginning. You see, his family disowned him, because he refused to be a clergyman ; it being a custom with the Herberts that the eldest son should be bred for the farm, and the second for the church. Therefore, when he went to London, he was so badly off, he was glad to work for any one who would employ him. He often used to say he got into a bad style of literature ; and what was worse, he made a name in that style, and that cost him all chances of advancement." And after this apologetic preamble, she added, humbly, "He wrote long stories for the common penny papers. I daresay you scarcely know what I mean, for such journals only go into kitchens."

"None the worse, for that matter," said Ruth, promptly. "I 've seen thirty-shilling novels that should only go into kitchen fires."

" No, I don't think my father cared for that alone." continued Agnes thoughtfully; "only he had to write in a particular way for these papers—to cram each story with twenty hair-breadth adventures, to make his people talk as real people never do, and each like—I scarcely know how to express myself—but every char_acter like one great capital letter, instead of a long word made up of many vowels and consonants, each modifying the other."

" All the devils very black, and all the angels very bright !" said Ruth.

" Yes, exactly so," rejoined Agnes, accepting my sister's shrewd definition. " How often he used to say that if he had known the end from the beginning, he would rather have swept a crossing than have rushed into literature merely to earn a piece of bread!"

"And was he never able to break these miserable trammels?" I inquired.

"Never—until—until just before his death," she answered, with a breaking voice : "and then a beautiful little simple tale of his came out in a first-class magazine. The number containing it was brought to him the day he died : and he read his own story, word for word, and smiled as if it pleased him." And here she broke down, very quietly.

"Did he say anything?" Ruth asked, presently.

"He put the magazine into my hands," she replied, raising her tearful face, "and he said, ' Agnes, that is the only legacy I can leave you. I wish I had gone to church with you now, my girl. If I have strength next Sunday, I will go.' But two hours after, he was dead."

We scarcely spoke again, until Phillis brought in our dinner. The afternoon passed in our usual sleepy, old-folks' way, but when tea and lamp-light banished our drowsiness, we found that in the meantime Agnes had made considerable progress with Ruth's knitting.

When Phillis came to remove our tea equipage she announced that Alice M'Callum was in the kitchen. " If you are not particularly engaged, sir, she has a message from her brother in London," said Phillis.

" Bring her in," directed my sister ; "and I hope she has brought the drawings which she promised to show us."

Alice came immediately; her pale face freshened by the healthy March breezes. In one hand she held a folded envelope, and in the other, a small, worn portfolio. Miss Herbert had resumed Ruth's knitting, but she looked up and smiled and nodded as our ex-servant entered.

Alice had brought good news. A little kindness is a very good investment when it secures us the first edition of all pleasant tidings concerning those we have aided. She had brought a sovereign from Ewen as his subscription towards the St Cross repairs, and she confided to us the history of this sovereign. Ewen had sold six little sketches at some picture shop in London, and the piece of gold was his payment.

"And I hope there are more in that portfolio," said Ruth, "for I want to see some. Take off your bonnet and shawl, child, or you will not feel their benefit when you go out again into the cool night air."

So Alice carried her wrappers to the sofa, and then returned to the table in her dark, tight dress, with its prim linen collar and cuffs. Agnes Herbert left her seat, and helped her to untie the knotted strings of her portfolio. When it was opened, she withdrew a little, that Ruth might have the best view.

The first which Alice displayed was the drawing which her brother had given to George Wilmot, a ruined boat on a moonlit wharf. It was a simple affair, the paper and other materials employed being of the very cheapest description. And yet there was something in the sketch which many a gilt-framed picture lacks. It made me think of the lives which at first gladden happy nouseholds, and yet end in corruption and misery on the seething shores of the river Thames. It was, somehow, like a prayer for such. I wonder if that was in Ewen's mind when he drew it. Very likely not. If the soul of an artist or a poet be once enlisted in God's service, I believe his brush or his pen becomes the unconscious mouthpiece of God's oracle. Over that picture Ruth lingered a long while.

The next was quite a different scene. A sunny, sloping meadow, with a river winding in the distance, one or two sleepy sheep in the foreground, and a single bird in the blue English sky. I knew the scene. It was the great field where I had first spoken to Ewen M'Callum.

"Oh I remember that!" exclaimed Agnes, startled.

Alice looked up, surprised.

"Have you seen it before?" asked Ruth.

"Yes," she answered, turning to Alice and adding, half-aside, "we chanced to come upon your brother whilst he was drawing it, and I remember it well, because afterwards we took the same subject."

Who were "we?" I wondered. But Alice only smiled, and seemed quite satisfied with the explanation, and passed on to another picture.

There were one or two other sketches of local scenery, all very beautiful. Then Alice produced two more drawings, the only ones which were mounted on cardboard. "These are a pair," said she, "and they are only in my charge. The others Ewen gave me, but these he asked me to keep for him. He did them in London, and brought them home on Christmas day.   I think he took the subject from some verses which he has copied on the back."

I took one, and Ruth took the other.   Mine represented a poorly furnished chamber, whose single ornament was an unframed portrait on the wall.   Before it sat a young man with a book on his knee, from which he seemed to have just looked up.   There were traces of laborious work about the figure, which showed our artist was a novice in this line.   Behind the drawing I found this verse, written in a close, dark characteristic hand :—

> " For like an angel's had her face
>     To his eyes always seem'd :
> On waking and on sleeping dreams
>     Her beauty ever beam'd :
> And the poor orphan boy, alas !
>     Was happiest when he dream'd ! "

Turning to the picture Ruth had taken, I found it represented a church porch.   The door was ajar, and one could see white dresses and gay flowers within.   Leaving the porch was a man, about seven years older than the hero of the other scene—and Ewen had evidently striven to preserve the character of the countenance, through the change from early youth to maturity.   The verses attached were as follows :—

> " He saunter'd up the rough-hewn steps,
>     The doors were open wide,
> And there,—before the altar old,
>     At her brave father's side,

With some one on her other hand,—
Stood Lady May, a bride !

.     .     .     .     .

" Ah, why ! ah, why ? that question came
To Fulke, without reply,
As he gazed on the village homes,
The blue, out-reaching sky,
The ancient church, the old red house,
And left them with a sigh."

As I read these quotations aloud, Agnes whispered to my sister, who responded, " Are they really, my dear ? " then addressing me, " Edward, Miss Herbert says those verses are taken from a poem which her father wrote in his last story."

"Oh, how strange ! " said Alice, smiling with pleased surprise ; "I wonder if Ewen knew it ! He never told me."

" What do you think of these two pictures, brother ? " queried Ruth.

"I am a bad art-critic," I replied. " They are very pretty, but, to my mind, scarcely as pleasing as the land-scapes."

" Their execution is not as good just because the aim is higher," said Agnes Herbert, eagerly. "I think Mr M'Callum's skill is scarcely equal to his ambition—as yet. But these are the best in the portfolio. Look at the two different expressions modifying the same fea-tures ! "

" I believe Ewen has taken his own reflection in the glass for his model," observed Ruth. " The face and the whole figure remind me of him."

"George Wilmot insists on the likeness," rejoined Alice, "but I can't see it, ma'am,"—pondering over the drawing,—"or, at least, a very little. Ewen is much better looking."

"Your brother is certainly a genius, Alice," I remarked.

"I always thought so, sir," she answered, very quietly indeed.

"Now, speaking confidentially, Alice," I said, "do you think Ewen would prefer some artistic occupation to his present office-work? Do you think it is a drudgery to him?"

"Oh no, sir," she replied, quite frankly; "I am sure he is happy. Indeed, I believe he greatly prefers things as they are. At Christmas I heard grandfather and him talk about something of the kind, and Ewen said the best life for a genius was one which kept him at a fair balance with everyday life. Those were his own words, sir. And he was not speaking of himself."

"I am sure he is right," said Agnes, warmly.

"Yes, truly," I responded, "a genius, to be above his fellows, must be a good, common-place man, and something besides. Is he higher than others for having what they have not, if he lack something which they have?"

"Ah!" said Ruth, "I never blame the good old woman who boxed King Alfred's ears because he let the cakes burn, while he pondered over his miserable country. Served him right!"

"But you would not have had him forget his country for the cakes," pleaded Agnes, gently.

"No; he might have watched them and thought of it while he did so. 'Twould have been good exercise for his eyes and his mind. And I daresay the dame's punishment did him good, and he was the better king for it afterwards," said my sister.

"But she need not have been so rough," Agnes remonstrated.

"That was the manner of the time," Ruth retorted; "if she had been a cruel woman she would not have given him any more cakes, and there would have been an end of King Alfred!"

"Ah, that is it," said the other. "I was sure you wouldn't think it right to spoil another's whole life for one instance of folly."

At this juncture, Phillis put in her head and announced, "Mrs Irons has come to fetch Miss Herbert."

"Perhaps you will like to come with us, Alice," said Agnes, as she assisted her in putting the pictures into the portfolio. "Then you will have the benefit of Mrs Irons' protection as far as the Farm—the loneliest part of your journey."

"Thank you, ma'am," answered Alice, "I shall be very glad, though I am not at all afraid."

"Neither am I," said Agnes; "but we may as well save our courage till we need it."

"Now, I hope you have enjoyed yourself sufficiently well to come again very soon," said I, shaking hands with Miss Herbert.

Miss Herbert penitently gave a suitable promise.

"And give our kindest regards to your grandfather,"

said Ruth, bidding good-bye to Alice; "and when you write to Ewen, tell him we wonder why we have no letter from him, and we suppose he has found so many friends in London that he has quite forgotten everybody at Upper Mallowe, except his own family."

Alice laughed gaily. "Ewen has not," she said. "Ewen never will. But he fears to be troublesome, ma'am."

"Then just tell him my opinion," retorted Ruth, "and then, I think, though he is Scotch—by descent—he can scarcely have sufficient obstinacy and pride to persist any longer in his own way."

Alice laughed again, and promised to deliver the message *exactly*, with an emphasis on the word. She perfectly understood my sister. Then they went off. And presently, as they crossed the garden, we heard their clear voices mingling with the harsher metallic tones of the severe upper servant of the Great Farm.

"Those two girls nearly realise the quaint old fictions wherein the maid was as much a gentlewoman as the mistress," I remarked.

"Is that such a wonder?" asked Ruth.

"Is it a common case?" I questioned, in return.

"No, but it should be," she replied: "and it would be, if masters and mistresses had a right idea of service."

"What do you think the right idea?" I asked.

"That man's whole duty to man is service," she answered, "and that, therefore, everybody is somebody's servant, and that he stands highest who best serves the greatest number."

"That lad Ewen is evidently a clever fellow," I observed presently.

"Yes, indeed, poor boy!" said Ruth.

And then we sat in silence, and I pondered over the pictures I had seen, and the talk we had held about them. And I wondered if Miss Herbert drew nearly as well as Ewen. "We took the same subject," she said. Who are "we?" Not her uncle, surely. No; my mind rejected that surmise. Who can "we" be? Is it not tantalising to hear a riddle, without its answer?

# CHAPTER XII.

N the first Sunday in April, St Cross was closed, and Mr Marten held service in the great room of the Refuge. This certainly had one good result; it led many parishioners to that place who had never been induced to visit it before, and, in consequence, several stray shillings found their way to its funds. Of course, the enlargement of the house, necessary for its proposed orphanage, could not be proceeded with while the building was needed for public worship; but I arranged with the builder that this improvement should be carried out as soon as the church was in a fair way of completion.

At the same time, it occurred to me to buy a piece of land close to the church green. The next time we met Mr Marten, we took him to survey my purchase. It lay on a gentle inclination behind St Cross, and commanded a fine open view of the surrounding country.

"I intend to build a house on it," I said.

"A fine, healthy site," he answered; "but are you not very comfortable in your present quarters?"

"Oh, yes, indeed," I replied; "ours is a thoroughly good old house, which suits us exactly. A house fit for birth, and death, and sickness, for making love and marriage—not that Ruth or I will require most of its capabilities, but a house is not a home without them."

"Then no new houses are homes, or at least very few," said the rector, dismally stroking his chin, and thinking of more than his words.

"I mean to try and make one," I responded. "Is there any reason why old houses should be better than new ones? In most things the world does not go backwards."

"No, nor in this, really," replied Mr Marten; "but a thoroughly good house costs money, and in this matter, cash seems scarcer now than formerly."

"I think we are getting to the root of the evil," I observed. "Money is much more plentiful now than it used to be, but every one pretends to be richer than he is, and if a man have enough money to build a real cottage, he builds a sham villa instead."

"And directly he gets fifty pounds a year more, he removes to a greater sham," said Ruth.

"The right method," I said, "is to build a place thoroughly good in its way, however humble that way may be. If it be only a barn, build it so that it may remain unchanged when the mansion is built before it. Why not follow the example of our fathers, and rear

houses so good and substantial that our successors shall
esteem it an honour to keep them up, and may gratify
their own tastes by enlarging and beautifying, rather than
by destroying ? "

"But then the march of fashion soon strides over
neighbourhoods," observed Mr Marten, "and the son
blushes to name where his father lived, and never does
so without the modification, ' It was so different then ! '
And yet I think if there were more right feeling in the
world, localities would not be mapped out as at present
—in one, outer life all colour and gilding ; in another, all
mildew and mist."

"You may well say 'outer life,'" said Ruth, grimly,
"for inner life is much the same queer mixture every
where. I believe there are as many heartaches in man-
sions as in huts."

"But might there not be fewer in both, if they did not
keep aloof from each other?" I pleaded. "Would not a
kindly interest in others' welfare be a healthy stimulant
to many an empty, irritable mind? And mere almsgiving
can never give this interest, which naturally grows from
near neighbourhood and habitual knowledge. And, on
the other hand, would not the world be spared many an
outburst of evil passion, if the despair which breeds such
were checked by the reassurance of God's protection in
a comforting human presence?"

"But still, some localities really grow unbearable," said
Mr Marten.

"Just because they are deserted," I answered. "If

O

people of means and cultivated tastes would stay in them, they could not become unbearable. And though cleanliness and elegance may cost more under these circumstances than under others, let wealthy men remember that the truest charity is that which works indirectly. There is far more self-denial and love in remaining on the spot, to confront the struggle which one's weaker neighbours *must* wage, than in flying from the scene of action, and then sending back a scanty supply of ammunition. Then, if exertion and example fail to ward off all the surrounding discomforts, let such as remain be cheerfully endured as God's discipline—far better than man's."

"Ah, yes," said Ruth, "if folks only stand steady in the path of duty, they will find penance enough without mounting Simon Stylites' pillar."

"Let us remember," I went on, "that in the few mixed neighbourhoods still left in London, however deep the poverty of the poor, we never hear of those frightful deaths from starvation and neglect which horrify us in parishes where the richest people are those just able to struggle on without assistance. Let us also remember, when we hear of aged people dying on the bare floors of empty rooms, that many of them have been industrious folks, though engaged upon those humble works to which the necessities of the labour-market forbid wages which will permit saving. Therefore they have had employers, from whom time and distance have separated them, and who only recall their old servants when they hear of their miserable end. I think it would be so much better if commercial men could condescend to keep to the places which keep them."

" But it must be very expensive and difficult to rear a refined family among coarse surroundings," said Mr Marten.

" Under present circumstances it is so difficult that it is almost impossible," I returned. " As a lonely bachelor I could reside in my house of business in the city, though I was only thought a lunatic for my pains. But as a married man I could scarce have done so. No, the mistakes which have been committed, cannot be hastily remedied. But where it is still possible that a neighbourhood be maintained as an epitome of God's world, with the rich and poor side by side, each to comfort and sustain the other, there let every thoughtful man beware how he begin the evil work of desertion."

" You see the rich draw the rich to them," said Mr Marten, "even in rural districts, and often in positive contradiction to the dictates of nature. Our village of Upper Mallowe is much healthier than Mallowe itself," he added, turning to Ruth, " for the one is on a hill, and the other in its valley ; but then, you see, Mallowe boasts a manor-house, and therefore every wealthy man in the adjacent country is anxious to live there."

" Not my brother, sir," remarked Ruth.

" Not your brother, thank God," Mr Marten was pleased to answer, (and I won't say I did not like to hear it !) " But even since my sojourn in this village, an aged farmer, retiring on a considerable fortune, and coveting a quiet little villa for him and his old wife to die in, immediately built the same in Mallowe proper. Nobody lives here except Mr Garrett, the farmers on their own land, their cottagers, and a few tradespeople, who go away as soon as they can."

"And the clergyman," I added.  "And no place is past redemption so long as the clergyman stands bravely co his post.  He should always live in his parish, whatever it be."

"So I think," replied Mr Marten; "only it is sometimes awkward when no house is provided," he added ruefully.

Ruth and I exchanged glances and smiles.

"What a discursive conversation we have had," I remarked, strolling about my new possession, "and it has all started from this little bit of ground, whereon I wish to build a house exactly suited to a well-educated family of moderate means.  I want it to be so good and so pleasing as to prove a suggestion for every future erection in Upper Mallowe, that people may say, 'Let our house be at least as comfortable as that behind St Cross, and then as much better as possible.'"

"But I don't like to see many houses alike," interrupted Ruth.  "To follow an example is good, but to imitate is bad.  God made no two minds precisely alike, so if two minds produce the same results, one is in slavery."

Then there was a pause.

"Mr Marten must dine with us to-day," I observed presently; "for to-morrow I must give my instructions for the plan of this house, and I want some hints."

"You must be a better judge than me," he said; "but I shall be very happy to dine with you nevertheless."

And so we adjourned to our own house, and when we had discussed a pheasant and a custard, and the cloth was removed, Ruth placed before us pens, ink, and paper, and then took up her knitting in a way that said she expected us to set about our business immediately.

"For what class of people is this house intended?" asked Mr Marten.

"For people with about two hundred pounds a-year or a little more," I replied.

"Then it must be built so that its proper maintenance will not make undue demands upon that sum," he remarked promptly, as if he had studied the exact possibilities of such an income, which very likely he had, considering it was his own.

"Certainly," I responded, "and so it must not be too large, and yet there must be several rooms, for the income does not fix the size of the family."

"No, indeed," sighed the rector, shaking his head.

"Well, isn't that a very good thing?" I queried. "Would you like poverty to deprive us of life's sweetest blessings? Which do you think the most fortunate—the poor man with loving children, or the rich man with none? I know my own answer to that question. But to return to our house," I added, taking up a pen and marking on the paper. "I think the door must be in the middle, so let that dot represent it."

"Ah, I like that," remarked the rector; "nothing is

better than a nice entrance-hall with rooms at each side."

"It must be broad enough to leave a good passage beyond a table and chair and hat-stand," I said, still drawing on the paper; "that is so handy when many messengers come who wait for answers, as in the case of most professional men."

"And how many rooms on the ground-floor?" asked Mr Marten.

"One at each side of the passage," I replied, "a study and a parlour."

"Then where is the kitchen?" interrupted Ruth.

"At the end of the hall shall be a door," I explained; "this door shall open into a small entry, with three other doors, those on the right and on the left opening into the garden, and that facing the hall into the kitchen. So, by opening the doors on the right and left, a current of fresh air may pass between the sitting apartments and the kitchen, whenever needed to cut off all over-salubrious culinary smells."

"Then all the bedrooms will be up-stairs?" queried Mr Marten.

"Certainly," I answered.

"Have you considered a staircase?" asked Ruth, "amateur architects never do."

"But I have," I replied. "I tell you the front part of the hall shall be wide enough for two people to walk abreast past a roomy table and a comfortable chair. This width is unnecessary at the back of the house. There a flight of stairs can rise to the landing, which will be above the kitchen entry and the back part of the hall, and will be lit by two windows, right and left, like the doors below. All the bedrooms will open on to this landing except one, which must be gained through another."

"I don't exactly understand how you arrange the stairhead," my sister observed.

" Neither do I," I admitted candidly; " but I suppose the architect will do so."

" I think I can see how it could be managed by means of a gallery," said Mr Marten, criticising my rough plan; " but as you say, these details are best left to professional skill."

" And how many bedrooms do you mean to have ? " asked Ruth.

" I think of five," I replied. " One for the heads of the family, extending over the study, one over the kitchen, two over the parlour, and a little extra chamber above the hall."

" Then you intend the study and the parlour to be rather large ? " remarked Mr Marten.

" Each about sixteen feet by fifteen," I answered.

" But I never thought a man with two hundred a-year could live in so large a house as this," he said, very briskly.

" I mean it for an income of two hundred exclusive of house rent," I replied.

" Oh, indeed ! " said he, in quite another tone.

" Shall you have the walls papered or wainscoted ? " asked Ruth.

" Wainscoted," I replied.

" It costs more at first, but it 's cheapest in the end," said my sister, " and it can be kept clean much more easily ; and wherever labour is saved, money is saved."

" And the kitchen shall have a red-brick floor," I went on, " and the hall shall be tiled, not with very smart tiles, which put ordinary furniture to shame, but good neat plain ones, so that the heart of the mistress need never be vexed by splitting oil-cloth or ripping carpet."

" How thoughtful you are ! " said the rector, with a grave smile.

" And build the house itself with red-bricks," put in Ruth.   " They look best with the green leaves in sum-mer, and in autumn and winter the sight is as good as a fire ! "

" It shall be built with red bricks, Ruth," I assented ; " that is another good old fashion which has fallen into disuse."

" Also on account of its cost," said Mr Marten.

" A short-sighted policy," I answered, " considering that houses are now made of inferior material, and then covered with paint or cement, which needs constant re-newal, and gives the owner the perpetual worry and mortification always caused by fading shabbiness."

" But I almost think two hundred a-year is too little to keep house upon," remarked Mr Marten presently.

" Too little for the fantastical existence of boarding-school misses and dandies," answered Ruth, " but just enough for the honest life of good women and brave men."

"But what service can a man secure with such an income?" asked the rector.

"The best service," replied my sister, "the service of love."

"What! set his wife to household work!" exclaimed the rector aghast.

"If I were a man I would not marry a woman who was unworthy of such work," said Ruth drily.

"Unworthy? No!" said Mr Marten. "But when a woman is highly educated"——

"What is the end of her education?" inquired my sister. "To play a little worse than a professional pianist?—to paint not so well as an artist?—to talk French so that foreigners can just guess what she means? If she can do better than this, she herself can add to the family income; but then, unless she be a wonder, the home will not be quite as happy as if she devoted herself to make the best of her husband's earnings."

"I could not endure that *my* wife should earn money," said the rector emphatically.

"I will tell you the plain truth, Mr Marten," retorted Ruth; "you would like to set up your wife as an idol, and then, like all other idols, she would break. Has a woman no soul, sir?" she added almost severely. "Is she neither to serve, nor to save, nor to earn? Will you leave her no way to heaven, sir?"

"I know good women feel with you," answered Mr Marten reflectively; "but I always thought it was the duty of the men who loved them to save them from themselves."

"'To what danger do their natural impulses spur them?'" asked Ruth, rather sarcastically. "On what precipice does a good housewife stand?"

"Oh, I don't mean danger exactly," said the rector; "but is not a cultivated mind likely to be dwarfed if set to work which could be as well done by an uncultivated one?"

"The simplest task is done better for real cultivation," answered my sister; "and the raw materials of education are just like seeds, quite valueless if they do not bring forth a crop."

"And let me remark," said I, "that most great and good women—and many who have been merely great— had their full share of the commonest domestic duties."

"Yes, truly," assented Ruth. "Was Grizel Baillie less a lady because she knew the worth of a farthing? Was Joan of Arc less heroic because she had doubtless scrubbed many a floor? Did not Emily Brontë blacken the grates in Haworth Parsonage? And upon my word, she was better employed then than when she wrote 'Wuthering Heights!'"

"Ruth, my dear," I said, "you will prejudice Mr Marten anew against domestic work, on the novel ground that it strengthens a woman's mind a little *too* much!"

"Well, if the woman be not a Christian, I'll own that is its tendency," she granted. "But if she be, no matter how strong her mind grows, she'll not forget her place, and her husband will be none the weaker for her strength."

"Then you don't think two hundred a-year a bad income to marry on?" said Mr Marten, smiling.

I must here observe that he had no idea we knew it was his own. That information we had obtained from the *Clergy List*, and I hope my readers will wait a while ere they condemn us for undue curiosity.

"I think two hundred a-year a very good beginning," I answered, "while energy is strong and hope is high. Nay, if all else were promising, I should blame one who, having so much, yet waited for more. For why did God give us hope if we are to avoid occasions for its exercise?"

"Reasonable hope," put in Mr Marten.

"And if an industrious and able man of thirty possess two hundred a-year, is it unreasonable in him to hope that he may have three hundred by the time he is forty?" I asked.

"But if not?" queried the rector, with a dubious smile.

"Well, I said, "should God deny a blossom to our hopes, and give us poverty instead of wealth, and sorrow instead of joy, He will not deny us hearts strong enough to answer, 'It is better so.'"

"Then what becomes of improvidence—is there no such thing?" inquired Mr Marten.

"Ah, truly there is," responded Ruth, "when a man marries a fool, or a woman does ditto."

"There are other kinds of improvidence, too," I remarked; "when a man marries without reasonable prospect of a permanent income, or without any little fund

to fall back upon in emergencies.   And yet I have observed that even these cases prosper better than they
seem to deserve."

"Should you speak thus to every one, sir?" said the
rector, carelessly sketching on a blank sheet.

Now, why did he try to make our conversation personal?   I was glad when Ruth answered for me,
saying,—

"Of course not.   Truths, like physic, must be administered to the right patients.   For what cures one, kills
another."

At that moment there came to our door a workman
from St Cross, inquiring for the rector.   So Mr Marten
bade us a hasty good-bye, and hurried off.   Orderly sister
Ruth instantly began to arrange the papers scattered over
the table.   Presently she paused smiling, and pushed a
sheet towards me—

"I declare he has drawn a lady's head!" said she.

# CHAPTER XIII

## THE FIRST OF MAY.

E learned that May-day did not pass unobserved in Upper Mallowe, but that it was a time much dreaded by all prudent fathers and mothers. The festivities were a mere degeneration of the old May-poles and dances, having forfeited whatever beauty and merriment those possessed, and retained only their riotous licence, thereby drawing to our quiet village all the disorderly characters within ten miles thereof. May-day was a sad date in many a humble cottage, marking the time when the only son first came home "not himself," or when the daughter conceived that fatal passion for flattery and finery which ultimately led her away and away,—God only knows where !

Mr Marten knew and deplored the evil, and it was he who first mentioned it to me, along with his own unsuccessful attempts to grapple therewith. He had preached about it, with stern and sorrowful lamentations; he had made personal appeals to the younger members of his flock, nay, when the fateful day came, he had startled the godless scene with terrible words of warning and condemnation. Startled it truly, but not to awed repentance, only to coarse jests and rude laughter. And now, when the time of trouble drew nigh, he came to me, saying, "What shall I do?"

"The Sunday before May-day," he remarked, "I always look round my church, and wonder which boy or which girl I shall never again see in the accustomed seat. It never passes without some such result."

"And have you never tried a counter-attraction?" I asked.

"Last year I got up a lecture on the 'Origin of Old Customs,' with illustrations," he answered, with a ludicrous expression of hoplessness.

"And who attended?" inquired Ruth.

"A few old people, and two or three very small girls," he replied.

"Did they like it?" pursued my sister.

"I cannot say," he responded.

"Did *you* like it?" she asked, pointedly.

"I might have preferred a walk in the fields," he answered, looking up with a rueful smile.

"Then judge others by yourself," said she.

"The only remedy lies in a counter-attraction," I remarked, "and it must be prepared very carefully, for each failure will make the matter more difficult. And in these things we must always remember that although it is sometimes good to unite instruction and amusement, yet the combination can never supply the place of pure play."

"Ah, yes," observed Ruth, "whenever I hear a child say it likes 'sensible games' best, I always think, 'You little idle simpleton, you'll choose differently when you've done some real work.'"

"Then you would ruin the makers of scientific toys," said Mr Marten, smiling.

"No, I would not," she answered; "they can make them for the schoolroom. Let a child learn about steam engines and so forth, but don't expect it to find merriment therein."

"Sir," I said, "will you clear your conscience from the burden of these May-day sports, and lay it upon mine?"

"Most gladly will I do so," he replied, "if—if I ought."

"I think you should," I answered, "and I will explain my reason. Perhaps I shall succeed better than you, just because I am not a clergyman."

"Is it so?" he sighed; "will people never believe it possible that a clergyman honestly wishes their good?"

"Not exactly that," I responded, "but their instincts cry out for 'fun,' and they have a notion that a clergyman will give but a diluted draught thereof, and will only tolerate that for the sake of the 'moral.'"

"And as there's never smoke without a little fire," put in Ruth, "so there's no popular notion which has not some reason for it. The sooner such reason is destroyed the better; only, till that time, there are certain whole-some movements in which a clergyman's best place is the background."

"Well, if you and your brother will kindly devise some successful May-day celebration, I am sure I shall be most happy to appear as your most insignificant guest," said Mr Marten, humbly.

"And then you will have a magnificent chance of con-vincing your parishioners you are none the less a man because you are 'a parson,'" I said. "I think it's a very good thing for all parties when a clergyman has an op-portunity of appearing among his people in an unofficial character."

And so we arranged between us that the rector should be kept as much in ignorance of our plans as any one in the parish, and that we should send him an invitation in due course, and away he went, declaring he should be quite restless and uneasy in his mind until it reached him, and adding that wonders would never cease, since he, too, was allured into eager expectation of the coming May-day.

So Ruth and I conspired together, and we took Agnes Herbert and the M'Callums into our plot. We settled directly that the festival must begin early in the day, and must be of a free, out-of-door character. There could be nothing better than the ancient custom of "getting in the may," which, owing to an early season, was now in beautiful blossoms. Strange to say, May-day at Upper Mallowe had been kept without any shadow of this usage, and the advent of God's flowers had been celebrated merely by rough dances, inane songs, gamb_ling, and intemperance. Surely it was not hard to find better ways of holiday-making. And I firmly believe that popular instinct will seldom choose the evil and reject the good,—if it only have a fair choice.

On the twenty-sixth of April, our invitations were issued on neatly-printed cards, Agnes and Alice filling in the names ot the individuals or families addressed, so that each invitation had a pleasant personal tone, and ran as follows :—

"Mr Edward Garrett hopes to see Mr John Jones and family, (as the case might be,) at the Oak on the Green, at nine o'clock in the morning of the first of May. Why should good old customs die out? Is not summer as great a blessing to us as to our forefathers?

'Can such delights be in the street
And open fields, and we not see't ?
Come, we'll abroad, and let's obey
The proclamation made for May.' "

Besides sending one to everybody in and about our own village, I sent a few cards to some old friends at Mallowe, among them the present owner of Meadow Farm, the only son of my Lucy's eldest brother.

The eventful morning arose bright and warm, and by half-past eight Ruth and I were at the rendezvous. I must mention that the Green lay behind our Refuge, so that its back gate opened upon it. Old Mr M'Callum and Alice had stocked the garden with every available seat, for the comfort of any elderly people who might honour the gathering with their presence. Indeed, the

P

whole house presented a holiday appearance, for in consideration of its famous "supper room," we intended to
close our festivities there.

Early as we were, many were before us, and amongst
them Mr Herbert and his niece. The farmer was in
his element, chatting with his labourers, complimenting
their blushing wives, and praising their bonnie children.
Bessie Sanders too was there, talking to Alice M'Callum,
and helping her to welcome some very aged village
matrons, who were saying "they wanted to see the fun,
though, dearie me, fun was getting hard work for their
likes, now-a-days." Anne Sanders was not there, but that
valuable member of society made her appearance about
noon, being, I presume, as soon as she could get ready.
I regret to say, she was the cause of the only breach of
propriety which occurred during the day, inasmuch as
when she arrived a small boy called out, " Hulloo, Jem,
here's a guy!" Of course I reproved the lad, but, except
to his good manners, there was no harm done, for Bessie
did not hear him, and Anne decidedly liked it, accepting
it as the malignity of an unappreciative world, instead of
blushing at the truthful description of her own slovenly
appearance.

As we walked through the assembled people, shaking
hands and exchanging greetings, a sound of sweet singing
suddenly reached us, and Mr Marten and the boys of
his choir came trooping across the green, trilling a merry
May-day carol. And did not we applaud when they came
amongst us !

And ever and anon as we lingered at the Oak on the

Green, while tardy neighbours joined us—some in a flutter which denoted they had not made up their minds to come till the last minute—Mr Marten and his choir boys lifted their voices and sang appropriate glees. But before ten we started on our rambles, Mr M'Callum remaining in the Refuge garden to dispense sundry simple dainties to such old people as had lost all inclination for pedestrianism.

Away we went : each free to follow his own tastes,—to run races, to search for hawthorn in sober earnest, to carry the babies, to go a little aside, whispering—dear me, where's the harm? When my Lucy said something which has done me good all my life, she did not speak in a room full of company ! As for Ruth, nobody was more popular or more delighted. She got on confidential terms with everybody. The courting couples seemed to feel she knew all about it, and so attempted no concealment. Wherever Ruth went there was quite a little bustle round her, but her particular companion was young Weston, and a fine-looking honest-hearted fellow he was, like his father before him.

Presently I noticed George Wilmot. Just as our whole party turned into a lane, so narrow that it reduced us to something like rank and file, he ran before, and then stood still and watched us pass. As I came up, I said to him—

"I hope you are enjoying yourself, my boy. Are you looking for anybody?"

"He doesn't seem to be here," he answered, eagerly watching as the crowd passed by.

"Who is he?" I asked.

"The gentleman who brought me to you, sir," he replied.

"Should you like to see him?" I queried.

"Yes, 'cos it's all so nice," he said, simply.

"What is that?" inquired Agnes Herbert, who happened to be beside me.

" Did you never hear that story?" I questioned in reply, and, drawing the lad along with us, I narrated his first arrival at our house.  She listened with very quiet interest, and just as my tale ended, her uncle came upon us, and claimed my attention.  But half an hour later I found the rough farm-lad still walking beside her, and, from a few words which I overheard, I discovered that her delicate womanly tact had made a far better mutual ground of their common acquaintance with London than I had done.

Long before noon the lads of our party were laden with may-blossom trophies, but I was glad to see these were only boughs, and that as no hawthorn trees were seriously broken, the meadows would look none the worse for our spoils.  Presently, as we came to a hedge, white with blossom, I discovered the reason for this thoughtfulness, by hearing Alice M'Callum's soft, Scottish voice lifted in gentle exhortation.  Where did she learn this tenderness for nature?  Very likely she has not read Wordsworth.  But who is most akin to the poet—those who know his words, or those who have his heart?

" What a pretty girl that is ! " remarked young Weston to Ruth, just as I joined them.

"Which?" queried my sister.

"The one with the Highland name," he answered. "She has a real pretty face."

"And as good as she's pretty," responded Ruth, "ay, and far better; only a man always begins at the wrong end of a woman's qualities."

"I fancy I've seen her before," said Mr Weston. "Will you say her name again?"

"Alice M'Callum," answered my sister: "and very likely you have seen her before, for she was formerly lady's-maid at Mallowe Manor."

"Oh indeed!" he said, with a slightly fallen countenance; "I remember now. There was some misfortune in her family."

"There was a sad accusation brought against her brother," I remarked, "who seems to me as fine a young man as I know. But he is now doing very well in London. As for Alice, the whole affair was only the trial-furnace which tests pure gold."

"But men seldom like tried gold in women's nature," said Ruth, rather sharply; "they prefer untried gilt. Perhaps because they know they don't deserve the other."

"Is Miss M'Callum now living at home?" asked Mr Weston, presently.

"When we first came here, she was our upper servant." Ruth answered. "She preferred our service to the Manor, that she might be near her grandfather. But she left us to live at our Refuge, where she is matron."

My sister had never before called Alice by this dignified name.

Here somebody called me away, and I was engaged with different members of our party for some time after, and when next I noticed young Weston he was climbing a steep bank to gather some pink hawthorn for the blushing matron of the Refuge.

"It is nearly time for me to go home, sir," she said, when she saw me.

"Very nearly, Alice," I answered.

"What! can't you stay with us?" queried Mr Weston, as he descended, panting, with a face which nearly matched his floral treasures.

"Alice has business at home," I said, smiling, and then I passed on.

In a few minutes I missed her—and him also.

The rest of us did not return to the Refuge until about one o'clock. Ruth and I knew what we should find there. In its back garden were two tables, groaning beneath the weight of huge joints and jolly pies, and enlivened by bunches of may, set in honest earthenware jugs. The lads cheered when they saw them. But there was not room for all to sit down together, so the juniors waited for a second "spread," and left their fathers and mothers' and uncles and aunts in our charge; and Miss Sanders and I provided for one table, and Mr Herbert and Ruth for another. Alice wished to wait upon us, but I bade her reserve herself wholly for the youngsters. As for Mr Weston, I found he had resolved to go or stay as she did, and they both lingered with us, till we sang the good old Doxology, and I wondered if he knew that was the daily custom in his grandfather's house!

There was such a constant flow of good-natured chatter round the tables, that I had neither eye nor ear to spare. There never were such victuals, so they said, and I heard one toothless old woman asking her "John" if the pie didn't mind him of what they had on their wedding-day? "It's forty-five years a-gone, but the taste of that pie brings it up better nor yesterday."

In about an hour's time, the young people took our places, presided over by Mr Marten and Agnes, young Weston and Alice. I daresay they did not talk about the repast, but deeds speak louder than words, and they did full justice to it. When they were deeply engaged with knives and forks, we discovered what they had done while we were at dinner. They had made a light arch over our garden gate and twined it with hawthorn, also fastening great bunches to the door-posts, so that the place looked quite a bower.

The day was warm and the sun was bright, so we old people were fain to rest ourselves on some turfy knolls and fallen trees left on the village Green. And when the young folks had finished dinner, they also felt rather tired, and were quite ready to join us. Then we had a little singing—good old songs which every one knows, and nobody tires over—"Home, sweet home," "Scots wha hae wi' Wallace bled," (that was Mr M'Callum's), "Poor Jack Brown," and so forth.

Later in the afternoon, Mr Marten paid a visit to the High Street, and brought back tidings that a few disreputable strangers were lounging listlessly about the inn. He also brought back an Italian organ-man with a monkey. The poor foreigner having heard some reports of festivity, had come down in hopes of a little harvest, and so in the end he was not disappointed, for Jacko's antics were a source of amusement to both young and old, and contributions in cash and kind did not fail.

In due time, tea and cake revived the spirits of the whole party, and effectually aroused any old ladies who were inclined to be sleepy. After tea we adjourned to the great room of the Refuge, taking with us the organ-man and Jacko, who by that time was on terms of personal friendship with most of the boys, who could understand his graphic gestures much better than his good-humoured master's broken English.

I hope nobody expects me to remember all the sports which enlivened the remainder of the evening. I recollect "Post" and "Proverbs," but in one or two other instances I blindly followed the instructions of the frank, smiling girls who volunteered to "teach" me, though I knew no more about the game when it was finished than when it began. In the course of the evening, a strange old gentleman and a young lady made their appearance, and Mr Marten introduced them to us as his old friends Lieutenant Blake, of the Royal Navy, and his only daughter, Marian. A jolly old sailor was Lieutenant Blake, and in ten minutes had quite caught the spirit of the evening, and sung sea-songs and spun yarns to such appreciative audiences, that some of the village mothers grew apprehensive lest their sons should be attacked with a seafaring fever. And two or three times in the evening, it did me good to hear Bessie Sanders laugh—not a careworn, middle-aged laugh, but one as buoyant and ringing as if she had no benumbing cross to lift the moment she passed her own threshold. And amid all the confusion of merriment sat the lonely Italian, with Jacko clinging round his neck, separated from us by the dread curse of Babel, but smiling at our glee, and murmuring melodious thanks for the little hospitalities we pressed upon him.

But at nine o'clock our friends began to depart, and by ten no one remained but the Herberts, Mr Weston, and ourselves, for Mr Marten had escorted the Blakes to their home. We arranged that the organ-man should sleep at the Refuge, and one or two destitute creatures who had hoped to make some forlorn pence, perhaps not over honestly, by the old village festivities, availed themselves of the same privilege.

But when Agnes Herbert was arranging her wrappers, she found she had lost a little fancy pincushion, which she carried in her pocket, and I really thought she seemed inclined to cry over her loss, trivial as it seemed.

" Don't ye remember when the little gal tore her frock in the 'edge, miss ?" asked George Wilmot ; " well, you hadn't lost it then, 'twas from it you took the pin to fasten up the hole. I'm sure of it, 'cos I noticed it's being so pretty."

" Then I daresay I foolishly laid it on the grass, and forgot to take it up," answered Agnes, "and it would soon get trodden down. It cannot be helped." But then I believe her eyes positively filled with tears, only she drew down her veil

"I knows where it was, miss," said George, eagerly; "'twas by the 'edge of the field aback of the Low Meadow. I'll go and look for it to-morrow."

"I shall be so glad if you find it," exclaimed Agnes, turning to him brightly, "but it doesn't seem worth much trouble."

"Yes, miss, if you wants it," said the boy.

And so that matter ended, and Agnes went off with her uncle.

Mr Weston accompanied us home, and supped with us, and Ruth and he made a duet in praising Alice M'Callum.

"I think she'd make a good wife," said he.

"So she would; but a good wife deserves a good husband," said Ruth.

"I hope she'll get a good one!" he ejaculated.

"Or else none," responded my sister.

"But, bless me, she'd draw any man's goodness to the top," said he.

"There's a great deal in that," answered Ruth.

And when Mr Weston went away he promised another visit to Upper Mallowe very soon, and I had not the least doubt of his sincerity.

"We have all had a very happy day, brother," said Ruth, as we parted for the night.

So we had. And we heard that, before the poor organ-man and his monkey, Jacko, left the Refuge, he insisted that Alice should accept a sixpence towards the funds of the place. "He pointed up to the sky," Alice narrated, and said, "Not to pay—but for thanks to Him there.'

And long afterwards, while chatting in sundry village parlours, I detected my invitation card stored among the small treasures of the house-mother's work-box. Ah truly, though

> "I 've heard of hearts unkind, kind deeds
>   With coldness still returning :
> Alas ! the gratitude of men
>   Has oftener left me mourning."

# CHAPTER XIV.

## AN OLD KNIFE.

EXT morning I went for a stroll, and after idly straying about for some time, it occurred to me that I would go to the field behind the Low Meadow, and see if I could find any trace of the missing pincushion. I was not very surprised when I found both George Wilmot and Agnes busily engaged in the search. It was the lad's dinner hour, and he had hurried over the meal, to gain a few minutes for the fulfilment of his promise. As for Miss Herbert, all I ever learned of her appearance on the scene was George's subsequent explanation that she was there "afore him," nor did she seem at all disposed to retire defeated. But just before I arrived, they had found, not what they sought, but something else.

They were so eagerly examining it that they did not notice my approach. George was sitting upon his heels, just as he had drawn back from a kneeling posture, and

Miss Herbert stood over him. They both started when they heard my voice, and the young lady turned and held out her hand, and George displayed his discovery.

It was a clasp knife, larger than the ordinary size, with a heavy brown handle, curiously carved, but much obscured by clay and dust, some of which George had rubbed away. The blade, red and blunt with rust, was partly open. I took it and tried to move it, but it was fixed in that position.

" I found it down among the long grass by the 'edge," said the boy. " I was feeling among the thickness, where we couldn't see, and I hit my hand agen somethin' hard, and says I, ' I got it, Miss ;' but when I took hold, I found it wor werry hard and straight, and stickin' into the ground, so I cleared the grass a bit till we could see, and there wor the knife a-standin' up, with the blade stabbed right into the earth."

" More than an inch of it underground," corroborated Agnes.

" I suppose somebody dropped it just as he had used it," I remarked, examining it.

" I think it must ha' been throwed a long way, sir," said George, " or it wouldn't have stuck in so precious hard and far. Knives is nasty things to chuck about that way."

Just then the church clock struck one, and Agnes touched his shoulder, and reminded him that he must hasten to his work, and not linger longer in her service.

" But you mustn't take that knife with you," I remarked, as he seemed about to put it into his pocket. " Half open as it is, any accident might easily cause it to hurt you dreadfully."

"But the handle's such a beauty," said the boy, "and it would make me late if I ran home with it."

"Then give it to me," I said, "and I will call at the Refuge, and leave it with Mr M'Callum for you."

"Thank ye, sir," he answered, cheerfully surrendering it; "an' if you please, Miss, I'll come back here in the evening an' look about again."

But instead of replying, Agnes exclaimed ecstatically, "Here it is! here it is!" and plucked something from a bed of briar, and eagerly held up a little purple leather thing, with white flowers painted on it. It was but an impulsive burst of the vivacity kept in chains within her. In a second, she was again her own quiet self, with only a flush of pleasure lingering on her face.

"I wish I'd found it, Miss," said George Wilmot.

"Miss Herbert will take the will for the deed," I remarked.

"That I'm sure I do," she responded; "and remember, you reminded me where I had lost it. But I must make haste home now." And after she had shaken hands with me, she shook hands with the little boy too; and so she went away.

"Now, my lad, run away to your work," I said. So counselled, George Wilmot set off at a fine pace. Country air and healthy work had already done him good. As I stood and watched him, it pleased me to think, "If his mother can see him, she must be quite satisfied."

I turned my steps to the Refuge, carrying the rusted

soiled knife openly in my hand. I did not waste two thoughts on it—a half-spoiled, old thing, only valuable because it pleased a boy's fancy. Coming across the fields, I approached the Refuge,—not from the High Street, but by way of the village green—and seeing its back-door open, I went in, and found Mr M'Callum and Alice both in the supper-room, packing up the crockery which had been used at the feast of the previous day. I laid the knife on the table, and was entering into its history, when an exclamation from Alice checked me.

"Grandfather, look !" she said, "it is his !"

As she uttered these words she did not raise her tone, and yet it gave me that thrilling sensation which homely folks call "the blood turning cold." Mr M'Callum walked to the table, and examined the knife with great deliberation; then suddenly dropped it, looked straight before him, and said—

"Sae it is, lassie."

And his voice was almost terrible in its expression of determined resignation to the worst.

"What is this?" I whispered, after a short pause.

"Only that is George Roper's knife," said Alice, meeting my eyes, and speaking very quietly, but with breaks in her sentences. "He was seen to take it when he left home on—the last morning. And it was missing when he was—taken out of the water."

"But how can you be sure it is his?" I asked, in my turn advancing to the table, and bending over the defaced thing, now invested with such dreadful interest.

"Yes, indeed, I can," she answered. "Before I went

to Mallowe Manor, Ewen used to bring it home for grandfather to sharpen for Mr Roper, because he did it so well."

"And you are sure Mr Roper's knife was never found after his death?" I questioned.

"Quite sure," she replied again; "for the police asked questions about it, and even searched over Ewen's things for it."

"Did your brother know anything of it?" I queried.

She shook her head.    "Ewen told me that Mr Roper had used a knife to cut some string during the regatta that morning," she answered; "and he thought he should have noticed if it had not been his usual one.    But you know, sir, it is so hard to be sure about things one is accustomed to," she added.  .

"Just so," I said.

"Halloo!" cried a cheerful voice at the still open back-door; "so yesterday has not tired you too much for morning visits, Mr Garrett."

It was our rector.    As I turned, I remember his countenance was particularly bright.    But the radiance sobered when he saw our anxious faces.    With very few words I detailed the facts I had just learned, and then handed him the knife.

He had naturally taken interest in a tragedy which involved the fates of two of his parishioners; therefore he remembered that, at the time of the murder, inquiries had been made concerning a missing knife belonging to the dead man.    He even remembered the description of the lost article which Bessie Sanders had furnished. And when he looked at it, he said, gravely—

" I have no doubt this is the same."

Then he rose from the seat he had taken, and carried it to the window for closer inspection.

" Ought anything to be done ?" I queried, following him, and speaking in a whisper.

" I suppose the orthodox course would be to give it to the police," answered Mr Marten, still twisting it about.

Alice caught our words, low as they were spoken, and all her woman-weakness rose within her, and, for a moment, it was stronger than her woman-strength. " Oh, Ewen, oh, my darling !" she cried, with a passionate tenderness which no happiness could have wrung from her. " If it is all to come over again, you were better dead, Ewen, my own brother !"

" Whisht, whisht, lassie !" said her grandfather ; " the Lord ne'er gies a cross wi'out poo'er to lift it. His holy will be done !"

" Even if the police had this, what can come over again ?" observed the rector soothingly. " The discovery of the knife has nothing to do with your brother."

" But it would bring up the old story and all the talk," said Alice more calmly.

" So it might," he answered, " and as I cannot see how it can possibly give a clue to the real culprit, I think we shall keep the discovery a secret,—if we can."

" Then Ewen need never hear of it," exclaimed Alice eagerly, with gleaming eyes.

"I think he should," I observed ; "the affair touched him very nearly, and he has a right to know all about it. Besides, should it be divulged afterwards, the concealment would pain him more than the disclosure."

"Poor Ewen !" sighed his sister, so softly that I saw the words rather than heard them.

"But I don't think we need unsettle him in London by writing about it," I added. "Time enough to tell him when he comes home for his holidays."

"Ay, ay," murmured the grandfather ; "it's ill putting worry in a letter."

"Mr M'Callum," said the rector, suddenly speaking from the window-seat, where he was still examining the rusty blade, "I don't recollect that any wound was found on Roper's body ?"

"There was nane," answered the old man, hobbling towards his questioner ; "there was nae mark o' violence at a', only the doctors said his wrists seemed to ha' been held in a tight grip. Na, the puir creatur had just been drooned."

"I only asked you," remarked Mr Marten, turning quite round, and quietly facing both the M'Callums, "because I believe there is blood on this knife."

"Ye dinna say sae, sir !" said Mr M'Callum astonished.

"With what knowledge we have now, this only deepens the mystery," I observed. "But we know Ewen and Mr Roper had high words before they parted ! is it possible they even came to blows ?"

"Came to blows ?—my brother ? Not at all likely, sir," said Alice, quite proudly.

" I cannot be certain these stains are blood," explained the rector; "but I know something of chemistry, for it was a pet pursuit of mine, and if Mr Garrett will accompany me, I will take it home, and make an analysis in his presence."

"It has occurred to me," I said, "that there is somebody else whom we must consult in the matter—somebody who is now the rightful owner of this knife—Miss Sanders—the nearest kin to the dead man."

"So we should, sir," responded Alice, though her lips tightened as she said it. Her sense of right had recovered its balance.

"And even if she will not take it," I went on, "yet with this terrible story belonging to it, of course we cannot give it to little George; so I must break my promise to him; but you may say I will send him another. I suppose he knows something of your household trial, Alice?" I added, staying behind Mr Marten, as she let us out.

"Yes, sir," she answered. "Ewen told him when he was here at Christmas."

"Why, then, George had only been with you a few days," I said.

"Yes, sir," she replied again; "but when he was scraping the snow off the High Street he heard something, and so he asked a question, and then my brother told him the whole history."

"How did he take it?" I queried.

An involuntary smile burst over Alice's face as she answered—

"He said he wished there was somebody to take up the police when they took up the wrong people, for they were always making stupid blunders. That was all, sir,"

Oh, terrible liberality of opinion learned in Ratcliff Highway! Is that how the majesty of the law looks there? So I suppose when the policeman tells a vagrant to "move on," the vagrant comforts himself with an adverse criticism, and does not think him such a canon of respectability as we do.

I accompanied Mr Marten to his home; and by his servant I sent a message to Ruth that she must not expect me for an hour or two, as I intended to lunch with him. After hastily partaking of this meal, the rector proceeded to his chemical inquisition. It verified his suspicions. The stains upon the blade were undoubtedly human blood.

It was rather late in the afternoon when we proceeded to Miss Sanders's house. The eldest sister admitted us —the brightness of yesterday scarcely faded from her face—and led us to the same little room where Ruth and I first made her acquaintance.

Presently Mr Marten unfolded our errand. Miss Bessie quietly took the knife, and set our last doubts at rest by pointing out a certain flaw on the handle, by which she could positively identify it as her cousin's property.

"Then we give it up to you, ma'am," said Mr Marten; "and shall you think it right to acquaint the police with i's discovery?"

" Need I do so ? " she asked.

" Not unless you choose," he replied ; " but it is the usual course,—only you remember that a young man was accused of Mr Roper's death."

" Yes, Ewen M'Callum," she said mechanically.

" Well," the rector went on, " the finding of this knife gives no clue to the guilt of any other person, and if the fact transpire, it can only revive the old accusation against him, certainly not in a court of law, but in the village, and much useless misery will surely result."

Miss Sanders was silent.

" You believe Ewen M'Callum guilty ? " I queried.

" I wish I could hope otherwise, sir," she said, quickly.

" We all think him innocent," observed Mr Marten.

" Of course the acquittal set him right with the world," she responded, rather bitterly.

" No, indeed it didn't, poor fellow ! " said I.

Her worn face, which had now quite lost the faint gleam of the day before, softened a little ; but she did not speak. Neither did we. The knife lay on the mantel-piece, her thin fingers resting over it.

At last she stirred, so suddenly that I almost started, and Mr Marten sprang up as if he understood that our visit was considered at an end. But Miss Sanders only moved to fetch her work-box in the depths of which she proceeded to deposit the dismal relic of her dead sister's lover.

" So nothing need be said about it," she observed, locking the box, and speaking in quite an ordinary tone.

"What a lovely evening it is, to be sure! Real summer weather!"

Mr Marten disregarded these remarks, which she evidently intended to cover her escape from any thanks. "The M'Callums will understand how much they owe you," said he.

"And you will do Ewen this great kindness, though you still believe his guilt?" I ventured to inquire.

"We cannot always govern our thoughts," she answered humbly; "but, God helping, we may control our deeds. And besides, I have no doubt George terribly provoked whoever brought him to his end."

"But if it were Ewen," I pleaded, "it would be easier to forgive the sudden crime than the persistent denial of it. In his nature, I could understand the one, but not the other."

"We need not puzzle ourselves about that," she sighed.

"Only I wish to make you feel his guilt an impossibility!" said I.

She shook her head with a sad smile.

"That does not matter while I act as if I thought him innocent," she replied. "I hope he is. I only wish that poor George had died without staining any soul with his blood. He did harm enough while he lived."

So, with a few more thanks we took our leave. Mr Marten returned to the Refuge, to assure the watchers there that all was well, and I pursued my way homeward.

It was truly a beautiful evening, and I found Ruth standing in the porch. As she greeted me, she added archly,—

" Mr Weston has been here."

"Indeed!" I said; "and wouldn't he wait to see me ?"

"Oh, he waited a little while," she answered ; "but when I told him that the girl who brought your message said she thought you and the rector were busy about some Refuge-business, he said very likely you would go there, and he might as well walk round and meet you ; but if he chanced to miss you, he would not return here, but would come again in a day or two.

When a young man promises to visit you soon, and then comes next day, and yet does not seem over-anxious to see your poor old face, what does it mean ?   And as I took my seat in my easy chair, I said to myself, "I wonder if Lucy's nephew is talking to Alice M'Callum at this instant?   He will see she has been crying.   Ah well I think showers ripen love even better than sunshine !"

# CHAPTER XV.

MR WESTON kept his second promise of "calling again soon," and very agreeable he made himself in his own simple country fashion. But he went away remarkably early. He said he was not going straight home. Two or three days after, when Phillis returned from buying some tapes for my sister, she told us she thought we should have Mr Weston to tea, for she saw him in the High Street. But he did not come. However, he arrived duly next week, and spent two or three hours with us. And when he rose to go, he found courage to announce openly that he intended to "look in" at the Refuge. He blushed a little as he said it, and stroked his hat.

Nobody made any comment—only Ruth sent a message to Alice. When next we saw Alice she remarked that she had received this message, and executed whatever its directions were, which I forget. Nothing more.

One evening still early in May, Ruth and I were taking a little stroll in the meadows, when we met Mr Marten. He was in high spirits; in fact, that was now his normal condition. I was very glad to see him, because, at that particular time, I wanted to consult him about the terrible coloured window of St Cross. I wished to get his consent for its removal. If I succeeded, I would substitute another at my own sole expense, quite apart from any assistance I rendered to the fund for general repairs.

Accordingly, I introduced the subject, without any preamble, candidly adding, that I was prepared for objections, inasmuch as I believed my own sister did not share my views on the matter.

"I'm glad you tell that, Edward," said Ruth, "for it is the truth. Why should people's nerves be so fine as to shrink from the sight of what HE endured? His own mother was strong enough to see it."

"Ah, so she was," I responded; "but, depend on it, she never spoke about it afterwards. And, Ruth, I fancy it would be those wrenched and worn with agony something like hers, who would shrink most from that picture, because they only would feel all its terrible meaning. I know _I_ don't, but it pains me for their sake."

"I daresay I do not realise its horrors more than you do, sir," said the rector; "but yet it pains me for my own sake,—or rather, it did so, for I doubt if it would have the same power now. I was often heroic enough to rejoice it was behind me!"

" Therefore while in that state of mind," I remarked, " had you been one of the laity, and doomed to confront it, you would have stayed away from worship."

" A pretty morbid state of mind it must have been," said Ruth. " I can't understand such weakness."

" Then thank God, my sister," I observed, " and so pity those who can."

" Surely *you* can't," she answered, somewhat sharply, as if resenting the possibility of such weakness in so near a relation.

" Not in my own spirit, God be praised," I replied; " but none the less I know it exists, as I know of blindness or palsy, or other evils I have never suffered, or of poetry or music, or other gifts which I have not— yet!"

" But such weakness, however pardonable, should be conquered, and not humoured," said Ruth, rather more gently.

" If you had a broken leg to be made whole," I argued, " would you walk upon it or rest it?"

" H'm—I don't know," she retorted; " I daresay I should use it more quickly than most people!"

" If it were mine, would you tell me to do the same?" I queried.

" You would not mind me if I did," said she, "for you are naturally lazy!"

" Can't you abstract all personalities from the question," I said, warming just a little, " and answer me fairly which you would recommend as the best course?"

" Well," she answered, "in the first instance I should

recommend the owner of the leg to take care it did not get broken, and I should say the same of hearts or spirits, or whatever region is the seat of the whims you're talking about."

" But, in all cases, some unavoidable accidents will happen," I pleaded.

" So they will," said she.

" Then granting that, which is the best and surest cure—perfect rest, or exercise, while the limb is in a diseased state ?" I questioned.

" Depends upon the patient," she replied, shortly. " If it were *my* duty to walk, then it would do me less harm than lying still; for that would set me in a fever."

" But if you were the nurse, should not you think it your duty to keep the invalid calm and "——

" Stop, Edward, stop," said my sister : " we need not argue it. You can do as you like about the window. I don't wish to hinder you."

" I always thought you could give an argument fair hearing, Ruth," I remarked, a little hurt.

" So I can—except when it proves me in the wrong," she replied, with a sly glance, which quite restored my good temper. " And see, here is Mr Herbert standing at his gate ;" for that moment we came in sight of the Great Farm.

Of course we stopped for a chat. If Mr Marten had been alone, I think he would have bowed and passed on ; but as he was with us, he remained to speak. Ruth's first inquiry was for Agnes.

" She's somewhere in the house," answered her uncle

"If you will step inside, Miss Garrett, I will call her. Gentlemen, will you follow?" he added, with a slight hesitation.

"Mr Garrett and I are consulting about some church alterations," said the rector, as an apology for declining the invitation.

"Well, can't you talk in our parlour?" returned Mr Herbert. "I guess Mr Garrett can, and I suppose you are not talking secrets, are you?"

"Oh dear, no," I said, "we shall be very glad to include you all in our consultation;" and with this I stepped up to the garden-path, and the rector followed in silence.

"A fine old place, to my mind, ma'am, though it's rough and old-fashioned," said our host, walking beside Ruth, and doing the honours. "But I've a right to say so. I was born in this house, and my father, and his father, and his grandfather, were born here before me. And our family has lived on the spot for two centuries, only the old house was burnt down, and the present one was built in my great-great-grandfather's time. But don't you fancy we belong to the gentry; we're only a good old yeomen stock—there isn't a better in the three nearest counties. And don't you fancy I'm proud of it. I'm no more proud of it, Mr Garrett, than you are of your money. You use your fortune to buy up all the hearts in the village by the kindness you do with it. That's your way. So I use my good old English blood; I keep 'em in their place by it. Bless you, if I let go that hold over 'em, I haven't got another."

"Wouldn't it be better, sir," I said, "if you used it to show them how successive honest and industrious generations, without any chance helps of fortune, lift their family above the low level of its fellows?"

Mr Herbert gave his good-humoured, coarse laugh.

"Let them find that out for themselves," said he. "If one does it, that's quite enough. I suppose my ancestor made it out for himself, and I'm glad his neighbours weren't enlightened on the matter. If they had kept pace with us, we should be no better off than if we had only kept pace with them!"

"But because your descent proves that honesty and industry may prosper apart from mere 'luck,'" I remarked, "it does not disprove that, in other cases, the will of God may set obstacles between the same qualities and success. Doubtless, if you review your family history, you will remember many instances where the well-being of the Herberts might have been damaged or destroyed, or at least hindered, by one of those commonplace misfortunes which happen every day to somebody. There are the M'Callums—high-principled people—who were prosperous after the frugal fashion of their country, and yet, through no fault of their own, they were forced to forego all the advantages of old neighbourhood and ancient respectability, and to begin a struggle for bare existence under new conditions in a strange land"——

"There!" exclaimed Mr Herbert, enthusiastically, slapping my shoulder, "that's what I always say! Good blood, like good wine, needs no bush. It speaks for itself. I knew that Ewen was above the common. He never said so; because he knew if the mettle was in him, it would not need his recommendation. But he did his work so that he never needed to be told that I was his master. I'm glad the yeoman blood is in him, sir. The best blood in the world. It made Great Britain what she is, sir."

The worthy farmer was evidently in happy ignorance of any difference between the Celtic and Saxon races, and I fear none of us was sufficiently well informed on the subject to care to begin his education in that particular.

" Well, so long as any blood, whether 'gentle' or simply 'good,' is never boasted, but quietly proved by deeds, the wildest Radical will scarcely complain," said Mr Marten ; " but certainly 'descent' is oftenest on the lips of those who themselves forget—

> ''Tis only noble to be good,
> Kind hearts are more than coronets,
> And simple faith than Norman blood.'"

" Pooh! who thinks anything of coronets?" interrupted Mr Herbert. " How were many of them earned?"

" Anyhow, many were earned most honourably," I returned; "and their value is, that they should be a spur to incite their wearers to rival the sires who won them. A great and good ancestor is as much a gift of God as any other blessing."

" And if the descendant prove unworthy, he changes that blessing into a curse," said the rector.

" So he does," observed Mr Herbert, with sudden gravity ; " but, to tell you the truth, I hate to hear about 'degenerate families.' Let every respectable family be considered extinct on the death of its last worthy representative."

"But some people have strange notions of worth," began Mr Marten, but he was interrupted, for, as our host uttered his last dogma, Agnes joined us, entering the great dining-room by one door, as we reached it by another. She looked a little scared, just as she had done on my first visit to the Great Farm, and she glanced from one to another as if she wondered what we were talking about. Her entrance broke the conversation, and presently Mr Marten introduced the subject of our previous discussion—the coloured window of St Cross.

"I say, Mr Garrett, can't you let well alone?" was the farmer's bluff query. "Any old thing is better than a new one, I'll engage."

"What is Miss Herbert's opinion?" asked the rector.

"I shall be sorry if it be taken away," she answered; "and yet I wish it had never been there."

"Thank you, my dear," I said; "that is the strongest possible argument on my side of the case."

"Is it?" she queried, smiling. "I don't quite understand why."

"I do," said Mr Marten.

And I think so did Ruth.

"Well, it does not matter to me what the window is," remarked Mr Herbert; "so you can settle it how you like, for my part."

"But you will not destroy the old window, will you?" asked Agnes.

"No, my dear," I answered, "we will exchange it for another."

"Will that be right?" questioned the conscientious rector. "Should we offer another what we reject ourselves?"

"Others may not be in our case," I replied. "In many churches there are several painted windows. In such our objection to this design does not hold good."

"Ah, I see that," assented Mr Marten.

"Then what shall you have?" asked the farmer. "Your coat-of-arms, eh, Mr Garrett?"

"Our family has never troubled the Heralds' College," I answered, drily, for I was rather affronted by his hint of self-glorification.

"I think heraldry out of place in churches," said the rector. "Need we take the most secular art on earth to adorn the House of God?"

"I don't quite agree with you," remarked Ruth. "An escutcheon is a family possession as much as a purse, and as a man may pour the one into God's treasury, so he may set up the other in God's temple, purely in the spirit of dedication,—'I and my house, we will serve the Lord.'"

"True enough," responded Mr Marten; "only I fear that spirit is somewhat scarce. But, at least, you do not think heraldry appropriate to a chancel window?"

"Certainly not," said Ruth.

"Do you think we shall have to order a window, Mr Garrett?" inquired the rector.

"I don't think so," I answered. "St Cross' window

is by no means unusually large, and many of the London ecclesiastical warehouses have coloured glasses which can be made to fit it by using wider or narrower borders."

"And who is to survey these warehouses and make the selection?" asked Mr Marten, rather blankly.

"You and I," I replied, laughing. "We will take the trip together."

"Oh dear," said he, "I wish I could get rid of the responsibility! What device do you think most suitable, Miss Garrett?"

"Well, certainly *not* two or three thin monks, each in a separate shrine, turning up his eyes, as if that promoted God's glory," returned my practical sister.

"Monks, Ruth?" I exclaimed. "I think you mistake. Surely they are intended for apostles?"

"If so, they are libels," she retorted. "Apostles, indeed! The apostles were all honest working men, and what reason have we to suppose they were so foolish as to wear pink and blue trailing robes, with embroidered edges?"

"I think some incident from the life of our Saviour would be far better," I remarked.

"Not with the usual treatment," Ruth replied. "There is scarcely one picture taken from our Lord's life which is not a LIE. Can their smooth, pink, feminine faces give any idea of One who wrought hard work, and lived in sun and wind? Are their delicate draperies consistent with the fact that He had not where to lay His head?"

"But I suppose art must have some licence in these

P.

things," I observed. "You see a painted window must be 'a thing of beauty.'"

"Truth first—and then as much beauty as you like," said Ruth.

"So say I," joined Mr Herbert, heartily. "But that is not the fashion now-a-days, madam."

"But there are subjects which admit of beautiful form and colour without any clashing with facts," said the rector. "I know a splendid window with emblematical figures of Faith, Hope, and Charity."

"And I'll engage the artist has painted them so that the most worthless women who ever enter the church are most like them!" answered Ruth.

"I confess I prefer scriptural subjects for church windows," I remarked.

"Certainly, if they are so treated as to convey God's truth," responded my sister; "for then they may be as useful as the sermon!"

"Do not the parables offer good subjects?" suggested Agnes, timidly.

"Yes, that they do," replied Ruth; "and as they are lessons which Christ set in stories, it does not seem inappropriate that we should set them in pictures. But they are not very common, are they, Edward?"

"I have seen them in some city churches, I believe," I answered; "in St Stephen's, Walbrook, for instance."

"But I don't like any great figures in a window," said the rector. "One cannot see anything else. If you will recall any ancient cathedral, you will remember there is nothing obtrusive about its coloured windows. They warm the light, and rest the eye, but they never stare one out of countenance."

"Well, I daresay we could divide the St Cross window into three parts," I said, "and about the centre of each part place a medallion representing a striking parable, and then fill in the ground with minute and richly-coloured devices."

"And what parables shall you select ? " asked Ruth.

"We must choose those which can best be illustrated," I answered. "I fear it would be hard to make the parable of 'the labourers' tell its own story in a picture."

"Perhaps the Good Samaritan will do for one," said Agnes.

"Yes," replied Mr Marten, "and the Prodigal Son for another."

By this time twilight had fallen, and Mr Herbert started up so suddenly, that some suggestion which was on my lips vanished completely from my mind, and I could never afterwards recall it.

"I don't know why we're sitting in the dark," said he ; "I'm getting quite sleepy, begging the company's pardon for saying so. Ah, here comes Mrs Irons with lights." And our worthy host stamped firmly down the long room, and closed the shutters of the end window with his own hands.

Meantime, Mrs Irons advanced to the table, and set down a very handsome, antique bronze lamp. Then she deliberately smoothed the table-cover, which did not really need smoothing, and at last inquired in her dry acid tones—

"Have you any orders, sir?"

"Now, you know all about it, Sarah," replied her bluff master; "only don't be long."

"I think we must say good-night, Ruth," I said, rising.

"No, you shan't," said the farmer in his peremptory way; "there's some ham coming in presently. Sarah will spread supper in a minute, Miss Garrett. She won't keep you waiting. She's an invaluable woman. Been in this house thirty years. Came here as my mother's maid. Found she liked the place, and concluded she would stay. Never was any danger of *her* sweethearts drinking up the ale in the kitchen. The only trouble she ever made was that she frightened all the men-servants away."

"Well, Mr Herbert," observed Ruth, with some asperity, "considering what specimens of womankind one sees in the bonds of matrimony, nobody can suppose that any woman is *obliged* to remain single on account of any ugliness, or even wickedness."

At this instant, Mrs Irons, carrying the supper-tray, and followed by a young attendant damsel, entered the room. While the elder servant spread the cloth, the girl arranged five chairs about the table, and Mr Herbert and his niece took their seats at either end. Mr Marten chanced to overlook this arrangement, and so drew up his own chair, and as Ruth and I sat down side

by side, an empty seat remained between him and
Agnes. When he perceived this he pointed to it, and
said, laughingly—

"Look, Miss Herbert, the ghost's seat!"

He had scarcely uttered the words before I saw he
wished he could recall them. And yet they seemed
harmless enough. But Agnes' face quivered, and she
glanced nervously at her uncle, while she gave the ob-
noxious chair a little ineffectual push. Mr Herbert's
face crimsoned, and he threw a fierce glance at the rector;
it was only a flash—next instant he turned round on his
chair, and shouted in a voice of thunder—

"Sarah, come back and take this——"

I think he was about to utter a word which our presence forbade, and as he checked himself in that particular, he also paused in his command. He got up, and
himself removed the chair, for Mr Marten sat perfectly
still, as if afraid that any movement on his part would only
make bad worse. Our host had scarcely returned to his
seat, when the door opened, and the dry, sour voice inquired—

"Did you call me, sir?"

"Yes, Sarah, I did," he answered, in quite a propitia-
tory tone; "but I made a mistake. Nothing is wanted,
thank you, Mrs Irons."

"Very well, sir," said the acid tones outside the
door.

Our conversation never recovered that shock. We
all left immediately after supper, and Mr Marten
walked home with us. Somehow, I guessed that he

knew the secret of the Great Farm, but whether he
kept silence because he supposed we knew it too, or
because he had learned it in the course of his pastoral
duty, in either case it behoved me to respect that
silence.

# CHAPTER XVI.

HAVING once arrived at the conclusion that we must take a journey to London, Mr Marten and I were not long in making the necessary arrangements. I wished Ruth to be of the party, but she would not " trouble us," as she called it, and so we were fain to go alone. And we started on the third morning after our visit to the Herberts, with nothing to take charge of except ourselves and a portmanteau, and two messages and one parcel, sent by Mr M'Callum and Alice to Ewen.

Ruth drove with us to the railway station, and when I saw her standing on the platform as we were whirled away, it seemed almost a revival of our old parting scene on Mallowe Common. But it was a revival with many improvements.

The rector had asked, "By which class shall we travel?" And it struck me that he would not have put this ques tion had he not wished to go second-class himself. So I gave him the answer I thought he wanted. And as the day was fine and warm, I found our second-class carriage exceedingly comfortable, and could not help reflecting that such men as Shakspeare and Dante would have esteemed it the height of luxury to travel in a vehicle now despised by many a paltry dandy, who is only kept in the flesh by his father's allowance.

During the earlier part of our journey we had three fellow-passengers. When I enter a train or an omnibus, it often seems to me that I must have known my fellow-travellers in some former stage of existence, where I unfortunately offended them. How otherwise can I account for the active animosity of the lady on my right, or the passive contempt of the gentleman opposite? Sometimes during the course of a journey, I contrive to propitiate them, but generally it is not easy. Nevertheless, I always do my best. So, on this occasion, as there was a newspaper in the hands of one of our party, a red-faced, important person—one of those who always suggest the idea of an intimate relationship with our national grandmother in Threadneedle Street—I presently ventured to inquire if there were any important telegrams from a certain foreign country, upon which the whole world was then intently gazing.

"No, sir," he answered, suddenly lowering the crackling sheet, and confounding me with the Gorgon gaze of stony gray eyes; "no, sir, there is not." And then up again went the closely-printed page, and down went my hopes of any reconciliation in that quarter.

Opposite sat a fair damsel of fifty, who seemed uneasy at finding herself the sole representative of her sex. I fear she thought I admired her, for I confess my eyes would wander in her direction, simply because I could not help wondering what she could possibly have been in her girlhood, and what she might eventually become before her career closed. I have heard of a great man who would not seek an interview with an early love in her middle age, because he wished to preserve her youthful memory. I always thought that strange, a sacrifice of feeling to sentiment. But I don't wonder at it, if he had learned to associate middle age with looks like that lady's. I think she had worn the bloom from her soul by fearing lest it was wearing from her face, and her spirits seemed quite exhausted by her vain contest with Time. I cannot think why any should fear his touches, when once they feel them. They may shrink a little beforehand, for unknown change is always sad. As the white marble is fair, so is the smooth young brow; but even as the one is ennobled by the sculptor's chisel, so is the other by the tracings of a good life. There is a beauty of dimples, and a beauty of crows' feet. We may put summer fruit on our winter tables, as a surprise and a rarity, but we do not choose it for our Christmas dinner. For all things there is a season, and what is seasonable is best.

As for our third passenger, I can only describe him as a pair of checked trousers, one straw-coloured glove, a black frock coat, a little reddish hair, and a low-crowned hat. I never saw more of him. He looked out of the window with the greatest assiduity. Perhaps he was shy. Perhaps he had been crossed in love. Perhaps he was in trouble. I shall never know. When our train stopped at a certain station he slipped from the carriage. The stout gentleman gave a sonorous cough, got up, threw down his paper—it was the *Standard*—and also alighted. The lady half rose, and then sat down, and then rose again; but when Mr Marten, kindly thinking to relieve her uncertainty, repeated the name of the station, she only answered with a freezing glance, and, gathering up a sea of fluffy frills and fringes, hastily quitted the carriage, leaving us alone.

As we moved on again, Mr Marten pointed to the newspaper, and laughingly remarked—

" That good gentleman left his journal behind him as a present to you, that you may look over the telegrams for yourself."

" Very much obliged for the favour," I said, taking possession of it.

" I dare say he meant to vex you," observed my companion.

" Oh, I hope not," I replied, " and it does not matter if he did, as I am not vexed, but quite the contrary, for I had no time to read the news before I left home this morning."

I found one or two reviews, and sundry items of political interest, and our discussions over these beguiled our time until the broad horizon narrowed, and knots of trim villas betokened the outskirts of the great city. Then gradually the fields vanished, and soon the newly-

planted trees of surburban gardens also disappeared, and
the train dashed on its resolute way amid a forest of
houses. On and on it went, cutting through the narrow
unknown arteries of our giant London, and the houses
crowded close upon its path and upon each other, for it
was the dreadful East End, where space is valuable—
more valuable than life? As we crossed the railway
bridges we saw the people swarming like insects in the
streets below. Through open windows, staring on the
dreary lines, we caught glimpses of sundry household
arrangements, patch-work quilts, boiling kettles, and
spread tables.

" Here every room is a home," I remarked.

" Don't say ' home,'" said Mr Marten, dismally shaking his head.

" Yes, I will say ' home,'" I replied, " for more are
homes than the reverse. The upper and middle classes
are too prone to judge the very poor by what they read
in the police reports. They have no reason to complain
if, in return, the very poor judge them, as I fear they
do, by the revelations of the Divorce Court. If you
take up any commonplace aristocratic fiction, you are
sure to find the conventional labourer, who gets drunk,
beats his wife, and starves his children, and only exists
to be converted by the angelic efforts of the young ladies
from the Hall. And if you buy any of the badly-printed
penny serials sold in the streets beneath us, you will be
equally sure to find the conventional nobleman, whose
mansion is a very charnel house, and who deceives and
seduces every girl he sees, until he is finally induced to

abandon his wickedness that he may deserve the hand of some peerless village damsel, whose virtue has resisted force and fraud alike. Now, one picture is as true as the other, or rather as false. I readily grant that in real life there are more ill-conducted labourers than wicked lords, because there are more labourers than noblemen. But unfortunately each class judges the other by the bad specimens, which, like all evil weeds, come into undue prominence."

"I did not make my remark in any depreciation of the poor," observed the rector; "only it seems to me that to keep one's mind pure and healthy and heavenward amid influences such as these, must be so hard as to be nearly impossible."

"Mr Marten," I said, "the modern school of sentimental philanthropists appear to forget that when Christ gave His opinion on the subject, He said, 'How hardly shall *they that have riches* enter into the kingdom of God!' Do not think I deny that this wretchedness is an evil, but I believe it does more harm to the soul of the rich man who allows it to be endured, than to the soul of the poor man who must endure it."

Just then the train stopped; it was not yet the terminus, but only a little eastern station, where many of the third-class passengers alighted. Close behind the parapet rose a tall old house. Its wide, low garret window overlooked the end of the platform. At this window stood a young woman, trimming a laurel in a red pot. She was a pretty girl in a coarse linsey dress. Presently a young railway guard came down the platform whistling, and when he saw her he laughed and nodded, and then stopped, leaning over the parapet. They could easily exchange a few words, but they had to raise their voices a little, and so I could hear what they said.

" Don't forget this evening, Maggie," said he.

" No, indeed," said she. "Shall you get away in time, Tom ? "

" Oh, yes," he answered. " Mind you don't make it late, Maggie."

" Mind *you* don't," she retorted.

" All right," said he. And then our train moved on, and left the little idyl behind ; and I looked at Mr Marten, and smiled, and he smiled back again.

After that, we were very soon at the terminus ; and when we were walking down the platform, who should we see alighting from another carriage but that fair damsel of fifty who had deserted us so early in our journey !

" She only changed carriages," I remarked to my companion. " So you see what she thought about us."

" Poor idiot ! " said Mr Marten.

" But I daresay we sometimes judge as unfairly," I added.

We took a cab, and drove to a comfortable old-fashioned hostelry in a quiet city close. There we dined, and after dinner, it being too late to begin our art expeditions for that day, Mr Marten went off to the Temple to visit a college crony, and I took a leisurely walk to my old house of business by the churchless city grave-yard. But by the quiet which I observed stealing over the streets, I feared that I should be too late to find my friends there. So it proved. Principals and staff had alike departed, with the exception of the old head-clerk, who regularly made a point of being the last on the premises. I was a great favourite of his, and he always treated me with that quaint patronage which confidential servants often extend to their employers. He took me into the familiar counting-house, where we sat down and chatted. He was a little man, whose wiry gray hair had a tendency to stand upright, and he had a habit of touching his auditor's arm when he wished to give particular emphasis to his words. He did so when he told me that the firm had bought the good-will of Barwell Brothers, and had found it a highly profitable investment. He did so when he told me that the junior partner was about to marry the senior partner's daughter; and he did so when he spoke of Ewen M'Callum.

"A fine young man, sir," he said in his little precise tone. "Of course, I know all about him. Whatever is told to the firm is told to me, sir, which, of course, you understand, Mr Garrett. So I'll own I suspected him at first, and I kept my eyes on him, but he had not been here a month before I saw that to pay him eighteen shillings a week was a sheer robbery on the part of the firm, sir. Now I'm not one for sudden advancement" (an emphatic touch), "but I talked it over with the principals, and we came to a conclusion. You remember we have on the premises, sir, a dinner-table for the boys—those young lads that get eight or nine shillings a week. Just

plain joint and vegetables, sir. Yes, yes, you remember.
We don't have it for the better-paid clerks, because they
may prefer dining with their wives at home, and if they
haven't got wives they can go to an ordinary, and suit
themselves *exactly*. So we made M'Callum free of that
dinner-table, which would make his eighteen shillings
go a great deal further" (another touch.) "He wrote
home of the arrangements, did he, sir? Yes, yes. he's
a grateful sort of lad. And no one could be jealous,
for the others' wages are all much higher. And now I'll
tell you a secret, sir. At Midsummer his salary will be
raised to EIGHTY POUNDS A YEAR!" (a vigorous poke.)

"I'm very glad to hear it," I said; "and as I must
not keep you from your family any longer, I will bid you
good-bye, and go and pay him a visit."

"But surely you will see something more of the firm
while you are in London?" observed the worthy man.

"Certainly," I answered; "I will be here as much as
I possibly can, but the length of my stay is very uncertain."

So I took my departure. I knew where Ewen lodged,
as he had written to us several times since Alice had
delivered my sister's injunction. I got into an omnibus
at the Bank, and rode to the "Angel," Islington, whence
I soon found my way into the Liverpool Road. Ewen
lived in a small cross street of humble but decent appearance. I soon found his number. There was a
plate on the door announcing that the landlord was a
tailor. The parlour window was screened by a respectable wire-blind, and had old-fashioned wooden shutters

outside. The establishment boasted both knocker and bell, and I chose the latter. Why need I alarm the quiet street, and throw the good housewife into an unnecessary flutter?

A plump, pleasant-faced woman opened the door. "Yes, sir, he's at home," she answered to my inquiry for "Mr M'Callum." "Will you step inside, sir; and what name shall I say?"

"Mr Garrett," I replied, advancing into the passage. The landlady ran up-stairs, and I heard her open the door, and announce me, and then Ewen's voice said, "Take the candle, please, for it must be quite dark on the stairs." But simultaneously there was a scuffle of feet, and a rush down the stairs, and a tall figure passed me in the dusk, and went out at the front door.

"Will you step this way, sir?" cried the landlady's cheerful voice, as she held the light over the banisters. I obeyed, and went up three flights of stairs. At the top Ewen welcomed me, took the candle from the woman, and led me into his room; and after our first greetings, and when I had repeated my message, and delivered his parcel, I found a moment's leisure to glance round it.

It was neither large nor small, and had two windows facing northward. It was clean and neat, but the furniture was singularly scanty. The floor was bare. In one corner stood a small, ascetic-looking bed, with a common deal washstand near it. The table was also deal; and there were only three chairs—two Windsor ones, and a cane arm-chair, in which Ewen had placed me. The rest of the furniture consisted of Ewen's box, (on which lay a shabby portmanteau,) a common look-ing-glass hung against the wall, and a homely set of book-shelves, with a decent array of worn books. I noticed a door beside the fire-place that I concluded belonged to a cupboard. But the region about the mantel had a brightness which, by its contrast to the rest of the apartment, reminded me of the little de-corated shrines one sees in Roman Catholic houses. There were three pictures hanging above it—two small ones unglazed, and one much larger, which boasted a very narrow frame. This one I could see was a head, but by the dim light of the solitary candle I could not distinguish more. The shelf itself was decorated by two plaster casts, and one or two bright bits of pottery, and at either end was a smart hand-screen. But there was a familiar look about the room which puzzled me. I had certainly never seen it before, nor could I recall any-thing like it, and yet it was not wholly strange. My observations were made in a minute, and then my eyes returned to my young host. Glancing at him as he stood in the centre of the room, I suddenly noticed that the two chairs were both drawn up to the table, on which lay two heaps of papers, indicating the recent presence of two individuals. Then I remembered the apparition in the passage.

"I fear I have disturbed you," I said; "did not a friend of yours run away when he heard of my arrival? I saw some one go out."

Ewen laughed, and yet looked a little embarrassed.

S

"Oh, he is staying with me," he answered.

"But why did he run away?" I queried; "I should not have eaten him."

"He did not wish to intrude," said the young man, rather stiffly.

"But a pleasant companion never intrudes," I replied. "If you know where to find him, pray fetch him back."

Ewen paused, and mechanically turned over the leaves of an open book lying on the table. Then he looked up, and said with hurried frankness—

"I must tell you at once, sir, that my friend is in such an unhappy state of mind that he generally shuns seeing or being seen."

"I am sorry he did not make me an exception to the rule," I answered, "for I might help him in some way. I think you say he lives with you?"

"At present," Ewen replied. "You see, sir, I am out all day, and then he has the room entirely to himself."

"Doesn't he go to business?" I inquired.

"He is an artist," said Ewen.

"Oh, indeed," I responded, involuntarily glancing round the bare chamber.

"This room has the advantage of a north light," explained the young man, "and the landlady is very kind and attentive. Her husband is a Scotchman, and new to London. I heard from one of my fellow-clerks that they let apartments. The rooms they showed me at first were nicely furnished and too expensive for me. But in the course of conversation, they mentioned this attic, and said they did not wish to go to the expense of furnishing it just now. And presently they said, if I could be satisfied with the furniture you see, they would let me have the room at a very low rent. And I have been here ever since."

"I see you stick to your art studies," I said, glancing at the etchings strewed about the table. "I suppose your artist-friend gives you a few hints."

"Yes, indeed he does," he replied; "some of his things are wonderfully beautiful."

"So are yours," I said.

Ewen smiled very sadly. "Mine are commonplace," he answered. "I always miss the idea in my mind. But I work and work and work upon them, and then they look elaborate, and so sometimes tempt the dealers to buy, while they stupidly reject his brilliant sketches, with genius in every dash of the pencil."

I glanced at this young man, with his passionate brow and intense eyes, and it struck me that very likely the dealers were right. But I only said, "Genius goes but a little way without hard work."

"And hard work goes but a little way without genius," he answered, somewhat bitterly.

I looked at him again. He was certainly paler and thinner than formerly. His hands had lost the hue they had caught in his days of out-door work. His manner had always been good, not, as people say, for "what he was," but intrinsically good, despite a little shy embarrassment; yet now he had gained an air which caused me to suspect that his companion was not without polish. But I also noticed that he looked much older, and like one who has passed through a severe moral struggle, where self-conquest was not gained without sharp suffering. I thought, surely this is not merely the trace of his artistic aspirations. And yet I knew that genius, before it understands itself, is often like that dumb spirit in the Scripture, which tore and wore its unhappy owner. So I said, cheerfully, "And your genius, my boy, combined with your hard work, will go a very long way. And when you are at the top of the tree, don't forget that I said so, but give me credit as a good prophet and a wiseacre."

He smiled a little more brightly.

"But I hope you do not forget rest and exercise," I added; "I need not hope you don't neglect business, for I have just heard your praises sounded at the counting-house."

"I think I give satisfaction there," he answered, meekly, "and I never sit up late, and I take two long walks regularly every week; I should not do justice to my work if I neglected those things."

"And yet you get through much drawing," I remarked.

"I could not live without it now," he exclaimed, with startling enthusiasm.

Then it had come to this! The spell was on him, whether for good or for evil. "My boy," I said, gently, "would you like to devote yourself wholly to art?"

"No," he replied, slowly and firmly; "but I suppose if I were a genius I should. And yet Milton did not live on 'Paradise Lost,' and Shakespeare made his fortune from his playhouse and not from his plays. And I'd rather get my bread like other people."

"Your friend does not think thus," I said.

"He did not think so," he answered; "but it would have been better for him, and for every one concerned, if he had."

I looked again at Ewen, for there was an undefinable something about him which filled me with wonder. He had certainly grown much older than the lapse of five months warranted; but it was not only that.

"Your friend is not in trouble?" I queried.

"Not now," he said.

"And you are in no trouble?" I whispered, softly.

"Why, what makes you say such a thing, sir?" he questioned in return, turning on me his old smile, which yet had a new solemnity that gave pathos to its brightness. "There ought not to be a happier man in London, sir, thanks to you."

"Thanks to God," I said—and I said no more; for, of all the delicate tortures which society tolerates, there are few more cruel than such remarks as, "You seem sad to-day," or, "You look ill." If mistaken, they annoy; if true, they sting.

After a little more conversation we parted. I would not promise another visit, for I scarcely knew what my plans would be. Yet, in my own mind, I felt sure that I should not leave the city without seeing Ewen again.

# CHAPTER XVII.

## MR RALPH.

N the morning, Mr Marten and I went off to one of the most celebrated ecclesiastical warehouses. I had not been in such a place since my boyhood, when I had carried a message from my good old master, relative to some simple piece of church furniture which he had ordered for the use of his parish church. I found the house much enlarged. In the old-fashioned days of my youth the garments of the sanctuary were so plain and so universal that they needed no display, but orders for them were quietly received at a desk, and the only matter for consideration was the precise quality of the silk or linen. But now a plate-glass window was stocked with clerical finery. Upon a dummy, like those in mercers' windows, stood a surplice with a cross embroidered on the collar, and over it was thrown a hood ostentatiously displaying the "Oxford" colours. We passed through this depart-

ment, and then we were shown into another, where we were detained some time, until the assistant who attended the sales of coloured glass was at liberty to wait upon us. In this place, I should have been fairly confounded but for the rector's explanations. I did not even know the names of the things about me, and when I learned them from the shopmen I was no wiser, until Mr Marten gave me the plain English for such words as "lectern" and "faldstool," "credence" and "piscina," and taught me that an "eagle" might be a reading-desk, and a "corporal" a cloth, and not a soldier!

"But it seems to me all rank folly," I said; "and I cannot understand how any sane man can upset the unity of the Church for such rubbish."

"To those who do so, it is not such folly as it seems to you," answered the rector. "In their eyes these things symbolise certain doctrines. For instance, that cloth which they choose to call a *corporal* is used to cover the bread at the Lord's Supper. Its name is plainly derived from the Latin *corpus*, or body, a subtle introduction of that doctrine of transubstantiation which changes our feast of *remembrance* into a *sacrifice*. Admitting the idea of sacrifice, an altar is needed, and where there is an altar there must be, not a simple ministry like that of the apostles, but a priesthood clothed with the mystic dignity and terrible powers of spiritual privilege—and able to brand with the sin of schism any who venture to expose its duplicity, or who dare to defy its encroachments."

"I don't think I could argue about it at all," I said;

"I can only say this doesn't seem like the New Testament."

"It is not, it is not," responded the rector, warmly. "It is a retreat from light into darkness—from realities into shadows—from the sermon on the Mount to the rules for building the tabernacle. And when and where will it end?" he added, mournfully.

"It will end in God's good time and place," I answered; "and, meanwhile, out of evil He can bring some good. Just now, let it stir our zeal to make His house a pleasant place, without turning His service into a mummery."

And so we went on to look at the glasses.

We were shown many specimens of that false and monkish art of which Ruth had spoken. We were assured that it was "admired," and "popular," and "devotional," (strange connexion of words!) We asked if they had no illustrations of the parables or miracles, and, with a sigh for our bad taste, our attendant owned they had; but they were not new, having been removed from a church about to be *restored*. They were shown us, and proved appropriate in shape. But as they were too large to admit of three in the St Cross window, we instantly decided on the Prodigal Son and the Good Samaritan, with a neat medallion representing an open Bible, for the centre of the triangular top of the window. A small device for the groundwork, and a richly-coloured border for the whole, were very easily selected, and so, having made all due arrangements, we left the warehouse and strolled leisurely back to our hotel.

Of course, we looked at the shops; now it is natural for every one to look at pictures and books, and occasionally, according to one's sex, at cravats or bonnets. Also it is pleasant to behold beautiful house-furniture, such as carved sideboards, inlaid cabinets, and stately mirrors. But what possessed Mr Marten to pull me up in front of a painted, cane-bottomed chair, bearing a label, "36s. a dozen," while he remarked, "That seems cheap; doesn't it, Mr Garrett? A dozen chairs go a long way in bedrooms." And a few minutes after, when I was admiring some photographs, and turned to call his attention to their beauty, I found he had wandered away to a china-shop, where he was gravely weighing the comparative merits of tea-sets, respectively priced "£1, 1s." and "£1, 5s." And at last, when he actually stopped to feel the thickness of some very cheap drugget, I slyly said, "Come, come, Mr Marten, we old bachelors need not trouble ourselves about such things." And he answered, hastily, "Oh, no," and hurried on.

Having brought our business to a satisfactory conclusion, we agreed to return to Upper Mallowe by the next day's early train. I felt that my few remaining hours in London were due to my old city friends, and as Mr Marten had many acquaintances of his own to whom he must show attention, I went alone to the counting-house by the churchyard, and saw the whole array of familiar faces, among whom so many years of my life had passed. Of course I saw Ewen, but only as one of the crowd. I went home with the senior partner, and dined at his house in Highbury Crescent, and spent a very pleasant evening, for every one was exceedingly kind. Nevertheless, I left before nine o'clock, and took a cab to the corner of a certain quiet street in the Liverpool Road.

The old-fashioned parlour-shutters were closed, and but for a light in the passage, the whole front of the house was dark. The same cheerful woman opened the door, and instantly recognising me, invited me to enter with a cheerful "Good evening, sir. Will you please to walk up-stairs? Mr M'Callum is at home."

I knocked at Ewen's door, and a voice, not his, cried, "Come in." So I entered. There were two figures seated at the table, with a solitary candle between them. Ewen had his back towards me, and when he heard my voice, he started up, glanced nervously at his companion, and hurried forward to offer me a seat in the cane arm-chair. I saw he was drawing. The stranger was reading. At first he did not look up, but while Ewen and I carried on that desultory chat which distinguishes unexpected visits, I found that he turned from his book, and regarded me with a curious scrutiny.

He was quite a young man, of not more than five or six and twenty. His face was remarkably pale, but his features were handsome, though a little worn for his time of life. I did not notice the details of his attire, but he had an elegant appearance, and his hands were white, and singularly fine in form. At first, I thought he was a little uneasy, though he only showed it by a statue-like stillness, scarcely seeming even to breathe. But after his eyes had twice or thrice met mine, this passed away, and presently he made some casual remark which fell in with the course of our conversation.

By and by Ewen quitted the room. I concluded he went to instruct his landlady to prepare some little hospitality. For a few minutes I and the stranger were silent. Then thinking I must not lose so good an opportunity, I observed—

" It gives me much pleasure to make the acquaintance of a young artist of whose talents my friend speaks so warmly, though I do not think he has ever chanced to mention your name "——

" Ralph—Mr Ralph," he interrupted, with a graceful bow ; " and I feel it a great honour to introduce myself to you, sir," he added hastily, with a strange emotion : " for I, too, have heard and—and heard again of the goodness of Mr Garrett."

" Ah, but you must not trust Ewen for my character," I said, smiling, " for I fear he exaggerates—yes, he certainly exaggerates."

At this instant Ewen returned, followed by a servant-girl with a little supper. It was a very simple repast, but it was quite a treat to me, carrying me back to the distant days when I gave such feasts to my few visitors, the dear friends of my youth, who are now all nearer God.

Our conversation during supper was not very brisk. Mr Ralph was decidedly taciturn, like one who does not care to conceal that his mind is not with his company. But this seemed an unconscious habit on his part, and perhaps arose from too much solitude. Whenever he spoke he was agreeable, though his words sometimes left an uncomfortable impression. Once or twice he was merry, and his mirth was saddest of all. It was as if a man, pursued by a relentless fate, from which he felt himself too weak to escape, recklessly turned and smiled in her direful face. I could not understand the intimacy between him and Ewen. It was evidently of the closest nature, no casual fellowship, entered into from community of tastes or motives of mere financial economy. Yet I could not pass an hour with these two young men without observing a great disparity between their natures. But there seemed a bond between them stronger than any difference of character, and firm enough to resist all change of circumstance. Their manner towards each other had none of the gushing enthusiasm of hastily warm friendships, but rather the quiet settled confidence one notices between brothers, old school-fellows, or tried comrades in war or travel.

"And did you two make acquaintance in London?" I found opportunity to inquire in the course of conversation.

"Oh, we knew each other a long time ago," said Mr Ralph. "Will you pass the ale, M'Callum?"

"School-fellows, perhaps?" I suggested, remembering that Ewen's early education had been received among lads of the apparent position of his companion.

"No; our acquaintance was of a very casual kind," he returned; "but one greets a familiar face when one has been lost in London.—A little more cheese, please, Ewen."

So I understood that the subject was to drop.

"I suppose you will ride home, sir?" remarked young M'Callum, when I rose to go.

"I don't think so," I answered, looking from the window. "This is a bright moon, and the streets are clear and quiet now."

"May I come with you?" said Mr Ralph. "I shall so enjoy the walk."

"Shall I come too?" queried Ewen, as if consulting his friend's pleasure.

"No, my boy," returned the other; "you have to rise early, and march off to business. You go to bed, and to sleep. I will see Mr Garrett safely to his hotel."

After receiving Ewen's home messages, we started off together. My companion offered me his arm. He had a fine, tall figure, and altogether what one calls "a good presence."

"What solemn grandeur hangs over London by night!" I said, as we walked through the moonlit streets. "Are you a native of the city, Mr Ralph, or did you come here to try your fortune?"

"I came here to set the Thames on fire," he answered with a light laugh. "And the Thames extinguished me!"

"Ah," I said, "London is the best place to teach a man his measure. A good lesson, Mr Ralph, and one that is never learned too soon."

"I don't know that," he retorted, laughing again. "When ignorance is bliss, 'tis folly to be wise."

"But when is ignorance bliss?" I asked.

"When knowledge comes too late," he replied.

"And when does knowledge come too late?" I queried.

"When you've done what you can't undo," said he, shortly.

"Then at least you can repent it," I observed. "It is never too late for that. If one's life is ruined, one's soul need not be lost."

"But when one has done all the harm one can," he answered gloomily, "it seems mere gross selfishness to try pushing into heaven at last!"

There was a something in his tone which chilled me as he uttered these dreadful words. Dreadful indeed they were—the very utterance of despair. They revealed a perilous nature, one that would slide down and down, and then use its most loveable instincts to excuse its never rising and struggling upward. He could actually see selfishness in seeking salvation! Well, perhaps his error was not worse than one much more common, when men fancy they have forsaken evil because they are simply sick of it. I tried to fight him with his own weapons.

"But whatever harm one has done," I observed, "he does a greater harm when he finally leaves his soul to destruction."

"Harm to himself or to others?" he inquired, laconically.

"One cannot harm one's-self without harming others," I answered. "'Nobody's enemy but his own,' is a false saying. By benefiting others one benefits one's-self, and by hurting one's-self one hurts others."

" Then goodness is pure selfishness," said he.

" Each has two selves." I explained in answer: " a lower self and a higher self, a temporary self and an eternal self. Each must serve one or the other. By solely seeking the gratification of one's lower and mortal part, one does harm in the world, and neglects one's own best interests. By following the dictates of one's nobler and immortal part, one does good in the world, and makes it a school of preparation for heaven."

" I can believe that," said Mr Ralph, gently, "because I have seen it."

" Now supposing that you were in the case we have in point," I went on ; "supposing that you had done as much harm as you could, and had caused much sin, and suffering, and sorrow—that is, if you will grant me the liberty of such an illustration ? "——

" Oh, certainly," said he, with a laugh.

" Then do you not feel that the very fear lest your soul was lost at last would cause more suffering, and more sorrow, and possibly more sin ? "

" Well, I think it might," he answered, nervously lifting his hat from his head ;—" yes, it would : there 's one or two that it would grieve, and there 's one who 'd say it was only what he expected."

" Then, if you left no reasonable cause for such fear, and so gave happiness to those who love you, and also taught your enemy more charity in future, would not you serve yourself and others at the same time ? "

He did not reply ; but walked by my side in silence. I felt I was carrying on the discussion at a great disadvantage; because I did not say that if it chanced there were none on earth who cared whether he went to God or to Satan, there was still One in heaven whom his absence would grieve, because it would show that he refused the salvation which He had purchased with a great price—even His own blood. And I dared not say this; because I was sure that my companion was as well-informed in the mere theology of the matter as myself. And the formal repetition of a fact whose truth can only be *felt* does no good—nay, it may disgust, by seeming but the easy parade of a glib lip-religion.

At last he spoke suddenly.

"Wandering a little from our subject," he said, "do you think that if a man makes some great self-sacrifices, he does not lose in the end?"

"If he do it for his neighbour's good or God's glory, I am sure he does not," I replied. "But he cannot make the sacrifice in this feeling. If he could, it would lose the very nature of sacrifice. And besides, God's compensations are seldom such as man in his mortality can appreciate. If one resigned his worldly prospects for the sake of another, God might recompense him by an early call to Himself. But till he was fairly within the veil, the touch of death would seem rather his Maker's chastening rod, than his loving Father's benediction."

"Do you—do you think it is right to allow another to make great sacrifices for one's own sake?" he asked, with a broken voice and with averted face.

"It depends upon circumstances," I answered, gently, or I felt I was walking blindfold over the youth's own history ; " but I should not refuse a friend's sacrifice merely because it was greater than I could ever make in return. Why should I grudge him a brighter heavenly crown than mine ? Only I should take care his goodness was not for nought. And, Mr Ralph, if ever a great sacrifice be made in our behalf, let it stand in our hearts as a type of His love who left His Father's throne for our sakes ! Let the human affection interpret the Divine love, and don't waste either."

The young man turned and looked at me—not with the face which he carried to the galleries and the picture dealers, but with the look which he surely had worn when he said "Our Father" at his mother's knee, years before ; —a look which might return and remain for eternity, if his eyes met the eyes of a good woman who loved him. The reckless prodigal laugh was silent ; the cynical artist sneer was gone ; the man's angel was in his countenance —the same angel·that had once been in the innocent child's face—only with the pathetic look of its long struggle with the reckless prodigal and the cynic artist. And.God had marked that angel all the time, and He would watch it to the very end ! It is because He is All-seeing that He is All-loving.

And then we walked in silence for the length of many streets, until at last we reached that leading to my hotel. There we shook hands ; and in our parting I made some simple remark in praise of Ewen M'Callum.

"Yes, yes," he answered, with singular fervour, "all you say is true ; but you don't know him as I do, that's all, Mr Garrett."

T

And so saying, he hurried off.

When I entered my sleeping room, I found a note from Mr Marten, intimating that a telegram had followed him from Upper Mallowe to London, urging him to hasten to Cambridge, to the dying bed of a young relative, a student there. He had received this on reaching the hotel during my absence, and in compliance with its entreaty he had started off immediately.

So my homeward journey was a solitary one.

# CHAPTER XVIII

### A NEW IDEA.

WAS very glad to find myself again in my quiet village home. My little trip to London gave us some new topics of conversation, and my sister was much interested in my account of young M'Callum and his friend. But she took a prejudice against the latter, and hazarded the uncharitable conjecture that he was "no good." When she saw Alice she threw out hints to this effect, which Alice received very quietly and without any reply.

Mr Marten's young relation did not die, but his convalescence was tedious and unsatisfactory, and as he had no other friend to attend him, our rector's absence from his parish proved a long one. A neighbouring clergyman came to us on Sundays, and gave us two sermons in the Refuge. But Mr Marten was at liberty by the time the church repairs were complete.

St Cross was re-opened on the second Sunday in July.

The weather was—just beautiful English summer; I can find no better words for it. Ruth and I set out at the first summons of the new peal of bells, which were among our improvements. I believe in church bells, simple, soft, and sweet,—a sound meet to echo in the sacred memories of childhood's Sabbath. If once linked with feelings of holy happiness, theirs is a voice which may speak where the preacher cannot come, and where the Bible is shut. And praised 'e God, they now sound so widely over the world that few can wander out of their reach.

When we arrived at St Cross, I was quite satisfied with the effect of our alterations, which, though sufficiently familiar to me while in process, I now saw for the first time tested by usage. The narrow path was widened and gravelled, and many evergreens and some flowers were planted about the graves. The porch was much enlarged, and the inner doors stood wide open. But it was the interior which was most changed. All the windows were widened, which destroyed the monotony of the white wall, and their opaque glass was exchanged for small clear panes, with one large coloured pane, bearing some appropriate device, in the centre of each window. Two new windows, containing more coloured glass, were opened north and south of the communion-table, thus brightening a portion of the building which had formerly been both dismal and ill-ventilated. The table itself was entirely refitted, and the candlesticks were gone— into the vestry! The tables of the law were re-written in legible characters, and over one was a scroll bearing a verse from the 103d psalm, " Like as a father pitieth his children, so the Lord pitieth them that fear Him;" and over the other was another inscribed with our Saviour's words, " Take my yoke upon you and learn of me : for I am meek and lowly in heart : and ye shall find rest unto your souls."

But *the* change was certainly the new chancel window. As the worshippers entered, one by one, or in groups, their eyes instantly fell on it, and each countenance brightened. Old Mr M'Callum, with his daughter and George Wilmot, were among the earliest arrivals. Bessie Sanders came soon afterwards, and presently Mr Herbert and Agnes. And just before service commenced, Mr Weston arrived, rather flushed, and in such a twitter that he did not notice the attendant who trotted forward to show him a pew, but precipitately took refuge in the M'Callums' seat, where presently he became quite at home.

The service was conducted in a very simple, spirited way, and Mr Marten's sermon did not attempt to " improve the occasion." Our young rector had sufficient judgment to conclude that "occasions" have a voice sufficiently eloquent to plead for themselves. And his sermon was very short, but full of those pithy truths which stick in the mind like arrows, and are not easily shaken out.

When all was over, the congregation was in no hurry to disperse. Some stayed to speak to others about the new window, and a few old people, whose sight was dim, drew nearer to the chancel to read the texts written above the table.

Mr Marten himself very speedily reappeared from the vestry, and it was then I first noticed that Lieutenant Blake and his daughter were that day among the worshippers at St Cross.   He walked off with them, and as I stood in the churchyard speaking to Mr Herbert, I saw the three pause to examine the skeleton of the house now rapidly rising behind the church, and in front of it Miss Blake turned and gazed around, and made some remark.   I fancy she said it had a very fine prospect.

"Well, my brother," said Ruth, as we sat down to our dinner that day, "you have certainly done *one* good work for Upper Mallowe."

"Yes, and only one," I answered, "for the Refuge is yours."

"Mine!" she ejaculated, "when all I gave was a few household things."

"You gave the thought," I said.   "The liberal deviseth liberal things."

"And I suppose the Lord will accept a plan, if it's all one can do," she replied; "and I have no money to give until I die, for as God prospered me just sufficiently to be independent, please God I'll never be dependent —even on you!"

"But you should not call even the church repairs my work," I said, presently.   "You must not forget that the village has been so liberal that my share of the expense will not exceed a tolerably moderate subscription."

"But then, if I gave the scheme for the Refuge," she answered, "you gave the scheme for the church, and you led the way, and took all the responsibility, whether it might prove great or small."

"Yes, I'll own that," I conceded; "I do so little good that I'll willingly acknowledge all I can."

"Now, I'll tell you what, Edward," said my sister, in that business-like tone which always means something: "you've fairly started the Refuge, and in my will they'll find a little endowment, which, with the annual subscriptions, will carry it safely on. And in the Refuge, I include the Orphan Home, which will cost very little, when once the additional rooms are made. So now I'll give you something else to do. Establish a village hospital, sir!"

"A village hospital!" I echoed, rather startled.

"Yes;" she answered, "what provision have our people in sickness? The very poor are dragged off to Hopleigh workhouse infirmary. Should you like to go there if you were ill? The class a little better off are taken to the hospital in the county town, at great expense of time, and money, and strength, just when they are all most valuable. You give ten pounds a year to that hospital. That ten pounds would be worth at least twenty, if you kept it in Upper Mallowe. And there would be no tedious recoveries, hindered by home-sickness, and no more deaths among strange faces."

"But don't you think the establishment of even a village hospital will be a somewhat complicated matter?" I ventured to inquire.

"No," she answered, decisively, " a country home for the sick is as different from a city hospital as Upper

Mallowe is from London. We shan't want six or eight wards, but about as many rooms. We shan't want a secretary, and a staff of Sisters of St Something or another, but just one experienced God-fearing woman, with two or three young girls between sixteen and eighteen years of age under her."

"Ah," I said, "I begin to see the possibility and the beauty of your plan, Ruth. Why, it may do great good in more ways than one!"

"With God's blessing, it certainly will," she answered. "At the present time, I know of a nice house standing empty. It is a detached cottage on the lonely side of the green, and it has eight well-sized and airy rooms. It may be either rented or sold, but it is dearer than the Refuge was."

"I'll buy it, nevertheless," I said.

"Yes, you can certainly afford that," returned my plain-speaking sister, "and then it will need serviceable, suitable furniture, and there must be maintenance and salary for the matron "——

"You mean the head nurse," I interrupted.

"Call her by the wise German name of 'house-mother,'" my sister went on,—"that includes all her duties; then there will be maintenance for the sick, and medical attendance. I think that is all the out-going. And the income will include subscriptions, the interest from your endowment, for I must leave that matter to you, my brother, and small weekly payments from the girls who assist the house-mother."

"Weekly payments *from* the girls?" I queried.

"Certainly," she answered. "It will be an excellent preparation for all branches of domestic life. Any lady interested in a young girl, or the girl's own parents, ought readily to give enough to purchase her victuals in exchange for such advantages. House-room and instruction will be gratuitous."

"But will one nurse and two or three girls be sufficient for the work?" I asked, dubiously.

"Except during epidemics," she answered, "and then funds for more aid will not be lacking. What is the average number of hospital cases in this little village at one time? Seldom more than five or six, and three or four of those not at all serious."

"But will people have confidence in such a homely affair?" I asked.

"Perhaps they'll laugh at it while they're in health," she promptly replied, "but when the head is sick and the heart is faint, there's nothing very reassuring in a line of pallets, and a long row of windows, and a gaunt white woman coolly naming one with a number. *Then* one longs for a roughly-plastered room, with the trees whispering outside, and familiar faces smiling within. *Then* they'll come to us, and, please God, they'll never laugh at us afterwards!"

"But who shall we choose for the house-mother?" I inquired. "Alice has little nursing experience, and she is too young: besides, the Refuge cannot spare her."

"The Refuge will lose her soon enough," said Ruth, significantly, "and then we shall find it tolerably hard to supply her place.'

"If Miss Sanders would like to become principal of our hospital," I observed, "surely she would suit it admirably. She is clear-headed and kind-hearted, and only God can fathom the depth of her patience."

"But what can we do with her sweet sister?" asked Ruth, with a wry face.

"We must get her a situation," I said.

"Ay, but will she keep it?" queried my sister. "If I wanted a servant, I would not have her, even without wages. I would sooner pension her."

"Then if the worst comes to the worst, we must pension her," I answered.

"A fine reward for idleness!" exclaimed Ruth, indignantly. "Very just towards poor Bessie!"

"Do you suppose Bessie would like us to pension *her*?" I asked, slyly.

"Ah, well, I'll own she would not," conceded my sister, "and I doubt if she would not carry her independence so far as to resent our doing as much for the lovely Anne."

"Nevertheless, if we get Bessie to like our hospital scheme," I said, "we will manage the rest *somehow*."

"Yes, somehow," assented Ruth.

Nothing more was said on the subject until Monday morning, when my sister, steadily true to her old principle of striking the iron while it was hot, took me first to see the empty cottage, and then to visit Miss Sanders. Bessie's face brightened softly as we unfolded our plan, though her words were simple and cool enough. "Yes, she should like it very much, but—Anne?"

"Make her a present of your business," said Ruth.

The dressmaker shook her head.

"Let her sell it to some young woman, and remain here as housekeeper," was my sister's next suggestion.

Miss Bessie smiled dimly, and shook her head again.

"At least try that experiment," I said; "it will certainly do no harm. We can but make some other arrangement if she do not suit the in-comer."

She reflected a few minutes, and then said, "It can do no harm. I beg pardon for being so slow, but the thought of a change rather confuses me. But—but I must speak to Anne before anything is decided."

She went to the door, and called her sister's name. It was but her proud determination to put the best possible appearance on her unhappy family life.

Anne presently answered the summons. She entered, with a grimy face, and a dress representing the fashion of bygone years. Ruth told our errand in a few clear words.

"You need not have asked me, Bessie," said she, turning to her sister. "Why should you consider *me?* Do what you think best for *yourself,* and I hope you will never repent it, but that you will be quite comfortable *at last.* Don't think of me at all," she added, turning to us, "anything will do for me. Some respectable young person will take Bessie's place, and I'll wait on her. I don't mind drudging *all day.* I'll do anything to please any one. I don't mind how I turn about. Since I'm only fit for mean work, I'll not make myself above it."

"No work is mean," said Ruth, rather fiercely, taking up her old argument, "except to a mean mind; and a mean mind makes everything mean."

"Well, I'm very glad you agree with our plans," I observed, rising, for I foresaw a useless tournament between Anne and my sister; "we shall press our work forward as much as we can, so prepare as quickly as possible for your approaching separation. Shall you bring away any of this furniture, Miss Sanders?" I asked.

"Only two or three little things which belong to me personally," she answered. She evidently desired to give Anne every advantage.

"Ah, that will do," I said; "we will provide all the rest. By the way," I added, when we were in the passage, and out of Anne's hearing, "I have not visited you since Mr Marten and I brought you that sad relic of your poor cousin. I suppose no new thought has struck you in connexion with that affair?"

"No, sir," she answered; "and I suppose you have not seen young M'Callum yet, to tell him about the knife?"

"I have seen him," I replied. "I went to London for a day or two, and I saw him there. But I told him nothing. It struck me that he was not very well, and I thought it best he should not hear of it till his own people told him in his own home. I hope you are not angry with my consideration, Miss Sanders."  .

"Oh, sir," she replied, "if every one considered others as you do, it would be a blessed world!" (Remember, my readers, that she measured my consideration only by her sister's, which was nothing at all.)

And so Ruth and I walked homeward.

"Our scheme is ripening fast," I remarked.

"Edward," said she, shortly, "I'm in a bad temper!"

"Indeed!" I exclaimed, "I am sorry for that."

"I daresay you are!" she said, "but that does no good. I'll always say that I'm selfish, and that I don't care for anybody but myself, and that I will have my own way! I'll do anything to be different from that Anne Sanders! No woman has provoked me so much since Laura Carewe. I'm in a regular passion! I feel as if I wanted to kick."

I knew that at that instant no words of mine would soothe my sister's ire, so I walked by her side in silence.

"And you never told me that you did not think Ewen was well!" she added, presently, with no abatement of asperity; "you leave me to find that out for myself. You come home from London and say nothing about it to Alice or me. Can I be sure you are not reserving something else; I've a great mind to go to London and see him for myself."

"My dear Ruth," I expostulated, "I said nothing because I thought it might be only my own imagination. He will have his holidays in a few weeks. So why should I trouble you or his sister? He would not like a fuss over a trifling ailment or a passing depression."

"You'd have made fuss enough had it been Agnes Herbert," said my sister, wrathfully. "You're always noticing whether she looks unhappy or no,— though depend on it she has nothing at all to trouble her except some fine fantastical sentimentality of her own. But women always get all the sympathy. They are the porcelain of humanity, of course, with all their delicate dandelion virtues which blow away at the first breath of every-day air!"

"Is that your description of Alice M'Callum and Bessie Sanders?" I asked, gently.

I knew Ruth heard the question, but she did not heed it, and presently started off on a new tack with—

"As I said directly I heard of him, you may depend upon it that new friend of Ewen's is no good. Some idle daundering good-for-naught" (when Ruth was excited she often used the graphic diction of the country-side) "who takes no trouble for himself, but just lives to trouble honest people. Talk about vampires! I believe in them. There are people who put all their self-made sufferings to suck the very life from other people, and never feel their sting themselves. Oh, well I remember your description of him, just a personification of your Childe Harolds and your Corsairs, and all your other rubbish, who might easily make a good riddance of themselves and their miseries, and not be afraid the world would stop without them!"

By this time we had reached home, and Ruth stepped off to her bedroom, while I went dismally into the parlour, marvelling at the mysterious influence which some natures possess of souring whoever comes near them, even as others always sweeten. The scolding Ruth had given me was all due to her glimpse of Anne Sanders. I knew that well enough.

In about ten minutes my sister reappeared. I had taken refuge behind the outspread newspaper. But she came up to me and put her hand on my shoulder. I looked up, and she laughed rather dolefully.

"The fit is over," she said, "and I'm sorry for the words I said. I'm afraid some of them are true. But I'm just as sorry I said them. Some women have hysterics and some have tempers!"

# CHAPTER XIX

### THE RIGHT OF REFUSAL.

RUTH proceeded very energetically with her hospital plans. She wished the house to be in readiness in case of any visitation of those sicknesses so often attendant on early or late autumn. Agnes Herbert was again her helper, in happy ignorance of the ruthless words which my sister had spoken in her anger, but for which Ruth strove to atone by extraordinary kindness and complacency. Very industriously the two worked and consulted together, with Bessie Saunders for an occasional third. Bessie sold her business very easily, for it was in good repute. So she took up her abode in the little hospital, and found plenty of occupation in putting up the furniture and preparing the house linen.

Meanwhile, the Refuge was in full vigour. Harvest operations had brought down the usual crowd of needy, unskilled labourers, who gladly took shelter there until they procured work. I liked to wander in the fields at their dinner hour, and have a chat about their winter life in London, and hear what they thought of their temporary home in our High Street. They did not know me, or my connexion therewith, and so I knew I should get the truth, and might obtain some useful hints for the future. But had they known who I was, I should certainly have suspected them of insincerity, for there was nothing but praise. Many a hearty Irish blessing did I hear bestowed on Alice M'Callum, "the purty girleen, with the face like the Holy Virgin's in the picture over the altar"—the out-spoken women adding, "We guess she won't be at the Refuge when we come again this time next year. Sure there is a big house down the hill with no want of anything, where she would be kindly welcome, for we have eyes in our heads, and we know what we know; and the ould gintleman will find it a lonely life without her. Heaven's blessing light on the both of them!"

Both Mr M'Callum and his grand-daughter were eagerly looking forward to Ewen's holidays. Through the exigencies of business, these were rather later than had been expected, but Alice bore the delay very patiently, feeling that she would have more time to enjoy her brother's society, when harvest was over, and the Refuge restored to its ordinary condition. Ewen's letters came regularly, both to the Refuge and to our house. Very nice letters they were—written in his close, neat, rather peculiar calligraphy—simply worded, half boyish and half manly in their tone. They had no fine sentences—nothing that any one would care to read but

U

those who knew and loved him. But then to such there was a strange sacredness about these simple letters. One could not bring one's self to destroy them. I kept all he sent me. They are in my desk now. Alice stored hers in her workbox. And you, too, my reader, have some such letters stored somewhere, though your fire may have devoured many clever ones, and perhaps even some with "autographs."

I must say that the medical man of Upper Mallowe entered very warmly into the interests of our little hospital. He was a young married man with a scattered, poor practice, and when he named a very modest sum as the annual price for his professional services at our sick home, I knew there was more real charity in the business-like agreement than in many a magnificent donation; and I think Ruth felt the same, for she sought his advice and concurrence in every question of arrangement and management, and it was wonderful how their views of such things coincided, though he saw everything from the point of scientific knowledge, while she saw all in the plain light of simple common-sense.

I was not admitted to the hospital until everything was finished, by which time Miss Saunders had gained a patient, and also a rosy-faced, obedient damsel to assist her. The patient was a middle-aged woman, an old resident in the village. Her malady was a rapid waste, and when I saw her the truth of my sister's words shone fully on me, and I felt how cruel it would have been had the worn-out invalid been doomed to the worry and excitement of strange sights and systems.

We found Bessie Saunders in the little sitting-room of the place, busily engaged with a basket full of that mysterious "white work' which always appears to excite a feeling of dignified and business-like elation in the heart of every true woman. She looked uncommonly well, and her plain dark violet gown showed to double advantage, inasmuch as it suited both her office and her person. By a skilful arrangement of her own little personalities, and a few simple ornaments with which Ruth had presented her, she had given the humble apartment quite the sociable look of home. We did not find her alone. Agnes Herbert came forward to greet us, with her hat swinging in her hand, as if her visit was no hasty one.

We went over all the rooms, one after another, kitchen and dormitories. As sickness must be, such a place seemed pleasant to suffer in. If it were possible for a life to be all so dreary that one could not remember a mother's smile, or a single "good time," still in these quiet chambers the passing soul might surely carry away one thanksgiving. The poor consumptive woman, sitting in her easy chair, almost too weak to speak, smiled kindly when she saw us. Oh, if we hope there are some angels somewhere in heaven who rejoice to know of us, let us be very gentle to the dying. They are starting for the land we long for. Let them take a good report of us.

"I only fear one thing," said Bessie in reply to my warm praises of all I saw—"I only fear Miss Garrett has trusted me too much, and that I fill a place which another might supply much better."

" Well, if we had given Miss Saunders a longer notice, she might easily have taken a little training at some great hospital," I remarked to Ruth as we walked homeward.

" Don't talk of what you don't understand, Edward," interrupted Ruth. " I won't say a word against the systems of the famous hospitals. Doubtless it is necessary for their nurses to be drilled like soldiers. There are not enough staunchly true women to supply their requirements, and that discipline may do a great deal of good to the shams whom they are obliged to receive into their ranks. Is not there something in Miss Saunders which makes her just Bessie Saunders, and no one else, —and something in me which makes me Ruth Garrett, and nothing more? And don't tell me we should be improved if that something was taken out of us. Would you like pictures painted in faintly differing shades of the same colour? Would you like all the flowers in your garden to be alike?"

"But, my dear Ruth," I pleaded, "would you like variety such as existed between those famous ladies, Betsy Prig and Sarah Gamp?"

" And, my dear Edward," retorted my sister ironically, " because one system is bad, it does not always follow that its opposite is perfection. And if *you* believe that any system can regenerate human nature, I don't. If Betsy Prig and Sarah Gamp existed under the old arrangements, depend upon it they have slipped in under the new ones, only of course they have changed their names!"

"Still, now-a-days," I said, "at least they cannot drink gin, and morally murder their patients."

" Those are very negative virtues in a nurse," replied my sister ; " but what I complain about is the modern cant of 'training.' You men don't let it get among yourselves. When once you are grown up, by which time your general or technical education, as the case may be, is completed, you find out what each other can do, and set each other to do it. If a man cannot become a clerk by simply passing upwards through the various grades of a clerk's duty, he turns to something else. There is no establishment where he may be artificially 'trained' at the public expense. But if a girl wishes to be a book-keeper, instead of expecting her to work her way like a boy, many employers request her to bring them a certificate of competency from some training class, where she has been stupefied by sham ledgers, and dazzled by precepts which she will never need to practise. Teachers are wanted for national schools, and instead of suitable women being chosen, and brought gradually onward through small schools to large ones, thousands of pounds are annually spent to make women competent, or rather what is called competent. Now there is always somebody exactly fitted for every work that exists in the world, and that somebody should be found for it."

"But, Ruth," I suggested, "in speaking of men a minute ago, you said, 'when their technical education is completed.' Now this 'training' simply comes in the place of that technical education."

"Then why isn't it paid for in the same way, and taken at the same time, close at the heels of common school days?" she asked rather sharply. "And mind you that in ordinary male employment, shop-keeping, clerkships, and so forth, there is no 'training' at all, only a steady working up from the lowest step of the ladder. It is a natural development of all they learnt when boys. And every woman's early life should have fitted her for something. Has not an elder sister had good discipline for a governess, and a tradesman's daughter for a business woman, and so on? And there will never be more exceptional women wanted than exceptional chances will provide. And yet ten chances to one, instead of making the best of each as she is, some wiseacre will set her in ' training' to become what she is not."

"But I'm sorry to say a woman's early life does not always fit her for anything," I said.

"Then I'm afraid nothing else will," retorted Ruth.

"But what is she to do?" I queried.

"Marry the first man who asks her," said my sister shortly.

"And is a woman who is fit for nothing else, fit for a wife?" I asked.

"No," she returned, "but she is quite good enough for any man who gives her a chance. But you are always asking me these sort of questions, Edward. Are you contemplating such a step for yourself?"

"Nay, Ruth," I answered, a little nettled; "I ask these questions gravely, and you turn them off with a joke. It is not a laughing matter."

" No," she said, " but it would do no good if I cried,
and my sex don't feel they need anybody's tears. They
think it is only the cruel injustice of the men which prevents them from filling the highest places in the land.
Very likely the Lord Chancellor does not know how to
make tea, and so a woman who does not know either
thinks she could be Lord Chancellor. We hear that it is
hard to obtain good nurses or thorough governesses, and
yet, forsooth, the ladies aim to become doctors and pro-
fessors."

" But may not the deficiencies you name arise simply
from want of training?" I pleaded.

"Then let them be trained by first painfully climbing
the lowest step of the ladder, and staying there until
they can mount higher without any help," she returned.
" Till the ranks of good nurses are filled, women need
not wish for opportunities to become doctors."

" But, Ruth," I said, " many women who would like
to be doctors would shrink from mere nursing, because
it is often foolishly regarded as a humiliating servitude."

"If a true gentlewoman by birth, breeding, or education, engages in any work, however humble," replied my
sister, " she does not sink to its lowest level, but she
raises it to herself, and it is thought better of for her
very sake. And mind, if women so scrupulously defer to a wrong popular prejudice, why don't they heed
that other prejudice, which has some reasonable founda-
tion, and hesitates before it gives a man's work to a
woman ?"

" But who shall define what is man's work and what is

woman's?" I asked, briskly, thinking I had hit upon a poser.

"The proper seed for every soil is what grows there without forcing," returned Ruth promptly. "I suppose a man or a woman may compel themselves to do almost anything, just as they may distort their limbs into unnatural attitudes. But you may always know when they are out of their proper place by the terrible bragging they make. An old bachelor does not boast of his ledger and cash-box, but he triumphs miserably in sewing on buttons and mending gloves. A woman does not publish a list of her seams and samplers, but she glories in her examinations and certificates."

"But may not that be because she has conquered, not nature, but merely custom?" I inquired. "Don't you really think that some employments now monopolised by men might fairly be shared by women?"

"They might be opened to women," she answered. "A steady, patient girl, who can manage delicate needlework, could manage watchmaking. And there are many other occupations now kept by men which are quite within the compass of a woman's abilities. But then I don't think the men would object to admit a woman. I have not forgotten my own early days, Edward."

"I am glad to hear you admit that women might have a wider sphere than at present," I said.

"I admit less than you think," she returned, "and even from my admission, I think you and I draw different inferences. I would not apprentice an indefinite number of girls to these employments, as is sometimes proposed,

It would be sheer waste of time and money. In five years' time nineteen girls out of twenty would have married, and thus wholly retired—at least I hope so—to the other business of housekeeping. As a body, women will never pass beyond the stage of raw learners. And that is one reason why men need never fear their rivalry."

" But, Ruth, don't you think it would be better if girls had other objects in life besides matrimony ?" I asked.

"Of course it would," she answered, " but putting it as you put it now, it is only twaddle. If you were a young man, would you like a girl to refuse you on the grounds that she had a good business, and so thought it her duty to keep to it?"

" No, I certainly should not," I replied.

" The fact is," my sister went on, " the people who start these movements proceed on a wrong track. They start with the belief that all women can follow occupations, for which not more than twenty per cent. are really suited. They ignore the fact that perhaps only one out of that twenty will require such occupation through her whole life. So they scare the men, and rouse all their opposition, by announcing that they will be beaten out of the field by female labour, equal in kind and superior in cheapness. Now, this equality in kind and superiority in cheapness are both fallacies."

" O Ruth," I said, indignantly, " will you say that women cannot work as well as men, when you know how well you carried on your own business ?"

" I know all about it, Edward," she answered, " and that is why I say it. Didn't I have Latin manuscripts sent me, and didn't I always take them to be copied by the old schoolmaster at Mallowe Academy, and didn't he allow me a small commission for giving him the job ? O Edward, Edward, that is how I succeeded. I knew what I could not do, as well as what I could !"

"But at any rate women's labour is certainly cheaper than men's," I said, presently.

"Mechanical labour of the sort we mean should have one price and only one," she returned. "If a woman devotes herself to these occupations, she cannot have time to cook her meals, or clean her room, or make her clothes. And so her existence becomes as costly as a man's. And remember, too, that the work which is easy to an ordinary man, requires a superior woman, in whose education much money and care have been invested. So she ought not to work except for a fair return on that investment."

"But those questions can scarcely be considered in the labour market," I remarked.

"And that's just why a woman should never take the question of her labour into the labour market," she retorted. "If exceptional work come in her way, and she be able to do it, let her do it quietly, and be thankful. When an able woman steps from the beaten track, they are not her friends who make a flourish of trumpets as if an army were about to follow."

"Then what do you lay down as the first principle in a girl's preparation for the future ?" I inquired.

"Develop all those powers and instincts which will make her a good mistress of a family, as she will most likely become," returned Ruth. "And even if not, after such rearing, she need not fear for a good and honest maintenance. Train her in industry, and patience, and energy, and whether she be single or married she will be always worth her place in the world."

"But still if some women have special talents for medicine or science," I said, "does it not seem a pity they should not follow them out?"

Ruth laughed.

"Of course, they can do as they like," she answered. "But I have noticed that those who best realise great responsibilities are always slowest to voluntarily incur them. And I observe that these lady-doctors are meant to attend upon women and children. Let me warn them that women will never trust women in that way."

"But is it not hard they should have so little confidence in their own sex?" I queried. "I wonder how it is!"

"Because women know what women are," answered Ruth; adding dryly, "It is not for me to deny that they might mistrust men as much if they knew them as well. But in the meantime, timid mistrust, however mistaken, injures a patient; while child-like confidence, however credulous, is half the cure."

Just at this moment, at the turn of a lane, we encountered Mr Weston. I say "encountered," for he paused before us and stared, as if it took him a moment to recall who we were. However, when he had collected himself, he saluted us warmly enough, and offered Ruth his arm

So as the path was sometimes rather narrow, I was obliged to drop behind, and soon fell into a reverie over our recent conversation. I am not very quick in discussion, and Ruth soon sets me down. Therefore, though to me her arguments are unanswerable, I am not sure they are so to other people. But even if there be a little prejudice in them, they are worthy of thought. And after all, what seems prejudice is sometimes truth. And certainly Ruth acts out her own precepts, and her actions seem always to the point. And I almost fancy that tests the goodness of precepts, as much as adding together the second and third rows proves a subtraction sum.

Walking behind Ruth and Mr Weston, I could distinctly hear their voices, but I did not listen for more, until my ear was struck by my sister saying—

" Well, sir, I have just been preaching down woman's rights ; but she has one right which I have never heard disputed—the right of refusal."

" If that is no secret, Ruth," I said, " I should like to know what it is."

" Mr Weston will tell you, if he wishes," she answered, walking on.

The young man turned and stood still. His honest blue eyes had the helpless look of a poor dog's, when it is hurt by its own master's foot.

" She's refused me," he said, " and it's all over ! " and then he walked on by my side, and, of course, I did not look into his face.

" We must all submit to these things sometimes," I

observed, presently; "ay, and often to far worse!" (For surely it was better to be rejected by Alice M'Callum than to be jilted by Maria Willoughby.) "But still, Weston, I should not have thought this of Alice. She ought to have guessed what you wanted long ago."

"Don't blame her, please, sir," he said: "she has never given me any encouragement; but yet somehow I thought she liked me, and—I've left her crying now. I thought she liked me—I did."

"Are you sure she does not?" I inquired more hope-fully. "What did she say?"

"She said—she said she'd never carry the cloud on her family into any man's house, sir. She's a fool, Mr Garrett!"

"You didn't say so?" I queried.

"No, and I don't say so, sir," he exclaimed, "except as if an angel lived in the world, we should very likely call her a fool! But I shouldn't have liked her to have sent me away without caring, sir; and yet now her caring makes it all the harder! What shall I do, sir?"

"Go home," said I, "go home, and be quiet. Things always prove better than they seem. And even if they don't, God and one's work remain, Mr Weston. Go home, and be quiet."

"Oh, sir," said he, forlornly, "could you bear it?"

"I have borne it, my boy," I answered. "Yes, twice—once in sorrow, and once in wrath and bitterness. And yet now, I would not change anything if I could. Go home, and be quiet."

"And this is the end of it," said Ruth, when I re-joined her, after parting from him; "and this is another specimen how—

> ' The best laid plans of mice and men
>         Gang aft a-gee. "

# CHAPTER XX

EWEN'S HOLIDAYS.

T proved that Ewen's holidays were not only later, but also shorter, than he had expected. The exigencies of business would only allow him a few days. So one fine autumn morning shortly after our meeting with Mr Weston, Alice came very early to our house to say that he had arrived at the Refuge late the night before. I thought her visit rather odd, as her brother would be sure to announce himself a few hours later. It was the first time we had seen her since Mr Weston's tidings, and despite her joy at Ewen's visit, she looked rather pale and grave, and so recalled all my first impressions of her. When she prepared to go away, Ruth followed her from the room, and presently I heard them in the next apartment, speaking in earnest whispers. At last the hall-door closed, I saw Alice go down the garden path, and then my sister reappeared.

"Can you guess why she came?" she inquired.

"No," I answered, "but I can guess she did not come without an object."

"She came to ask us not to name Mr Weston to Ewen," replied my sister, in that whisper which comes so naturally when any secrecy is enjoined.

"I can understand all her reasons," I said. "It is a beautiful piece of unselfishness. But I wish she had forgotten to enjoin our silence, for then I should have spoken. Now, we must decidedly yield to her wishes."

"And the poor girl is fretting dreadfully about the change in her brother," Ruth went on. "It makes me quite anxious to see him."

"Oh, Alice forgets that he has been living a sedentary town life," I replied; "and, besides, Ewen's is not the style of face which ever displays robust health, once the first bloom of boyhood is past."

So all the morning I sat at home waiting for him. But he did not come. When dinner-time came and passed without his appearance, I grew a little vexed. And when Ruth broadly took his part, and invented such good reasons for his non-arrival, I grew vexed with her also.

"You would not like it if I fidgeted you because Agnes Herbert neglects me," said Ruth pointedly. "And she has never been here to tea since the night when Alice showed us those pictures."

I had no answer to make, but after dinner I went out, saying to myself that if everybody had forgotten the old man, he would at least take care of himself, and get a little fresh air. That is not often my train of thought, and I am very glad of it, for I found it was not at all conducive to happiness, and I went along grumbling to myself at a fine rate. I took my usual route, through the meadows flanking the road to the village. Between their bordering of trees, now lightened of half their wealth of leaves, I caught glimpses of the Great Farm. But in the field immediately facing the house (it was the one behind the Low Meadow), I almost started to see him whose apparent negligence had thus put me out of temper. He stood, leaning against a tree upon a slight elevation. His arms were folded, and he was so rapt in gloomy reverie that he did not observe my approach. When he did so, he started, and then stepped forward to meet me. All my pique vanished when I saw his face. If it struck me as sharpened and wan when I saw him in his twilight garret, after a day spent in crowds of faded London faces, it now seemed tenfold so, as I saw it under the trees, facing the glowing sunset. Nay, more, he wore a look of acute pain, no mere fleeting expression, but one which had lasted long enough to fix a hard line about his mouth, which was not even broken by his smile. His face recalled the face of a companion of my early manhood who underwent a severe surgical operation. The sufferer endured without groan or sigh, but his countenance bore the stamp of that anguish till the day he died, years afterwards.

"Alice has told me about the knife which George Wilmot found in this field," he remarked presently.

I glanced at him, thinking that perhaps the revival of painful associations had something to do with the look

X

he wore, but, on the contrary, his face seemed to clear as he went on.

"I am very glad of its discovery."

"Why so, in particular?" I asked, quietly.

"Every little detail throws light on the story," he answered, rather dreamily.

"*This* does not enlighten me at all," I said.

"No," he replied, "but any item may tend to disprove or to prove anything that is said."

"*What* is said?" I inquired, testily.

"Oh, nothing," he answered, in some confusion.

His manner perplexed me. If he had spoken with such embarrassment during our first interview on the hill overlooking the river, I should have doubted his innocence. Even now, my confidence shook just a little, and we walked side by side in silence.

"That is the door of the Great Farm," he said suddenly, turning in its direction as a slight sound met my ear, so trifling and distant that I scarcely noticed it.

"You seem to know it well," I observed.

"You remember I once worked round the house, sir," he replied, with almost a dash of haughtiness in his manner. "I think Miss Herbert and her dog Griff are coming this way, sir."

So we stood still and waited for them. The great, substantial grey dog, her constant attendant, came bounding towards us, but instead of paying his usual compliments to me, he leaped upon Ewen, and overwhelmed him with the most demonstrative professions of regard.

His mistress came up almost breathless. "Oh, it is
you," she said when she saw Ewen, and there was a disappointed sound in her voice which was not at all complimentary to the young man. "Griff seems to recognise
you," she added more graciously.

"He recognises something," he replied, caressing the
dog. "Griff, Griff, poor, faithful old fellow !"

"And how are you going on in London, my boy?" I
asked presently ; "as well as before, I hope."

"Oh, yes, sir," he answered. "I wrote you that my
salary was raised at Midsummer."

"Yes," I returned, "and I knew it beforehand. But
what are you doing as an artist?"

Ewen was on my right hand, and Miss Herbert on
my left. She bent a little forward as I asked this
question, and he rather drew back, and replied very
precisely :

"I succeed better than I hoped. I have illustrated
one or two poems in some journals."

"I hope they pay you well," I said.

"I am satisfied, sir," he answered, with a slight
smile.

"Beginners often fare badly," I said, shaking my
wise head ; "however well they work, they are generally
paid only as beginners."

"Then there's something to look forward to," replied
the young man, with one of those quick turns by which
he sometimes reminded me of my sister. "Oh, I find
people very kind," he went on, "and they are more
ready to notice things than one would believe. A

gentleman whose poem I illustrated asked about me, and invited me to his house, and then he called on me and looked over all my drawings, and then he asked us to a little party of young artists and authors. He is a well-born, wealthy gentleman, who can afford to show these kindnesses."

Agnes listened with intense interest.

" Does Mr Ralph illustrate too ? " I asked.

" Yes, and he does it beautifully," Ewen answered.

" Yet the gentleman did not notice his work," I said, slyly, " and so Mr Ralph had to wait for his invitation till he made his personal acquaintance."

I wanted to put the young man on his mettle in defence of his friend, and I did not fail.

" His oversight was only an accident," he answered eagerly.

" Did he see Mr Ralph's drawings when he visited you ? " I inquired.

" Mr Ralph did not offer to show them," said Ewen.

" Very well, my boy," I returned ; " but whether it was his own fault or not, your invitation was earned and his was only honorary."

" The gentleman could see Mr Ralph was his equal," returned Ewen, with his strange new dignity of manner. " His presence at his house would not need the explanation that he had drawn this, or written that."

" And how is Mr Ralph ? " I inquired presently.

" He is much better, sir, and he sent his most dutiful regards to you," he replied, returning to his old simple manner.

"I'm afraid Miss Herbert thinks us rather rude," I said; "our conversation must be a riddle to her. Let me explain, my dear, that Mr Ralph is a young artist who lives with our friend here, and who seems to have seen a great deal of trouble."

"Indeed!" said Agnes. "Griff, Griff, come away, sir. You are quite troublesome to Mr M'Callum. Really, sir," she added, bending forward and addressing Ewen, "he seems as if he thought you had seen some friend of his, and so leaped up to whisper inquiries in your ear. See, up he goes again! Griff, Griff, come away!"

Her words were simple and natural enough, though she seldom said as much to a comparative stranger; but she spoke with a singular formality and emphasis, and presently, as if she thought she had not shown sufficient interest in my explanation, she remarked—

"'Ralph' sounds odd for a surname. It is much more natural as a Christian one."

"Yes, certainly it is," replied Ewen, with a warmth of assent quite beyond the subject.

"And how do you like London?" she asked in a few minutes, and without waiting for a reply, added another question: "Have you ever met any one you knew before?"

I answered for him. "I know he has met one, for he had some old acquaintance with this very Mr Ralph."

"Yes, I knew Ralph before," he assented, for the first time naming his friend without the prefix "Mr." "Ralph thinks of going abroad next spring," he stated presently.

"Going abroad!" exclaimed Agnes, so sharply that I started.

"Does he think he will find more scope in a new country?" I inquired.

Ewen shook his head. "I fear he will go only because he is weary of the old country," he replied. "Poor fellow, I own he acted foolishly in some things, but he has been punished as if folly were a sin, and the shadow of all he has lost hangs constantly over him. He fancies he will escape it. I think it will go with him. But, as he says, at any rate Australia or Canada will be as home-like as England is now, and there is not one who will suffer by his departure."

"But suppose he is mistaken in all this!" exclaimed Agnes, in a voice full of tears. Poor girl, I knew her sympathetic and emotional nature!

"I tell him he is mistaken," said Ewen with earnest solemnity; "but I only wish I could prove it to him."

And then we wandered on in silence, till I broke the spell by claiming Ewen's company for my sister's tea-table, and informing Miss Herbert that Ruth made certain comments about her long absence from our house. Agnes replied that she should come to see us in a day or two, and she was sure she would come oftener, only she feared to be troublesome. She made this answer with a bright, eager look on her sweet face, and then she turned to Ewen and said in that pretty petitioning tone which women use when they have some dear little trifling request to make—

"Mr M'Callum, I have long wished to write to a dear

friend in London, but I do not know the exact address. If I direct it as well as I can, and send it to the Refuge under cover to you, will you, if possible, supply the omissions of my superscription? I think you will be able."

"Certainly I will do what I can," he answered as if he sincerely felt the commonplace commission to be an honour and a pleasure. Then they shook hands,—a regular hearty, honest shake. And she turned away, calling the reluctant Griff to follow her.

It was nearly tea-time when Ruth welcomed our young guest. We partook of the meal in the twilight, for it was a very fine evening, without that autumnal mirk and chill which makes artificial light and artificial heat alike grateful. The young man seemed to have recovered his spirits, and consequently his face had lost that haggard hunger which had so startled me at our first meeting. Nevertheless, when the lamp was at last brought in, and Ruth took up her knitting, I saw she stole many a glance at him, as we sat conversing about his promotions, and the cheerful prospect before him. Suddenly she said— "Don't let the bustle of London life make you an old man before your time, Ewen."

He laughed, a little constrainedly. "Do you see any symptoms, ma'am?" he queried lightly.

"Yes," answered my candid sister. "You are nearly ten years older since this time last year. Now I should not speak of this, if it were anything you could not help, but I believe it can be helped. Nobody has any right to be spendthrift in his energies and emotions."

" But, Ruth," I said, " business sometimes compels "——

"I don't say any one is not to be 'diligent in busi-ness,'" she interrupted. "But I believe the metho-dical exercise energy gets in business proves only strengthening development, at least while energy is young and fresh. And besides, if it be spent for any adequate return, it is well spent. If a clock wear out in keeping time, it has done its work. But if it be worn out by the hands whirling round the dial sixty times a day, then it is wasted. And so is all energy expended in emotion."

"Ruth," I exclaimed, "do you mean that one may prevent himself suffering?"

"Yes, I do," she answered; "at least to a certain degree. Mental pain is subject to the same conditions as bodily pain, which any one can either alleviate or aggra-vate. If a man unbinds a wound, and thinks about it, and reads about his disease, and twists the hurt limb to test the extent of the injury, he suffers for it. So if a man sets up a sorrow as a shrine where he may worship, and walks round it to survey it from all sides, and draws all his life about it, and reads fiction and poetry to see what others say of the same, then he also suffers for it."

" But sorrow should scarcely be shunned like a sin," I said.

"And it should not be courted like a virtue," she re-turned. " God-sent sorrow is an angel in mourning. But any sorrow which we may rightfully escape is not God-sent. Sometimes, in old days, I 've wished to cry, but couldn't, because I had to go into the shop. And by the time the shop was closed I was braver, and did not want to cry."

" But the tears would have been a relief," I said, " and you certainly suffered no less because they might not come."

" But I was stronger for the self-control," she answered, " and you remember—

'Not enjoyment and not sorrow
Is our destined end or way ;
But to act, that each to-morrow
Finds us farther than to-day.'

But though I quote poetry," she added, turning to Ewen with a smile, " I don't advise you to read it. It's not that you want now. Build with granite before you clothe with creepers. Read Bacon, and Montaigne, and Rollin, and Shakespeare. He's a poet, you say? Yes, my dear, but he's a dramatist. He does not tell us how bitterly he feared Anne Hathaway would reject him. He says nothing about himself. He was above it, he had better things to say. So he don't make us, his readers, think of ourselves, rather he lifts us out of self. But leave all other poets till you are growing bald, then you will want them to remind you of what you were. If they moisten your eyes then, it will do you good. Why, Mr M'Callum," she said, pointing to our book-case, " there are books on those shelves which I have never dared to read since I was eighteen until—not very long ago !"

My dear, enduring sister !

Ewen stayed with us that night until nine o'clock,

and we saw him two or three times afterwards during his brief holidays.  But that visit was the only lengthened one which he paid us.  For I would not give him a set invitation, as I knew his punctilious conscientiousness would accept it, however much he might prefer the society of his grandfather and sister.

But I met him in my walks, and one day, as we were strolling down a lane, rather silently, it occurred to me to inquire if Miss Herbert had forwarded her promised letter.

"Yes," he answered so briskly that I thought he was about to make some further remark, but he did not.

"And I hope you can help her with the address?" I said.

"The letter has reached its destination by this time," he replied.

"I am glad of it," I observed, just for the sake of politeness.

"So am I," he responded, rather dryly.

"Miss Herbert is a very lovely girl," I went on in my prim old-fashioned way, "but having spent so much of her life in London, I almost think she suffers from the monotony of country existence."

"Perhaps she does," said Ewen, "but though one can see when something is wrong, it is hard to guess rightly what it is.  Now, I see there is something amiss with Alice, and yet I supposed Alice was so happy!"

"And so she is," I answered, "only, as the healthiest are sometimes ailing, so the happiest are sometimes sad.  Life, like a portrait, must have its shadows.  But the good are never miserable, though they may suffer very keenly through the sins of others, or for their sakes."

"Ay, and how far may that suffering extend?" he asked rather bitterly.

"Never farther than the valley of the shadow of death," I answered.

That was the last time I saw Ewen before he returned to London. On the day of his departure I proposed that we should take a walk towards the station, and so have a chance of seeing the last of him. But Ruth said, "No, leave him to his own relations. Partings are long remembered, and so they may like to remember they had it all to themselves."

# CHAPTER XXI.

## A PROGRAMME.

HAT year we enjoyed a singularly fine autumn, with but little mist or moisture; consequently it was a healthy season, and the resources of our little hospital were not prematurely tried. Also, it furthered the speedy and satisfactory completion of the Refuge orphan rooms, which were at last put in perfect readiness for any who might need them during the coming months. Over these things Ruth and I had many a quiet chat in the dusky twilight of our parlour, and we thanked God we had not quite done with the world, however the world had done with us. When I say "world," reader, I do not mean that narrow crust of society which is often implied thereby. I mean God's whole creation, "the earth and the fulness thereof."

Nevertheless, we were rather lonely that autumn. We saw nothing of Mr Weston after our memorable interview in the meadows. He did not come again to St

Cross, but in the course of some incidental conversation I heard with regret that he had been seen at the Puseyite church at Hopleigh. But it was still early in October when Mr Marten paid us an afternoon call, and promptly accepted our invitation to tea. And though he stated he had a little difficulty which he wished to discuss with us, he looked so flourishing and content, that it was very plain the "difficulty" gave him no undue disturbance. Indeed, it proved to be only a feeling on his part that it was the duty of the leaders in the parish in some way to direct their juniors' evening occupations and amusements during the coming winter.

"In short," he went on, "if St Cross is to maintain its ground, we must certainly do something. The Hopleigh people are very energetic in this matter. They have established a series of lectures, penny readings, &c., varied with entertainments and *soirées* and concerts. Besides these, they have opened classes, presenting a very attractive course of study for almost nominal fees."

Just then I happened to glance at Ruth behind the tea-urn, and I saw a storm gathering in her face. When Mr Marten ceased, there was an ominous pause. Then Ruth said, grimly—

"If you give children sugar-plums every day, they are never a treat, and they spoil their teeth into the bargain. That's a figure of speech for you, Mr Marten."

"Why, Miss Garrett," exclaimed the rector, "surely you don't disapprove of innocent and improving recreations?"

"I disapprove of 'gadding about,'" she answered,

severely. "I disapprove of everything which makes folks at home when they are out, and strangers when they are at home. In short, I disapprove of dissipation, whatever mask it may wear."

"I hope you don't see things in this light, sir," said Mr Marten, turning to me.

"Not altogether," I replied, "but I am a slow person, and I weigh matters very leisurely."

"I wonder what had become of my business if I had taken to lectures, and classes, and so forth!" exclaimed my sister.

"Ruth, Ruth," I said gently, "remember that we must not carry our personalities too far in these affairs."

"Well it's one way of getting at a bit of truth," she returned, "and I always fear to advise others to do what I never did myself. It's like holding out a cup and saying, 'I know that would poison me, but I think it will be good medicine for you.'"

"You must remember, Miss Garrett," said the rector, "that some homes are not very attractive. Think of the many one-roomed homes, with few books and no intelligent conversation."

"Mr Marten, Mr Marten," I repeated warningly, "has that good song gone out of fashion,—

> Be it ever so fondly,
> There's no place like home?'

But at the same time I willingly grant that home is often all the dearer for short absences, even as such short absences are more enjoyable for the sake of the dear home where they will end."

"And again," Mr Marten went on, inclining his head in acknowledgment of my words, "there are many young people who are utterly homeless."

"That is true," said Ruth, "but for the sake of the future they should be encouraged as much as possible to form homely habits. If bachelors or spinsters cannot settle to books or work in their lonely rooms, I fear they will fret at the stay-at-home ways of comfortable matrimony, when once its novelty has worn off."

"Well, I'm sorry to find you see another side to this matter," observed the rector; "for to me these evening lectures and classes seemed such a splendid means for mental improvement and moral elevation."

"Can you give us any details of the Hopleigh programme?" I inquired; "for until one knows all, one may differ about theories rather than facts."

"Oh, I can tell you all about it," he responded, briskly tugging at his pocket. "See! I came armed with all necessary documents!" and he produced sundry printed bills, and spread them out on the table.

"Take one by one, and read each aloud, please," requested Ruth, suddenly shifting her knitting needles and beginning another row.

I have a strange notion that my sister's knitting is to her strength of mind something like Samson's hair to his bodily prowess. Whenever we two are in argument, I have a wild wish to snatch that mysterious web from her agile fingers. Besides, its very continuance

daunts one with the reproach—"Behold, in spite of all
your idle clatter, these needles go on, and so does the
world!"

"Which shall I take first?" queried the rector.
"There are a prospectus of the classes, a programme of
the lectures, and a list of the discussions."

"Read whichever you like," said I.

"Then I'll read the paper of the classes," he answered;
and so began the sheet with its very heading :—

"Hopleigh College.    Under this name it is proposed
to establish a course of evening classes.    The subjects
chosen, with the names of the gentlemen who have
kindly undertaken to teach them, will recommend themselves.    Monday, Latin and English Composition (by
Mr Senecca Moon) ; Tuesday, French (by M. Vert);
Wednesday, Elementary Singing ; Thursday, Writing and
Arithmetic (by Mr Senecca Moon) ; Friday, Reading and
Elocution (by Mr O'Toole); Saturday, Advanced Singing.    Hours from eight to ten o'clock.    Fee for one class,
two shillings each month ; for the whole course, eight
shillings.    Entrance fee, one shilling.    Intending members are invited to enrol as soon as possible.    Under the
especial patronage of the Rev. Ambrose Angelo, Rector
of St Cyprian, Hopleigh."

"You see, Miss Garrett," the rector commented, when
he had finished, "this is not even innocent recreation,
but improving study."

"I doubt whether it is either 'improving' or 'study,'"
she answered, taking up his words a little tartly.    "I
suppose girls are included in these classes.    I wonder if

the clergyman would like his own daughter to run through the streets after nightfall in that way."

"A distinction must be made between certain ranks, madam," returned Mr Marten, rather stiffly.

"That is what I always say!" assented Ruth. "But let the distinction be in acquirements rather than in manners or morals."

"But some of these classes go to the very rudiments of education," pursued the rector: "reading, for instance, and writing and arithmetic. If by some evil chance these were neglected in childhood, would you suffer the girl or boy to go on in ignorance, Miss Garrett?"

She answered thoughtfully, "No: reading and writing are almost like two extra senses. They are worth some sacrifice. But what poor servant girl, sensible in spite of her ignorance, would venture to 'Hopleigh College?' And would she study A B C in the first hour, and then learn how to spout 'My name is Norval' during the remainder of the time! And would she be much at ease in the society of the smart shop-girls, who would come to practise rant, and who would attend the French and Latin classes on the other evenings?"

"But I think these institutions are really for the benefit of a higher class than common servants or ploughboys," said Mr Marten; "and for such how serviceable is French, and how useful the power of writing a correct letter!"

"Thorough French is a valuable acquirement," returned Ruth, "and a good letter is a sure sign of a sound education. But mere 'lingo' is ridiculous, and a 'phrase' epistle is an abomination. Perhaps you will add, that

Y

even superficial French may be useful in business; but if poor M. Vert is willing to teach it for two shillings a month, can the scholars expect to make it more profitable than the master?"

"But M. Vert, who is a working professor, would not teach at that rate, except for a consolation-fee from the committee," explained the rector.

"I hate that false method of cheapening good things," answered my sister. "If an acquirement be worth anything, it is worth its price, and let those who desire it deny themselves to pay that price. All who can derive advantage from it will readily do so. Those who want pearls dive for them, and shall others take them to throw before swine?"

There was a pause. Then I inquired what were the other arrangements.

"They have a fortnightly lecture," replied Mr Marten, taking up another paper. "The Rev. Ambrose Angelo will deliver one on Ecclesiastical History; and Mr Senecca Moon, the principal of Hopleigh Academy, will give another on Meteorology. On two evenings there will be Readings from Popular Authors by various gentlemen, among them, Mr Daniel O'Toole and Mr Smith —— ["Rather vague," murmured Ruth.] And on Christmas-eve there will be a vocal and instrumental concert, for which, the bill says, 'many ladies and gentlemen have promised assistance.'"

"I think the lectures are too dry," I said; "and they are certainly subjects of which 'a little knowledge' is very useless."

" But how nice to hear about a word which ordinary folk cannot pronounce !" observed Ruth, ironically, laying down her knitting, and taking a book from the little bracket which always stood on her work-table. " Met-e-o-ro-lo-gy," she repeated, turning over the leaves. " Dear me ! I fear Dr Johnson's ideas on the subject were nearly as misty as mine ; for he only defines it as ' the doctrine of meteors.' "

" But I must say I like the ' Readings from Popular Authors,' " I remarked. " In themselves they are amusing, and they are well calculated to awaken a desire for further information."

" That is quite true," said my sister ; " but they should only be entrusted to people whose age and position qualify them for the teacher's desk. Otherwise the parish school-room simply becomes the scene of bad amateur theatricals."

" Then what do you say to the concert ?" inquired Mr Marten.

I answered—" Only this : that men are always too ready to speak lightly of those women who, having real musical gifts, display them for hire to maintain themselves and their dependents. The gift may stir in their souls, the remuneration may mean home and household happiness, but the audience listens and applauds and slights. It is not right ! Publicity is a dire necessity to those women—the dark side of their profession, which must be accepted with the bright one. But what of girls who, without their gifts, and unneeding their pay, court the common eye and the common clap? Sir, I belong to

the old-fashioned days, when a woman's pretty accom-
plishments were kept for those who loved her, and when
a young lassie, safe and happy in the retreat of her
father's house, would have blushed to see her name
printed in bills, and stuck up on walls and shop-win-
dows."

"And the old-fashioned notions were certainly right,"
said my sister, with a little sigh ; " but in spite of them
all, there were young girls, and young girls then, as now !
Yet need we meddle with what we cannot mend ?"

"We only criticise these matters to guide our own
actions," I answered.   " Have you any more announce-
ments, Mr Marten ?"

" There is also a discussion-class," he replied, with a
slight hesitation.   " The paper says it is held in the boys'
schoolroom at Hopleigh, every Friday evening, at eight
o'clock, and it announces the four discussions for the
month of November.   The first will be opened by your
friend Mr Weston, of Mallowe, the subject being, 'Is
not the single state most conducive to happiness ?'"

Ruth and I both looked up in such startled amaze-
ment, that it might almost have betrayed the confidence
the young man had reposed in us.

" Can any one attend these discussions ?" my sister
asked, quietly.

"Oh, certainly," returned the rector ; " and the other
subjects are, 'Was Robert Emmett a patriot ?' opened
by Mr O'Toole ; ' The advantages of Co-operation,' by
Mr Smith."

" The exciseman, I suppose ?'" queried Ruth.

"I believe so," said Mr Marten; "and the Rev. Ambrose Angelo closes the list with the knotty question, 'Is the Protestant church a Catholic church?'"

"And now," I remarked, "we must come to the point, and consider what part of this intellectual machinery we can best adapt to St Cross."

"Don't have any 'discussions,'" said my sister, shaking her head; "they only encourage a parcel of foolish boys to spout nonsense, which they will wish forgotten when they are grown older and wiser."

"I cannot say I like them," assented the rector, "for I think they only give occasion to a certain order of minds to display their powers by triumphantly making the worse appear the better cause."

"We will put them out of the question," I said, "and let us reflect what we can do in the way of evening classes."

"Let us have two," rejoined my sister, "one for youths, and one for young women; and let the instruction be confined to reading, writing, and simple arithmetic, and let each class meet twice weekly. It is hopeless to teach reading by one lesson a-week."

"I am sure I shall be very happy to take one class," said Mr Marten.

"That would be a mistake," answered Ruth. "Your attentions would be voluntary, and you would either demand no fee, or the fees would be devoted to some parochial use. Now honest young people don't like to be recipients of charity. Besides, amateur teaching, like everything that is amateur, is none of the best.

Let somebody be paid to teach, or, better still, let him receive the fees, and it will become his interest to make the classes as attractive and serviceable as possible."

"It must be a low nature that would not do so without such stimulus," observed Mr Marten.

"Ah, but we must not ignore the natural propensity towards evil," said my sister; "and I don't see there is any wrong in making the right easy and pleasant. For which reason, I will promise a prize for the best girl-scholar. And it shall be no sham prize either."

"And I'll promise one for the best boy," I added; "and now what shall we do about the lectures?"

"In the first place, don't have them too often," said my sister. "It only destroys their interest, and all home-comfort into the bargain."

"Let us have them but once a month," I said, "and let them be genuine 'recreations.' I don't think that poor tired heads are benefited by hearing dates and statistics. Mine never was. Let us have something to draw out blithe, honest, innocent laughter, which leaves the heart larger than it found it. Let us have tears sometimes, those sympathetic tears which are the best cure for our own unspoken sorrows. In short, let us be as *human* as possible."

"And shall we never have a concert?" queried the rector, rather regretfully; "and music is *so* popular!"

"And such an agent for good," I rejoined, warmly; "though I don't think any of God's blessings is so fearfully perverted. The exercise of that gift which we specially connect with the glories of heaven, but too often becomes a temptation to vanity and frivolity, and worse!"

"Ah," said Ruth, "I went to a village concert once, and I saw the singer girls sitting in a row in their best dresses, which were too fine for their owners' pockets, and in one or two cases not very modest in taste. And when I heard the village audience—their little world—whispering of the beauty of this one, and the dress of the other, and the voice of a third, I could not forget the old saying, that a 'woman's true honour was not to be spoken about!'"

"Then let us always have singing at the lectures," I said, "just as we have at church. Let us take some familiar airs, such as 'Rule Britannia,' 'Auld langsyne,' and so forth, and sing them in the course of the evening, the assembly standing, and all who can, joining."

"Ah," said Ruth, "I think that might give a greater love and taste for music than a few young people on a platform practising airs and graces, and striking up, 'In Celia's Arbour,' and so on, which means nothing at all to ignorant people like me, who listen with our hearts instead of our ears."

"And then we can always conclude with the dear old doxology," I remarked.

"But may not that seem rather irreverent sometimes?" queried my sister.

"Never!" I replied, "if we have been merry, we shall sing,—

'Praise God from whom all blessings flow.'

and include our mirth and laughter among those blessings. The same apostle who asks, ' Is any among you afflicted ? let him pray,' adds, ' Is any merry? let him sing psalms.' "

There was a short silence, which Ruth broke by saying,—

" Edward, at Christmas-time, let us have a genuine party ; not a tea-meeting, nor a *soirée*, but a thorough old-fashioned hospitable party, with games and forfeits, and music, and all good cheer. We have no room in this house sufficiently large, or I should like it to be in a private dwelling even better than in the great room of the Refuge. But I fancy Mr Herbert could be brought to favour that scheme, and his noble dining-room would be the right place."

" At anyrate, we can ask him," I said ; " and then, if he will not consent, we can but take refuge in the Refuge ;" and I laughed at my own little joke.

" And are you quite satisfied with all these plans, Mr Marten ? " I inquired presently ; " I almost fear you think them too homely and simple."

" No," he answered, starting from a reverie into which he had fallen, "for I was just thinking that when we clergymen enter upon our duties, fresh from collegiate cloisters, we are too apt to forget the claims of home, and to ignore the heavenward end of secular duties, and I fear many of my brethren persevere in this mistake to the very end. They do not realise that they are only set aside for a special purpose, and so they constantly strive to draw people from their own line of work and study into theirs."

"Yes," returned Ruth, "and even more, they often seem to forget that God made the world, and so speak of His appointments as if they were hindrances on the road to Him. They literally say, with Thomas à Kempis (hand me his book, Edward,) 'O that thou mightest never have need to eat, or drink, or sleep: but mightest always praise God, and only employ thyself in spiritual exercises: thou shouldest then be much more happy than now thou art, when for so many necessities thou art constrained to serve thy body.' And the good man constantly repeats that mistake in his otherwise beautiful 'Imitation of Christ,' forgetting that He worked in the carpenter's shop, and went to the marriage feast, and wept at Lazarus' grave. How different from the Scripture precept, 'Whether ye eat, or drink, or whatsoever ye do, do all to the glory of God!' The one comes to us like a draught from a cathedral crypt, and the other like a breeze from the hills!"

And so our long consultation drew to an end, and when the rector had departed, and we had drawn our chairs close together to partake of our cozy little supper, Ruth gave me a sly side glance, and said—

"We will both be present when Mr Weston opens that wonderful discussion!"

# CHAPTER XXII.

## COMING EVENTS AND SHADOWS BEFORE.

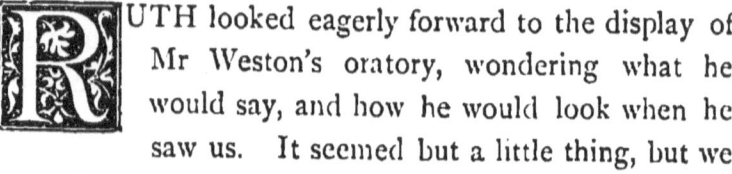UTH looked eagerly forward to the display of Mr Weston's oratory, wondering what he would say, and how he would look when he saw us. It seemed but a little thing, but we knew it concerned the futures of two whose welfare we desired, and besides, we had now reached that happy resting-place when the feelings are only stirred by the interests of others. And so I was quite ready to echo my sister's expectations and conjectures.

But our sympathies and counsels were destined to be evoked in other directions besides. About noon on the day of the discussion, Agnes Herbert paid us a visit. I saw her cross the garden at a brisk pace, and when Phillis admitted her, her step in the hall was less noiseless, and her voice higher than usual. In short, her whole aspect had brightened, and the very expression of her face went far to fulfil the prophecy which the flicker-

ing firelight had revealed to me a year before.   She had
donned her winter garments, and her bonnet was enlivened by a ribbon of pure scarlet, in place of the sombre
mixtures which she had hitherto affected.   Altogether
she was as much changed from her former self as is a
darkened room when ·the curtains are suddenly drawn
aside to admit the sunshine.

And yet she was the bearer of uncomfortable tidings,
with the misery of which she strongly sympathised.
But there was the difference.   At an earlier date, her
sympathy would have been true, but listless—the sympathy which sits down by the sufferer, and says, " It
is a weary world—let us endure together."   Now it was
aroused and active, busily inquiring, " What can be
done ? "

The evil was nothing more nor less than Anne
Sanders, and the misfortune was, that the young stranger
who had taken Bessie's place, had called at the hospital,
complaining that she must resign her position : she
found the business good, and the house comfortable, but
the housekeeper was like the fly in the ointment, which
spoiled all.   She could not enter into Anne's shortcomings ; they were of that almost indefinite kind which
pervade life, and make it unendurable, without leaving
any distinct mark.

Agnes had also visited the hospital, and had found
Bessie in great trouble about this disturbing communica-
tion.   Bessie seemed to have placed much confidence in
our pretty friend.   Perhaps she preferred to open her
mind to a young creature of whose sympathy she was

sure, yet who could not fancy she claimed more than sympathy. Doubtless it soothed her lonely heart to let her memory wander back to those earlier days when her kindred was not centred in the narrow, selfish sister, who could neither love nor be loved. For she had evidently spoken to Agnes of the dead Katie and her unhappy lover, and of all the pleasant budding hopes which had once promised fairly to bloom into realities. As Miss Herbert repeated the sorrows of Bessie Sanders, I could see her feelings were touched, and there was earnest solicitude in her question :

"What can be done?"

"Does Miss Sanders suggest anything?" I inquired, in return.

Agnes looked up deprecatingly. "She says it will be her duty to go back to Anne, as of course Anne cannot be received at the hospital," she answered. "But oh, Mr Garrett, do you think it can be God's will that any one should submit for ever to the ceaseless tyranny of an evil nature?"

"Whatever Mr Garrett may think, Miss Garrett does not think so," replied Ruth; "and besides, Anne is not benefited by Bessie's sacrifice. When kindness fails, severity may succeed. Let her leave Bessie's successor in undisturbed possession and go into some lodging in the village, until she can find a suitable position."

"Will she ever do so?" I queried, shaking my head.

"I don't know," answered my sister. "But that

scheme will certainly gain us a little time; and very often the world comes round to those who will but wait."

"Yes, I think it does," said Agnes, with a bright glance, like that of one suddenly assenting in the solution of an old problem.

"I will put on my bonnet and shawl, and go about the matter directly," remarked my energetic sister. "I won't ask you to come with me, Agnes, for that miserable woman is likely to put one out of patience with human nature, and you are young, and must endure it for a long time."

And so Miss Herbert and I were left together. The newspaper was on the table, and I took it up and started some topic of public interest. I forget what it was, but it was something about which I held peculiar notions, and I began to explain them, meantime holding up the paper, and interspersing my oration with sundry sentences therein, which I thought to agree with my views. I talked on with great animation, till I made some observation which called for an answer. Then I paused; but none came. I dropped the paper. Agnes sat opposite me, her scarlet strings untied, and her hands, loosely holding her gloves, lying in her lap. But her thoughts were not with me and my politics, for her lips were parted with a soft, slight smile, and her eyes had the far-off look of young eyes when they gaze into the future, and fancy they catch glimpses of angels walking in its mists. But the rustling paper recalled her to the present, and she

hastily tried to take up the broken thread of my discourse. But where it had fallen, there I let it lie; and
so there was silence.

Suddenly she rose and came towards me, and stood
beside my chair. Then she paused, and I did not look
at her till she whispered in a very girlish voice—

"Mr Garrett, you are not angry?"

"Angry, my dear!" I exclaimed; "am I such a can-
tankerous old stick, that you imagine anger is my natural
condition?"

"No, sir," she answered, with a little laugh. "But I
was so rude a minute ago, and I can't excuse myself, for
I was only thinking about my own affairs!"

"Well, my dear," I replied, "and if you would talk
about them, and let me have a share in them, I 'm sure
I would not trouble you with the leading articles."

"I want to ask your advice and help," she said, with
downcast eyes.

"O-ho," thought I, "must the old bachelor intercede
with the stern uncle?" But I merely said, "I can only
say, Miss Herbert, that you are heartily welcome to the
best I can give."

She went back to her seat, as if to gain a moment to
choose her words. I was all attention. And this was
what she said—

"I should like my father's best writings to be collected
and made into a small volume."

I had expected something very different; but I bowed
my head, and assented. "A very dutiful wish, my dear.
And have you any hope of its fulfilment?"

"I have gone very carefully through his pieces," she said, "and I have selected the best. You see I remember his opinions of them," she added, as if excusing her temerity, "and I have made copies of them, embracing alterations which he wrote on their margins, and I have added two or three which remained unpublished when he died. I think they will make a very nice book. But I should not like to send it to a publisher without somebody else seeing it. Will you look over it, Mr Garrett?" and opening a little leathern reticule, she produced the manuscript, and handed it to me.

It was of considerable size, and the writing was not of that deceptive, scrawling kind which spreads two or three words over a page. It was firm, compact calligraphy, not as characteristic as Ewen M'Callum's, but as easy to read as print. I have a respect for good writing, by which I mean *plain* writing. Illegible scribble is selfish and rude, implying that the reader's time is less valuable than the writer's. In literary matters, I cannot but think plain writing must be advantageous; for even editors are human; and the man who can wade through a manuscript novel when he must pore over every word, need be above the frailties to which ordinary flesh is liable.

"Have you spoken to Mr Herbert about your wish to publish this?" I inquired.

"Yes," she answered.

"And he consents?" I queried.

"He leaves me at liberty to do so," she replied: her conscientious nature drawing a distinction between consent and mere permission.

"You will pass the day with us, my dear?" I said.

"Uncle said I might," she returned; and thus she accepted my invitation, and put aside her bonnet and mantle. I continued to look over the manuscript, and when next I glanced at my fair companion, she was seated in the easy chair, busily employed in—what? Darning stockings! I think my head gave a little involuntary shake. There was a change in the girl—a change which made her think of housewifery and practical life. God bless her! What jumps my heart always gave whenever Lucy Weston talked of what she would do if she became the mistress of a house! But Agnes Herbert is not like Lucy. Her nature is perhaps stronger, but she is not half as sweet.

"You wish to be paid for this book, I suppose," I said, still turning over its leaves.

"Oh yes," she answered, decidedly; "and it will be as money left me by my father,—the nest-egg of my fortunes, sir;" and she laughed, but not quite merrily; and neither of us spoke again until Ruth came back.

"I have settled it all," exclaimed my sister, as she came in; "and Anne Sanders is fairly lodged in a room in the High Street, where she can disgrace nobody but herself. The young dressmaker helped her to pack up her belongings, and she parted from her quite kindly, just because she was so glad to part from her! And such a mess as her things were, I never saw. There were good lace collars run to rags for want of a stitch; and cuffs, and mantles, and bonnets all suffered to lie useless, because she was too idle to alter and re-model. Oh, I spoke to her! 'You'll be sorry for your life when it's too late!' I said. 'What have I done?' she cried out. 'What have I done?' 'Miss Anne Sanders,' I answered, 'you have done *nothing:* and that is your crime; for whoever does nothing, does evil; and I wish you were a little child, that I might give you a whipping?'"

And my sister dropped into a chair in an exhausted way quite uncommon for her, and then drew a long breath, like one who has just gone through unusual and straining exertion.

But the minute she sat down, her quick eye observed Agnes' work. "I'm glad to see you so well employed, my dear," she said; "and are you a good darner? Let me see! Yes. And do you like it?"

"I don't always like it," answered Agnes; "but just now I do."

"Then you should always like it," retorted Ruth. "Don't form the habit of whims, and fits, and starts. When you like your duty, praise God for the blessing; and when you don't like it, pray God for His help. Anyhow, do it all the same."

"But can we always be sure what is our duty?" asked Agnes, very softly, while a faint shadow crept over her face.

"I won't deny there are some puzzling cases," returned Ruth; "but we needn't vex ourselves about them until we've done the little bit that is quite plain before us, and few of us get through that. And what are you reading, Edward?" she inquired. "Poetry? In Miss

Z

Herbert's writing? Child," she asked, severely, "surely you don't write poetry?"

"No, indeed," said Agnes, laughing. "It is my father's."

"Ah, I'm glad it's not yours," answered Ruth, taking the book from me. "If a woman lives poetry, that is quite enough. If she write it, I fear lest it evaporate at her fingers' ends. Thank God you're not a genius, Agnes; but don't thank Him in the Pharisee's fashion. Genius is God's great gift; but too often it is over-heavy for a woman's hand."

I fear Agnes had a somewhat quiet day, but I don't suppose she regretted our silence, since we were absorbed in her father's writings. Generally, when a tale or a poem touched either of us, it was handed to the other, and perused in silence, and then commented on. But once, Ruth raised her head, and said—

"Edward, listen;" and so she read:—

### "NOT WITHOUT HOPE."

They say you are not as you were
  In days of long ago :
That clouds came o'er your sun at noon,
  And dimm'd its golden glow.

Yet every gentler word I say,
  Each gentler deed I do,
Is but a blossom on the grave
  Where sleeps my love for you.

And can a weed bring forth a flow ?
  Or blight bear beauty? Nay,
This darkness is but short eclipse
  To surely pass away.

Though one by one my early friends
    Have faded from my prayer,
Your name was always first and last,
    And still it lingers there.

I love but dearer for my fears
    And prayers for such a one :
I think God does not love us less
    For costing Him his Son.

And I believe when death shall break
    This spell of human pain,
The love that I to God entrust
    He'll give to me again.

"There !" said Ruth, with a swell of suppressed emotion in her voice. "Nothing can improve *that*, Edward."

So I thought then. I have read it since, and not cared for it at all, except for the memory of my first impression. But my sister's reading put a soul into the dry bones,—yea, her own soul, for was it not the story of her life ?

"I remember when my father wrote it," said Agnes thoughtfully : "I was but a little girl, and I thought it must be quite true. And when my hour came—my hour was between the sunlight and the candles,—I asked him who it meant; surely not mamma, for he had always told me she was safe in heaven, waiting for us. And then he first explained to me that genius must rise beyond and above its own experience,—must let itself out of itself, and alike comprehend the calm of a saint's heart and the tortures of a malefactor's conscience. In short, he taught me that the power to do thus is genius itself. But he added, he did not believe even genius could catch the secrets of a character above itself, and that a man's loftiest conception revealed the highest possibility of his own nature. He might degrade it, but it was still in him,—his ideal,—the image of God as reflected in the mirror of the individual soul. I did not understand him then, and I fancy he only spoke to clear his own thoughts from misty silence. But I remembered his words, and I think I understand them now. And I think they are true."

"I think so," I replied; "and if so, then the higher a man's best conception, the wider the range below it. And thus he who gives us Brutus, gives us also Bardolph."

"Of course," said Ruth, "or a man's mind would be like Isaac Newton's door, with a large hole for the cat, and a small one for the kitten."

There was a moment's pause. Then Agnes said, " Ewen M'Callum will be a great man."

"I believe so," I answered.

"But what makes you say it?" queried Ruth.

"Because he has the greatness which makes a man great even following the plough," she replied with flushing face and quivering lips, "and then he has genius to be the voice of that greatness. Some great souls are dumb, and only God can understand their signs!"

"Has your London friend, to whom he carried your letter, made any acquaintance with him?" I inquired.

"That is how I learn to praise him!" she returned. "I hear enough—enough—to make me speak as I do, but—they—say there is something beyond—something I must not know, which eclipses all I may know. And

from what I do know, I can believe him equal to anything."

She spoke with some excitement, which betrayed itself
in the reiteration of her words.  Then with great energy
she resumed her darning.  Glancing at Ruth, I saw she
was gazing at Agnes.  She, too, could see the change in
the girl—a change which, as the day wore on, grew more
manifold.  There was no further outburst of the enthusiasm pent within her, but her mind, her whole nature
was awake.  She forestalled my sister's movements ; she
asked the recipe for a pudding which appeared on our
dinner table ; she took an active part in each domestic
matter.  Ruth was charmed.  If Agnes would have remained in our house for the evening, I am sure my sister
would willingly have foregone even the long-expected
discussion.  But Miss Herbert was resolved to return to
the Great Farm before tea.  She sustained her new
character to the last moment of her visit, showing Ruth
her winter bonnet, and proudly explaining that it was
but a renovation of last year's, and that the fashion
of its shape and trimming were all due to her own
skill.

"She has in her the making of a good housewife,"
said my sister when she was gone ; "and I think it will
come out.  But she's not the woman to be a manager
for management's sake."

"For whose sake then ?" I asked, slyly.

"For the sake of some worthless man," retorted Ruth ;
"and the more he gives her to manage, the better she'll
like him.  Did you see how her fingers twittered about

her engaged ring every time she dropped her work?
Engaged ring, indeed! Engaged rubbish!"

So we set off to Hopleigh in our little pony-chaise,
and we reached the school-room of St Cyprian in such
very good time that nobody else was there. Slowly, the
audience straggled in. At last came Mr Weston. He
lingered in the outer room to speak to an acquaintance, and while so doing, I saw his eyes fall on us.
Just then, some of my sister's old friends from Mallowe
entered and surrounded us, and hid him from our sight.
Presently the assembly got into order: there was expectant silence, but no Mr Weston. Then an attendant
mysteriously stepped about the room, adjusting windows
and blinds, after the fashion of attendants, to screen un-
punctuality. Again expectant silence, but still no Mr
Weston. At last the Rev. Ambrose Angelo, a spare,
sallow youth in a very prim collar, stood up, and said
that he feared some unforeseen circumstance had prevented the appearance of our estimable friend, and that
the discussion must proceed in the absence of its promoter. His motion was seconded, and the discussion
proceeded. It proved no discussion at all—only an
outpouring of sentiment, none of the speakers, on either
side, ever forgetting the presence of the reverend gentleman—a saintly and confirmed celibate of five-and-twenty
—a novice in the class of life to which he had been
raised by the liberality of a theological college. For
how, in the light of his mild spectacled eyes, could any
farmer or tradesman dare to suggest that a littered noisy
family room might be nearer heaven and a better school

for self-denial than his ascetic chambers, with their sacred pictures and crosses, and their constant influx of illuminated texts, wherewith the young ladies of St Cyprian faithfully fortified the piety of the Reverend Ambrose?

When the discussion was over, and it was satisfactorily proved that God was best served by a state of things which would bring His world to a speedy end, the assembly dispersed, and we heard many conjectures about the non-appearance of Mr Weston.

"He was here," said somebody; "for I spoke to him outside."

"He must have been sent for afterwards," remarked another; "but it's strange he did not leave a message; only perhaps he did not expect to be detained."

"Ah, his good sense came back to him," whispered Ruth, gripping my arm, "and he could scarcely send that message into a roomful of people!"

"A wasted evening, Ruth," I said, as we re-entered our dwelling.

"No, indeed," she returned; "we have saved an honest man from making a fool of himself!"

# CHAPTER XXIII.

## AN ANONYMOUS LETTER.

NOT very long after that memorable evening when Mr Weston was conspicuous by his absence, I paid a visit to the M'Callums at the Refuge. That morning's post had brought me a letter from Ewen, and I always gave them the benefit of the last news from him.

I found the High Street in a low bustle. Curious faces peeped from doors and windows. The object of interest was an old-fashioned, ungainly carriage standing in front of a little hosiery shop. Now, it was above this shop that Ruth had found lodgings for Anne Sanders.

Mr M'Callum himself was at the gate with a comical smile on his cheerful old face.

"It's an ill wind that blows naebody guid," said he, admitting me; "but it's no often there's a guid wind that blows naebody ill."

"What is the matter?" I asked.

"There's just an auld leddy come to fetch away Miss Bessie's sister," he replied. "She's an auld widow cousin of their mither's, an' she's never luiked on the sisters before. But she says, for the credit of the family she'll no hear of the puir lassie being left to fight her ain way in a sair warld. She has nae end o' siller, and mayhap Miss Anne will come in for it a' i' the end."

Looking across the road, I could see the lady standing in the hosier's shop—a little woman, quaintly dressed, with her face almost hidden by a hood-like bonnet.

"Does she live far from here?" I asked.

"She lives in a queer little house on the side of Mallowe Heath," he answered.

"In the parish of St Cross?" I said. "Then I suppose I have seen her at church?" for there seemed something familiar in the little figure.

"Na, na," returned Mr M'Callum, "she doesna gang to the kirk, but to a chapel on the Heath, where she's the richest and greatest leddy. She has neither child nor kith or kin save these Sanderses—but she isna the body to mind. Money canna buy love, but it can buy fear, and she has a mighty hard high spirit that's weel satisfied wi' that, puir body."

"Does Miss Sanders know of her sister's removal?" I asked, still watching the small angular form, with that uneasy interest we always feel when our memory is stirred we know not how.

"She's over in the house wi' her the noo," replied Mr M'Callum. "But it's a blessed change to hae that fulish, ill-conceited being ta'en respectably aff her hands. What culd she do wi' her? She's ill to go and ill to guide. But that aye gaes wi'out saying, for the waur the fule, the better the mule."

"Do you think the old lady knows the character of her adopted friend?" I inquired.

The old man's merry eyes gave a sly wink. "I dinna think she cares," said he. "Whan ye're a certain age, and a crackit auld body tae the bargain, ye maun hae a body-servant, and whan ye hae tried a' the lasses i' the toon, and they hae a' run back to their mithers, and said ye might keep their bit wage sae ye let them gae free, then ye're owre glad to find onybody left. Miss Anne wad suit nae service, and the auld leddie would suit nae servant, and by the blessing o' God they hae found out each ither!"

Then I proceeded to give the grandfather his boy's messages. And I asked where Alice was. She was up-stairs at needlework, he said. In bygone days she would have come down directly she heard my voice, but the poor girl was just now passing through those trials which honest hearts bear best in solitude and silence.

While we stood at the gate, George Wilmot came in from his morning's work. In Mr M'Callum's words, "the laddie was shooting up," and his blue eyes had gained quickness without losing their frank honesty. Now, when he was addressed, they did not fall and his answer was ready, though the blush still came. As the wise old Scotchman said, "There was guid gowd in the callant, and guid gowd will aye brichten."

Just then there was a bustle at the hosier's door. It was the moment of departure. Bessie came to the door-step, and there the two sisters shook hands. No warmer salutation. Bessie was very pale. Anne was fussy, and dropped her gloves, and ran her umbrella at the side of the carriage. Bessie gave her arm to assist her aged relation down the steps. Then I first saw the lady's face. It was a yellow, dry face, with wizened lips and faded eyes, and no white in the thin, withered hair. But then I knew it had once been fair and comely, a face which I had coveted to confront me on my own hearth—ay, a face which I had once kissed truly and tenderly; alas! a face which afterwards I had almost cursed—for that haggard shrew was the remains of Maria Willoughby! Thank God that Lucy Weston was my first love, and lives safe with Him!

When they were gone, Miss Sanders crossed the road and spoke to us. She only said all had happened very fortunately, and she hoped Anne would be happy, and inquired after Ruth, and sent her dutiful regards to her. Then she drew down her veil, and went away.

"She has lost her torment, and yet she seems sad," I remarked.

"It's hard to hae kin to tease one," said Mr M'Callum; "but it's harder to hae nane to please one. I reckon she'd give ten years of her life to hae a richt to ilka body who had a bit o' love in them."

But after the arrival of George Wilmot I feared lest I was keeping the good man from his dinner, so with a very few words more I left him, and went homewards in

a somewhat sobered and saddened mood.   However I
had parted from Maria Willoughby, I could not forget
how we had once met, and her re-appearance, an em-
bittered, loveless old woman, sickened my spirit like a
breath of clammy air from a tomb.   What said Mr
M'Callum?—that money could not buy love?   Ah, she
had love once without thought of buying, and she threw
it away !   Does its ghost ever visit her?   There are
houses which stand so foul and neglected that passers-by
say, "Surely they are haunted."   And so there are faces
which warn us not to ask the secrets of the hearts behind
them.   Poor Maria!  poor Maria!

But just at my own gate, I was roused from my reverie by the stout voice of Mr Herbert.   His niece was
with him, and they had come to pay us a visit.   Somehow, Mr Herbert had heard of the proposed gathering
of the people of St Cross, and he had actually come, un-
asked, to offer the use of his great dining-room for the
occasion.   I think he conferred the obligation in return
for the little aid I had rendered Agnes ; for I had trans-
mitted her father's book to a friend of mine in Paternoster
Row, who promised to give her a hundred pounds for
it.   The transaction was managed by Agnes and me, and
it was never mentioned in the presence of her uncle, and
he never mentioned it himself; but from his manner I
concluded his niece had kept no secret, though both he
and she preferred a tacit silence on the subject.

"You and your worthy sister and Mr Marten can invite the folks—who you like and as many as you like—
the more the merrier," said the bluff farmer.   "The

whole house is at your service, and so are Mrs Irons and the girls, and I 'll provide the victuals—don't fear I shan't have enough."

"We shall certainly want the whole house, sir," returned my sister : "kitchen, parlours, dining-room, and all, for everybody must come ; and I 'm sure you 'll welcome nobody so kindly as some who will be most at home by the kitchen fire. We won't place anybody, but we 'll give everybody a chance of placing himself. There are some that we should rise up before, Mr Herbert, who would not thank us if we put them on cushioned chairs and Turkey carpet."

"You're a wise woman, Miss Garrett," said he : " and for my part, if I could only sit in my own kitchen, I shouldn't be sorry. My great-grandfather was a better man than me, ma'am, and he sat there. Ah, ma'am, if we kept to the old ways we should be none the worse."

"But at which old way shall we make a stand ? " asked Ruth dryly. "The oldest ways in England were woad and acorns, and Druids and sacrifices."

"Now, it strikes me you are laughing at me, Miss Garrett," said the farmer, good-humouredly ; " I thought you liked the old ways too ? "

"I like some old ways," Ruth answered, " but along with the good old ways there were bad old ways, and somehow I think the good old ways live longest. I don't believe the world grows worse, Mr Herbert."

"Then do you think it grows better ? " he asked rather quickly.

She shook her head: "I won't say that either," she replied, "but I think it is like a child growing up. Its evil passions are still there, but they are kept under more restraint."

"You are a clever woman," he said, "and you get beyond me. I just like to keep in the beaten track, and do what my people did before me, and then, at least, I'm safe."

"I don't know that," returned Ruth, carrying on the figure, "you may be going over different soil, where a light wheel would travel better than a heavy one."

"A heavy wheel may be sometimes slow, but it's always sure," said he, "and that reminds me a waggon of mine is now at the wheelwright's, and I had best go and see after it."

He left Agnes behind him, saying he would send Mrs Irons to fetch her in the course of the evening. The girl had not expected this prolonged visit, and, as she had brought no work, she asked us to provide her with some, and so I set her to sort and endorse a basketful of old letters which I wished to keep. The task lasted all day, though she went through it with alacrity, and we were just going over the last papers, when there was a hasty rap at the door, and a moment after Phillis hurriedly announced "Miss Sanders," adding in a whisper, "She is crying, ma'am, and all in a flutter."

Bessie entered. She had lost no time on her toilet, for her bonnet was not tied, and her shawl was only thrown hastily round her. She had an open letter in her hand, which she laid before Ruth, and then stood, breathless, unheeding the chair which Phillis set for her.

My sister perused the document in silence, then, with a flash of astonished intelligence, she said, " Edward, listen to this," and read—

" DEAR MADAM,

" I feel it is my duty to tell you that the boy known in your village as George Wilmot, and now living at the Refuge, is the son of your dead cousin George Roper, who was privately married in London under an assumed name. With this information to start from, I think you will soon trace a likeness between the two. I only disclose this as I think it will give happiness to both you and the lad. In token of my good intentions I enclose a sovereign for George Wilmot, not as a present, but as part payment of an old account between his father and me. And I can only sign myself

" ONE WHO HAS MUCH TO REGRET."

" There it is!" exclaimed Bessie, dropping the piece of gold on the table, and then, sinking on a seat, she gave way to a storm of hysteric tears and laughter, among which the only intelligible words were, " loneliness— ended—thank God—thank God!" She forgave her cousin's faithlessness to her sister's memory : she forgave his hidden marriage, and the deception in which he died. She thought only of a new right to love, of another call to live and labour!

We all examined the letter. It was in delicate upright

writing, evidently the disguise of a refined, but perhaps egotistical hand.   The postmark was St Martin's-le-
Grand, and there was no stationer's name on the
envelope.   The writer had known how to secure secrecy.
Yet there was a simplicity about the letter and its enclosure which seemed to ensure its truthfulness.   Evidently
Bessie Sanders did not doubt it.   Presently she grew
calm, and then arose, saying—

"I must go to the Refuge, and fetch him."

I prepared to go with her.   Just as I put on my hat,
Agnes Herbert whispered—

"Please take me with you, and leave me at the Great
Farm as you pass."

I looked down at the girl, and was startled by her
ashen face and wan eyes.   "My dear," I said, "I fear
you have done too much to-day."

"I am a little tired," she answered, "but it's not for
that I want to go home; only if I go with you it will
save Mrs Irons a walk."

So she went with us, and we left her at her uncle's
gate.   I half-expected she would ask me to call in on
my return, and tell her what passed at the Refuge, but
she did not.

The M'Callums and George were all comfortably
seated in their little sitting-room.   Our very appearance
at that untimely season startled them, and our errand
startled them more.   They would fain have doubted the
letter, but Bessie was terribly in earnest, and had brought
her sister's portrait, and there certainly was a likeness
between it and the half-pleased, half-frightened boy, who

submitted rather timidly to his relation's caresses, and then stole back to Alice M'Callum.

Wherever his future home might be, Bessie implored that he might return with her that night, until at last, with quivering lips, Alice prepared his little outfit. Then the old man blessed the boy, and Alice kissed him—quite calmly, until the garden-gate clanged behind the happy woman and the astonished lad, and then the gentle "matron" sat down, and wept bitterly—almost as bitterly as a mother when her firstborn is carried from her arms to his grave.

"You must not grudge him to Miss Sanders," I said as gently as I could; "she has nothing. You still have your grandfather and Ewen."

"Yes, I know," she sobbed. "And Ewen will never tire of me, but oh, I must keep away from him. For he will rise—rise—rise, and I must not keep him down. I must make him think I don't care much for him, and can be quite happy without him. And I thought we should have George always!"

"Wisht, lassie!" said old M'Callum; "the Lord gives and the Lord takes awa', and a' ye've to do, lassie, is to bless His holy name."

"And you have not lost George," I pleaded. "Even if he live with Miss Sanders, still he will be close to you, and he will not forget that you are his old friend—his first friend."

And just then it struck me it was a good thing his relationship to the Sanderses had not been known on his arrival at Upper Mallowe, for though Bessie's heart was

2 A

soft enough towards him now, when she saw him subdued, mellowed, and somewhat instructed, her charity was not as tender and catholic as Alice's, and she might have shrunk from the uncouth coarseness of the mere tramper boy.

"And he *is* George Roper's son," Alice exclaimed suddenly, her tears ceasing, as she started up to set the supper dishes, "and it was his father's knife he found in the hedge—and Bessie Sanders believes our Ewen guilty—and now——"

"But George does not," I interrupted, "and George never will—and your brother's innocence may be made manifest yet. This very evening gives us an instance how secret things are brought to light."

I said no more, for I knew her woman's heart was very sore—smarting with the old ache of her brother's sufferings, and the newer pang of Mr Weston's love affair. At another time she would rejoice in the joy of Bessie and George, but just now it mocked her—as a laugh in the streets mocks the watcher by a dying bed.

So I returned home, musing at the wondrous providence which weaves together such varying threads of human life, and suddenly the question forced itself upon my mind—"Is it possible that he who led George Wilmot to our house a year ago is the same who now sends this letter?"

# CHAPTER XXIV.

## A QUESTION ANSWERED.

THE weeks following that mysterious letter from London brought with them no interests stronger than the opening of the evening classes, and the preparations for our great Christmas gathering. We issued our invitations ten days beforehand, believing the expectation of pleasure sure to be its very essence, and then we tried our hardest to prove equal to the occasion. The village tradesfolk were gladdened by the liberality of Mr Herbert's orders, and half the girls in the parish were pressed into his niece's service, to assist in the decoration of the chambers. Agnes worked valiantly : whenever we called we never found her post deserted. Sometimes her colour-box was open, and an illumination in progress ; or else she was tying up posies, or stringing holly-berries. Nay, a few mornings before the entertainment, when the freedom and easiness of hospitality had extended so far that I found the house-door open, and nobody about, I was guided to my hostess by the sound of singing in the dining-room. Her voice came ringing through the long corridor, and she sang a song of her father's ; for I remembered the words, as I half-involuntarily paused to catch them :—

> " There's ane they dinna ken aboot
>     For naebody kens him noo,
>   An' he used to say—Oh I daurna tell !
>     But he meant it all for true.
>
> " An' if I ken I'm a blithesome lass
>     Wi' a winsome way or twa,
>   It isna for a' the neebor's talk,
>     But because he telt me sae."

The song ceased when she heard my footstep, and she turned towards me a face rosy with the exertion of rubbing-up the oaken table.   She was a pretty, quaint figure, in her blue print dress, with the sleeves rolled back from her round wrists, and her hair pushed up on her broad, flushed brow.   Nevertheless, knowing there were three servants in the house, I half-wondered to find her so employed.   I think she caught my thought, and perhaps that accounted for a certain piqued, almost defiant, expression on her face,—

" Playing the housewife, Miss Herbert ?" I said.

" Good earnest play," she answered, and resumed her cloth, and went gallantly on with her polishing.

" My dear," I remarked presently, " I fear you will tire yourself."

" So would the servant," she replied with a laugh. " And the less I do it, the sooner I shall tire.   Have you never heard of the poor exiled woman who carried her calf every day, while her strength increased with its weight, till at last she still carried it when it was a cow, Mr Garrett ?"

" I have heard the story," I answered, " and though I doubt its exact truth, yet its principle is quite correct. ' Strength according to our day ' is a scriptural promise. And we none of us know what we can do until we begin to try."

" Oh, I think I could do anything if I had a very strong motive," she said.

" Anything ?" I echoed. " That is a wide statement, my dear."

" I mean anything within reason," she replied ; " any household work, or travelling, or matters of that kind. There's a pleasant excitement in exertion."

" But there is a reaction too," I said.

" Do you think so ?" she queried, rather heedlessly, still rubbing away. " Now, when this table is finished," she added presently, " the sight of it will be quite a treat to me, because I shall be proud of it. And yet, I daresay, the housemaid will laugh aside at my performance. But I think we enjoy things for their relation to ourselves. and not for their own perfection."

" I believe that is universally true," I answered.

" And so I think poor people enjoy more than rich ones," she went on. " I don't mean *very* poor people, but those who have to work hard, and to plan a great deal. What pleasure lies in buying a dress when you can afford any price, and can send it anywhere to be made up? But it is quite another thing when you have but a certain sum to spend, and must take a lively interest in getting the best and prettiest for that sum!"

"I should say you have a talent for management, my dear," I observed.

"I think I have,"—with a bright glance as if in acceptance of a valued compliment, then a little sigh,— "I'm almost sure I have."

At this moment, a ruddy servant put her head into the room, saying, "Please, miss, Mrs Irons says she's a beginning of the pastry,"—adding, in an apologetic aside, "you remember, you wanted to see it, miss."

"Yes, Mary, and I'll come," returned the young lady. "But will you go over the house and find my uncle, and tell him that Mr Garrett is here? And then you will kindly excuse me, sir," she added, dropping one of her slight, half-courtly, half-quaint curtsies, as she left the room.

I remained in the house more than an hour, chatting with Mr Herbert. Before my departure, he took me to his farmyard to see some rare fowls which had just arrived from a London auction. Now the kitchen windows, wide and low, overlooked this farmyard, and though I kept my eyes as strictly as possible, I was not upon my guard until I had caught a very distinct glimpse of a slender form in a blue print dress, with pretty bare arms plunged into the floury contents of a great brown tub.

I did not see Agnes Herbert again until the night of our gathering. We intended to be among the earliest arrivals, but there were many before us, and Agnes was duly at her uncle's side, playing her part as hostess, and looking as quiet and pale as if there were no such things as oak tables and rolling-pins. Her part that evening was not altogether easy. It was necessary that each promoter of the entertainment should have a line of duty particularly his own. Mr Herbert busied himself among the farming people, with all of whom he enjoyed an honest, kindly, despotic popularity. Ruth was, as usual, most at home among the young folk, and my powers were just equal to pleasing the very aged, and the little children, who, God bless them! are easily pleased. And in all these departments we found able seconds in the rector, and Mr M'Callum, and his daughter. But there were still a few who held aloof, tasty spinsters, or genteel young married people of the trading or *employé* class, who were heard to remark, " how nice it was,—how charming to see all distinctions merged for one evening : how much good must follow any opportunity for the different orders of society coming together, and learning mutual respect," and who then immediately looked askant at the other guests, and sat down apart, or in forlorn little coteries, in which the only common feeling lay in the texture of dresses, or the whiteness of hands. Yet these people had to be conciliated,—their want of sympathy but recommended them for conciliation, and there was no one less likely to arouse their prejudices than Agnes Herbert. So to her charge they were committed.

She did not flinch, but I knew her soul shivered

within her, as she moved from one chilly presence to another. At first her face was very white, and her courtesy appeared constrained, but gradually her courage seemed to rise in very scorn of her shallow, frivolous companions. And then they, who would steadily have resisted the sweet suing influences of her purest nature, were suddenly conquered by the outburst of her strength. And so she, who, warmly received and rightly understood, would have sat aside happy, and unnoticeable, now, chilled and defiant, stood forth the beauty and wit of the evening. Beauty and wit: they are terrible crowns for a woman's wearing. I almost think they are a crown of thorn!

But not all my interest in Agnes could exonerate me from my own duties. Indeed, while observing her, I had somewhat flagged in my narration of the adventures of the famous little crook-back of the Arabian nights wherewith I beguiled a large circle of toothless old ladies and open-mouthed children. That night I made a reputation as a story-teller. After the crook-back, I gave the Ugly Duckling. After the Ugly Duckling, I briefly narrated the story of Alexander Selkirk. I was encored, and I repeated my performances to increased audiences. I was applauded,—yes, touchingly applauded,—for one wee damsel of seven summers gave me a kiss, and said she loved me, oh, so much! Am I a weak old fellow to repeat this? Ah, but the little lips were soft, and the little face was—what Lucy's grandchild's might have been!

What a quiet peaceful world it seemed among those

grandmothers and their darlings ! Nobody can say what
tragedies have stamped their lines on the worn old faces,
but then their agony is over. They may have been
weary, but their rest is nearly reached, and like travellers
idly waiting at a station, their minds are free and open
to little amusements and trifling cares. And the children!—for them the fleecy snow is still a solemn and novel
mystery, and morning and night, Saturday half-holiday
and Sunday service are variety enough,—the dear little
children, who hold life carelessly, like a toy with an unknown secret shut inside it ! And after all, it is our own
fault that we are not as light-hearted and content. They
trust all to their parents. Cannot we trust God ? Is it
best to be in the outer court of the temple, or within
the veil ? When father and mother forsake us, does not
God take us up ?

Then my story, and the laughter of my hearers, were
hushed for the music. None of the working men or
women dreamed of speaking while the young ladies were
" at the piano." But many of those who thought themselves far better born and bred, whispered, and flirted,
and commented, as if the sweet sounds were nothing
but an accompaniment to their own shallow minds, a
very good background to cover the gaps of their feeble
wit ! And yet, poor things, they all thought they had
" a taste for music," and so I suppose they had, as much
taste for that as for anything, since doubtless they would
chatter in front of Raphael's Transfiguration, and interrupt the reading of Wordsworth's " Immortality." For
after all, taste is not emotion. Taste is the education

of the senses, and the senses are part of that body which some day we shall throw away like a worn-out garment.    But emotion is the stirring of the soul, like the angel's touch on the waters of Bethesda.

Agnes neither sang nor played ; she could do both, but she did not.    The general performances were very commonplace, by which I don't mean simple or well-known, but rather the contrary, mere musical gymnastics, clumsily performed.    But Marian Blake, the daughter of Mr Marten's friend the lieutenant, sang a very sweet touching Scotch ballad about a young laird going to the wars, who never, never came back, and how his lady-love sat with his mother and sisters, and loved them for his sake, and would not despair of his return till her heart was comforted by very patience, and heaven was nearer than earth.    Mr M'Callum told me, "he minded his mother sang it when he was a bit bairnie, but it was ane of thae sangs which were aye fresh, like God's ain blessed flowers."    Like such songs, and like such flowers, is Marian Blake herself.    And Mr Marten stood beside her while she sang, and smiled upon her when the song was over.    And it seemed as if a breeze from Eden blew through the crowded room.

But it was not Eden.    For glancing from the pretty playful group around the piano, my eyes fell on Alice M'Callum, resting from her hospitable labours and self-surrendered to the spells of sweet sad music, and her face was so unutterably sorrowful, that it startled one like the discovery of a grave in a garden.    Whenever the door opened, she looked towards it, not expectantly, but yet

with a light in her eyes which hopelessly darkened as
each tardy arrival proved—not whom she longed for.
As I watched her, I could have said bitter words of young
Weston.   For among our other friends, we had sent him
an invitation, and he had not even answered it.   I had
hoped his silence arose from a reluctance finally to decline
it.   But his absence seemed to indicate another cause.
I felt my anger towards him was very illogical, for he had
been refused by the woman whom he had honoured, and
so he had a right to turn utterly away from her.   But I
pleaded testily with myself, "Genuine love has no rights.
He knows why she refused him, and he is a coward to
give her up ;" and then I half-smiled to think how Alice's
wan face would fire with indignation if she knew what
hard names I silently bestowed upon him.

Supper came at last.   The long tables fairly groaned
under the substantial dainties provided by our liberal
host, and the parents were obliged to chide their
youngsters for too eager exclamations of "Look at the
puddin'," and "Oh, the jolly pies."   Of course, such cries
must be reproved, but nevertheless one likes the frank
British boy, who is not above making them.   Then there
was a fine tangle before each got into his place at table,
but it was accomplished at last, and I found Mr Marten
had seated Miss Blake at my right hand, and I was very
much obliged to him for so pleasant a companion.   Ruth
was placed opposite Mr Herbert, and George Wilmot
slipped into an empty place beside Alice M'Callum, and
when she whispered something to him which made him
glance towards his cousin Bessie, I was glad to see that

Bessie answered the glance with a smile and nod, which set the boy's conscience at ease about deserting her. After her first hungry joy over a new guest to her empty heart, Miss Sanders's magnanimity had re-asserted itself, and she never grudged her kinsman's love for his old friends.

It was a very merry meal. There was a great deal of talk, and to judge by the laughter there were some good jokes uttered, perhaps no worse because not original. Even the genteel people grew convivial, and contributed their mites to the general entertainment, warming so far as to tell some tolerably good stories, none the less amusing for such prefaces as, " On my uncle's estate in Shropshire," or " While my cousin was Canon of Close Cathedral," about which one need not be over-severe, for doubtless the vanity pleased themselves, and I'm sure it did not hurt any one else.

But when supper was nearly over, and many plates were pushed a little way, and the bustle of helping and serving was quite done, a light thin voice spoke up from the far end of the table. There was an instant hush, as there always is in mixed companies when a woman makes an audible appeal. It was the village chemist's bran new wife, a flaxen frivolous London girl. And this was what she asked :—

" Mr Herbert, I am so fond of romances that you must tell me the history of that mysterious picture with its back to us. I'm sure it has a history. Is it the portrait of some naughty ancestor ?"

There was a silence—a silence to be felt—the breath·

lessness of expectant people. My own eyes seemed rooted to the table before me. Suddenly another voice broke the spell—it seemed a strange voice with just a familiar note, and it said,—

"The picture is only a portrait—not a good one— of my cousin—my cousin Ralph."

It was Agnes who spoke. As I looked towards her, there was a bright spot on her cheek, but it faded instantly. Mrs Irons had walked up the room from her station at the door, and now stood behind her young lady's chair. By this time, the faces round the table showed the foolish inquirer that she had trodden on dangerous ground, and with the blundering tactics of a weak mind, she proceeded to a stammering apology, far worse than her offence.

"I'm sure I didn't know I shouldn't ask. I thought it was something dead and gone. I'd no idea there was anything unpleasant now "——

"Nobody says there is," returned Agnes, with the awful dignity of a quiet nature aroused, and so saying, she rose from her seat, thereby setting us an example to do the same, and thus put an end to an embarrassing situation.

It was fortunate for the success of our gathering that this unhappy incident occurred at its very close, for it would have put a check to all geniality. Some pitied the rebuked questioner, but the majority felt for the family thus forced to display its skeleton, of whose existence nearly everybody seemed quite aware. Anyhow, a chill had fallen on the whole party. No tone rose

above a whisper, and with a sense of relief I heard Mr
Marten announce that we would separate after singing
the ever-beautiful and always appropriate Evening
Hymn.

And I went home, feeling I had an answer to my old
riddle, " Who are ' we ?' "

# CHAPTER XXV

## A HOUSEHOLD SKELETON.

THE next morning rose dank and chilly. I got up with that strange sensation of dreamy unreality which often follows unusual exertion or excitement. The landscape from my chamber window was not cheering. A heavy rain had fallen in the night, and the panes were dabbled with drops from creepers around, while beyond lay field below field, all in the heavy dull green which characterises winter moisture. To-morrow was Christmas-day, and all my little seasonable remembrances lay in the hall below ready for despatch, but somehow the seasonable feeling was not in my heart, which felt as cold and dank as the meadows outside.

But I cheered a little when I entered our snug parlour, where Ruth was already seated, with a knitted crimson shawl enlivening her black dress, and the great Bible before her on a corner of the breakfast-table. It was a

curious fact, that during our walk homeward the night
before we had not even mentioned the incident of the
picture.   Such is the strange reticence which sometimes
seizes one regarding any subject of which his mind is
particularly full.

But I could tell by my sister's very movement that she
now intended to break this silence.   And, sure enough,
as she handed me my first cup of tea, she said,—

"Depend upon it, Edward, Ralph Herbert is Ewen's
Mr Ralph."

"I don't doubt it," I answered ; "but how strange it
is that through all our intimacy with the Great Farm, we
have heard no allusion to this missing member of its
household !   And yet I remember Mr Marten once made
some slight remark about ' young Mr Herbert,' but I afterwards supposed I had misunderstood him, and since then
I had forgotten all about it.   Do you think Mr Herbert
was angry with Agnes for her frankness last night ?" I
inquired, after a pause.

"He was half-angry and half-surprised," replied my
sister.   "He liked her dash of the Herbert spirit.   You
know we all like to recognise our own streak of the old
Adam in another.   And, after all, since he chooses to
keep the thing there, to provoke questions, I don't see
how she could have acted better than she did."

I had my own thoughts on the subject.   I remembered
the conversation of that afternoon when Agnes Herbert
had joined Ewen and me in the fields behind the Low
Meadow, and I doubted whether the young lady had
answered for her uncle, with a wish to preserve as much

propriety as possible, or rather with a woman's desperate resolution to speak up for the absent, who could not defend himself. I remembered the letter with which Ewen had been entrusted for a friend in London, whose address she did not exactly know. I even remembered more than this—something which I banished from my mind as soon as it entered it, for, as I always say, (as I once said to Alice M'Callum,) coincidences are but fancies till proved by facts, and facts once obtained, coincidences are no longer anything.

"But what must this Ralph be," I remarked, "for his very picture to be thus disgraced in his own father's house?"

"He needn't be so very bad because of that," returned Ruth; "some parents choose to stamp children as prodigals whom others would think angels. Before you condemn the black sheep of a family, you must make sure that the shepherd is not colour-blind."

We did not prolong the conversation. We had nothing new to say, and we should only have gone over the old ground, making wild guesses as to possibilities and probabilities. Besides, it was Christmas-time, and therefore my housewifely sister was more than usually busy, and during the whole day the parlour was only honoured by her presence at intervals few and far between. I was dull and lonely enough. The Christmas annuals were in the house, but I could not read, for there was a story being acted out, only a few yards off, which absorbed all my interest. I should have been glad of a visitor, but none came. I knew perfectly well that none were likely to come. Ewen would be at the Refuge that evening, but he would only arrive by a late train. And, as Christmas-day fell on a Friday, I concluded he would remain at home till the Monday following, and so I could not expect to see him, except at church, until Saturday or Sunday; and I knew, too, that Mr Marten was busy—for was there not a sermon to be preached to-morrow? and also duties to be done beforehand to provide for a blank day, for had he not told me he was going to spend Christmas with the Blakes? Oh, the Blakes, indeed! Ah, the Blakes, to be sure!

But a visitor came at last; only, with the usual contrariness of visitors, not till I had ceased wishing for one, for my lonely hours wore wearily away, until evening brought my sister back to her accustomed seat, when it became my pleasing duty to read her extracts from the seasonable literature, and to enlighten her with my sensible criticisms thereon. And we were in the height of an edifying discussion about the naturalness and propriety of a certain hero's mode of courting a certain heroine, when there came a vigorous pull at our door bell, and then there was a pause in our dialogue till Phillis came to us, announcing, "It's Mrs Irons from the Great Farm, ma'am, and she says she wants to speak to you about a message from her master."

"Then show her in here," rejoined my sister.

Mrs Irons obeyed the summons with the noisy sound of thick sensible boots. She only came a step or two into the room, and then stood still. I have said she was a big gaunt woman, and she wore a clinging sage-green dress and a large-patterned shawl, with a worn boa tied round her neck, and half-hidden behind limp black satin bonnet-strings. When Phillis set a chair for her, she promptly took it, and forthwith pulled off her cotton gloves and loosened her boa, in consideration of the near neighbourhood of our blazing fire. But after her first tart " good evening," her mouth remained shut as closely as a steel trap.

" I wonder Mr Herbert can spare you from the Farm this evening," said Ruth, by way of opening the conversation.

" Ah," rejoined our visitor, " but there be some things that even meat and drink must bide for—not but what the puddin's ready, and the mince-pies made, and only the fowls a-picking, and the girls *are* fools if they can't do that between them ! "

" I hope Mr Herbert and his niece are quite well ? " I inquired.

" Yes, they 're quite well, sir," she returned, " for that's the answer they 'd give ye theirselves. But it don't become Sarah Irons to beat about her master's bush. Only, ma'am," she added, turning to my sister, " I hopes you'll consider what a servant 's told to say, she must say, but them ain't always her own words."

" Every one understands that," answered Ruth.

" Yes," said Mrs Irons, " I think even master does. For he says, ' You tell them what I say, Sarah ; ' but, says he, ' you can give your own version of all the ins and outs.' "

" And what did Mr Herbert say ? " asked my sister.

"He said, ma'am," resumed Mrs Irons, solemnly, "'Will you ask Miss Garrett to help me to keep a young girl from a-sacrificing of herself to a vagabond?' Now, I knows the master often uses stronger language than he means, mem; so, says I, 'Vagabond, sir?' But he only says, cross-like, 'Yes, Sarah, vagabond, or anything worse that you can think of.'"

"And who is the young girl, and who is the vagabond, Sarah?" asked Ruth, gravely enough, though I thought I could detect a budding smile.

"The young girl is our Miss Agnes," answered the worthy woman; "and, lack-a-day! by that hard name the master means his own son, young Mister Ralph."

There was a silence.

"The master reckons you know about him?" she said presently, in a questioning tone, "because Miss Agnes has often been here. But I reckons you don't, for she's not one to talk much where she feels most."

"She never named him," answered Ruth.

"Well, ma'am," returned Mrs Irons, her tongue evidently unlocked, "it's a long story. It began long before Master Ralph was born or thought of—bless me, more than ten years before. It had begun when I first entered the Great Farm, in the old lady's days. Not that she'd be a very old woman if she were alive now; but when young ones come on, those behind 'em are always called old. A fine woman she was, too, and had been a beauty, and was a real lady to the last, with hands too white to touch a rough thing"

"Never mind that," said Ruth, rather testily; "it can't have much to do with the present time."

"Yes, it do, ma'am," answered Mrs Irons, a little affronted, "for she was that high and delicate in her mind, that she could not abide anything but the finest; and when I first saw her, she was mighty angry with her youngest son because he wouldn't be a parson, but ran off to London, and took to scribbling for his daily bread. You see, the patron of St Cross would always give it to a Herbert, if there was one ready. And Madam Herbert would never see her boy again, though he were her favourite before, being softer-mannered than the master. She wouldn't let him come to her dying bed, and she left behind her a written paper, forbidding the master to give his brother stick or stone that had belonged to her. You know, mem, it was very hard for her to see a stranger put over the village where her son might ha' been, and the Herberts have never been so well looked on since. And she was a real lady, who could stick to her dignity."

Mrs Irons paused, but Ruth gave no encouraging sympathy, though she would not openly check the ugly, honest woman's sincere though mistaken admiration for the false, vain beauty, who had once been Laura Carewe. Then Mrs Irons resumed :—

"When Madam was dead, master got married to quite another sort of lady. At first I wondered how he could bear to see her sitting in his mother's place, for she was a little quiet thing, nothing to see and nothing to hear; but he was marvellous set on her. And by and by I liked her too, as she grew at home in her own house. But, bless her! she was only there a year. For when Master Ralph came she was took away the very next day. She seemed to get over it all right, and was glad it was a boy —and a fine boy he was too—the finest baby I ever saw. And the master was so proud, and went about on tip-toe a-hushing of us all. But the second day the young mistress called me to her, and she a-lying on her bed, like a tired angel a-resting on the clouds. And she says, 'Take him, please' (that was the dear baby); 'I can't have him any longer. You must take care of him for me, Sarah.' And then she just lifted up her head, and kissed him as I took him away. And half-an-hour later she was gone." And the hard voice failed, and the pale, gray eyes were dim with tears for the young mother who had been in her grave more than five-and-twenty years.

"The master was dreadfully cut up," she went on presently, "and after a bit he took to the baby almost like a woman, and would sit in the dining-room the whole evening a-nursing and playing with it; and there was a rare work if anything ailed the child, which wasn't often, for he was a fine little fellow, and did not seem to fret after his mother. But when he growed up, and could walk about and talk, the master had that determined spirit that he'd make himself be ever so stern with the boy for fear he'd spoil him. And stern enough he were, though perhaps no more than was good, if there'd been a mother to put it all straight again. But there was only me to take the child's part, and I was nobody.

However, in the course of time, things righted themselves, and the lad never said his father nay, and there were no words atween them. And when he came of age, if you'd asked the old rector—the one afore Mr Marten—for a model of the fifth commandment, he'd have pointed out our Mr Herbert and Master Ralph. Of course, the young master had plenty of time to himself, and he and his father did not see much of each other except at meals and late o' nights. And soon after the coming o' age, Mr Herbert's brother sent down word he were dying in London."

"Agnes' father?" queried Ruth.

"Yes," resumed Mrs Irons, "and master showed me his letter—master isn't the man to misdoubt a woman who has lived in his house thirty years! A rare, fine letter it was, sayin' he would never have reminded the Herberts of himself, but he was leaving a daughter who wouldn't disgrace any kindness they might show her. Master and me started for London that very night, but it was all over before we got there. And there was the old Madam's son a-layin' dead in two bits o' rooms, in a street off Soho Square, in a house so packed up with lodgers that there was always one or other creeping about on the staircase,—him who might have been rector of St Cross and had half the parish at his funeral! And there was Miss Agnes, stinting her tears that she might stitch her 'broidery to pay for the supper she set before us. But the master snatched it out of her hands, and told her that was done with for ever. And directly after the funeral, he took her home with us to the Great Farm, and somehow—mayhap, because nobody'd ever looked so at me,—the minute she and Mister Ralph met, I thought how it would be, and I wondered if it was joy or rue the master was planting in his house that night. Mister Ralph was at home a good deal more after that, and in the fine weather he and his cousin were much out together. She was fond of drawing, for she'd learnt it somehow in London, and was over-glad to practise it in the country; and the young master himself had always a turn that way. I mind they had a tiff once, because he was out two or three hours every evening, and wouldn't tell her where he went, till at last he brought home a fine drawing, and told her how he had been to a class at Mallowe, and what praises he got from some artists who'd been a-visiting the teacher. And she was so pleased, that before he could stop her, she ran off to tell the master, thinking no harm, poor dear! And then there was a fine piece o' work; and that was the beginning of the strife. For it set the master a-thinking of his brother's folly; and he said the Herberts should have nothing to do with scratching or scrawling, 'cept to pay for 'em, if they wanted 'em. But it was hushed up for that time; and very soon after, I saw Mr Ralph's mother's keeper-ring on his cousin's hand—and Sarah Irons is not so thick in the head but she knowed what that meant—and the master seemed mighty satisfied, and fonder nor ever of his niece."

"She wears that ring still," I observed.

"She do, and she'll wear it in her coffin," returned Mrs Irons: "and I says, 'God bless her!'—though it were no great fancy I took for her at fust, with her face over white and worn for a young thing, and I even thought Mr Ralph might ha' found a better missis for the Great Farm; but I did not guess how it would be, and he knowed best after all!"

"And what happened to bring all this household happiness to an end?" I asked.

"The young master would not turn into his father's mould," answered the good woman, with a sad shake of her head. "He could not take to the farm, but wanted to go to London and be an artist, which his father would not hear on. And Mr Herbert said hard things of daubers and such like, and, lack-a-day! Master Ralph had an answer ready about bumpkins and clod-hoppers; and 'atween the two, Miss Agnes was always scared and striving, and I used to catch her crying, because the young master got to shun his home, and almost seemed careless of her. And other times she were quite cheerful, because she thought things were mending. But it come to an end on New-year's-day, three years a-gone. Miss Agnes were in the kitchen with me, when master and his son came in, and we heard high words atween 'em, and master shut the dining-room door with a bang; and I would not let Miss Agnes go in, because I thought they'd settle it best theirselves. And all of a sudden Master Ralph came out, and came to the kitchen, and caught hold of his cousin and kissed her hard and fast, and never seemed to see me, and then walked straight out at the door; and while we both stood struck, a-staring at each other, there was the master calling us in a voice fit to raise the dead.

"He was standing by the fireplace in the dining-room, and there was a chair upset on the ground. Master's face was white, and I'd never seen his face white afore,—for, in ordinary, he turns red in his passions,—and he put dreadful words on Master Ralph, and said the old Herberts of Mallowe had come to an end. And then he noticed his son's picture on the wall, and he up and struck it in the face, and turned it round to the wall— never stopping to lift it from the nail, and you may see the hanging string is twisted to this day. And then he caught his niece's hand, and was drawing off her ring— the very ring he'd once put on his wife's finger,—but she snatched her hand away, and for the minute she seemed the strongest of the two, and her voice was as loud and shriller! But the next minute she was down on the floor at his feet, a-begging of him like a little chidden child. She'd kept her own, and that was all she cared about; and master never said another word about the ring."

Mrs Irons paused for a moment.

"He was calmer-like after that," she went on, "but he told us we were never to set it any more that he and Master Ralph were father and son. 'Sarah,' says he, 'there's nothing in this house for him—not even room to stand on the door-mat. Mind, your master says so, whom you've served faithful this thirty years!' I don't know how it was,—whether it was a feeling for the only baby I'd ever nursed, or the sight of poor Miss Agnes— but says I, 'Yes, sir; I'll mind, except so far as I can't disobey my dead missis' orders to take care of her boy for her. The words of the dead last long, sir,' I said, ' for there's no asking 'em to draw 'em back.'

"And then, somehows, we went off to our own rooms for the night; but I left the door on the latch, if so be the young master might come back, and things straighten in the morning. But, sure enough, I heard the master go and fasten it up with his own hands. And in the dead of the night, just as I was dropping asleep, a-dreaming that Master Ralph was a baby in my arms, Miss Agnes came and roused me like a spectre. It was on her mind that her cousin might destroy himself, and we be never the wiser; and so, to quiet her, I had to promise that first thing in the morning I'd go out and ask about him. But when I was out a-trailing about the village, I didn't know where to go, nor who to ask. I thought the lad had likely taken the last train to London, and it struck me that the new rector—I mean Mr Marten—who had just come from there, might put me in the way to track him. So I went and told him just as much as I must, and as little as I could. And then I wondered I hadn't had common-sense to do what he did—to go to the railway station, and ask if young Herbert had left there by the London train. And the guard said he had. And then Mr Marten did more than I bargained for. He called at the Great Farm, and had a long talk with the master. I thought the place would be too hot to hold me after that. But the master never said one word about what I'd done. And the rector never called again—never till that evening when he came with you, sir."

"And did Mr Ralph make no effort to communicate with his cousin?" I asked.

"O yes, indeed," she replied. "The morning of the second day there came a letter telling her where he was, and full of fine hopes of his future, and sure that his father had done the best thing for him when he turned him out of the Great Farm, and so on. Miss Agnes never named the letter to her uncle, but she let it lie on the dining-room mantel for two whole days, and he looked at the envelope, but said ne'er a word. And be sure, she answered it by the first post. And so things went on for a time."

"And did you never hear what was the quarrel between father and son?" inquired Ruth.

"Mr Ralph wrote that it was about difficulties he was in at Mallowe—money difficulties, and that his father would not help him unless he promised to give himself up to the farm, which he wouldn't, and then the master washed his hands of him. I'm feared he'd been rather reckless that time when he was a'most driven out of his own home. But he wrote he should soon work it all off, and would be wise in future."

"And when did this state of things end?" I queried.

"Well, six months after he left home, in the middle of summer, he wrote word he expected he should be at Mallowe in the course of a few days, and if so, and he could send a message when he arrived, would his cousin ask me to come with her to meet him, so that they might have a little walk and talk together—the two poor dears! And he wrote his letter, which she showed me, so simple and straightforward, that I thought he was surely in the right way, and I should be obeying his dead mother if I helped him to this bit of comfort to encourage him on. And then Miss Agnes and me were in a regular flutter at every knock that came to the door."

With all her earnestness, worthy Mrs Irons had a bit of the art of a story-teller, for she paused at every climax.

"And did you see him at last?" I asked, to prompt her.

"He never comed," she answered, and there was no letter from him long over his usual time, and I thought Miss Agnes would waste away to nothing, and her soul would get free to go and watch over him wherever he was. At last there was a letter, for me, not for her. It said he'd been in France and very ill, and I was to tell his cousin she was to forget she had ever seen him, for she should never see him again; he was not fit to come within her sight; he wasn't even fit to write to herself, but I was to give her that letter to do what she liked with, though it was written to me. I thought that seemed as if he half hoped she'd still care to have it. But it had no address, and his poor writing was so bad! And in a postscript he said she was to take off her engaged ring, and give it back to his father. and to love and honour him always, and in everything, for whatever the master had cost him, he had only saved her from misery, and now she was all that he had in the world.

"I shan't ever forget her face, when she read it," Mrs

Irons went on. "I watched her, for I was feared. But there came a sort of glory on her, and she looked up with a light in her eyes, and said, 'I will never do it, Sarah. Now for the first and last time, I disobey him. I will never take off his ring, and I will never give him up! And I will love and honour my uncle always and in everything, just for his sake—Ralph first, and he next.' And all that day she bore up better than I did."

"Ah," murmured my sister, "there is a comfort in the strength of love."

"I dare say there is, ma'am," answered the honest woman; "but if so be, it's a comfort that doesn't warm the heart enough to cheer the body, and it was woeful to see how Miss Agnes wore away, and how she'd stand at the window a-watching for the post that never brought her nought. She'd been a lively 'sponsible girl before, · always at her books, or her pencil, or her needles, and I think she tried to keep on with them, but there were nothing to force her, and she couldn't force herself. And it seemed weary work for a young thing to sit waiting and waiting, like old folks wait for death. I often thought it might be a good thing for her to be back in London, a-earnin' of her own living."

"And what was the next you heard of young Mr Herbert?" I inquired.

"Nought for more than a year," she returned. "Winter had come round again, and it was nigh Christmas, when one night, quite late, I heard a tapping at the little window beside the back-door. Miss Agnes were a-bed, but it came over me who it was, and I went out quite softly, not to waken the master, nor nobody. And it were Master Ralph, sure enough ; but he would not cross his father's threshold, and I had to talk to him in the yard. He'd been to Mallowe, he said, a-trying to get some money he had lent long ago to a young fellow there, but he couldn't ; and would you believe it, sir, the master's only son was that hard driven, that he hadn't a penny to take him back to London ; and he spoke so weakly and looked so white, that I asked a straightforward question, and he owned to old Sarah, who fed him when he was a baby, that he had not touched aught since a cup of tea in the early morning. He said he was sure he could not eat anything if he had it, but I knowed what that meant ; and I just made him go and sit down in my wash-house, and then carried him some sandwiches, and a cup of wine. It wasn't my master's victuals I gave," explained the faithful creature, " for the wine I'd bought with my own money to give some to a poor consumptive creature in the village ; and I put two shillings into the purse my master gives me for house expenses, which were over and above the value of the bread and meat I took. Master Ralph would scarce touch it at first ; but once he began he ate like a famished dog. And it seemed to call him back to life and feeling like ; for before he took it, he'd spoken as cold and dry as if it was nothing, his coming so to his own father's house. But when he'd done, all of a sudden, he put his arm round my neck and dropped his face on my shoulder, and cried as he scarcely ever did, even when he was a child. I felt the hot tears a-falling quick on my hand. I hope you'll excuse my being so affected, ma'am," said the worthy woman, wiping tears from her hard-lined cheeks ; " but I 've had nobody of my own since I was twenty years old, and I 'd had him from his dying mother ; and he seemed to belong to me more than any one else. And when he was a little bit quieted, he told me he had been in the neighbourhood once or twice afore, about this same little debt ; and he'd walked round and round the Great Farm, but hadn't ventured to come nigh it, and he 'd only come at last, to ask me for enough to take him back to London ; for come what might, he did not want to starve in his native place. And I made him take all the money I had in my work-box, and a rare bother I had to make him take it. Though he knowed I had not lived thirty years in service for nothing, still he wouldn't touch it, till I said he might pay me again directly he could, and with in-terest too, if he liked. And all the time he kept asking about his cousin, and made me promise not to tell her of seeing him in such trouble,—at least, not directly; and ' I hope she forgets me,' he said, poor dear, and looked so down-hearted, that the truth came out afore I knowed it, and said I, ' Don't you think it ; she 's as true to you as if you 'd never parted, and she always will be ; and you 'll live to talk it over, some day, sir,' I said. But he shook his head, and said no, that wouldn't ever be ; and he was sorry he 'd cross'd her life to darken it. But I told him it was all settled in the will of God ; and says I, ' Even if you never come together, the young missis will not be an unhappy woman, if she knows you 're com fortable and settled in yourself. If you 'd keep trouble from her, keep it from yourself, sir,' I said. And then he went away."

"And did you never tell Miss Herbert of this visit?" I inquired.

"Not till quite lately," she answered. "About June I got a post-office order for the money I'd lent Mr Ralph, but even then I only told her I'd reasons of my own for saying her cousin was alive and well. And in the autumn, when young M'Callum came down for his holiday, Miss Agnes found out the two were living together in London. And Mr Ralph has written to her since then, and she has put his letters on the dining-room mantel, just as she did at first. She has told me he is doing pretty well, and she's not said a word further. But master and me, we've eyes in our heads, and we can put two and two together, and didn't she set-to, and get ready that book of her father's, and sell it? And hasn't she taken a mighty interest in the cooking and the house-work? And doesn't she try how little she can spend on her dress? And isn't she reading a book about Canada? And after the way she spoke up for Mr Ralph last night, the whole village'll talk. Master knows as well as I do that there's something in the wind, and so he sends me here to ask you to help him to stop it."

"And you don't come quite willingly, Mrs Irons?" queried Ruth.

"Well, I don't, ma'am," she answered, candidly; "and I'd come less willingly if I thought you or the master either would be able to stop it."

"You think of the young man," I said, "but we must

2 C

give some consideration to the prospect before Miss Herbert."

"I don't see why the two need be thought on apart," returned Mrs Irons, her native asperity again rising to the surface. "There's a lot of fine talk about female influence and out-of-the-way things, but all I say is, if God puts a man's soul in reach of a woman's hand, and she throws it away, it may go to the wicked place, but she's scarcely fit to go to t'other one! Yes, you may all say what you like!" she added, standing up, and shaking out her skirt, with a disclaiming gesture; "but if any of you change Miss Agnes' mind, then God help Master Ralph, and I've made a mistake all along!"

"Whether she be right or wrong in this matter," said Ruth, after our visitor had departed, "she is a good woman."

"I should say there is a fortune of insufficiently-claimed affection lying waste in her heart," I remarked.

"No matter," answered my sister, "it will ascend pure to God!"

# CHAPTER XXVI

EWEN.

CHRISTMAS-DAY again; not an honest Christmas, like the last, with frozen ground and peeps of pale sunshine, but Christmas in a wet green robe with an umbrella. The choir boys came under our window, as before, but Ruth despatched them after one short hymn; "it was not worth while for them to stand there getting wet," she said. Nevertheless we managed to attend service, and despite the unfavourable weather, St Cross had a good congregation.

Mr Herbert stole a glance at us as he entered his pew. His niece followed him, quite unconscious of the revelation of the preceding night. Then I looked towards the M'Callums' accustomed seat—the old man and his two grandchildren were there, and I noticed that George Wilmot and his aunt sat with them, and then I remembered hearing they intended to spend Christmas together. Bessie Sanders was surely a true-hearted woman, for if she had yet any lingering doubt of Ewen, she certainly did not allow it to bias her actions. The worried look has left her face, and it is a finely-cut, powerful countenance, a quaint contrast to the round, ruddy visage of her nephew, with his clear, simple, blue eyes. I have good hopes of that boy, and I think he will atone to his aunt for all the past.—"At eventide there shall be light."

When the joyful service was over, and I turned to leave our pew, I saw at the back of the church, one whose presence made me greatly glad. It was Mr Weston, looking older and graver than he looked before. He waited for the M'Callums. In the porch I saw he was introduced to Ewen. They all walked down the church-yard together, and there I lost sight of them, for the Herberts arrested our progress down the aisle, and we had their company for our homeward journey. What a strange significance did their conversation acquire from that revealed secret ! And yet, after all, the significance may exist rather in the fancy of the hearer than in the mind of the speaker.

In the road we overtook the M'Callums and their friends walking in a kind of cluster, as one can in the country, whenever it would be rather invidious to get into couples. We all exchanged salutations. I had for-gotten to ask Mrs Irons if she supposed her master knew of the friendship between his son and Ewen. Anyhow, Mr Herbert was as genial as ever towards both grand-father and grandson. Perhaps he argued with himself that it was no business of his if they chose to befriend fools and beggars. But to Alice he was decidedly civil, and very interesting and pretty she looked in a demure, plaintive little flutter caused by the presence of her rejected suitor, who, for his part, soon dashed into a bucolic argument with his brother agriculturalist of the Great Farm. Ewen alone walked a little apart, as if there was something in his lot which as yet he could scarcely cast into the simple merriment around him. I saw Agnes steal one or two glances at him, but he did not seem to notice her, though I almost fancied his pale cheek—it was very pale—reddened a little. At the end of the lane, our party broke into three groups, breathing good-byes and good wishes as if there was nothing in the world beyond a walk from church to Christmas cheer — no old tragedies, no hopes more wearing than fears, no endurance, no dead or jarring notes in the anthem of life. And then Ruth and I went home together.

We had our quiet dinner, she at one end of the table and I at the other, and then we drew up our chairs in front of the fire, and talked softly of all that had happened in the year—of the Refuge, and the Orphanage, and the May-day feast, and the hospital; of the M'Callums and their fortunes, and the trial of Agnes Herbert. And our talk was broken by short silences, when each gazed mutely at the red embers in the grate, and saw diverse things therein—perchance trees meet for whispering beneath, or the form of a woman-angel, or haply the turret of the old clock-house of Mallowe, or a rough pauper's grave. Shall I ever speak of these things to my sister? No, I think not—not in this world.

We had finished our tea, and were again lost in silence, when there came a gentle double rap at our front door. It was actually Ewen M'Callum.

He took a chair between us, and explained that he intended to return to London by the first train next day, and so ventured to pay us this unexpected Christmas visit.

"How did they spare you from the Refuge?" asked Ruth.

"Oh, they're all very merry there," he answered, with a grave smile. "You know they have Miss Sanders and George, and Mr Weston has stayed also. They'll not miss me."

"Need you return to London so soon?" I inquired.

"It is best for many reasons," he replied.

"And how is Mr Ralph?" I queried. "Ewen, we know his other name now."

"You do?" he said quickly. "Mr Ralph is very well, sir."

"Why did you keep him a secret from us?" I asked.

"He wished to be kept secret from every one," Ewen answered, gravely. "And I kept the secret until I was forced to betray him to his cousin."

"How forced?" inquired Ruth.

"Mr Garrett asked about 'Mr Ralph' in Miss Herbert's hearing," he replied, "that gave me an excuse. And I was very glad of it, for Ralph kept losing all hope and interest in life, and thinking he might throw himself away anyhow, like a useless thing."

"Do you think he has great affection for his cousin?" I asked, in my prim old-fashioned way.

Ewen turned to me with glowing eyes. "I should think he has!" he said. "It's just her memory which has kept him afloat above the lowest depths. It's just her memory that's kept in him a bit of faith in man or God; and yet it was just her memory—thinking that he'd lost her—that made him stand where I found him last spring—on London Bridge, looking over and wondering if"——

There Ewen paused.

"His love should have given him courage to live worthily of her, come what might," said Ruth.

"One would think so," observed the young man, reflectively; "he should not have lost heart so soon; but yet it must have been a dreadful trial. It's hard enough to love her,—I mean it's hard enough to love such as her,—hopelessly from the beginning; but to have hope in one's love at first and then to lose it, oh, we can't guess how bitter that must be!"

"That's right," remarked Ruth; "when we measure our own temptations with our neighbour's, let us always think his the sharpest."

"But Ralph Herbert voluntarily resigned his cousin?" I said.

"He thought it was his bounden duty under certain circumstances. He still thinks so," Ewen added.

"Then he still despairs?" queried Ruth, a little satirically.

The ghost of a smile crept over our visitor's face, and that was his only answer.

"And so Mr Ralph meditated a leap into the river," continued my sister in her pitiless tones, "and he thought that was dying of love, while it would be simply death by feverish impatience and a cold bath."

"Shakespeare says something like that, my dear," I observed.

"Yes, I know he does," returned Ruth, "and I dare say he says something like any remark *you* make, if it happen to be worth hearing. I always grow ill-tempered over any of this Lord Byron kind of romance. If I knew any one dying of love, and enjoying the sensation, I'd give them a good dose of physic, or a sound caning. Or if they were really such fools as to be slipping away without knowing it, I'd cheat them into learning a language, or a good tough science."

"Like Wordsworth's gentleman who collected and dried flowers," I remarked.

"But Ralph never thought he was dying of love," said Ewen; "he was only broken down by misery."

"By the way, you look much better than you did the last time you were here," observed my sister, rather abruptly disregarding Ewen's last remark, and turning towards him.

"I am much better, thank you," he said.

"Then you knew you were ill?" pursued Ruth. "Alice was quite alarmed about you."

"I never said a word to her," he answered.

"Why not?" she asked.

"Where was the good?" said he; "she would have wanted me to give up my work, and my drawing, and so forth."

"And why should you not?" I queried.

"Because I suppose it is a sin willingly to do aught to shorten one's life," he answered, with a quiet smile, "and if once I called myself sick, I should die."

"Did you have any medical advice?" I inquired.

"Ralph made me go to a doctor," he replied. "He said if I wouldn't he would write and tell them at home, so I went once, though I don't much believe in doctors, and I heard what was the matter with me, which I knew beforehand, and I was told to do certain things which I could not do, or I shouldn't have been ill. But I did my best towards them, as I had done all the time, and in due time I recovered, as I felt I should from the first."

"Ah," said Ruth, "it takes much to kill young folks, or nobody would reach thirty."

"But they grow old folks in the struggle?" remarked Ewen.

I thought he gave a little sigh, and I glanced towards him. The look of pain — of forced endurance — was gone; but it had taken its bloom with it, and had left its own traces behind. There were lines now which gave a noble character to the always handsome face : lines, which his future wife will declare are half his beauty, though she may give a little sigh to think she did not know him before they came ! For I hope Ewen will have a wife some day, though I fancy he does not hope anything of that sort just now. And perhaps he will carry those lines with him when he goes to the Better Place. For we must not measure heavenly beauty by earthly beauty. Is it not a face "more marred than any man's" which gazes at us from the glory of the Father's throne?

"And if they do 'grow old' in the process," I answered, repeating his words—for there had been a pause—"it is none the worse. It is not the boys and girls who do the work of the world. They may be its flowers, but the middle-aged and elderly are its fruit and its corn."

"Young folks are often over-willing to die," remarked Ruth, folding her hands and gazing into the fire, "and God seldom wants us when we want death. He knows we don't want to go to Him, but only to get away from the world. And we're not fit to go to Him till we're quite willing to bide his time."

And then Ewen said "Good-bye," and went back to the Refuge festivities.

"I'll never say again that men choose gilt when they might have gold," said my sister, after he was gone. "The women are quite as bad!"

"What do you mean?" I asked.

"I mean what I say," she returned; "and if you don't understand now, you may in time. And haven't we spent a sentimental evening, for two old people who never fell in love in their lives!"

Oh, Ruth, Ruth! I hope you did not take my silence for assent to that last statement of yours, though I hadn't courage to contradict it. But it does not matter much, for you didn't mean it!

# CHAPTER XXVII.

THE weather did not mend, and we were un-
visited prisoners in our house until after the
New Year. But at the end of the first week
in January, there came a glorious day,—not
bleak with wintry cold, nor rough with wind, nor yet
heavy with the stifling moisture of unseasonable heat.
It was almost like the first day of spring—a little too
early—escaped from the prison-house of the year, before
the storms were passed; as Noah's dove left the ark
before the flood was over. We knew—and so did the
birds—that it was too bright and fair to last,—that to-
morrow might bring back the mist and rain. But we
shall have little pleasure in this life if we do not treasure
all the little bits we can find. Do you suppose Noah
threw away the olive-branch because it was not a tree？
And so the birds twittered, and we went out.

We went up the road towards St Cross, choosing that

direction for two reasons,—because it was hilly, and so secure from any latent moisture, and because we wished to visit my new house behind the church. It was now completed, or at least very nearly so, for the locksmith and the varnisher were the workmen now employed.

As we toiled up the ascent, we were arrested by a cheerful salute from behind, and turning round, we found Mr Marten and his friends the Blakes hastening to overtake us; and we waited till they came up.

"We have intended you a visit ever since Christmas," said the rector, as he shook hands; "but the weather has always forbidden it until to-day. We have just been at your house, and the servant told us where we should find you."

"Then let us all return instantly, and have a comfortable luncheon," I answered.

"Oh no," returned Mr Marten; "we can chat as we walk, and have the benefit of the fresh air and exercise besides. We have not had a long journey—only as far as the High Street."

"Have you been to the Refuge, then?" I asked.

"No," he replied with a slight hesitation; "in fact—in short"— Speaking briskly at last, "Mr Garrett, I planned this morning visit as a fitting opportunity to introduce Miss Blake—as my future wife."

We made a slight pause, and congratulated the young lady, who was duly diffident and blushing. And I think the rector was a little disappointed to find we expressed no surprise.

"It is no new happiness to me," he said. "We both

thought best to keep it quiet until our circumstances justified us in commencing preparations for the event. I have looked forward to the pleasure of telling you my good fortune ever since the first of May last year; and Marian and I hope to be married on that date this year, which will allow us five months to make our very simple arrangements."

At this juncture, Lieutenant Blake kindly enlightened us on the purpose of that morning's visit to Upper Mallowe village. "We've been looking over a house," said he, with a wink intended to be highly comical.

"But you have not taken it?" I asked hastily.

"No," answered Mr Marten, shaking his head with a dash of his old despondency; "but we must. There is no better one to be had. Do you know it?—that small gray house, at the angle of the High Street and Pleasant Lane?"

"Which lane's name goes by the rule of contrary, as most names do," put in the gallant old sailor.

"Have you looked at any others?" inquired Ruth.

"Yes," he replied; "we looked at a cottage in the lane by the Low Meadow,—a very pretty cottage too, but that situation is damp. The kitchen walls were discoloured by it. Then we looked over a house, on the high road to Mallowe,—a nice house, but it was only to be let on lease; and that arrangement is not always convenient for a clergyman. And there are no other unoccupied houses in the neighbourhood."

"Except that behind St Cross," I remarked, carelessly.

"Ah, but that is above our means," said he.

"You see I built it for an income of two hundred a-year, exclusive of house rent," I observed.

"Ah, I remember you said so," he responded.

"And I fixed on this income, because it is that of the rectors of St Cross"——

"I beg your pardon," he interrupted, "we receive only two hundred, inclusive of all personal expenses."

"And I intend this house as a gift to the rectory of St Cross," I continued, not heeding his interruption, "and my solicitor in London is at the present time engaged in preparing the necessary deeds."

And then we made another little pause, and went through another confusion of acknowledgments and congratulations, which were all very pleasant to hear, but would make very stupid reading, and I interrupted them by proposing we should all go and survey the "Parsonage." I wanted to fix that name to the house; I did not wish it to be the "Rectory." Whenever a thing is well expressed by a Saxon word, why should we not use it in preference to one springing from a Latin root? When there is not a Saxon word, let us take the Latin and be thankful; but why should we seek abroad for what we can find at home?

We soon reached the building, and we lingered just a moment to criticise its exterior. Its red-brick front was slightly relieved by the stone copings and window-sills, and Miss Blake exclaimed delightedly at the little trellis-work porch, which I had caused to be erected, thinking that one of brick or stone would be far too heavy for the

modest size of the building; while I was determined to
have a porch of some kind, that any guest might find
the house a true refuge for shelter or shade even before
its door was opened.   Then we all walked up the gravel
path, between two plots of ground, which now gave but
a barren suggestion of future beds.   In the porch, I
invited all the party to turn and survey the beautiful
view below—lovely even now in leafless January.   The
back of the house did not command so fine a view—the
country there was flatter—therefore I had given it the
larger garden, so that the future household might rejoice
on the one side in the telescopic magnificence of valley,
river, and distant hill, and on the other, in the micro-
scopic beauties of flower and leaf.   I explained this as we
stood in the porch, and then we entered the hall.

The tiling of the floor was laid in a neat pattern of
buff and black, and the walls were engrained as oak, and
varnished.

"They will wash over and over again, Lewis, and
then look as well as ever," said Miss Marian, stroking
them quite lovingly; "and, papa, there will be no little
marks like those which are always on our hall paper at
home, though nobody knows how they come.   And here
is a nice fixture hat-rail; and see! a lamp-bracket, and
a lifting-flap for a table!   How charming!   There are
only one or two chairs wanted to perfectly furnish the
hall."

We passed on to the room destined for the library.
I drew their attention to its being painted in a pale buff.

"I told my brother to choose a perfectly neutral tint,"

said Ruth, "that you might not be limited in your choice of carpets and chair-covers. Now if your tastes be gay, you can have blue or green, or pink, if you like."

"I think we will have brown leather chairs here, Marian," observed the rector, thoughtfully: "they are expensive, but they wear well."

"What wears well is never expensive," said my sister; "for granting that you have in hand sufficient money for the first outlay, how can you invest it better than by buying what will last?"

"And see, Marian," said Mr Marten, "here are glass book-fixtures, with little cupboards below, at each side of the fireplace. I think these will hold all the books I have at present."

"I thought they would receive a tolerable library," I observed; but the rector did not heed my words, for he was reflectively stroking his whiskers and planning the furniture.

"I wonder, Marian," said he, and paused—"I wonder," he repeated, "if we might make this room at once library and dining-room."

"That would be very pleasant," said the young lady; "for then the other might be quite a drawing-room."

"Don't think of such a thing," observed Ruth, emphatically. "You think, Mr Marten, that because you will always join the family meals, you will lose no more time if they come to you than if you go to them. Remember, meals must be set on the table and removed, and the pitiless servant will come and clear away your papers when you are in the middle of a sentence."

"But if we have our meals in the other room, where can we ask visitors?" inquired inexperienced little Marian.

"My dear," said Ruth, "the question is, who is most important, a morning caller, or the master of the house? Shall you keep a room at the service of the idle guest who *may* come, or shall you cultivate the peace and comfort of him who gives the household its very existence?"

Marian's lip almost quivered.

"I know which you wish to do," said my sister quite gently, "and I know the proposal came from Mr Marten himself; but if you take my sincere advice, you'll not think of 'drawing-rooms.' What you want is a nice, snug, pretty parlour which will be quite a pleasant change for the rector when he leaves his book-room. And let me remind you, my dear, that whenever the parlour is particularly engaged by dinner or tea, then the library, in its turn, will be free to receive a visitor until the other room is at liberty."

"But still there are grand 'occasions' in all families sometimes," I said; "and a little due provision for these when furnishing a house often saves much future worry and annoyance."

"Ah, suppose I bought a sideboard and a dining-table for this room?" queried the rector. "I could put my desk on the table, and it would give a delightful surface for my papers and reference-books; and then the room would be quite prepared for any emergency, and yet need not be used for convivial purposes except on the arrival

2 D

of those guests for whose sake I should keep holiday myself."

"That will be very convenient indeed," I assented, "for this reason especially, that when respected visitors are to be entertained, the mistress of a small household must generally superintend the arrangement of the dining-room herself, and it is not always pleasant to do so in the room where the company is seated."

"'Um, I suppose not," answered Ruth, as if conceding to a common human weakness; "but, for my part, I can't see why she cannot go through that as gracefully as through her performance on the piano."

"A great woman could, but I think I could not," said modest little Marian ; and Ruth was mollified, and smiled kindly upon her.

Then we adjourned from the library to the parlour, where the wall tinting was gray. There we held a discussion about carpets, and Ruth strongly recommended a good one of a small pattern, as least likely to display the unavoidable marks of wear and tear. In this room Miss Blake was in her element, walking from side to side, and imagining all possible kinds of furniture in all possible positions. I found she had already sundry treasures designed for the decoration of this peculiarly feminine domain—such as pictures, china, and miniature statuary —about which she held half-whispered consultations with her father the lieutenant, whose stereotyped answer was, "Yes, that will be certainly best, my dear. What pleases you will be the right thing ; you 've a nice taste, and so had your mother, Marian."

Then we surveyed the bedrooms, making very wise
sanitary remarks thereon, and the rector observed that
"for the present" (how I liked that!) Marian could have
one of them for a little boudoir or study of her own, and
she said she would have the small room above the hall
—guided to that choice by its pretty fancy window. It
was delightful to find that the new parsonage was certainly exactly to the taste of the first pair who would
make it their home.

Lastly, we descended the stairs, and went into the back
garden. It was not large, though of considerable extent
for the size of the house. Beyond causing the ground
to be put in a good state, I had not done much with it.
I was too much of a Londoner, by education, to know
much of the theory or practice of gardening, so I had
resolved from the first to leave this matter to the taste
of the future master. My sister was not so ignorant ;
she was quite able to enter into a conversation about it
with Mr Marten.

"By all means, plant some dwarf fruit-trees, sir," said
she ; "they give us three pleasures in the year—the
beauty of their blossoms, the beauty of their fruit, and
the sweetness of the dessert. I don't know why they
are depreciated while flowers are so admired, unless,
indeed, it is because they are useful ; for it is only too
common to say, this thing is made for use, and that for
ornament. And if anything be both useful and orna-
mental, its use is used, and its beauty is never observed!"

I fear the bride-elect did not hear these remarks, for
at that moment she came towards Mr Marten, saying,

"Lewis, isn't it *almost* a pity that the kitchen windows look into this garden?"

"Why so?" asked my sister, a little quickly, (for she knew I was the architect of the house—which, by the way, Miss Blake very likely did not, since Mr Marten would scarcely have mentioned such a circumstance, when he never supposed the building had anything to do with them.) "Why is it a pity, Miss Blake? I would not give much for the comfort of any house where the kitchen was not as pleasant to look at or to live in as the parlour. There's real beauty in a well-scrubbed floor and a white dresser, with its stand of bright copper and tin, and its rows of plates. And it is a beauty that never tires one. And why shouldn't a kitchen be as pleasant as a parlour? It is just what I say about the fruit-trees and the flowers," she added, turning towards Mr Marten. "A kitchen is thought meanly of because it's the most useful room in the house."

"The most useful to the commonest wants of our nature, certainly," said the rector, scarcely liking to give it unqualified supremacy over the library.

My quick sister caught the reservation. "And where would be the highest aspirations of our nature if those commonest wants were unsupplied?" she asked triumphantly; and the reverend gentlemen smiled, and did not answer.

The betrothed couple seemed unwilling to leave the premises, and presently Ruth drew me a little aside and whispered that they might wish to go over the rooms again without our intrusive presence. The suggestion was full of kindly sympathy, but this was the mask it wore : "We had better leave them to themselves, Edward. I daresay he has some nonsense to say to her, which we must not hear."

When we two were once more at home, chatting in the twilight, my mind reverted to our poor Agnes, whom we had not seen since we had learned the secret of her short history.

"Ah, Ruth," I said, "I only wish her future was as full of the promise of peace and comfort as is little Marian Blake's."

"Have some more sensible wishes, Edward," rejoined my sister,—"wish that chickens swam, and peacocks flew, and that everything changed its nature. One wish will be quite as rational as the other."

# CHAPTER XXVIII.

T was not until the latter end of January that we had a visit from Miss Herbert, though we saw her two or three times in the interval —meeting her in the lanes or at the Refuge. During that time Alice M'Callum was never seen beyond her own threshold, except on the way to church. She was not ill: her duties were performed with unfailing diligence ; she was only taking to herself one of those spiritual disciplines which are far more painful than any of the jagged crosses or hair shirts of fanatic devotees. She said nothing, and we said nothing; but we heard the story from Mr Weston, who now made ample atonement for the neglect he had recently shown us. After the first paroxysm of disappointment, he had tried, as we knew, to take his rejection coolly—to alienate himself totally from his recent pleasant associations—nay, even to disparage the blessing which had proved beyond his reach.

But he could not do it. His better nature triumphed. His heart softened towards the innocent woman who had suffered in his suffering. And even when his renewed pleas were still set aside by the same gently stern answer that "it could not be," he did not now turn his back on Upper Mallowe in wrath and bitterness, but still visited the Refuge as a friend might, but not without an unspoken hope that quiet perseverance in patient waiting would win its own at last.

He had made a call at our house, and was just leaving us, on the day when Agnes Herbert at last arrived. They passed each other in the garden with a silent salutation; for their mutual acquaintance had never advanced beyond a knowledge of each other's names. Then Agnes joined us in the parlour.

Of course, whatever Mr Herbert might intend, we did not mean to thrust our counsel on the girl. The knowledge Mrs Irons had given us might somewhat influence our conversation with her, and it would give us the advantage of perfect information should she of her own accord seek our advice or sympathy. We could do no more.

Tea-time passed by in the most comfortable and commonplace manner — how those adjectives always belong to each other! Once or twice I thought Agnes was a little abstracted; once or twice I fancied she was about to speak, and then reserved her remark. And the event proved I was not mistaken. While Phillis removed the tea-tray, and the ladies settled themselves for the evening, I went into the back parlour to seek a book.

The door between the rooms was open, and I heard Agnes say, very softly, and with some apparent effort—

"Miss Garrett"—(a pause)—"I daresay you were surprised to hear I have a cousin Herbert!"

I thought silently, perhaps her long absence from our house had been caused by doubts whether she should make this allusion, or wholly ignore the incident of the Christmas gathering.

"I was rather surprised," said Ruth.

"I think my uncle has told you all about it?" asked Agnes.

"Well, my dear, he has caused us to be told," acknowledged Ruth. "Did he tell you so?"

"He did not exactly tell me; but I fancied it from something he said," observed Agnes.

There was a silence; then my sister remarked—

"I hope, my dear, you will do nothing rashly."

"I don't want to be rash," said Agnes; but there was a querulous tone in her voice.

"My dear," Ruth went on, "a strong, unselfish young love is a very noble thing, and not at all to be pooh-poohed and pushed aside, as it too often is. But nevertheless, my dear, it is a young thing, and therefore it needs guidance and restraint, else it may be like other young things which defeat and destroy themselves by their own wilful strength."

"I don't feel very young!" said Agnes, with a sigh.

"Only because your feelings are so strong that they wear you out," replied Ruth. "When you are really old, your heart will never feel as weary, because it will never exert itself as much.".

"Ought that to make one long to be old, or not?" queried the girl. "The peace of indifference does not seem very enviable."

"My dear," said Ruth—[In all this conversation I noticed her words were gentle, and her tones soft]— "My dear, when the time comes that you will find neither your tears nor your smiles are as eager as they are now, you need not bemoan that your heart is worn out and dead. It will only be at rest after its struggle, and it will awake as fresh as ever, and need rest no more!"

There was a short silence till my sister asked, "When did you last hear from young Mr Herbert?"

"At the end of last week," Agnes replied. "I shall write to him to-morrow."

"I understand," pursued Ruth, "that the young man himself feels you ought not to sacrifice your future to his present."

Agnes answered very slowly, "If he wishes to give me up for my sake, why should I not wish to keep him for his sake? A woman is nothing if she be not unselfish. And yet I can't say I am quite unselfish. Perhaps I can provide for my own truest happiness better even than he can."

"My dear," said Ruth again, "it is quite possible you mistake yourself. Twenty years hence you may sit at another hearth, and ponder over this conversation, and thank God for leading you to a sober happiness you don't dream of to-night."

"I may," returned Agnes, in the same slow tone, "for we never know what we may become. The day *may* come when I shall find all my happiness in fine tables, and chairs, and carpets—many women do." Then with sudden energy she added, "But I pray I never shall."

"Ah," said Ruth still gently, "but even in the midst of their own dreams young things must not forget that life has many treasures and duties beside that love which is courtship. That must pass away. It can be but the glamour of the dawn. The working hours come after."

"I don't think I ever knew that glamour," answered Agnes, "I did not feel much like a girl when I first came to my uncle's farm. I was weary, and frightened, and sad, but Ralph had patience with me, and did little things to please me. And I never had a brother, and he never had a sister, and I had been accustomed to come and go alone, and it seemed so different to have him. I have grown another being with Ralph. I was very narrow and cold before."

"I can understand that," said my sister, "but it says nothing special in praise of your cousin. His very faults may have corrected yours. Your toleration may have grown larger merely to admit him, and your patience may have increased because he gave it practice."

"I know that Ralph has faults. I always knew it," cried Agnes, "and that is why I think I never knew the glamour. Every one must have faults, and Ralph's suit me. I can see them and bear them. After every little quarrel we ever had I loved him better."

"My dear, my dear," said Ruth, a little startled by

this outburst, " I believe all that you say ; but your heart is very warm and enthusiastic, and perhaps you love Mr Ralph better than you might if he deserved it more."

" Don't say ' deserved it more,' please," answered Agnes, "for if he had stayed at home, and his father had never quarrelled with him, and none of his friends had deserted him, I don't think I should have loved him less, though I might have made believe so, even to myself."

" You believe your cousin a genius," pursued my sister, " and a genius made doubly interesting by persecution and misfortune. But in all this there is no satisfactory basis for love. Genius is worth nothing without stable principles. Nay, more, genius needs uncommonly stable principles, or it will overbalance the whole character. A cart-horse will go steadily where a racer will gallop to destruction and death."

" Yet the racer might pause the soonest, if a voice that he loved called him," whispered the girl.

" Then, again," continued Ruth, not heeding this parenthesis, " I know that persecution and misfortune continually attract that pity which constantly leads to love. But remember, a brave heart shrinks from pity, and takes its troubles and conquers them silently ! Thus some whom the world calls most fortunate God knows to be really martyrs, while mistaken human sympathy reserves itself for those who sit in sackcloth and ashes, which they richly deserve, but which they could take off directly if they chose, only that they have a morbid taste for misery. And yet, Agnes, *you* did not pity Anne Sanders."

"Miss Garrett, you don't compare Ralph with *her* ?" queried Agnes, indignantly.

"No, my dear, I do not," answered my sister, "for I know what she is, and I do not yet know him; and I know that she has contrived to alienate all hearts from her, while your cousin has secured at least two—yours and Mrs Irons', and I think Ewen M'Callum's beside."

"You will like Ralph when you know him," said Agnes, softly.

"I hope I may," returned Ruth. "I almost think I shall; but I scarcely think I shall respect and honour him."

"He is but a young man," said his defender.

"There are some young people whom I respect and honour," answered my sister. "But I fear your cousin is one of those characters which are constantly called ' victims to circumstance.' I grant that he could not help your uncle's aversion to his tastes; and I do not say that he should immediately have put aside those tastes. But he should have carried them out modestly and gently, doing his utmost to disarm his father's opposition. Now, from what I hear of his conduct, it tended to justify and confirm Mr Herbert's prejudices. I see these truths pain you, Agnes; but it is better you should hear them now, than learn them when it is too late."

"But, then," said the girl, with a checked sob in her voice, "if it had not been for my uncle's prejudice, Ralph would not have been tempted to do as he did."

"If the devil had not tempted Eve to eat the apple, we should all be in Eden to-day," returned Ruth.

"Ah, I know it is not a sound argument in that way," sighed Agnes; "but I mean this, that some who are flattered and caressed, and called the ornaments of their family, might have fallen as Ralph did, if they had been tried as he was."

"Still a false argument," said my sister; "for I believe all have their trials, and that too at their weakest point. If adversity be our ordeal, and it ruins us in one way, prosperity, had it been allotted to us, would ruin us in another."

"Oh, I cannot argue about it," cried the poor girl. "I only know that Ralph has nobody but me, and I will not desert him,—let any one say what they may!"

"But a groundless love is like a rootless plant," said Ruth,—"fair enough for the time, but easily carried away by a passing hand or a breath of wind."

"A groundless love?" queried Agnes, with bitter daring. "Is love well grounded on a pretty face or a sweet voice, or a thousand pounds, or a family connexion? I love Ralph because he loves me, and because he has nobody else to love him!"

There was a pause. "But, my dear," said Ruth, "it is very easy to sit quietly in your uncle's comfortable rooms, and work out a pretty romance for yourself. But romance is seldom very easy living. It generally develops itself in cheap marketings, and common dresses, and frowsiness. Romance can seldom afford to be perfectly clean, and sometimes it teaches the way to the pawn-broker's back door, and imparts other valuable information which does not inform the mind so much as it breaks the heart. It is only in novels that penury has white dresses and spotless table-cloths, and does not become jaded and gray, and drawn about the mouth!"

Agnes laughed that half-reckless laugh which is so sad from sweet young lips. "I know what penury is," she said; "I know all about it. I have borne it before; and for his sake, I can bear it again. If I were a man, I would not accept a love which feared such things. And after all, I believe many a woman would joyfully pay this price—ay, and double!—if so she might marry the first whom she ever loved!"

Ruth drew a long breath—something like a sigh.

Just then I heard by the rustle of Agnes's dress that she rose from her seat and crossed the room to my sister's side; there I think she kneeled down. They both knew perfectly well that I was within hearing of every word, and that I could not escape from the back parlour except by passing through the front one.

"Miss Garrett," said Agnes, and somehow I fancied she laid both her hands on my sister's arm, "let me do what I can. Ralph will be so much better with some one always to love and care for him"——

"And for this hope you will sacrifice everything?" said my sister, and then I think she took Agnes's face between her hands.

"No, not sacrifice," sobbed the girl. "I don't sacrifice anything; it is my delight—my glory!"

"But we must never set aside one duty for another," said Ruth. "How can you desert your uncle?"

I wish I had seen Agnes's eyes when she answered, in

a solemn whisper, " Can I serve the father better than by serving his son?"

Then there was a long pause, with a low sound of tears, and then total silence,—till suddenly there was a general movement, and Agnes remarked, with a forced attempt at her accustomed voice, that it was nearly time for her to go home. Upon which I availed myself of the opportunity to return to the front parlour, and found my sister knitting as busily as usual, while our young visitor was extricating her veil from some entanglement with her bonnet, preparatory to dressing herself for the homeward walk, that when Mrs Irons called for her, she might not be kept waiting.

"And so Mr Marten is to marry Miss Blake," she observed, by way of passing remark, as she stood before the mirror, settling her bonnet strings.

"Yes," said Ruth ; "how did you hear about it?"

"Mrs Irons told me yesterday, when she came from shopping in the village," Agnes answered. "I suppose she heard it there."

"We only knew it at the beginning of this month," said my sister. "Did Mrs Irons also hear of the destiny of the house behind St Cross?"

"Yes," replied Agnes, half-turning from the glass, and so displaying her tear-stained face. "I am sure *they* ought to be very happy,"—this a little bitterly.

"My dear," said Ruth, "there is an old truism, that after all none of us would like to change ourselves into the people whom we envy. Each has something which he values above anything that others have. This may sound very trite ; but that's a word which fits most old precepts. Now, I think that if a maxim fits ourselves, it is just as new as if it had never been used by any one else."

" And there will be another wedding soon, will there not ?" queried Agnes, after a pause. "And I should think that will be a very happy one. Is not Mr Weston of Meadow Farm to marry our Alice M'Callum."

" Who told you that ?" asked Ruth, sharply.

" My uncle said he thought so," replied Agnes. " It was a wonder to hear him speak about such a thing ; but he likes Mr Weston, and Alice is a great favourite of his. He said it would be a most comfortable marriage, and no great rise for the bride, let people say what they would ; for she was a farmer's daughter, and he was a farmer's son ; and a little difference in fortune was nothing between the two." And Agnes smiled dimly as she repeated her uncle's words.

" Your uncle and you have both made a mistake," said my sister, rather dryly. " At present there is no prospect of such a marriage. Alice refuses to enter another family while the stain of that old accusation rests upon her own. Instead of the happiness and prosperity which you imagine, there is nothing but disappointment and trial and patient endurance."

" Is it really so ? " queried Agnes. " But surely Alice is wrong ! She should feel that a man who loves her at all will only love her better for anything which makes others undervalue her."

"Men and women love very differently, my dear," said Ruth, with a shake of her head.

"But poor Alice, how I pity her! It stings us so when those we have envied need our pity," sighed Agnes. And when she went away I think she was strengthened to bear her own troubles, because there were tears in her eyes for troubles which were not her own.

"Miss Herbert resisted all your arguments, Ruth," I remarked, when my sister and I were once more alone.

"Yes," said Ruth shortly; "and I like her the better for it. Of course she is a simpleton; but such simpletons are the oil which keep the world's wheels from grating hopelessly."

"Then do you think she will realise her loving hopes?" I questioned, rather sentimentally.

"'Twenty years hence," said my sister, "she will be a quiet, timid, middle-aged woman, a little faded, and a little given to defer overmuch to 'Mr Herbert,' who will in general patronise her very kindly. But perhaps sometimes he will say, 'Little woman, where should I be without you?' And then Agnes will have her reward. And I think her children will rise up and call her blessed. And she will have a harder life than many a noisy woman who fancies herself a victim to her zeal for public good; and in heaven, maybe, she will have a brighter crown."

Ah, my pretty Agnes, I gave one or two sighs, to think of you, in your future struggles, and yet I could not wish you acted otherwise than you did. "Should you like a daughter of your own to have such a fate?" asks

2 E

some critical and prudent mother.   Well, if a daughter
of my own met a destiny like Margaret Roper at her
father's scaffold, or like Lucy Hutchinson outside her
Puritan husband's prison, or like Anita Garibaldi in her
hunted death, my heart would be pained, but I should
not wish them other than they were.   There are pains
which are sweeter than any pleasures.   There are natures
which choose the palm as the fairest flower which earth
can offer.

# CHAPTER XXIX

## THE HISTORY OF THE MYSTERY.

T was the second day after Miss Herbert's visit, and the first day of February. The weather, which had been tolerably fine for the last two or three weeks, was revenging itself. The rain descended in torrents, driven about by the wind, which, like a changeable, passionate woman, now sobbed among the leafless trees, and then scolded down the chimneys and round the house. But it happened Ruth and I were provided with abundant indoor occupations, for we had just received the annual accounts of the Refuge, and their various items gave us plenty of material for reflection and discussion. By evening I had drawn up a balance-sheet, and a most satisfactory one it was, with a tolerable surplus at the right side, which would enable us to extend our sympathies more courageously in the coming year. As for the little orphan home, whose accounts were included in

those of the Refuge, its expenses for the future would be small indeed, now its erection and furniture were fairly paid. Its benefits were already shared by two little sisters, who paid their weekly board by their labours at the village dressmaker's, but who would have been but poorly off if thrown entirely on their own exertions.

So we passed a very pleasant day, and I was in such a comfortable and cheery mood that I did not shrink from contemplating the dreary aspect out of doors. So I pulled aside the red curtain, and lifted the blind, and stood between it and the cold, damp window, and reported to Ruth that it was a " dreadful night "—" not fit for a dog to be abroad ;" and then I thought how London looked at that hour—how the City men jogged home through mirk and mud, and the gaslights flared on shining pavements, and poor women went a-marketing with broken shoes that lapped the puddles as they passed along.

But my reverie was suddenly interrupted by the sound of rapid wheels coming down the lane, and a fly-lamp flashed like a will-o'-the-wisp through the darkness of the garden hedge. A voice called sharply, and the vehicle stopped at our gate. Somebody came up the garden path, and there was one of those quick, urgent knocks which make the heart leap, and the feet hurry to the parlour door to anticipate the servant's announcement.

Phillis ran so eagerly to the parlour, that she nearly flew against me. " Oh, please, sir," said she, " it's young Mr M'Callum !"

He followed close behind her, with a white, anxious

face, which made me instantly think of my old friends of the firm. "Come in, Ewen," I said, taking his cold hand : "what is the matter, my boy?"

"Ralph Herbert is not here?" was his questioning response.

"Certainly not," I answered. "Is anything wrong?"

"He has left our place in London," said Ewen. "They tell me he started off almost immediately after I left home this morning."

"Not a very long absence," observed Ruth.

Her cool words seemed somewhat to reassure Ewen. It is pleasant to think a danger may exist only in one's own excited imagination. But, in a second, he recalled the more tangible reasons for his fears. "I left home before the first post came in," he said, "and our landlady says there was a letter for him. And I know he had an important appointment in town for this evening, when he was to receive payment for some pictures. And he wanted the money."

"And he hasn't kept that appointment, or made any arrangement about it?" queried my sister.

"No; I went to the gentleman, to learn if he knew anything," explained Ewen; "and, finding he did not, I made as good an excuse as I could, and came straight down here. I had chanced to leave business very early to-day, or I should not have been here to-night."

"Did you fancy he might be in the village?" I asked.

"I thought it just possible," said the young man. "I think this morning's letter was from Miss Herbert. I know he expected one from her."

"Is it likely there is a reconciliation," I said, "and that he is at the Great Farm ?"

Ewen shook his head.  " I fear not," he answered.

" If there had been good news, he would have left a note for me."

" A thoughtless omission, under any circumstances," said Ruth ; "tacking trouble to trouble's tail."

" What do you propose, Ewen ?" I asked.

"I must go to the Great Farm," he said, with a long breath ; "and I thought, sir, if you will go with me—but it's such a shocking night—only poor Miss Herbert !"

" I 'll go," I answered.

" Have you kept the fly, Ewen, asked my sister.

" O yes, ma'am," he replied—" it's waiting at the gate."

" That's right.   You have sense." said Ruth.

We soon rattled through the dense darkness of the road, into the broad light of the lamp over the Great Farm door.   It was not until Ewen rung the bell that I marvelled what would result from our daring to disturb Mr Herbert on such a subject.

Mrs Irons admitted us.   " Heaven help us !" she cried, when she saw my companion.   " It's something wrong with Mr Ralph !"

" Hush, hush!" said Ewen, "and tell us, is your master within?"

" No, no, he isn't," she answered : "he's away, at a farmers' dinner at the 'Red Lion.'   Miss Agnes is in the dining room ; but, whatever it be, don't show your face, Ewen M'Callum, till Mr Garrett goes in first.   And tell me what it is—for I nussed him, I did, sir."

"It's nothing yet," said Ewen, soothingly. "I hoped he might have been here before us, Mrs Irons."

"Then it's missing, he is?" wailed the poor old soul; "and the Lord ha' mercy on Miss Agnes!"

I went to the dining-room, and, in answer to my knock, Agnes gave a soft "Come in!" There was a blazing fire in the wide grate, but otherwise the room was but dimly lighted by a shaded lamp, whose rays scarcely travelled to the pictures on the wall. Agnes sat in front of the fire, her slight figure almost lost in the roomy depths of her uncle's great arm-chair. There was a basket of white work beside her. She rose when she saw it was a visitor; and Griff, the dog, stood at her feet, and wagged his tail.

"Mr Garrett!" she exclaimed, surprised. But, as I came forward into the light, her face inexpressibly darkened, and she was totally silent.

"Sit down, my dear," I said; "I have only a question to ask."

She stood still and awaited it.

"Have you heard from your cousin Ralph during the day?"

"No," she said, with great eyes.

"He left home unexpectedly this morning," I said, "and he has not returned. And so Mr M'Callum is anxious about him—perhaps unduly anxious—that is all."

Ewen entered softly. Till then, he had waited at the door. Agnes looked blankly at him, and spoke no word.

"Mr M'Callum thinks your cousin had a letter from you this morning," I said.  " Is he right?"

" Yes," she answered.

I remembered Ruth's recent conversation with her. Might it be that had given a tone to her letter which had worked this disaster ?

" My dear," I began gently, "was there anything in that letter which could possibly cause this?"

She looked at me for a moment, only half comprehending, and then exclaimed, "No, no, nothing at all. O God ! if there had been, what should I do now?"

She turned to Ewen.  "What shall we do? What can I do ?  Where can I go?"

The young man bowed his head.  "Whatever can be done, shall be done," he said ; "I will do it."

"Perhaps it is only an accidental mistake," I remarked.

" It may be, it may be," exclaimed Agnes eagerly. " I am so glad uncle is out.  He need not know yet.  If it be nothing, he would only be so angry and dreadful ! And if it be anything, let us keep it till we are quite sure."

To prolong our visit was useless, and only wasted time. With a promise that anything we might learn should be instantly communicated to her, we took our departure. She came with us to the outer doors, and stood on the step till we drove off.  It would have relieved her to have rushed out in the darkness—anywhere—anywhere— better than the silent dining-room, and the waiting and the watching—the woman's part in the tragedy of life !

" Let us drive to the inn in the High Street," said

Ewen, "and ask what visitors they have. He may be there, intending to send to his cousin to-morrow morning."

We did so. We were shown into the tap-room to take a silent survey of two unconscious young men sitting there, smoking pipes and reading sporting papers. Neither of them was Ralph Herbert. When we left the inn, the weather had cleared, and we dismissed our fly, and walked slowly down the High Street to the Railway Station, consulting as we went. Now the Police Station was in this High Street. Of course it was a very small unpretending affair, suited to the modest requirements of a quiet and respectable village. But to-night there was a vague air of excitement about it. The resident policemen were indulging in a dignified gossip with another official, and they suspended their chat as we came up, and looked at us with unusual interest. I nodded to one of them whom I happened to know, and we passed on. Our intention was to make inquiries of the guards at the railway station. Ewen had not done so when he arrived, in case Mr Ralph had simply found reason to visit his home. Even now, we wished to make our inquiries as cautiously as possible, not to awaken unnecessary curiosity. So I went up to an intelligent-looking guard, and asked him if he happened to know young Mr Herbert.

"Young Mr Herbert?" repeated the man. "Yes, sir; he came up from London by the train to-day, sir."

"Thank you," I answered, "that is what I wish to know. By which train did he come."

"Let us see," pondered the guard, giving his cap a little jerk from his brow. "My wife had just brought me my dinner, for 'twas her said, 'Tom, there's the young squire.' So 'twas the one o'clock train, sir."

"Thank you," I replied, leaving him a little consideration for his civility, and then returned with my news to Ewen. It only increased the mystery, and not knowing where else to go, we slowly returned up the High Street. The little group still stood about the Police Station. A new idea struck me. I disengaged my arm from Ewen's and accosted the policeman, whom I knew.

"Is anything the matter to-night, Mr Jones?"

"Nothing in particular, sir," said he.

"Because we are looking for a young friend who came into the village to-day; but whom we cannot find."

"Indeed, sir," said the man civilly. But one of the others jogged his elbow and suggested, "Ask the gentleman what's his friend's name, Jones."

In response to this, I said at once, "It is young Mr Herbert."

"Then it's all right, sir," answered Jones, with a quick side-glance at Ewen. "The young gentleman's safe inside."

"Inside the Police Station!" I exclaimed, and Ewen uttered a peculiar and inarticulate ejaculation.

"He gave himself up," explained our informant; "and between you and me, sir, I shouldn't wonder if he's a little turned in the head. For he walked straight in, as jolly like as possible, and says he, 'Here, Mr Jones, I know all about George Roper's death in the

Low Meadow. Just put me in your cell for to-night, and bring me up before the justices to-morrow, and I'll tell 'em all about it.' He wouldn't enter into no particulars with me, sir, so I was obligated to put him under arrest, knowin' as the job was brought in a murder, and nobody was convicted of it;" with another side glance at Ewen.

"This is most extraordinary," I said. " Cannot we be permitted to see him ?"

" Certainly, sir," granted the civil official ; "we'd ha' sent to the Great Farm for him, or to any other friend's, but he wouldn't let us. I'm glad you've found him out. It's a dirty thing to have a prisoner like a rat in a hole with the dogs arter it, and no one to take its part. But, begging your pardon, sir," added the man, turning to Ewen, and continuing the same civil tone he had used through the interview, "if you won't take it amiss, I thing *you'd* better not see him. Ye see folks will remember old stories, and it might look like what the lawyers call *collussion*."

I saw the force of this advice, and urged it upon Ewen, until he reluctantly accepted it, saying that he would go back to the Great Farm, and tell Miss Herbert of her cousin's safety, and then return and rejoin me in the High Street.

Leaving him to carry the painful news to poor Agnes, I followed the policeman to the safe-room of the little station. The place was sufficiently clean and comfortable. The cell opened at the end of a passage, and was lit by a small lamp placed on a bracket above the door.

The voluntary prisoner sat on a bare bench beside a little fixture-table in the middle of the room.

"Here's a gentleman come to see you, sir," said Mr Jones, ushering me in.

Ralph Herbert coloured, and started up. I fancy he thought it might be his father, for his face relaxed when he saw me, and he held out his hand saying, "How did you find me out, Mr Garrett? You should not have taken the trouble to come here."

"I am here for your cousin's sake as well as your own," I answered gravely, for I thought he scarcely realised the horror of his position.

"Poor Agnes!" he said, passing his hand over his face, "and she does not know about it yet!"

"She knows something," I replied, "and she will know the rest in a few minutes. Ewen came down here and raised the alarm of your disappearance, and we tracked you to this place, and now he has gone to the Great Farm to tell her. I hope she will bear it well."

"Ewen will soften it as much as he can," he answered, sadly.

"And now," I said, taking a seat on the bench beside him, "we must make some preparations for to-morrow. They tell me that you profess to have the secret of George Roper's murder."

"I have the secret of George Roper's *death*," he replied with an emphasis, raising his eyes and looking me full in the face. "There was no murder."

"Ewen was not the last who saw Roper alive," he continued, after a moment's pause. "I met him after they parted. I had come from London expressly to meet him, because there were some accounts between us. I owed him a small sum, and he owed me a much larger one, and I wanted him to deduct my debt from his and pay me the surplus, which was a very serious affair to me just then. He was not sober. He paid me two or three pounds very easily, but I wanted a little more, which would have squared our accounts. Then he taunted me, and used dreadful language. He was always very violent when not sober. I told him I could not waste time and money in journeys from London to Mallowe, and that was why I wished to settle the matters between us. I can't think why he was so fierce, but he flew at my throat like a wild animal, and I felt something prick me, but I caught his hands and wrenched an open knife from them. I held him with one hand while I threw it as far across the fields as I could, that he might not regain it. It took all my strength to keep him, and when I saw my own blood trickling down my dress, I turned sick and faint, and I put all my powers into one effort, and threw him full-length on the path. 'You murderous madman!' I said, 'lie there while I fetch somebody who will stop your mischief for the future.' I don't know what I meant myself, for I never really thought of making a disturbance in my own father's village. But I suppose he believed me. I looked back when I cleared the field. He had not attempted to follow me. He was sitting at the edge of the stream, and he shouted after me, 'I shan't be here when you come back. You've taken the knife, but you've left the water.'

I took no notice of his words then, but went across the fields and bound up my own wound, which was very slight.   I walked the whole way to London, for I wanted all my money to carry me to Paris, where I had a commission about a picture.   I never knew of Roper's death until weeks afterwards, when I read an announcement of the discovery of his body in an old newspaper."

"Then you saw the accusation against Ewen, I suppose," I queried.

"No, I didn't: it was not in that paper," he said, eagerly.   "I had suffered a great deal from many causes, and though I never dreamed that Roper's death could be thought other than a suicide, yet I regarded myself—and I regard myself still—as his murderer, through the foolish threat which drove a frenzied, drunken man to his end.   I tried to lose my own identity.   For more than a year I suffered horrors I can never describe, until, through inability to work at my art, I was driven to the point of destitution.   Then I ventured to Mallowe to try to recover another small debt due to me.   I dared not attempt to present myself to any one who knew me. One night, when I was lurking about in the darkness, I met you and the rector.   Another winter night—and that was the night when I stole to my father's back door and his good old servant fed me like a beggar man—I encountered George Roper's son.   I saw his father's face in his, and scarcely needed the proof of the name of Wilmot—for I knew all the story of the deserted wife in London—and I daresay you can guess I wrote that letter about him only lately.   Then I struggled on again in

great misery, and in the March following that, I met
Ewen M'Callum."

There he paused and drew a long breath, like one re-
counting the history of his own rescue. I knew *how* he
had met Ewen, but I said nothing.

" He took me home with him," he continued presently,
" and he heard all my story. He did not tell me his
then ; but when I grew a little better, I asked so many
questions that it all came out. Then I wanted to come
here and tell all I knew, but he would not let me."

" Should you have allowed him to hinder you ?" I
asked.

" Perhaps not," he answered, looking at me ; " but he
set it before me in this way :—That the accusation
against him was only a suspicion,—that it had lost its sting,
—that it no longer injured any one,—that my new story
would only transfer the suspicion from him to me,—that
it would drag my family through the agony from which
his had just escaped. But still I did not like to give
him his will. And then he begged and prayed it of me
for Agnes' sake !" And the young man raised his eyes
to mine, with a strange mist in them. " And so I let
it be. And you know, when I first saw you in London,
I asked you if it was right to let one make a great sacrifice for another. Perhaps you remember what you said ;"
and he threw his arms upon the table, and dropped his
head upon them.

" Then what makes you reveal this secret at last ?" I
inquired, as gently as I could.

He replied without raising his head. " In the letter I

got this morning, Agnes told me that Ewen's sister refused to marry while the supposed crime rested on her brother. I could not allow that. I should be worse than I am if I could, and less fit than ever for Agnes. I came here directly. They may not believe what I say. They may think I killed the poor man. They may do what they like with me. But in case of anything, will you do something for me, sir?" he asked, looking up again; "will you write to that address, and explain things?" and he placed a card before me. "It is a young man who is going out to Canada. He was to take me with him. He has a little money, and means to farm, and I know enough about agriculture to be useful to him; for I find it is no use trying to live by my art. I mistook a taste for a talent. I found that out long ago; but then I couldn't go back."

"Does Miss Herbert know of this plan?" I asked, pocketing the card.

"Yes," he said; "and we thought when I'd been out there a year or two, I might come home and fetch her. But that's all over now;" and he sighed heavily.

"Please, sir," interrupted Mr Jones, opening the door, "here's two ladies come to see you next."

They were Mrs Irons and Agnes. I doubt if either of them even noticed my presence, and I withdrew before the first agitated embrace was over. I found Ewen in the entry, looking unutterably white and fagged.

"My boy," I said, laying my hand on his arm, "you have acted most nobly towards that unfortunate man."

Those were the first and last words I ever breathed on

his unselfishness. It was above the praise of men—meet for the approval of God.

"Won't you come home and sup with us?" I asked, presently.

"No, thank you. I'll go to my grandfather's," he answered. "Poor Alice will be glad of this. I thought she had quite got over the trouble, until my last autumn holidays, when I saw she was still pining."

For his sister had kept her secret; and he did not yet know what Ralph Herbert had learned, and that, in his self-sacrifice, he had nearly sacrificed her. But that night of dolour and darkness at the Great Farm was the dawn of light and joy at the Refuge.

He had taken one or two steps away, when he turned back, and said, calmly enough—

"Don't call Ralph 'unfortunate.' One life has one blessing and another life has another; but he has the best! Good-night, sir."

I watched him hastening down the splashy road. And thus the woman's love clings to the frail man and leaves this good one alone! Is it because he knows the way to heaven without her guidance?

# CHAPTER XXX.

### THE JUSTICE-ROOM.

ARLY next morning I made it my business to lay the whole case before a respectable solicitor at Mallowe; and that gentleman, together with Mr Marten and I, were in due attendance at the justice-room. Ewen and his grandfather were also there, and young George Roper accompanied his aunt, who was present to produce the hitherto mysterious knife, which now gave such proof to Ralph Herbert's narrative. Agnes too came, in my sister's charge. But her uncle was conspicuous by his absence. He had been apprised of his son's position by the rector; and Mr Marten said, the muscles of his face had twitched sadly when he heard it, but he only said, " My son, sir ? I haven't a son. It can't concern me."

It was a sufficiently commonplace scene,—the shabby justice-room, with its worn oil-cloth, and its rows of wooden chairs, and intent faces turned towards the two old gentlemen invested with the majesty of the law; kindly enough old gentlemen, who drank port at dinner, and had dainty lady-daughters and strapping sons of their own to stir their elderly hearts, but who yet seemed strangely separate from humanity when they sat down in their awful arm-chairs, and said commonplace things through the Oracle of Justice, and sprinkled magisterial snuff over the papers of the reporter beside them. That dreadful reporter, too,—whom some fear more than God or their own conscience,—he was only a lank lad of twenty, with red hair. Once or twice, as the inquiry lengthened, I noticed him adding up the lines of his report. and it struck me he was thinking of the sum he would gain by the job.

By two o'clock it was all over. There was no evidence against Ralph Herbert, but every reason to credit his story, and to believe that Mr Roper had met his death by his own rash act. The justices shook their heads very much over it, and administered little parental reproofs all round, admonishing Mr Marten and me for having dared to conceal the discovery of the knife from the proper authorities :—"Very wrong, very unwise, gentlemen ; though we can understand your motives, gentlemen, and respect them. But it is not a safe course of action." And sniff, sniff went a pinch of judicial snuff.

There was a little chamber opening from the justices' room, and it made a convenient refuge for all the more interested spectators. Only one did not avail himself of it. Directly the magistrates pronounced their opinion, Ewen rose from his seat and softly left the place.

In that little brown room, with its solitary window looking on to a square flagged court with a broken pump in the middle, the two cousins met. Her face was just a little whiter than usual, and perhaps he held her hand a second longer than he held mine. That was all. He was as reserved as her; and yet, a minute afterwards, I think the recollection of her manner troubled him. It was an utterly mute greeting. There was something to be said between the two,—but not then,—not there.

"Mr Herbert will return with us to our house," said my sister. "You will come also, Agnes, will you not?"

"I must go home to my uncle now," she answered quite calmly. "So, good-bye, Ralph! I shall see you again before night."

They shook hands again, and he went with her to the door. When he rejoined us, his face was sadder and more concerned than it had been at any time during the morning.

"She has given me up," he said, as we ushered him into our parlour. "For her sake, I ought to be very glad, but I can't."

"Wait awhile," answered Ruth rather grimly, "and don't show your selfishness before you must."

My sister utterly refused to be won over to the side of Mr Ralph. Except one or two curt remarks, she was courteous to him, as a stranger and in trouble, but no more. Immediately after our early tea, she announced that she should pay a visit to the Refuge. She had scarcely departed on this errand, before Agnes fulfilled her promise of an evening visit. Of course, directly she entered, I left the room. I am an old man, but my memory is not yet decayed. I remember how it troubled me when Lucy's father called us that evening in the fields, and when her mother chanced to stand at her side the next morning. To this day, I wish it had not so happened.

I went up-stairs to my own chamber, and tried to read. Sometimes, in the profound silence, I caught a tone of the earnest talk in the room beneath me. I heard Ralph walk up and down after the fashion of perturbed or excited people; and so the time wore wearily away, until Ruth knocked at the hall-door, and then I went down and admitted her, because I did not wish her to interrupt the pair in the parlour. So I mysteriously beckoned her into another room, and then explained myself.

"There's no peace anywhere because of some courting couple," said she, very tartly. "I have just been driven from the Refuge, because Mr Weston chose to arrive. As for these two, they have had enough. Been here ever since I left, you say? That's two hours. I shall go in, whether you will or not."

Somewhat under protest, I followed her. Ralph was in my arm-chair, and Agnes was seated on a very low stool beside him. She had been crying, but now she smiled and was very rosy.

"Tell them, Ralph," said she.

"I spoke to you about Canada, last night, sir," he began with some hesitation. "My friend starts next month, and we hope to be ready to join him—Agnes and I?"

"My uncle has given permission," she whispered.

"And, of course, he thinks we encouraged you!" said Ruth, severely.

"No, he doesn't!" she answered, warmly. "I told him all about it."

"And you asked his consent?" I queried.

"I told him all about it," she replied humbly, "and he said I might do as I liked;—I was of age, and he wouldn't hinder me."

Was this some secret relenting—some hidden joy that God had given one faithful friend to the son whom he had deserted?

"Then let me wish you happiness, my dear," I said, laying my hand on the brown head, bowed low enough in this moment of womanly triumph; "then let me wish you all peace and happiness after your trial and sorrow —the sweet sunshine after the rain!"

Ralph Herbert turned to my sister. "*You* say no-thing," he said, in a tone of sorrowful reproach.

"Yes, I do," she answered, more kindly than she had spoken before, and laying her hand gently upon his. "I don't say, May she never regret this day!—for she never will—but I pray that on your dying bed you may remem-ber it with thanksgiving, and not remorse!"

"God helping me, so I will!" he said solemnly. And I am sure he meant it.

# CHAPTER XXXI

THE very next day after the inquiry, Ruth had a petition presented to her.

It was Mr Weston's. He came—shyly enough, but with the confidence of eager hope —to beg my sister to join him in persuading Alice M'Callum to leave the Refuge in a month's time. This was how he stated the case, with a blush and a roguish smile.

"Leave the Refuge!" said my sister, with arch innocence : "then where is she going, sir?"

He made a fine boggle of an answer, which was intended to embrace excuses and reasons for his own haste. "If she'd said 'Yes' when I asked her first, I should have named a day in early spring," he stammered ; "and why shouldn't it be now as if it had never been ? She's looking fagged and white, and the change of scene 'll do her good. And the Meadow Farm's quite ready for its mistress. And what things does she want ? Can't she get them when she's there ? Only she says you won't like such a short notice."

"Oh, I am not the person to be considered," said Ruth drily. "You'd better not consult my pleasure, or I shall say I don't like any notice at all!"

Mr Weston took the little joke in good part, and laughed heartily. "You're right, Miss Garrett," he answered, quite jovially. "I should not like *her* to give *me* notice."

"Should you not?" queried Ruth. "Ah,—I have heard some people are never so happy as when they are miserable, and I suppose that is why they rush into matrimony, although the 'single state is most conducive to happiness.'"

Mr Weston reddened a little and laughed again. 'Don't laugh at a poor fellow for saying the grapes were sour when they seemed out of his reach," said he. "*I* always pitied that fox in the fable."

"Well, he *was* pitiable," rejoined my sister; "but if he had gained the grapes and then praised them, I should have told him he was a coward before."

"When he has gained the grapes, he is so fortunate that he can afford to be called anything," said the young man, good-humouredly.

The simple kindly farmer was far further in Ruth's good graces than the polished son of the Great Farm. She actually went with him to the Refuge, and had a long conversation with Alice and her grandfather, for Ewen had returned to London that morning with Mr Herbert. And when Ruth returned, she brought the news that the old adage that one wedding makes another was fulfilled in this case, and that there would be two marriages at St Cross, while the primroses were out in the churchyard.

And for a whole month, I was a quiet shadow in the background—a person with no valuable opinions on the subjects in hand—linens, and dresses, and ribbons. I heard that Mr Weston wished to place in Ruth's hand a considerable sum of money for the disposal of his bride, only Alice would not hear of it. She said, he must take her with what she could get herself, and he said it didn't matter to him, so I think her bridal attire would have been exceedingly simple but that Ruth's wedding gift was the wedding dress. Mr Weston was not at all offended because Alice accepted *that*. It was a gray silk, rich and delicate, but suited alike to the bride's loveliness, and the bridegroom's position.

After all, her wedding came first. The Herberts' was fixed a single day later. Ewen arrived the evening before his sister's marriage, and said Mr Herbert would not come until the eve of his own. And Ewen tried to keep his face bright for his sister's joy. But all the more it haunted me with that inexpressible pain which often makes weddings more sad than funerals,—the suffering of Life instead of the peace of Death.

It was a laughing spring morning, and in homely phrase, the village was "alive." St Cross was crowded, for the M'Callums were old residents, and rendered none the less interesting by the melancholy circumstances through which they had so innocently suffered. When the bridal party stood in the chancel, I heard an old lady whisper that it was a "pretty wedding," and I think she was right. In the immediate circle the fine o'd grandfather, the comely bridegroom, the sweet bride, the little orphan bridesmaids in their fresh muslins, and the grave handsome groomsman—all were pleasing and picturesque after their own fashion. And, standing behind these, Ruth and Bessie and young George Roper did not spoil the scene. And the background was made up of eager interested faces, all bright in the sunshine, which poured in through the clear windows and brought with it a sweet breath from the budding trees outside. And then the solemn service which folds the joy of man in the sanctity of God, and the happy tears, and the fond kisses, and the poor trembling maiden signature in the vestry. And then the merry bells, telling heath and hamlet that God has consecrated another home—and the ride through familiar faces that nobody sees—and the dainty meal that nobody tastes—and the good byes —and then the silence afterwards.

Agnes was not at the wedding. It was her last day at home. A very sad last day—when she might not weep nor smile except as her wont—when she must go about everything as if to-morrow, and the next day, and the next would be the same. Her uncle knew it was her last day in his house, he had only said "Very well" when she told him so, and by this silence, she knew to be silent herself.

After the morning's excitement I sat listlessly at our window, watching for Ralph Herbert, who was to be our guest for that night. I did not know whether to expect a visit from Agnes, and I was very pleased when she entered.

"I hear the wedding went off well," she said. "I have written a letter to Alice, that she may receive it in her new home to-night."

For I should have mentioned that this simple country

bride had gone straight from her old home to her husband's house, as he could ill spare a long holiday at this time of year, when his fields needed their master's eye.

" Very thoughtful of you, my dear," I answered, " and what finery have you there ? " for she had a small parcel in her hand.

" Only all my trousseau ! " she replied, laying a dainty pair of lilac gloves upon the table, and looking up with an arch smile about her lips and pathos in her eyes.

It was quite true. For her honeymoon was to be passed in no luxurious hotel, her home would be no fresh flowery bride-chambers. By nightfall after her wedding she would be in the seaport town whence the American ship sailed. By the next sunset, she would be on the sea—drifting to a new life in a rough settler farm. And so it was an emigrant's outfit and not a bride's, which filled the great boxes that encumbered our hall.

She had not been with us many minutes before she rose to go.

" Will you not wait to see your cousin ? " asked Ruth ; " he will be here presently."

" No," she said, " I must go—back. Tell him I left him my love, but I want to stay with my uncle as long as I can. I only left home now because he was out among his men."

I walked home with her in the twilight, speaking of the arrangements for the morrow. Nobody but those concerned knew what was about to happen. The honest labourers who touched their foreheads as Agnes passed, little dreamed it was a farewell salutation. There was something unspeakably touching in the girl going so brave

and so lonely from one life to another, not even knowing her own courage and loneliness, but, with the sweet
perversity of womankind, only the more reliant on Ralph's
protection because it was but a cipher—all the prouder
of him because there was little to be proud about !

When I shook hands with her at the gate of the Farm,
she held my hand a little, and probably thinking this was
our last moment of undisturbed converse, she thanked
me for all that Ruth and I had tried to do for her—
speaking so eagerly and fervently of all the past, and yet
looking so confidently and quietly into her strange dim
future, that my heart was strangely stirred. But she
made one omission which pained me. In her rapid
anxious review of all to whom she owed any kindness,
she never even named Ewen, to whom, especially for
Ralph's sake, she owed so much. And I interrupted
her to say—

"Nobody has shown you or Ralph more than the
common kindness of humanity—except young M'Callum.
I hope you quite understand what he has done. *He*
deserves thanks."

"Understand what he has done ?" she echoed, "thank
him ?   Mr Garrett, Ewen M'Callum is a saint, and I am
only a woman !"

And she turned and obeyed the deep bay of Griff,
impatiently awaiting her within the house. I stayed at
the gate until she crossed the garden, and fairly closed
the house door behind her. But she never turned her
head.

And that was the night before the wedding.

# CHAPTER XXXII

UR breakfast party on the wedding morning was somewhat constrained and silent. Ralph had joined us very late the night before, and we had then no time for conversation, nor did we seem inclined for any when we gathered round the table for our morning meal. We were in our trim for the ceremony, that is to say, I wore my neatest tie, and Ruth her best silk dress, for no further attempt at gala attire was possible. The parlour, too, was "tidied" in Ruth's strictest sense of the word; not a shred of work or writing remained about, and the china bowls and vases were duly filled with fresh primroses and hyacinths. That was the extent of our preparation. But when Phillis brought in our toast and new-laid eggs, I thought by her glance at our visitor that she had a shrewd guess at what was going forward, though she had heard no remark to lead her to such

conclusion, and though there was nothing in the refreshments which Ruth had ordered to awaken conjecture. For there could be no sugary wedding breakfast, with cakes, and champagnes, and trifles, but a repast of savoury joints and poultry, substantial enough to carry the young couple to their sea-port destination.

There was a solemnity about the aspect of affairs which crept over each of us. The very morning was solemn—not cloudy, but with a low-toned steady sunlight, and a cool still air. The shadows on our garden plot did not dance, but lay straight and still. The parlour too, with the signs of ordinary life all banished, had a conventual air, consistent with bated voices and silent smiles. But even silent smiles were lacking. Yet when I thought of all this day was in Ralph's life, I could not wonder at his pale grave face, or the reddened lightless eyes that told of a sleepless night. True, he had achieved a great happiness—to him, unworthy as he felt himself, had fallen that good gift which Solomon tells us comes directly "from the Lord." But I liked the youth no less because he took his blessing with awe and trembling, nor because he did not prepare to leave his fatherland with a laugh upon his lips. Alone, he might have gone recklessly enough. Going alone, he might have said his native country cast him off, and so turned his face to another shore, and never looked behind. But now that one went with him, nothing fearing, he felt tenderly for the old place that spared him its best, and his heart yearned over the very fields where he had walked and talked with one so pure and true. I dare

say his feeling was something like that expressed in
those lines of an old song, which I remember once
reading, where one emigrant says to another—

> " 'Tis not the future makes me grieve ɪ
> But though the past is sad,
> I weep my grateful thanks to God
> For pleasant times I 've had ! "

Of course he made one at our little service of family
worship. It is our custom to hold that service immediately after breakfast. Ruth and I agreed that it was in-
considerate to summon servants to such a duty before
they had taken some refreshment after their early household work. At the risk of being thought a monotonous
formalist, I must explain our form of worship. I take
our prayers from the Book of Common Prayer—first, the
general confession of sin, then the prayer for all conditions of men, concluding with the collect for the preceding Sunday, and that is all, except on any special occasion, when I take a special petition from the Litany.
For a Scripture portion I read the New Testament lesson
for the day. I have often noticed how strangely appropriate these appointed portions seem, and never more so,
than when on this 4th of March, I found it my duty to
read the fifteenth chapter of St Luke's Gospel. As I
announced it, I involuntarily glanced at Ralph. He
did not need to seek it—his Bible opened at the place,
for the page was marked by a dried spray of that delicate
fern which is, I think, called " maiden hair."

When we rose from our knees, it was time to prepare

for church. Ralph was the first to depart, Ewen would join him on the road—the only wedding guest beside ourselves. We waited at our window until Agnes appeared, coming steadily and gravely along the road. Then we left our house, and she came up to us with a quiet simple salutation, and took her place by my sister's side. But behind her, followed an attendant on whom we had not counted, even the great dog Griff, walking with a dignified solemnity fit for the occasion.

"Yes, he must come," said his mistress, responding to our glances. "Griff goes with us. Ralph arranged that. Griff is a faithful old friend, and must not be left behind."

"But what will he do at the church?" I asked, in dismay.

"He will wait in the porch," she answered.

I scarcely liked to ask about her parting from her uncle, but presently she raised her eyes and said, "I have said good-bye to uncle. He did not give me a chance of saying a word; but he knows he is not likely to see me again, and he spoke very kindly." And there the low voice faltered, and the brown eyes filled with tears, which did not overflow, as very sad tears seldom do.

We went up the churchyard way, and entered the silent house of God, with its long, misty sunbeams slanting over the empty pews. Ralph and Ewen stood in the chancel in the coloured light of the stained window. The rector saw our entrance through the half-open vestry door, and he came out, gowned, and went behind the communion rails.

There was a moment's silence—a pause—before the mysterious gate through which two lives would pass into one. Agnes was the calmer of the two, with her pale face and veiled eyes, for I saw Ralph grasp the rail before. him, like one thankful for any support, while his eyes wandered vaguely to the scrolls above the table, and his lips moved in unconscious recitation of those words, whose full, sweet meaning scarcely seemed for him : "Like as a *father* pitieth his children, so the Lord pitieth them that fear him."

Then the service began—the service which I had heard only the day before, but which, however solemn then, now seemed to have a new and thrilling minor key. I could scarcely trust my voice in the few simple responses, but there was one whose tones rung out clear and firm in each. It was Ewen. Somehow, I could not look at him. Without a glance, I could see his figure standing behind the bridegroom, generally erect, though the head bowed a little once or twice. Ah, the wedding might seem dreary in its solemn love and daring, bare of all those sweet little charities which generally drape such scenes in mists of tearful smiles and smiling tears, but many a bridal, with troops of congratulating friends, might envy that one loyal and true wedding guest, poor indeed, lowly as yet,—though I think the day may come when Agnes will be proud to say who stood behind her bridegroom—but who bravely brought all he had, even his own heart, and laid it as a willing offering on the marriage altar.

One or two hearty sobs, startling the rector's eyes

2 G

from his book, warned us that some interested spectator
had stolen upon our solitude; and when all was over,
and we left the vestry, where Agnes had signed the
name that she need not change, and Ruth had kissed
her, and I had blessed her, and Ewen had touched her
hand—very lightly—and said never a word, then we
found Sarah Irons seated on a back seat, indulging
herself in a "good cry." And I was glad to see that
Ralph Herbert did not shrink from the honest servant's
fond embrace. Ah, surely henceforth every woman,
however plain and homely, will be sacred to him for
the sake of one! The old Crusaders held their chivalry
in the name of "Our Ladye." And should not every
man be gentler and braver for the sake of the woman in
his heart, whether her image stand at a hearth or in a
shrine?

"I've left a letter for you from the master at your
house, sir," whispered Sarah, detaining me a minute
after the young people passed out. "O' course I don't
know what's in it, but it can't part 'em now, thank
God!"

No bells, no whispering faces, no huzzas, only the
breeze stirring a little in the new-budded boughs, and
one or two villagers looking from their doors, with
a little wonder and curiosity, to see the squire's son
and niece once more walking together, and that as
quietly and soberly as if it were quite a matter of
course.

According to instructions, we found a substantial
meal spread in our parlour, and Phillis in watchful,

conscious attendance. The letter from Mr Herbert lay beside my plate, and I did not venture to touch it until dinner was over. I might have spared my fears.

"DEAR SIR" (it ran),—"I have just parted from my niece Agnes, who has been a good and dutiful niece to me, though not as wise as she might have been. Now, I do not like that the last daughter of the Herberts of Upper Mallowe should leave her home with no portion but the beggarly produce of a book of verses and stories. Therefore I enclose ten fifty-pound notes, which I hope will be useful to her. I would have taken care to bind this sum upon herself, but she's one of those women you can't take care of, because she's determined to throw herself away.—I remain, yours truly, RALPH HERBERT, sen."

I silently placed the letter and its enclosure before the young couple. They read it through, and looked at each other.

"Ralph," said Agnes, very softly, "now you may go and say good-bye to uncle."

"He will not see me," he answered sadly; "and, besides, we have no time."

"He will see you if I ask him now," she returned; "and we will go on our way to the station."

Their boxes had all been despatched there in a cart, and so the little journey was to be made on foot. At the gate of the Great Farm, Agnes turned and said, "Mr Garrett and I will go in together."

But we found the hall door open, and so Ralph advanced into the porch, and stood there to await his fate, while my sister and Ewen lingered beyond the garden palings.

The strange stillness of the early morning had passed away, and there was a lively breeze astir. It swept through the open hall and lightly rustled the curtains of Agnes' deserted parlour, and I heard the low of cattle from the meadows behind the house. But Agnes did not heed the familiar sights and sounds, she walked straight forward to the dining-room ; its door, too, was open, and the room was in a flood of fresh spring sunshine. At the far end of the long table, just before the quaint window, with its treasures of blooming hyacinths and crocuses, sat Mr Herbert. He did not heed our footsteps—perhaps he did not even hear them. His arms were spread over the table, and his head was laid upon them. I don't know whether it was owing to the strong light or to his attitude, but, for the first time, I noticed many white hairs among his glossy brown. Agnes stopped to notice nothing ; she went straight up to him, and sat suddenly down on the floor, and laid her cheek on his knee.

"Uncle !" she cried.

He started up, half bewildered, and caught her in his arms. "My darling, my pretty one !" he exclaimed. " But you're not mine now ; I could not keep you."

"Uncle !" she cried again, putting her arms round his neck, the tears raining down her face. "Uncle, my husband wants to thank you for all your kindness to me. Let him come !"

Mr Herbert half shook off the clasp of those gentle

arms, but they were firm with the might of love. If he did not own Ralph as his son, she chose him for her husband! He hesitated, and Agnes kissed him again, and her tears fell on his hands.

" Let him come !" said he.

I went softly, and led him in. I did not re-enter the room. Nay, I closed the door behind Ralph, for there are some scenes which strange eyes ought not to see— some words which only God may hear !

. . . . . ` .

Half-an-hour afterwards they came out — all three. They walked together to the station, and Ewen and Ruth and I followed behind. On the platform stood old Mr M'Callum, and George and Miss Sanders. George had a nosegay for Agnes.

Mr Herbert was almost inclined to go with them to the seaport, but he did not. "It's parting either here or there," he said, "so we 'll get it over at once. But somebody 's going to see you off, I suppose ?"

" I am," said Ewen. " I will be with them till the last !"

" You 're a good fellow," responded the farmer.

A shriek from the engine, and Agnes, already seated in the carriage, placed her hand in her husband's. Ewen sat opposite. Another shriek, a smile, nods, and a burst of tears, and they were off. And we heard Griff's growl, as the dog-carriage passed us.

God bless the bride and bridegroom ! And God bless Ewen ! He smiled as he looked from the window ; and so I know how men smile at the stake or on the rack.

And yet he will be all the better for this anguish. A pure love never harmed any man. Love and sorrow have sung the world's sweetest songs, and painted its fairest pictures, and achieved its greatest deeds. So some day, perhaps, Ewen will make a picture of an emigrant ship, and the agony which was in his heart he will paint in the faces there, so that they shall stir the souls of all that gaze thereon into that human tenderness whence grows

> "That best portion of a good man's life,
> His little nameless, unremember'd acts
> Of kindness and of love."

Oh, let us thank God for the love and sorrow of genius! Yet, let us thank Him reverently, as we thank Him for all the blessings which come to us, by the sacrifice and pain of others. We take the flowers that blossom from the thorny stems, but they long for the time when the Master's eye shall see that the fruit is ripe, and His hand shall gather it in. I remember one verse in Agnes' father's book :—

> "Oh 'tis hard to hear them praise us for the music we have learn'd
> From the sobs we choked within us, and the hidden tears that burn'd ;
> When the poet goes to God, sure he leaves his harp behind,
> For the song they sing in heaven is of qu'te another kind."

# A POSTSCRIPT BY MISS GARRETT.

Now Edward has finished his love-story, I hope he will listen to me when I want to talk to him about the Refuge or the Hospital. For it seems to me uncommonly like a love-story, though it professes to be a record of what an old man and woman are able to do, when they sit down to rest and take breath before they go into the King's presence.

We've heard from Agnes and Ralph. They are settled in Canada, and Agnes says they are doing very well; but how is one to believe her? I shall not be surprised if Mr Herbert goes out after them. For in this world, wonders never cease. The other evening when I was at the Great Farm, in the dining-room, where that portrait's face is now decently turned forward, he almost cried while he pointed out a mark on the rug, worn by Griff's paws, where he used to hold on when Mr Herbert tried to push him away to make room for his own feet. Now if that is not rank sentiment and just like people, I don't know what is! I should not have pushed the poor dog aside, and then I should have had no mark in the rug to cry over, and so I suppose people would say I had no feeling! But I don't care what they say.

Bessie manages the Hospital famously, and her nephew

lives with her. Phillis is matron at the Refuge now, a..
Mr M'Callum says she does very well indeed. The
man would not leave his poor people even to go and .
in the chimney-corner at Meadow Farm, where Alice a:.
her husband live in great happiness and prosperit
They have a little daughter, and Edward and I are the
godfather and godmother. Alice thought she should ]· ·
named after me, and so did I, but Edward said sl
must be a " Lucy," because that was a family name w
the Westons. Family name, indeed !—I dare say he c.,
a great deal for family names ! But as he says nothii
I don't take any notice. If it pleases him to keep
secret, let him think he keeps it, that's all !

Ewen does not come very often to Upper Mallowe,
at least he does not stay very long when he does come.
He does not go to the counting-house now, but is " an
artist all out," as his grandfather says. But he says he
will return to business the moment his art is a labr · to
him, because it is not right to turn God's gift i ɔ a
machine. He is a very. fine young man, but I he .hat
people say he is stern and haughty. Nobody ever
believes in a volcano, which keeps itself to itself, and
does not rampage and destroy everything around it.

But I can't write any more, for the Refuge bills are
just sent in, and there's a basket of linen to sew for the
Hospital. It's very well to write about work, but it's
better to do it !

LONDON: PRINTED BY VIRTUE AND CO., CITY ROAD.